CRACK AT DUSK: CROOK OF DAWN

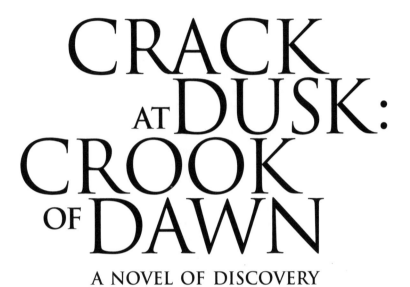

CRACK AT DUSK: CROOK OF DAWN

A NOVEL OF DISCOVERY

BY

PRISCILLA COGAN

TWO CANOES PRESS
Hopkinton, Massachusetts

Two Canoes Press
PO Box 334
Hopkinton, MA 01748
http://www.TwoCanoesPress.com

This book is a work of fiction.
Names, characters, places, and incidents
are products of the author's imagination
or are used fictitiously.

Jacket and book design, typography and electronic pagination by
Arrow Graphics, Inc., Watertown, Massachusetts.
Cover illustration by Lois Beardslee
Author's photograph by Duncan Sings-Alone

Manufactured in the United States of America

Publisher's Cataloging-in-Publication
(Provided by Quality Books, Inc.)

Cogan, Priscilla.
    Crack at dusk : crook of dawn : a novel of
discovery / Priscilla Cogan — 1st ed.
    p.   cm.
    Includes bibliographical references.
    ISBN: 1-929590-05-9

1. Teton Indians—Michigan—Fiction.
2. Shamans—Michigan—Leelanau County—Fiction.
3. Psychologists—Michigan—Leelanau County—Fiction.
4. Veterinarians—Michigan—Leelanau County—Fiction.
5. Leelanau County (Mich.)—Fiction.
I. Title.

PS3553.O4152C73 2000   813'.54
                    QBI99-1414

"Poem for Beginners," from THE COLLECTED POEMS OF ROBERT CREELEY,
1945-1975, by Robert Creeley. Copyright © 1983 The Regents of the University of
California. Used by permission of the University of California Press.

Glossary of Lakota words in the back.

ACKNOWLEDGMENTS

For the gifts of love, time and energy and, most of all, for his compassionate wisdom, I want to thank:
> Duncan Sings-Alone.

For the Lakota teachings:
> George Whitewolf

For their steadfast support of the writing:
> Polly Parson, Katie Rock, Dianne Foster, Brooke Schiavi, Darlene Arden

For their useful criticism and editorial suggestions:
> Jody Rein, Rebecca Chown, FAB, Denell Downum

For the Stone Song:
> Wild Goose and his inipi community

For the bold cover art that catches the sun going and coming:
> Lois Beardslee

For the wonderful help of their reference staff:
> Traverse Area District Library

For local wildlife and landscape information:
> Rick Wilson

For advice on accounting and other matters:
> Barbara Henins, Mike Schwartz

And, finally, for all those therapists and clients who, confronted by the trauma of evil, labored to share their hard-earned insights about the healing process.

*To those extraordinary individuals who,
in the language of their own journeys
and the crucible of psychotherapy,
dared to reenter the gates of hell
to retrieve their tattered humanity.*

*There will be those who will say
this cannot happen today.*

You and I know better.

PROLOGUE

TELL THEM, HAWK

The spirits of old times do not come to me any more. . . .
The old life is gone, and I cannot be a young man again.

—LITTLE WOUND, 1905
Lakota Belief and Ritual

"Tell them, Hawk, that We are still here."

Eyes shut, Hawk groaned, but there was no pity in the words.

"Tell them We are in the rocks, breathing. We are in the trees, talking. Tell them that the winged ones can pierce time and space and that the fins stroke ancient prayer songs across the ocean floor. Tell the two-leggeds that they are not the endpoint of Creation. The crawling things will eat their bodies too when they are dead, long after their vaults and statues have crumbled into the Grandmother. You tell them that We are still here."

Hawk's left ear ached; his body shook in chilled spasms. He did not recognize the voice. It was dark and he could see nothing.

Into his ear, another voice sighed, "Come. As you arrive at the end of this twentieth century, We shall show you its beginning." Strong fingers gripped his shoulder but the faces remained in shadow. Hawk rose to his feet, weak and afraid, but he knew better than to resist.

In the flap of a wing and the breath of a wind, he breezed across rolling prairie toward an isolated cabin, sheltered by a cottonwood grove. He passed through ill-chinked walls, as if neither the wood nor he held any substance. Draped over the cabin windows, tacked-up fabric endeavored to keep out winter's reach.

In a semi-circle of rude wooden chairs, four old men huddled around a sputtering fire. Their faces appeared like prairie landscapes, earth-dark and reddish brown, rivuletted with wrinkles outlining prominent noses and hillocked cheekbones. From shoulders slumped by age to the hinge of the men's knees, frayed army blankets mantled their lumpy forms. Bowed, skinny legs poked out; their feet all turned toward the pitiful flames.

An assortment of medicine articles dangled from their coarse woolen shirts and pants. By the speech patterns and the presence of the *Chanunpa Wakan*, Hawk guessed that the men were Lakota elders. They smoked the Sacred Pipe and did not acknowledge his presence.

A question had been asked to which each man now offered an answer.

"We must have offended the *Wakanpi*," said the first man, his eyes reflecting the dim light. "We grew blind and did not recognize the Evil Ones as our enemy. The white man came as Their messenger. We grew deaf and did not ask the good *Wakanpi* to protect us. Now our people are hungry, cold, and full of grief." He passed the Pipe to his neighbor.

The second man lifted the Chanunpa. "Every day another word is lost, unspoken. The sacred language will not survive our silence. We are letting the words of our ancestors slip out of memory. The whites—they are stealing our children away to boarding schools, beating them if they speak in the tongue of their grandparents. Soon, the young ones will no longer be able to understand us." He smoked, then handed on the Pipe.

The third man touched the warm bowl of the Chanunpa to his fore-head. "In the old days, we did not know of the Great Spirit of the white man. I think He must be very powerful but I cannot hear Him. I have called for Him to speak to me, but He says nothing. I have become a Christian and taken a new name. I go to church every Sunday. Still, their Great Spirit does not choose to talk to me. What have I done to hurt Him so? In the darkness I cling to my Chanunpa, but the ways of our ances-tors are like smoke scattering before a prairie wind."

The fourth man, the oldest one of all, elongated a deformed left arm to cradle the Pipe as if it were a fragile infant. He puffed in silence. The last of the burning tobacco rustled with each inhalation. At last he spoke, his words echoing in Hawk's ears.

"I take my Chanunpa out to pray at night. I sing the old songs. I conduct the Pipe ceremony as has been taught to me from seven generations. I pray for my people and wait for an answer."

He paused, knowing that the last ember of tobacco had burned cold. "But the Spirits don't talk to me anymore."

The old man gamely rose and blew the Pipe's ashes into the fireplace. Turning toward the others, fierce pride resonating in his deep voice, he proclaimed, "And still I cry out, 'Mitakuye oyas'in.'"

ONE

THE LAST DAY

Time flies over us, but leaves its shadow behind.

—NATHANIEL HAWTHORNE
The Marble Faun

"Where am I?" Hawk jerked awake in the morning's early light.

"You're home," Meggie O'Connor answered, leaning over him. She sponged his forehead with a damp cloth as if to wash away the fever that possessed him.

"Where have you been, Hawk?"

"What day is it?" He tried to sit up, but the effort made him dizzy. He flopped back onto the pillows.

"It's the last day of the old year, December thirty-first. Tomorrow marks the new year, the twenty-first century, the next millennium."

Hawk looked confused.

Meggie talked slowly, as if he were one of her psychotic patients, orienting him to time, place, and person. "I am Dr. Meggie O'Connor —your lover, the therapist for your late cousin, Winona, and the guardian of Chrysalis, the family estate here in Leelanau County. You are Slade Spelman, formerly the handyman around here. You are also

Hawk, a storyteller of Native American tales and a medicine teacher of Lakota rituals. Fifteen months ago you arrived in Michigan to spend time with Winona, your teacher. Is there anything else you would like to know?" She was grinning.

He wasn't *that* feverish and she knew it, but he played along with her. "Tell me how long we've been lovers."

"Not until you let me take your temperature." Thrusting a digital thermometer in his mouth, she perched at the bed's edge.

Like an old schoolmarm, she lectured him. "You've gone and caught yourself a virus. Right now a host of perverse agents are attacking your immune system, invading your cells, and co-opting the reproductive processes to spawn another generation of nasty little viruses. They don't mind killing off some of your cells in order to gain power over you and spread their influence. Your body is at war, Hawk."

"I've got better things to do," he slurred, trying to sit up.

Gently but firmly, she pushed him back down onto the pillows. "You're not doing anything for a while. Now keep your mouth shut until the thermometer begins to beep. You're going to stay in bed and recuperate. Better that you stay isolated and resist passing the virus to others."

The thermometer chirped like a cricket.

Meggie seized it and held it to the light. "Your temperature is up to 103.5."

Biting her lower lip and frowning, she picked up the telephone receiver and dialed a long number. "Hawk's got a high fever, Mom."

In response to questions, Meggie replied, "No muscle aches, but his eyes are watery, filmy. Yes, he does have a cough. No, it doesn't produce much."

She held the receiver down and asked him, "Mom wants to know if it's green or red."

"What?"

"Your sputum, what you cough up. Does it have a color?"

He shook his head.

"No. Okay, Mom. Thanks. Talk to you later." Meggie hung up the phone. Her eyes softened as she looked down upon his hangdog face.

"My physician mother said that if the fever gets much higher or if you become confused and comatose, I'm to take you to the hospital."

Hawk croaked, "You mean when I'm at the point of death. So what am I supposed to do now?"

Meggie retreated to the bathroom for a second and returned, handing him two capsules and a glass of water. Laughing, she reported, "Mom said to take two Tylenol and contact her in the morning. You must feel like shit."

"Um," he agreed. The thermometer's confirmation of his fever suddenly made him feel worse. All he wanted to do was to close his eyes and return to sleep, without revisiting the dream world.

"So, where were you?" Meggie asked.

It never failed to surprise Hawk how well she read him, as if somehow she could bore into his brain and pluck out his thoughts. He had never before known a woman like her—smart, physically strong, independent, loving, with a fierce Irish-American core. Spontaneous and playful, yet solid as granite. Dependable. For him, home would always be where he could look into her face and find his own bearings. Meggie possessed an open smile that could warm a room and green eyes that could either spark in anger or sport with mischief.

"It was only a dream," he rationalized.

"No, it wasn't. You're the one who taught me about the power of dreams. You were moaning and groaning with this one. I think you'd better talk about it." She folded her hands and waited.

"There were four old men," he began, "and it was at the beginning of the twentieth century. . . ."

He rushed through the telling of it, not wanting to immerse himself in the despair of elderly men watching their traditions and way of life dissolve from tribal memory. The dream was so vivid he felt a twinge of fear, as if the sheer horror of their experience could suck him back, abandon him there in another time, another place. Meggie listened, wiped his brow, and studied his troubled eyes.

When he had finished, she said, "No dream, Hawk. It was a vision. You've taught me that much."

Feebly he nodded. Now all he wanted to do was sleep. He closed his eyes but they suddenly blinked open.

"How long have we been lovers?" She had not yet answered his question.

Her first reply was quick of wit. "Not long enough."

Her second reply sprouted more slowly from the heart. "Have you ever felt like you've known someone all your life but that he or she simply hadn't yet arrived? As if there is a room inside each one of us with a *Vacant* sign hung upon the door. It's the self longing for its partner. And then one day, that special person arrives, key in hand, to make a claim upon that space and its lodger. The key fits and the doors inside the house spring open to other rooms you never even knew existed."

Meggie dropped her eyes from his gaze. "I think we were lovers long before we ever met, Hawk." She tucked the blankets around him and smoothed his long black hair away from his eyes.

As she spoke of their love, a variety of expressions rippled across his face from wide-eyed puzzlement to squinting skepticism, from furrowed doubt to smiling comprehension.

"It wasn't a key, Meggie, that opened your heart."

"Oh? If it wasn't a key, what was it then?"

"The flute. Do you remember that night, Meggie, when my mallard flute called to you from deep in the woods? How the notes shimmered into your bedroom window and sparkled all over you? If a man knows the right song to touch the woman's heart, there's no way she can resist him."

He grinned. "You were as good as mine that night."

"Ha," Meggie snorted. Hawk was the equal in blarney to any Irishman. But she remembered that evening with perfect clarity. And although she didn't believe in the power of spells, the flute's notes had danced love and mystery right across the forest bed into the lodgings of her heart.

A cold nose upon her leg interrupted Meggie's reverie. Fritzie, her wire-haired fox terrier, was bidding for attention. She rubbed his ears and gruffed, "Oh, I suppose you want to make your claims upon me too."

Fritzie wagged his tail, meandered over to his own bed, gingerly lowered himself into it, and rolled over onto his back—four stiff legs poking into the air, defying gravity.

Meggie laughed. "Go to sleep, both of you. I'm going downstairs to cook some chicken noodle soup."

Hawk closed his eyes. He was home where it was safe to be sick. The virus could go ahead and kick ass. He had faith that Meggie's soup and homemade bread would restore him back to life.

He hadn't needed to inform Meggie that the Spirits still lived.

Before her death, Winona had taken on the task of educating Meggie, presenting her with experiences that contradicted the psychologist's comfortable twentieth-century, scientific assumptions.

An old world view for a new millennium.

With that thought surging through his feverish brain, Hawk tumbled back into a fitful slumber.

* * * *

Into the morning's stillness, nine-year-old Adam Stands-By-Dog Arbre, Winona's grandson, thrust open the creaky front door. Stopping all motion, he cocked an ear but no one stirred in the sleeping house. With a long box tucked under his arm, he maneuvered his pudgy form outside and trudged over the hard-packed snow to the sweat lodge area. Nose to the ground, his mixed-breed hound padded after him.

Arriving at the lodge, Adam reached in, pried up a stiff carpet piece, and dropped it upon the frozen ground. Kneeling down upon the make-shift rug, he peeled off his mittens, blew hot air on his fingers, and cracked open the box. He knew that while other kids were probably playing happily with their new Christmas toys, none of his friends had received a present as extraordinary as this one.

It had been a good Christmas for him. His father had given him a compound bow, along with a promise to teach the boy how to track deer through the Northport swamp. His mother had gifted him with clothes: Two flannel shirts, three pairs of pants, and Western boots. His younger sister, Eva, had beaded a belt buckle for him. The design was somewhat off-balance but the intention was good. What he had really wanted for Christmas was a horse, but he could see that was not going to happen any time soon.

On Christmas day, Hawk had handed him the long plain box, saying, "This is for you, Stands-By-Dog. Your grandmother, Winona, would have approved."

Adam remembered how his mother, Lucy, had studied him when he first opened the box. Although not privy to the reasons, he had been well aware of the tension between his mother and his grandmother when she had come to stay with them. Of the same flesh and blood, they had chosen to pursue different life directions. Adam's mother was always lecturing him how Native Americans had to learn to "accommodate" to the modern world, but he never really knew what she meant by that word. He understood better the meanings of his grandmother when she told him that he belonged to the first people on this continent and never to forget it.

He sorely missed his grandmother. Winona had died over a year ago. For a long time thereafter, when he'd come out to the sweat lodge area to pray, she'd materialize out of thin air to talk with him. Never appearing to anyone else, her presence had made him feel special. Then one day, she'd announced she couldn't visit him that way any longer. She didn't say why. Since that time, loneliness had shadowed his heart and dogged his steps.

He had quit praying then, except in the inipi ceremonies. It had not gone beyond his notice that other kids didn't take time out of their days to make prayers. Some older teenagers had even persuaded him to smoke cigarettes and drink alcohol with them. Once he had gotten so drunk he'd puked up a storm. His mother would have killed him if she had ever found out. At school, June Tubbs agreed to be his girlfriend, whatever that meant. He prided himself on growing up, even dreaming of the day that he might possess his own horse. Still, the emptiness trotted after him. His grandmother no longer talked to him.

Past losses, however, did not distract him from present treasures. Adam dug his fingers into the box, extracting Hawk's gift—a small version of the social pipe, the chanunpa. "In the old days, the young Lakota were given little boys' pipes to learn how to handle the chanunpa with respect," Hawk had said. "It's not done much any more, but it was a good custom. You must smudge yourself and the chanunpa with sage before you pray with it."

Even if he didn't have the words, Adam now possessed his own pipe with which to pray. He had promised his disapproving mother he would not smoke it for pleasure, only for prayer. For the first time in a long time, that special feeling once more wrapped around him.

* * * *

All over the Leelanau Peninsula, people were rising to the last day of the old millennium. In the Tubbs household, Katja was the first one up, frying kielbasa and cooking a batch of pancakes for the family which included her husband Paul, son Robert, and daughter June. She had managed to pull off a small miracle—persuading Paul to celebrate New Year's Eve at a polka party in Cedar. The time was soon coming when tax work would occupy all his attention.

Dr. Bev Paterson, Meggie's colleague, had decided to meditate for world peace on New Year's Eve, somewhat in the same spirit as her recent efforts to endure a period of chastity to raise her *kundalini*. She couldn't help observing that the more she abstained from sex, the more she became obsessed with it. The more her *kundalini* rose, the lower her focus of observation zoomed when around the male gender. "I must simply try harder," she murmured before sinking back into a delicious, sensual sleep.

Lucy Arbre, Adam's mother, rolled over in her bed to gaze at the handsome face of her Ojibway husband, Larry. Their life in Peshawbestown, Michigan was easier than it would have been if they had chosen to live with her Oglala Lakota people at Pine Ridge reservation, South Dakota. The Leelanau Sands Casino and hotel had brought good times to the small reservation on the Leelanau Peninsula. Back home at Pine Ridge, Lucy knew there were a lot of her people in houses that were cold, the plumbing bad or nonexistent, the food scarce at the end of the month, too many parents deep into alcoholism, and the elderly having to struggle to make it from day to day. Winter could be especially grim out on the Plains. She guessed that was why *Waziya*, Grandfather of the North, was so often perceived by her people as cruel and pitiless in His dealings with the two-leggeds. His home edged the land of the ghosts.

She gently shook Larry awake and said, "Today, let's buy some blankets at the Traverse Bay Woolen Company to send back to Pine Ridge. It'll be a good way to begin the new year."

Sam Waters, the Suttons Bay veterinarian, rubbed his eyes and peered out the window onto the white, hilly landscape. It wouldn't be long before people would be crowding into his clinic. They'd come in droves when they discovered it wasn't enough to simply cuddle and feed their Christmas pets. Nail-biting adults would demand that kittens, who had shredded the curtains, be declawed. Owners of young labs would come in howling that their dogs' clumsy tails had swept family heirlooms off the table. People with tropical fish would gasp and sputter about how difficult it was to keep their aquariums healthy. Phlegmatic farmers would want to know why the old horse kept coughing in the cold winter air. Or why the neglected parrot refused to talk or the overcrowded, caged minks had stop eating. *Life in the animal world is never dull*, he reflected.

Sam rolled out of bed, shrugged on an old plaid bathrobe, let out his golden retriever to gambol in the snow, brewed up a pot of coffee, and took down his briar pipe from the mantle. One of the joys of being a bachelor, he reasoned, was his ability to live his life according to his own rhythms. He lit the tobacco and sat back on an old stuffed chair to savor the sweet smoke.

All over the Peninsula, such were the morning rituals of people preparing for the change from one year to the next, one century to the next, one millennium to the next. A time to remember the years before, to hope for the years to come, to grieve the past and greet what was to arrive, to give thanks for their blessings and to still the fear that always lurched backwards from the future, this was a time which belonged to no time, when nothing was certain and all was possible.

As time's wheel inexorably cranked another notch on this special New Year's Eve, the two-leggeds all over the country launched themselves into an orgy of celebration, blowing their horns, throwing confetti to the air, shouting down the minutes to midnight, and joyfully forgetting that:

> Into every night crawls the dawn.
> Into every day creeps the shadow.

TWO

NEW YEAR'S DAY

Be nice to your friends. If it wasn't for them, you'd be a total stranger.

—ANONYMOUS

Hawk's temperature registered 102.4.

Meggie shook the thermometer. A judgement call—whether to drive down the fever with medication or let Hawk's internal fire burn out the virus. Provided that the body wasn't overwhelmed by fatigue, the internal battle, and well-intentioned modern medicine, it possessed its own healing process.

"How do you feel?" she asked.

"I've had better days." He exhaled deeply and began to cough, a futile gesture. Nothing much was stirring in his compacted chest.

Sympathy conquered her better sense. She handed him two Tylenol with a glass of ginger ale. She knew that while the pills would help him sleep, prematurely depressing the fever might also prolong his illness. Modern pharmacology often robbed the body of its natural defenses.

"I don't think it's the flu, Hawk. You aren't showing aching muscles and joints—just fever, rheumy eyes, and a rattle in your lungs."

"I'm dying," he moaned. "Only a heavier dose of sympathy will save me." His feeble attempt at humor made her smile.

She gave his hand a squeeze. "What you need most is rest. I'll come back up and check on you in another half hour."

Slipping back into the sanctuary of sleep, Hawk was oblivious to the incessant ring of the telephone.

Meggie ran downstairs and grabbed the cordless phone. It was Bev on the line. Crooking the receiver between neck and chin, Meggie extracted a quart of milk from the refrigerator, flour and sugar canisters from the pantry, and a box of baking soda from the cabinet shelf.

Bev griped, "If, as you say, Meggie, that what happens on New Year's Day signals what will happen for the rest of the year, I pity both of us. You're having to play nurse to a sick soul while I suffer withdrawal pains from the carnal comforts of men."

"Perhaps all it means is that you'll develop your spiritual side this year." To the measure and mix of flour, sugar, milk, and salt, Meggie added baking soda without which there could be no leavening of the bread.

"What spiritual side?" Bev scoffed.

Meggie's hands plunged into the stiff mixture. "Come on, Bev. You pretend to be a lot more cynical than you really are. At one time or another, we all ask: Who am I? What's really important?"

"Ha," Bev spouted. "You and I both know that any search for spiritual meaning on my part is solely propelled by my desire to understand Karl Young. Good God, why did I ever fall in love with a minister? I've always been a devout atheist. Is this one of life's cruel jokes or what?"

Meggie folded the dough onto itself and punched it down. "Winona would say that the Trickster Figure is playing with you, having fun at your expense."

"Why me? I'm not Indian."

"No, but you're a human being. The Trickster Figure teaches us two-leggeds how to regain balance in our lives by placing us into impossible situations. Either we grow stronger for that or we make utter fools of ourselves in the name of pride and power."

Bev fired back, "Phooey. I don't believe in Evil Spirits any more than I do in a God who gives a damn about how I live my life."

"But the Trickster Spirits aren't the same as Evil Spirits." Meggie massaged the dough. "While the Trickster Spirits may make humbling sport of us, They are always trying to teach us not to puff up and take ourselves too seriously. The Evil Spirits, on the other hand, are malevolent in nature."

"Come on, Meggie," Bev scoffed. "We've entered the twenty-first century. It's too simplistic to say that there is Good and there is Evil and it's clear which is which. Or that there are these Trickster Spirits running around, sticking out their feet so that we human beings fall flat on our faces."

"But what about Karl?" Meggie asked. She adjusted the receiver under her chin.

"Well, of course, *he* believes in both God and Satan. It's an article of faith for him as a minister."

Knowing that Bev couldn't see her over the telephone, Meggie fashioned a round button nose and added toothpick whiskers to the bread loaf. She pricked the ears canine high and, with the flat edge of a knife, carved a supercilious grin around the lower jaw line. Cautiously she opined, "The Trickster Spirit was preying upon Karl last year."

It hadn't been but a few months since Bev's lover had quit his Northport and Leland congregations in disgrace. His romance with Bev had been the last in a long line of extra-marital affairs. The parishioners were dumbfounded by the revelations of their minister's extracurricular activities and his betrayal of his wife, Andrea. After the great debacle, Karl disappeared into a monastic retreat to meditate on his failings as a human being.

Meggie was aware that others had not known of the childhood sexual abuse in Andrea's background. Or how the specter of that abuse had haunted every moment of the Youngs' marriage, telling and retelling the repressed story in the cold echoes of their relationship. Andrea Young had neither possessed the words nor the images to speak the terrors of her past; only in her bones, her flesh, and her ability to hide could the story be inferred.

"Why bring in a Trickster figure when Andrea was the one to fire the pistol?" Bev believed that people, not Spirits, had to be held accountable for their actions, no matter the circumstances.

The discovery of Karl's adulterous affair with Bev had unraveled Andrea's slim thread of emotional control. She ended the caricature of their marriage by shooting her husband in the leg, disappearing, then divorcing Karl.

There was no compassion in Bev's words. "I don't blame Andrea for being angry at Karl, but she didn't have to shoot him."

Meggie remained silent, remembering back to the tumultuous days following the incident. Ashamed, Karl had refused to implicate Andrea as the one who had wounded him. No one really understood why the minister's wife had chosen violence as a way to end the marriage.

But Meggie knew.

Andrea Young had been her client in psychotherapy. *She had wanted Karl to understand how it felt to live life as a cripple*, Meggie thought.

Bev changed the topic. "Why dwell on past history when the future is right around the corner? In the next few weeks, Karl's coming back."

"What do you mean?" Meggie slipped the coyote loaf into the hot oven.

"The bishop visited him at the monastery. It seems that fewer and fewer people are choosing to be ministers and so the church can ill afford to have someone with his experience demit and leave the profession. Despite all his personal problems, Karl is one hell of a good preacher."

"I'm surprised he plans to remain in the church."

Bev laughed. "He says what else can he do? But since the divorce, my thinking is that he's free to pursue other interests."

"Such as?"

"Me, for one," Bev teased.

"Karl has his work cut out for him."

"Well, he's going to have to catch me first. Don't forget, Meggie, in the Christian world you and Hawk are also considered pagans." Bev paused. "Isn't it strange how a man of the cloth who calls himself 'a fool for Christ' ends up with you as his best friend and me as his lover?"

Before Meggie could answer, Hawk began calling from the upstairs bedroom. "I've got to go, Bev," she apologized.

"Do you need anything? You're more worried than you let on about his fever."

"He's picked up a virus somewhere. The fever has to break real soon. You know me, the eternal optimist in all things."

"Yes," Bev interrupted, "but I also know that you find it difficult to ask for assistance. If things get worse, swear to me that you'll call for help."

"Okay," Meggie assured her.

In the new year, that was a promise Meggie would learn to keep.

* * * *

"I solemnly swear, Katja, that I will take the children and you to Disney World *after* tax season. But you and I both know that for the next four months I'll be leaving home early in the morning and getting back late. There's no use arguing about it or disturbing our last free day together." Paul Tubbs stood in the doorway, hands on his hips, as if expecting a rebuttal.

Katja shrugged her shoulders. It was an old fight with them. "Four months is a long time. It'd mean a lot to Robert and June if you could simply take off two nights a week so that we could play a board game or go to a movie in Traverse City."

"Honey," he softened his voice. "I can't ask the other accountants to do my work. I'm involved with the kids' activities during the other eight months of the year: Soccer practice, school recitals, fishing trips on the lake. Four months isn't that long a period. It won't kill them."

To a child, four months is like a lifetime, thought Katja.

* * * *

Already the afternoon shadows were tracking across the peninsula when Sam Waters and his retriever arrived at the veterinary clinic in Suttons Bay. His staff was on vacation. A clutter of bills littered his desktop, the examining table sported a multitude of stains, and magazines sprawled in disarray about the waiting room. He desperately needed to hire another part-time worker.

Sam fingered his unopened mail. A computer-generated letter suggested in large type that *Sam Waters has just won 3 million dollars!* Into the trash basket he dumped the letter.

Other pieces of mail drew his attention: A local protest over the placement of police communication towers, another low-interest credit card, a request for money from his college alumni association, and finally one hand-addressed, penciled letter. He slit open the envelope and extracted a sheet of paper.

Dear Dr. Waters,
    I need a job after school. I'm real good
with animals. As long as I don't have to put them to
sleep or nothing, I'd be willing to do anything. I'm a
real hard worker.
        please?
            Daisy Bassett

Sam dropped the letter on his desk. It sure would beat having to advertise the position, but then again he wasn't sure that Daisy was up to handling the responsibility of answering phone calls, scheduling appointments, and keeping the clinic from becoming a disorderly mess. She was a high school student, old enough for a part-time job and good with animals, but her speech could be rough and her temper quick. Would his main assistant, Jillian Townes, ever forgive him for hiring a teenager? Jillian would have to be the one to train Daisy and coach her in the use of respectful English.

"please?" Daisy had written. Not "Thanks" or "Sincerely Yours" or some such nicety. A kid's plea. Sam rubbed the inside of his dog's ears. "Well, Taffy, I guess we'll try out the girl and see if she can be of help here." Sam penned a note to Daisy, suggesting a time for an interview in the following week.

Against his leg, he could feel the gentle slap of Taffy's tail. "So you agree?" He could swear the retriever nodded in response.

"please?"

That single word in a strange place kept nagging at Sam, as if scratching at his door for attention.

He would post his reply that afternoon.

* * * *

Although the air was frost cold and ice patches lingered on the roads, Adam bundled up in his new flannel shirt, winter jacket, and mittens, jumped onto his bicycle, and headed toward the Leelanau State Park. He pedaled at a leisurely rate so that his dog, Shunka, could keep up a steady lope behind him. They turned off the main road and headed past the small airstrip.

The woods of the park were tall and deep. He dropped his bike behind a park shed. Together with Shunka, he headed down a familiar lowland trail. After a few minutes of hard walking, boy and dog arrived at Mud Lake where a regiment of branchless, dead gray trees stood at ghostly attention, waist-high in frozen water. On the surface the ice had worn thin, cracking along diagonal lines as if outlining a battleground. It was the kind of place—part swamp, part lake—that would attract frogs, turtles, mallards, wood ducks, a boy, and his dog. Shunka loved water. His tail strutted from side to side with enthusiasm.

Adam studied the prints of raccoon and fox that led to the water's edge. He was hoping to catch sight of a bear print, for a brown bear had been sighted making its rounds of Northport sheds and garbage pails, causing much local consternation. People believed that the bear must have wandered over the ice from the Upper Peninsula to Northport at the northernmost tip of the Leelanau Peninsula.

Shunka was exploring too. The swamp yielded pungent, primordial smells of rotting stumps, compressed pine needles, leaf mold, water, and wood soaking into each other. Gingerly, Shunka stepped onto the ice, following a scent past the stiff army of wooden soldiers to an open area where the forces of water had weakened the siege of ice.

Ice plates, cracking along the seams, caught Shunka's attention as the ground shifted and split beneath him. Immediately the dog wheeled back toward land but his hind legs broke through the thin ice and sank into the grasping cold fingers of the lake. He scrabbled with his front paws to pull himself up but the ice kept shredding in front of him. He barked high with panic.

From the woods, Adam looked up to see his dog disappearing into the lake's dark sucking mouth. Shunka was his best friend.

Pudgy legs flying, Adam skidded across the ice. "It's okay; it's okay," he called out to the flailing dog.

In the slush hole, Shunka frantically splashed water. Out in the open there was nothing for Adam to grasp, to hold him firm on the unstable surface. As he neared the dog, Adam lowered himself onto the thin ice and bellied up closer. He made a grab for Shunka's collar but the dog pedaled away from him.

Shunka's movements steadily grew more lethargic in the tomb-cold temperature. Adam would have to act fast. Inching closer to the hole, mindful of the hairline cracks that were starting to spider around him, the boy lunged once again with his right arm. This time his hand snagged the dog's collar.

Yanking, hauling with his arms, the boy scooted backwards on his belly dragging the choking dog. Fissures on the surface snaked after him like an underwater serpent moving in for the kill. Shunka sputtered and thrashed but could not break free of the water's suck. Adam lifted up on his knees for better purchase, still holding onto the collar, still propelling backwards, wondering if they would ever make it to the solidity of Grandmother Earth. But the ice mercilessly broke behind him, around him, in front of him. The boy felt his feet plunging into the freezing water. He flung out his arms and thrust his body upright.

The water was knee-high. They had reached the shallows.

Exhausted, Adam released his grip on the collar. Shunka scrambled out of the water on his own four feet, the boy trudging behind him.

The hound collapsed on the ground, shivering. Adam peeled off his jacket, unbuttoned his new flannel shirt, wrapped it around the dog, and rubbed his fur to restore circulation. He put his jacket back on to keep warm. He knew he had to get Shunka up and moving to the parking lot.

He pulled up the dog's hind quarters, then the front, dragging, coaxing the dog back along the trail, using his shirt as a leash. Adam's feet were cold and numb, turning to icicles in the slosh of wet pants, boots, and socks.

Adam spotted his bicycle leaning up against a signpost. He looked around. A black van was parked at the other end of the lot. Exhaust plumed up from the back.

Adam let Shunka fall back to the ground and plodded over to the van whose windows had steamed into a frosty glaze. He rapped on the driver's door. A window rolled down and out poked the round face of a middle-aged woman, smoking a cigarette.

Her arms were plump; her head, barely clearing the steering wheel, sunk into a triple chin. Her hair, flecked with gray, was straight and stringy but her eyes, while sharp and focused on him, hinted at merriment. He recognized her as a clerk at a Suttons Bay store.

"My dog . . ." he explained, rushing through the story of the breaking ice.

"Would you like a ride?" she asked. She indicated that the van had room enough for him, the wet dog, and the bicycle as well.

Shunka needed no second persuasion to jump into the back seat. The woman poured her hefty body out of the vehicle to help Adam load the bicycle. With gratitude and relief, the boy climbed into the vehicle and relaxed against the seat.

"It's too cold a day to be out wading in the swamp," the woman scolded. "You live in Peshawbestown, don't you?" Her voice was full of concern.

He nodded.

The car was quickly taking on the odors of wet dog, damp socks, stale smoke, and tired boy.

"I know you," the woman said. "Your mother's a nurse and your dad works at the bingo hall. My name is Emily." She extended a hand to him.

"Mine's Adam."

"You hungry?" She reached behind her and pulled out a bag of oatmeal raisin cookies. "Go ahead. Eat as many as you would like."

Adam wolfed down two cookies. Shunka yipped, wanting to be remembered. The boy broke off a piece of cookie and reached back. Shunka's mouth grabbed the cookie and bolted it down. His ears perked up.

"Your dog's coming back to life." Emily gave Shunka an admiring glance.

"Thank you for the cookies." Adam remembered his mother's admonition to be polite.

"You're welcome," she answered. "I'll drive you to your place." She backed up the van and headed out of the parking lot.

The fear that had lodged in his heart and coiled in his muscles began to recede as the gray-haired woman and the black van sped him homeward toward safety.

That night, Adam took out his pipe and headed toward the sweat lodge area where he offered his pipe toward the night's darkness. "Grandfather," he announced, "I made a new friend today. She's old enough to be a grandmother."

And then Adam smiled.

THREE

RECIPES

Recipe: 1. *A formula for compounding a medicine or remedy.*
2. *A formula for cooking.*
3. *A method or procedure for doing something.*

—WEBSTER'S THIRD NEW INTERNATIONAL DICTIONARY

"That's it," Meggie exclaimed. "Your fever is still above 100. I'm taking you to the physician. Something else is going on."

"No, I can't," Hawk protested. His face sagged with the fatigue of illness after five days of fever. He was growing restless and coughing more; huge whoops and wheezing sounds thundered and crackled from his chest and lungs.

"Why not?" Meggie stood there, hands on hips.

He looked away, as if embarrassed. "I don't have medical insurance. Can't afford it."

"What about Indian Health Services"

He shook his head. "You have to be officially enrolled in a tribe to use them. You forget, Meggie, I'm a mongrel—Lakota, Apache, Cherokee, Irish, and Scottish. What tribe is going to claim me? It's bad enough that in the white world you're not an Indian unless the Bureau of Indian Affairs says you are. But what's worse is that often my own Lakota people say the same goddamn thing."

Meggie was only too aware of the painful politics in the Native American world as to who was a *real* Indian. As if blood quantum were a true measure of one's identity. It seemed to her that the issue always boiled down to the meat and potatoes of money and tribal services.

"I'll pay the doctor. I'll not be getting a good night's sleep until we can find out what's wrong with you. Come on." She pulled back the bed covers, threw him his clothes, and drove him to the Northport Medical Clinic.

Listening to Hawk's rattling breaths, the physician assessed, "Could be pneumonia. Could be a bad bronchial infection. X-rays are irrelevant, as I'd treat you the same way for either condition."

"Two Tylenol and call me in the morning?" quipped Hawk.

The doctor smiled and shook his head. "No, Tylenol's not going to do it. I'm giving you a heavy antibiotic. Take it for four days; if the fever doesn't disappear, come back to the clinic." He gave Hawk an initial dose and scribbled a prescription. They were in and out of the medical clinic within an hour.

"Hey, Dr. O'Connor," Hawk muttered, easing back into the front seat of Meggie's Toyota, "I thought you told me that an antibiotic wouldn't cure a virus."

"That's right," she replied. "It's like a war. The first assault upon the self was the virus. Your immune system mobilized for the battle: Hence, the fever. But all that effort to protect the body took its toll and the secondary lines of defense weakened. The next assault came from behind the lines." Meggie paused for dramatic effect.

"Meggie, don't give me that New Age line that I'm responsible for everything that happens to me," Hawk groaned.

"I'm not," laughed Meggie. "But in every one of us there lurks a swarm of bacteria. Some are very destructive and just waiting for that weakness, that moment of opportunity, to strike when our attention is directed elsewhere. So, while there may have been success in fighting off the viral invaders, the bacterial saboteurs in you went to work, giving you either pneumonia or, at least, a bronchial infection. That's where the antibiotics come into play. They're the big guns of medicine, the tanks of an allied force that will beef up your offensive line to wage war."

Hawk peered at Meggie with a skeptical eye. "I have one question about the expense of modern medicine and your military metaphors," he said.

"What?" Meggie sped toward Suttons Bay, rather pleased with her analogy.

"Am I the impoverished third world country on whose soil the battle is being fought?" He tapped his chest and began coughing.

Before she could answer, he added, "And I wonder what my powerful ally will demand of me in payment, once the battle is won." He arched his eyebrows over at her and blew his nose into the tissue.

"Oh, that's simple," she replied. "Dinner. A whole week's worth."

"But I don't have the money to take you out seven nights in a row. Except for love, I am a poor man."

"You don't understand, Hawk." She momentarily turned her head away from the road to look straight at him. "You're going to *cook* supper every night for seven nights. When you're well, that is." A touch of feminine condescension lurked at the corners of her smile. Her eyes turned a deeper green.

Hawk was trying to suppress a smile. "But I don't know if I can meet your strict culinary standards, being a third world country and all. You always want gourmet food."

"Beans every night won't do. You'll simply have to learn how to cook other dishes."

"Beans are good for you." Hawk appealed to her low-fat sensibilities.

"After a meal of beans, I end up looking like I'm seven months pregnant. We'll compromise. I'll buy the food. You cook it. No beans. Besides, you'd look cute in a chef's hat." She added, "With nothing else on."

Leaving off Hawk at the house, she was pleased that she'd be able to make her afternoon appointments. In downtown Suttons Bay, Meggie and Bev shared a set of offices with a view toward Lake Michigan and the beach. Apart from the county mental health agency, Dr. Meggie O'Connor and Dr. Beverly Paterson were the only psychologists on the Leelanau Peninsula. Their private practice of psychotherapy blended work with children and adults, individuals and families.

For the most part, Meggie preferred that Bev handle the marital cases that came their way. "In marriage therapy, it's like you are always looking for the lowest common denominator between the two people," Meggie told Bev. "In individual psychotherapy you can help a person realize his or her maximum potential."

But Bev loved the complexity and emotional intensity that feuding couples brought to her office. She reasoned that since she had never been married, she wasn't biased either toward marriage or toward divorce.

Families were a different matter all together. Meggie enjoyed the ebb and flow of energy in family systems, the internal structures and hierarchies that had developed over time, the stories each family member brought to the therapy process.

What Meggie cherished most about being a psychologist was the precious opportunity to work with emotionally disturbed children. It puzzled her that many psychologists, such as Bev, did not enjoy psychotherapy with the young child.

"They're not like adults, Meggie," Bev complained. "You can't sit down with them, face to face, like civilized human beings, talk about feelings, and work out the issues. Children are either sticking their fingers up their noses or scuffing my white couch with their muddy shoes. Give me a pimply-face teenager any day."

But children, Meggie knew, had a language all their own to express their fears and sorrows, their joys and excitement, and their unique perceptions of the world around them. When an adult was able to crack the code of the child's language, the result was often immediate—trust and alliance. Something sacred would then occur between Meggie and the child. She never took the gift of their stories lightly.

* * * *

A week later, all that lingered of Hawk's illness was a diminishing cough. The virus had run its course and the antibiotics had defeated the bacterial infection. Hawk was well enough to start paying off war reparations.

"Here's the first recipe," Meggie said, handing him a three-by-five-inch card. "I thought I would start you off with something simple. I'll be home around six and ready to eat about seven. Everything you need is here." Her eyes flirted mischievously.

"Why are you leaving so early this morning? I thought you didn't have clients until this afternoon." Hawk enjoyed their mornings together. Except for a few story-telling engagements at libraries and schools, there was a paucity of winter jobs for him and an excess of free time.

Meggie took once last sip of her coffee. "I'm giving a presentation soon at the Gertrude Gold Clinic in Traverse City and I need to prepare for it without any distractions. They tell me that the old lady herself may come to hear my lecture."

Hawk squinted dubiously at the recipe. "Maybe I could work out a monetary arrangement with you after all."

"Nope. A deal's a deal." She picked up her bulging briefcase. "Besides, you still need to stay indoors. That cough of yours . . ."

"Is nothing," he interrupted. He stifled the urge to clear the tickle from his throat. "I don't need to be babied by any woman. Especially a white woman."

Meggie blew him a goodbye kiss over the kitchen table and shut the door behind her. Hawk stood there, scratching his head. What did he know about cooking? Apart from two previous attempts at marriage, he had done very well eating fast food or canned beans. He sat down at the breakfast table with a cup of coffee and studied the card:

LOW FAT CHICKEN POT PIE

1 large package of chicken pieces
12 oz. bottle of herb/garlic or lemon/pepper sauce
1 (10.5 oz.) can low fat cream of chicken soup
1 lb. bag of frozen vegetable medley
1 tsp. thyme or tarragon
black pepper to taste
Pillsbury refrigerated pie crust

Peel off all skin/fat from chicken. Cook in herb sauce for 45 mins. in 350 oven. Cut up 2 cups of chicken, save rest for other dishes. In large bowl, mix diced chicken and some of the sauce with the soup, vegetables, and spices until moist. After covering the bottom of the 10-inch pie plate with uncooked pie crust, pour in mixture, fit dough on top. Cut vents in top crust. Bake 45 mins. in 375 oven.

"Easier said than done," grumbled Hawk. He extracted the pie crust from the refrigerator and reached for the rolling pin way back on a lower cabinet shelf. His arm bumped a higher shelf; a wobbly tower of stacked metal cookware toppled with a loud clattering to the kitchen floor.

Hawk did what any man would do in the same situation.

He cursed.

F O U R

WORD PLAY

Naked Truth used to walk the streets, bare and unadorned. People either paid him no attention or turned away from him in disgust whenever they saw him. Then, one day while feeling rejected, he came across his friend, Parable, dressed in fine clothing and surrounded by well-wishers.

He complained, "Why is it that you get so much attention, while I, actual truth, get none at all?

Parable replied, "Because you walk around, plain and unadorned. No one likes to meet Naked Truth face to face. Let me help you."

Parable dressed up Truth in some of his most beautiful garments. Lo and behold, everywhere Truth appeared in his beautiful, new outfits, people stood up and paid attention to him.

Truth remains the same, with or without the adornments, but most people cannot bear to come face to face with Naked Truth. Therefore, truth often can only enter into people's hearts when clothed in a parable.

—THE MAGGID OF DUBNO

Employing large body movements and gestures, Hawk recited the *Pine-Gum Wolf* story to a special group of elementary school children. Behind him, a female translator pantomimed his movements and signed his words, for all the children were deaf and most were unable to hear his voice.

"And Rabbit screamed to the silent pine-gum wolf, 'Get out of my way or I'm going to hurt you.' But the pine-gum wolf didn't move or say a word. So Rabbit took his right front paw and hit the wolf as hard as he could. And do you know what happened?"

Hawk's right hand shuddered in the air as if glued to some invisible being. Some of the children signed. Some spoke out loud, in the oval pronunciation of the totally deaf. "He's stuck."

"And Rabbit got so mad. Angry as he could be. He struck the pine-gum wolf with his left front paw but the wolf held onto both front paws.

"'You'd better let me go or else,' Rabbit cried out. He lifted his powerful right hind paw and kicked the wolf, but he couldn't free his paw. Then he thrust out his left hind paw and that, too, stuck to the pine-gum wolf. Oh, what rage he felt.

"'You're going to be sorry,' Rabbit yelled. Bringing his neck back, he head-butted the pine-gum wolf with all his strength."

In front of the children, Hawk jerked his neck forward at an unnatural angle. Their eyes shifted from him to the signer and back to him again, not wanting to miss any expression, any gesture. They grinned at Rabbit's predicament.

"All the animals came out of hiding to see who had been stealing their water from the community well. It was Rabbit, all entangled in the sticky trap of the pine-gum wolf. They laughed at Rabbit and left him there for a long time, dangling from the pine-gum wolf.

"And that is how the animals taught Rabbit never to steal from them again. Because when you refuse to work with others, you can't expect to share in the rewards of their efforts. Rabbit didn't know how to be a team player.

"At this school, you are learning how to work together so you won't end up a lonely fool, like our friend, Rabbit."

Hawk clapped his hands together to show the kids that the story was over. An eerie silence ensued. Then the children lifted their hands over their heads and wiggled all ten fingers. It dawned on Hawk that this was the way the deaf applauded.

Hawk next brought out an assortment of objects for the children to inspect. His large drum excited great interest. When he drummed the heartbeat of Grandmother Earth, two boys lay down and put their heads on the side of the drum to feel the vibrations. The children's hands fingered the stone-age axe head, the carved wooden war club, the fringe on Hawk's deerskin outfit. They correctly guessed that the mallard tube was a flute. Through signing, they asked him to play it for them. It was a request that surprised him as the sound of the flute was high and soft, unlikely to be heard even by the partially deaf children.

He warned them that the sound might excite their female teachers, as it was a magical love flute. "When a young man takes a deep liking to a young woman, he makes up a special song for her," Hawk explained and the translator signed.

"When he plays that song outside her tipi, it sets her heart to fluttering. She can't resist coming outside toward the song and the flute. And soon, the young man is asking her father if he can marry her. So, only if you will take responsibility for your teachers and watch them closely with an eagle eye do I dare play this flute."

The children nodded with great enthusiasm. Their eyes bored into their teachers.

Hawk lifted the flute and began to play. Two of the younger teachers grinned and began to sway back and forth, as if pulled closer by the flute. It didn't seem to matter that one of the teachers was totally deaf herself.

When he finished the song, Hawk lowered the flute and took a slight bow. The children peppered him with questions about Native Americans. "Do they still live in tipis? Do they still kill people and take scalps? What do they wear under their dresses?"

And just before Hawk left the large classroom, two blushing eight-year-old girls, totally deaf, ran up to him and signed, "When you played that flute, our hearts fluttered too."

*　*　*　*

Bev was ecstatic.

Karl had returned from the monastic life, limping back into Traverse City. The bishop had assigned him to a supervised church position at some distance from Northport and Leland where a senior minister could keep an eye on him. He had rented a small apartment on the east side of the city.

"I'm on probation for a couple of years. If it works out with this congregation then I'll take over when Rev. Atherton retires. This is my last chance in the ministry, Bev. I've got to keep my nose clean."

"What do you mean?" Bev was suspicious.

"No fooling around, for one."

"But you're divorced, free and clear." Bev could feel a touch of agitation burbling in her stomach.

"The church doesn't approve of premarital sex." Karl pressed his lips together. "Besides, I have discovered that chastity has heightened my spiritual awareness. Made me a much stronger man. Sex had become too important to me. It's better this way."

"But, but . . ." For once, Bev was at a loss for words. Chastity hadn't worked any such miracles for her.

"But what?" Karl asked.

"What about us?" Bev blurted out. "Are we to endure a Platonic relationship or what?"

Karl sat down on a couch opposite Bev and picked up her hand. "Why don't you tell me more about what *you* had in mind."

Bev drew back. "You're playing with me, aren't you?"

He grinned. "What makes you think that?"

She reached over to give him a shove but he grabbed her two hands and pulled her over to the couch. Slowly, he drew her body closer until her lips were almost touching his smile.

She didn't know whether to butt him with her head or to kiss him. "Karl, what are you doing to me?"

"I'm flirting with temptation," he answered.

"You're a thief," she said, leaning down and planting a kiss on his lips.

He released her hands and wrapped his arms around her waist. She eased her hands down below his shoulders.

He fingered her hair. He stared into her eyes and at her face, admiring the pout of her lips and the fabric stretching into creased folds over her breasts. His hands ran down the whole of her figure, past the outline of her hips, down her strong thighs, to the round bones at her ankles. He pulled off her shoes and stroked the arches of her feet. "Oh, it's been so-o-o long."

"But what about chastity and your spiritual life?"

He rolled his eyes heavenward. "Oh Lord, forgive me for what I am about to do."

"That's it?" Bev was incredulous.

His hands reached up inside her blouse and unhooked her bra. Running his hand over the mound of her left breast, he observed, "Your cup runneth over."

Bev burst out laughing. How could she resist a man who, despite all the grief in his life, found such joy in sensuality and maintained such a wicked sense of humor? When she touched him, it was all fire and glue that bound them together. If loving him was the craziest thing she had ever done in her life, well so be it. She would willingly play the part of the fool.

Karl was stealing her heart all over again.

*   *   *   *

"I got caught shoplifting two years ago, but I ain't been in trouble since." A mass of straight bangs covered Daisy Bassett's eyes as she stared at the clinic floor.

She's not an unattractive youngster, thought Sam, *but can I trust her?*

Daisy sported a silver earring in her right nostril and a purple streak in her mousy brown hair. A black leather jacket squeaked as she shifted her position on the chair. Every once in a while she'd crack a hidden piece of gum in her mouth.

"Irreparable goods," Jillian had sniffed when he mentioned that he was going to interview Daisy for the part-time position.

But Sam had a soft spot for wounded animals and damaged humans. His calling was to be a healer and if anybody needed help it was this teenager girl gawkily sitting before him. If he hired her, he knew that Jillian would come around.

"I love animals. It's people I can't stand," Daisy muttered. "I don't mind cleaning cages or nuthin.'"

"But you'll have to be working with the pet owners when they come in for their appointments. The job requires that the person set up appointments, make telephone calls, and answer questions besides working with the animals," Sam warned her.

Rather than confront the nature of her apparel, he added, "You'll also have to wear a lab coat so that your own clothing doesn't get stained. And we can't have any profanity or cigarette smoking here."

"No smoking?" An anguished look squinched her eyebrows.

Sam shook his head. "Not good for the animals. Or us."

"Geez, I dunno." Lines furrowed across her brow. She pursed her lips together. "Hell's bells."

"Remember, no swearing. Do you think you can do it?" Sam leaned forward toward her.

She sat up straight, stared at him. "You're shitting me, aren't you?"

"No. The job's yours if you would like it."

"God damn," she exclaimed. "Okay. When do I start?"

* * * *

"Grandfathers," cried out Adam that evening by the sweat lodge. "My new friend, Emily, has invited me to come to her house on Tuesday or Thursday afternoons. She doesn't live too far away, if I cut through the woods. I've already been to her place a couple of times. I didn't tell Mom about her, because Mom would want to know how I met her and all that."

He lifted his small chanunpa. It was becoming familiar to his hands. "I give thanks for the gift of this pipe. Emily's kind to me. She wants to know all about my life, my friends at school, the pipe, and our ceremonies. She says someday she would like me to show her this pipe. Grandfather, she says that I am like a grandson to her, that my visits make her happy. Mitakuye oyas'in."

F I V E

FORTY-ONE

Not what we give, but what we share—
For the gift without the giver is bare;
Who gives himself with his alms feeds
     three,—
Himself, his hungering neighbor,
     and Me.

—JAMES RUSSELL LOWELL
The Vision of Sir Launfal

On her forty-first birthday, Meggie awakened to the smell of freshly brewed coffee, scrambled eggs, bacon, orange juice, and an English muffin toasted to perfection. Hawk set the tray down on a small table and climbed back into bed with her.

"Happy Birthday, old woman."

She cut him a glance. "Just remember, Hawk, you're older than I am. But thank you for cooking my breakfast."

He reached over and stole a piece of bacon off her plate. She pretended not to notice. He took a sip of her black coffee. Still, she said nothing. He picked up the buttery English muffin and nibbled on it. Finally, Meggie couldn't restrain herself. "Touch my eggs and you're dead."

"Okay." He backed off, laughing at her. "Do you want all your birthday gifts right now or piece by piece during the day?"

"How many did you get me?"

Reaching below the bed, he dragged out a large, soft package wrapped in crinkled brown paper adorned with the words *Leland Mercantile*.

"I used the paper bags from the grocery store," he explained.

Meggie was curious. She tore open the paper and unfolded a soft deer skin.

"Brain-tanned." Hawk brought the hide up to Meggie's face and touched it to her cheek so that she could feel the velvety texture.

"It's really nice, Hawk. And so unusual." Meggie hadn't the slightest idea what she was going to do with the present.

"I knew you'd really appreciate it," Hawk enthused. "But it's not the only gift I have for you."

"Oh?"

Hawk leaned over the edge of the bed and pulled out a box. He placed it in her hands.

A weighty cardboard container but small. A piece of sculpture? A music box? There was just no telling what Hawk had gotten her. The man was always full of surprises. She lifted up the lid and extracted a white soap stone, three-legged mortar, and pestle. What to say? It wasn't like she needed one. Her food processor did the job of grinding a whole lot faster and easier than any mortar and pestle.

"Interesting," Meggie said.

"It's exactly what you need." He grinned. And before she could ask him what he meant by that statement, he pushed a shoe box in her direction.

"I'm not even going to venture a guess as to what this contains," Meggie sighed. Hawk was having fun at her expense. She pried off the lid. Nestled inside the box were zip-locked bags of colored beads, black paper needle holders, an amber ball of beeswax, several spools of white thread, and silver earring wires. She studied Hawk's reaction.

He beamed. "Well, if you can teach me to cook, certainly I can instruct you in the fine art of beadwork. But that's not all." He set a second shoe box on her lap.

Cautious, not knowing what to expect, Meggie peeked inside the rattling box which contained a leather hole punch, sharp scissors, an awl, and a set of larger needles. Getting into the spirit of the game, she smiled at him, saying, "This is what I always wanted, Hawk. And to think I had to wait forty-one years to get it." Good God, would these presents never end?

"Just two more gifts for my birthday girl." Hawk hefted a heavy grocery bag onto the bed. Meggie teased apart the top of the bag, reached in, and hauled out a plastic bag of dried corn. "Okay," she said, not betraying her confusion, "What else do you have for me?" She had dispensed with the niceties.

Hawk slipped his hand into the pocket of his bathrobe and pulled out a small royal blue box. "This is a present from both your parents and from me."

Into the palm of her hand he set the velvet box. Eagerly she thumbed it open and to her delight it was a ring—a diamond offset by two dark red rubies. "Oh, Hawk, it's beautiful," Meggie exclaimed.

She held the ring in her fingers then began to slide it over the ring finger of her right hand. Hawk stopped her. "That's the wrong hand," he said. He slipped the ring on the finger of her left hand.

"But . . ." she began to protest.

"It's your wedding ring, Meggie. Your mother sent me the diamond when it became clear to her that we were planning to get married. It was your great-grandmother's diamond. I bought the two rubies. At the core, you'll always be Irish-American: That's the diamond."

He then pointed to the rubies. "But, by God, you're the captive of this red man." He encircled her with his arms and kissed her long and deep.

When she came up for air, she spoke. "It's beautiful, but I do have one minor technical point to bring up."

He looked at her.

She continued, "We're not married yet."

"What do you think all these presents are for?" he asked.

Her eyes inventoried the deer skin, the awl, the beads and earring wires, the mortar and pestle, the bag of corn. It was beginning to dawn on her that they were part of some larger scheme.

"You tell me," she suggested.

Patiently, he explained. "There's a lot of work that goes into the traditional Lakota blanket ceremony. The deerskin is for pipe bags and medicine bags. The beads are to make earrings, belt buckles, pipe tampers. The mortar and pestle are for grinding corn by hand. I have to make *wasna*, buffalo pemmican. You have to grind corn for the ceremony. We must give every wedding guest a present of thanks-giving, because you and I are the lucky ones. We have to share our good fortune and happiness with others. So, we'll be busy every night making presents for the giveaway at our wedding."

"Maybe a Methodist ceremony would be easier?"

Hawk didn't pay her any mind. "Laughing Bear has agreed to do the ceremony."

Meggie tried again. "Would you like to inform me *when* we are going to have this wedding?"

"March 21st, the Spring Equinox, when night and day are equally weighed and time goes tipping toward the morning. It will be a good time for us to get married." Hawk had obviously given it some thought.

Two months away.

It certainly sounded to Meggie as if they had a lot of work ahead of them. As much as she would enjoy teasing Hawk about having a tradi-tional Lakota ceremony, it would never occur to her to marry him in any other manner. The Chanunpa Wakan nestled in the center of their love for each other. The Sacred Pipe had helped heal the wounds of the previous year, when Meggie had lost their baby and Hawk had tem-porarily lost his way.

In two months' time she would become his wife.

"Forever," he spoke. "We will be married by the Pipe, for eternity."

Mischievously, she arched her eyebrows at him. "Eternity is a very long time."

The golden light of morning glinted in through the eastern window. Like a new bride, Meggie held out her left hand and watched the translucent diamond play in the cast of the sun, surrounded by the dark and mysterious red rubies.

"Look, Hawk." The ring twinkled and then, catching a full ray, burst a rainbow onto the bedroom wall, an arch of dazzling but distinct colors.

SIX

DERANGEMENTS

Here comes February, a little girl with her first valentine,
a red bow in her wind-blown hair, a kiss waiting on her lips,
a tantrum just back of her laughter.

—HAL BORLAND
Sundial of the Seasons

The pristine face of January's snow began to blister and pale before the uncertainties of February's bluster. Whereas the skies in January had been bright and full of winter's sparkle, a gray shroud now descended over the Leelanau Peninsula and its restless inhabitants. The land popped and crackled with the incessant drip of rain. Miniature glaciers retreated across fields and farms, uncovering a sodden mat of beaten brown grass. Bare, gnarly trees twisted toward the heavens, grasping for a touch of the evasive sun. The limbs of fir trees hung low, earthward, as if imprinted with the memory of heavy snows and the harsh face of *Waziya*.

During the long February evenings, as he and Meggie applied themselves to craft work, Hawk often spoke to her of spiritual matters.

"Winona taught me about the Good Spirits and the Trickster Spirits but not much about the Evil Spirits," Meggie confessed.

"That's because she was a wise woman. To know too much too soon can make one reckless, dangerous," Hawk said.

"You don't mean booga wooga stuff?"

Hawk laughed. "Yes, that's exactly what I mean."

"Evil spells?" Her voice was incredulous.

Hawk nodded.

A moment's silence. "Hawk, do you *really* believe one person can cast an evil spell upon another?"

"Yes."

"Okay, I can understand people doing all kinds of things out of the mistaken belief that they have some special power. But you don't really believe the spells work, do you?"

Again, Hawk nodded.

"But that's crazy thinking," Meggie protested. "You mean if I am angry at someone, I can do a Lakota ritual and hurt them?"

"I've seen it happen," he said, "but there's a price to be paid for doing that kind of work. The evil can come back onto someone in your family and hurt them as well. That's one reason I don't mess with any of those rituals."

"But if they were effective, people would be doing them all the time."

"That's why all medicine people have protective medicine," Hawk explained. "If you can keep strong and balanced, the spell will probably not work. The Pipe protects you as well as the sage. That's why I smudge every day. I'm . . ." Hawk thought a moment, looking for the analogy. "Every day I'm boosting my immune system so the ugly germs of mankind won't hurt me."

"Apparently your protection didn't work out so well when you got sick."

"But what you said made sense, Meggie. The virus had upset my internal balance so that the bacteria already in me made me even sicker. That is the true genius, the push of Evil's power. It is like a snake that insinuates into one's self, so that we then manufacture our own self-destruction."

"Ouch!" Meggie stuck herself with a needle. "I'm a total klutz," she complained.

When she made mistakes in the beadwork, and there were many, he told her not to worry. "Even the best Native American artist tries to include one error in the piece. It is our way of showing that we two-leggeds are not perfect."

He also told her that there was one upstairs room in the house that was now off-limits. Unbeknownst to her, Hawk had been spending many daylight hours in that room.

"Why? Does it have to do with your medicine?"

"Don't be nosy. It's none of your business." He tried to divert the conversation, but by the crackling fire and the darkness of the moonless night, Meggie recited the story of Blue Beard.

"A wealthy brigand, he forbade his wife from entering into a particular room of the castle. When she disobeyed him . . ."

"She must have been Irish American," Hawk interrupted.

Meggie shot him a hushing look and continued, "When she opened the door, she discovered the bloodied skeletons of all his former wives."

"Ouch." Hawk pricked his finger with a beading needle.

"So, what dark mystery are you hiding?" Meggie probed.

"I've already told you everything about my former wives."

"So what's in the room, Blue Beard?" Meggie was not about to give up.

"It's a secret. Can't you leave it at that?" He gave her a sharp, warning look.

Meggie considered his request for a moment before giving answer. "No. If you don't tell me, I'll find out for myself."

"It's your wedding present, if you must know." Hawk slumped in his chair, annoyed that Meggie had teased out part of the secret. "And you're just going to have to wait until it's finished before you see it."

∗   ∗   ∗   ∗

Meggie didn't really mind the doldrums of February. Not only did she have a wedding to anticipate, it was the time of year when nature's gloom sent many a client scurrying her way.

Couples who had renovated their homes in the previous Michigan spring, frolicked and eaten cherry pie in the lush summer, golfed and gone apple-picking in the brilliant fall, skied and visited movie theaters in the sparkling winter, could no longer tolerate the sight of each other come February. The endearing little habits that mark a person as surely as a signature grew tiresome and loathsome in the marital confines.

If winter was over and February was simply a transition to Spring, then everyone could have endured the days of gray with grace. But the people of the Leelanau Peninsula knew that winter hadn't really disappeared. The weather had simply transformed the crystalline snow to glazing ice by night and sucking sop by day. The snow would recycle several times again before the true revolution of spring. But the storms would now come unexpectedly, in punishing, unforgiving fury. The blizzard blankets of snow would lay down quick upon the earth and seep into the freezing mud of February.

* * * *

Jillian stomped into the Suttons Bay Veterinary Clinic, scraping the muck from the under-soles of her boots. Daisy followed, cuddling a coal black rabbit to her chest. "Look, Dr. Waters, what we found huddling on the side of the road."

"Not we," scoffed Jillian. She turned to Sam. "There I am, moving at a swift fifty miles-per-hour on M22, and Daisy begins leaping up and down in the front seat of my car, yelling at me to stop and turn around. God almighty, I thought she was having an epileptic seizure."

"But we couldn't leave this little guy behind," Daisy interrupted. "He was shivering by the road." She stroked between his two long black ears.

"Needless to say," continued Jillian, "we almost caused an accident, but I dutifully turned around back to where she was pointing. The rabbit didn't move, even when the cars whizzed by. I thought he was road kill."

Daisy passed him over into Sam's hands. The veterinarian peered into the dulled eyes and felt along the paws and legs. "Nothing seems to be broken. Obviously someone's lost pet rabbit. We'll watch him for the next forty-eight hours, keep him warm, and feed him. Daisy," Sam addressed the concerned teenager, "I'm going to make this rabbit your special responsibility. Now it's time for you to be getting off to school. We'll expect you back this afternoon."

"Can't I stay here today to look after him?" Daisy hated school and sought any opportunity to skip class.

Sam shook his head. "Part of our agreement was that you would attend your classes full-time. In return for that, Jillian gives you a ride to town in the morning and you have your job with us every afternoon. So scoot."

Jillian opened the door.

Daisy reluctantly departed, shouting over her shoulder, "I'm going to call him Buster."

Jillian shut the door. "You know what's going to happen, don't you, Sam? Every lost and orphaned animal will end up here, brought in by that girl. Already we have two kittens, one mangy dog, and a turtle with a cracked shell. Now, unless you rapidly enlarge the facility, we're going to run out of room."

"I know, Jillian. You've been very patient. But did you notice, she didn't utter a single swear word today? That's progress, isn't it?"

"Today has hardly even begun, Sam." Jillian scored her words with skepticism. "Are we a veterinary clinic or Suttons Bay's newest day care center for wayward youth and lost pets?"

It was a futile argument. Her job was to remind Sam about reality and help keep the business fiscally sound. Not the easiest of tasks. Sam had the softest heart of any man she had ever encountered.

"But you've given me a good idea." Sam paused before taking Buster into the back room.

"I always give you good ideas, Sam."

"I'm going to make all these orphans Daisy's special project. I'll ask her to figure out how to find them good homes once we've brought them back to health. Responsibility can instill a sense of accomplishment and personal pride in a young person." Sam smiled, pleased with his plan.

"That's what we call a *two-fer*." Jillian hauled out the appointment book, the stack of appointment cards, and a can of pens and arranged them on the counter.

"What?"

"A *two-fer-one* solution." Before Jillian could elaborate, the front door flung open and in lunged a muzzled Rottweiler, yanking his leashed owner across the door sill.

"Sit," shouted a rough looking man in his late thirties. But the dog had spied Buster and, from way back in its throat, emitted a ferocious growl. A tug of war ensued between dog and man until the man threw his weight upon the dog's back and forced it into a sitting position. Sam quickly removed Buster to a back room cage before returning to the waiting room.

Jillian was already writing down information in a new file folder. "The Rottweiler is two years old, in good condition, but untrainable, according to Mr. . . . ."

"McCutheon. It's worse than that. He's a biter and always has been. Keep him chained to the dog house, but it don't do a damn bit of good. He's a killer, I'm telling you. Yesterday he got loose, tore after a twelve-year-old kid on a bicycle. Went right for the boy's throat. Luckily, the boy raised his arm in time. He's got a circle of bite marks there. This is the third time the damn dog has attacked someone. You got to put him down, Doc. He's just plain mean."

The dog's eyes rolled and his ears flattened.

"Do you want to be there when I put him to sleep?" Sam hadn't yet set up the equipment.

The man shook his head. "No. I don't have no love for the dog. No matter how much I discipline him, he's got a vicious streak in him a mile wide. I'll come by tomorrow to pick up the muzzle." The man paid his bill and left.

Jillian reminded Sam that he had scheduled an afternoon euthanasia for a sick cocker spaniel.

Sam joshed, "Are you suggesting I do a two-fer?"

"I'm simply trying to make you more efficient."

Sam winked. "You know I couldn't run this place without you."

"That goes without saying, Sam."

In mid-afternoon Daisy reappeared, hung up her leather jacket, and donned a white lab coat. Jillian informed her that Sam wanted her to come up with some plan for all the orphan animals. "We can't keep them forever," Jillian warned.

Daisy collected Buster from his cage, rubbing the soft fur against her cheek. "Isn't he a beauty?"

Jillian looked up from her computer. She had to agree there was a certain bunnified charm to him.

"What if we took a photograph of him and tacked it up on the bulletin board here as 'Pet of the Month'? We could write a description and say that he's up for adoption. We could even charge money for the adoption." Daisy's enthusiasm grew with each word.

"One pet a month? At the rate you're collecting the animals, the intake will far exceed the outflow. That's where mathematics comes in, girl. You figure." Jillian was always pointing out the benefits of higher education to Daisy.

Daisy counted on her fingers, then declared, "A 'Pet of the Week' will about do it."

Jillian continued, "After you clean the cages and ask Sam if there is anything else he needs, I want you to sit down and compute how much we're spending on food and shelter for these orphans. That will tell you how much we need to charge for each adoption. I want you also to think about where we can advertise, without charge. This is your project."

Daisy's eyes gleamed. She had lots and lots of ideas about where potential owners could be notified. Her school, the IGA, maybe even in a weekly church pamphlet. She'd advertise the dog first. That way, Buster could stay at the clinic longer. Careful to secure the gate into the waiting room, she deposited Buster on the office floor.

"Boy, he's coming back strong," she announced.

Jillian didn't pay attention. Her eyes were affixed to the computer screen. Behind the counter and located in the waiting room sat three people: One constraining a tri-colored collie, another stroking a brown Manx cat, and the third holding a green, slow-blinking iguana. Buster hopped over toward Jillian's right leg while Daisy searched the back rooms for the cleaning equipment. The rabbit sniffed Jillian's ankle and peered up into the dark sanctuary of the pants' fabric. He suddenly did the unexpected. Up, up he leapt inside Jillian's pant leg, almost making it to the safe perch of her knee.

Jillian shrieked, jumped up, shook her leg violently. Out shot Buster, skidding sideways onto the floor. Both Sam and Daisy came running. Startled, the collie began barking. The Manx cat arched its back and hissed at the dog. The iguana slithered out of its owner's grasp, scuttled across the floor, and disappeared down a loose air duct.

"What's the matter?" voiced Sam.

"Oh my gosh, is he hurt?" yelled Daisy. She grabbed Buster and examined him.

Jillian narrowed her eyes at Daisy and ordered, "Take that rabbit out of this room now."

Daisy didn't dare say anything. She retreated to the back rooms, Buster safely cradled in her hands.

Jillian lifted up her hands, rolled her eyes in dismay, and patted her hair back into place. "I'm all right, Sam. You can go back to work." She turned toward the counter where one of the three customers was trying to catch her attention. "Yes?" she asked, letting her breathing slow down to normal.

A woman in her thirties, the owner of an art gallery in Suttons Bay, looked at Jillian, anxiety crisscrossing her face, and hyperventilated. "Napoleon, my iguana, is gone." She pointed to the opened air duct on the floor, the grate having been dislodged.

"I'm sure he'll surface when he feels it's safe." Jillian tried for a smile and missed. "I'll be right back," she groaned. She burst into the examining room where Sam was vaccinating a Samoyed puppy that was being held down by its owner. "I need to talk to you, Sam."

He looked up from the puppy who was flinching from the sting of the needle.

"Now," commanded Jillian.

In the back rooms, Daisy deposited Buster on the floor and shut the door to Jillian's area. "Now you be good." She wagged her finger at the rabbit. Buster quietly sniffed and explored the corners. Daisy gathered up a mop, a bucket filled with cleaning fluid, a roll of paper, and a white waste container. She did the cat cages first, humming snatches of popular tunes, convinced that the animals enjoyed the sound of her voice.

When she entered the canine quarters, the cocker spaniel and the rescued dog wagged their tails. At first she didn't notice the Rottweiler, so concerned was she to give special attention to the spaniel whom she knew was going to be put to sleep that afternoon. "Hey baby," she crooned, opening the door to stroke the cocker who was too sick to stand up. His tail flapped against the bottom of the cage; his feverish tongue licked across her palm. Daisy tried not to think about what was going to happen. Then she heard the low sound from the corner. A groan or a growl, it wasn't clear. She turned and saw the Rottweiler, watching her with intense eyes.

"Oh, who are you?" Daisy shut the door to the spaniel's cage and moved toward the large enclosure. She noticed the tight bite of the muzzle on the Rottweiler's jaw.

"That's the problem, isn't it? Does it hurt you?"

The dog studied her, twitching its ears back and forth. Daisy imagined that the Rottweiler found her sympathetic. It couldn't hurt for her to loosen the muzzle some, she reasoned. She opened the door to the cage, wondering what kind of illness had brought the Rottweiler to the clinic. The dog stood there, not moving, as Daisy approached him. Bringing up her fingers alongside the leather muzzle, she unbuckled its tight hold. "There you are, Big Guy."

Before she could reattach the buckle, the Rottweiler shot out past her, the muzzle flapping open, straight for the cornered rabbit. His massive jaws opened and Buster's head disappeared into the dog's mouth.

Daisy screamed and threw herself upon the dog's neck, yanking him back, but the Rottweiler refused to let go. Back and forth, back and forth, he shook Buster's body with great enthusiasm.

Sam burst into the room, yelling, "What now?" Seeing the mayhem, he grabbed the dog from behind, forced him to release the rabbit, and shoved him back into the cage.

Buster flopped to the ground, bloodied and broken. Not an ear twitched. Daisy didn't need to touch him to know that he was dead.

She burst into tears. "It's all my fault." She grabbed onto Sam and began sobbing into his shoulder.

He patted her on the back. "That dog is here to be put down."

Daisy looked up at him, tears streaming down her face. "But it was my fault."

Sam shook his head. "The dog is a killer."

Daisy wiped her eyes on the back of her white sleeve. "You mean he was born bad?"

"Are animals and people born bad or do they get made that way? You can take most animals or children and shape them towards gentleness or towards meanness. But sometimes, Daisy, there are those individuals who seem born to take pleasure out of hurting others and it can't simply be explained away by bad training. This guy here," Sam nodded toward the Rottweiler, "has a history of killing animals and attacking people. You were lucky that you didn't get hurt. I don't want you fiddling with any more muzzles. Okay?"

"But what about Buster?" Daisy's lower lip began to tremble.

Sam picked up the dead rabbit and dropped Buster in the animal disposal container. He sighed. "I'm sorry, Daisy. I only know how to help the living. I don't have the power to bring the dead back to life."

*   *   *   *

"You've got dirt on your forehead," Bev said to Karl over a cup of mocha java at Bacchus and Brie. She licked her thumb and reached over to clean off the smudge. He threw back his head and held up his hand to block her thumb.

"No," he laughed. "That's ash. It's Ash Wednesday, don't you know?"

"Karl, you forget. I'm an atheist. What do I know about your occult rituals? Or why you go around with a gray stain in the middle of your forehead?"

He explained. "After Palm Sunday, the palms are burned. The ash is then saved for months until Ash Wednesday. It's a way some Christians publicly acknowledge the beginning of Lent."

Bev blew on her coffee. "I'm not sure I want to know, but I'm going to ask anyway. What's Lent?"

"It's the forty days and forty nights before Easter. It's a time of meditation and prayer and, for some Christians, a time of fasting and abstaining from a favorite activity."

"I'm warning you, Karl," Bev shook a finger at him. "I refuse to become a nun."

"But when you really want something, Bev, your prayers become intense and alive with meaning."

Bev didn't know whether Karl was teasing her or being serious. It didn't occur to her that maybe he was doing both at the same time.

SEVEN

FIRE IN HER EYES

To tell the right story at the right time is the equivalent
of approaching the heavens with the fiery chariots.

—STEVE SANDFIELD, 1996

Emily brought over a large glass of milk and a dish of chocolate chip cookies to her round oak table. Elbows firmly planted on its wooden surface, Adam leaned forward, his feet dangling from the tall chair. He was hungry after a long school day.

"I brought my new pipe with me," he announced, beaming. He slid the pieces out of the pipe bag, fit the dark wood stem into the salmon-hued bowl, and circled the chanunpa in the air. "But you can't touch it, if you're at the time of the month when . . ." Adam's cheeks reddened. He was too embarrassed to continue.

Emily's stout belly jiggled with laughter. She ruffled Adam's hair, saying, "It's been a long time since I've done any monthly bleeding. But thank you for the compliment."

He passed her the assembled pipe and picked up a cookie.

Emily adjusted her half-glasses. "An interesting color to the bowl," she said, then half-whispered, "The tint of flesh, the taint of blood."

Adam overheard that curious comment. Remembering his mother's admonitions not to talk with a full mouth, he swallowed before speaking. "Hawk says that's the color of our people."

"Who is Hawk?" Emily flashed interested eyes as she turned the pipe over in her hands.

"My mom's cousin. He teaches us 'bout ceremonies and stuff. He's got a trailer at our place but he doesn't stay there much anymore." Adam let out a huge sigh.

"It sounds like you miss him." Emily's kind words wrapped around him.

Adam's eyes shifted to the table. The corners of his mouth arched downward. "He's got a girlfriend now."

"You don't like her?"

"Oh, she's okay. Don't really know her. He says he's gonna marry her."

"But you'd rather he was back living in that trailer close to you, I bet." Emily smiled.

Adam nodded. "It's just that he knows a lot. My grandma taught him. And he doesn't come around much anymore, unless it's for Pipe ceremonies."

Emily carefully transferred the pipe back into Adam's hands. "I ask a lot of questions, don't I? Thank you, Adam, for showing it to me. Do all tribes use the pipe?"

Adam sipped his milk, shook his head. "White Buffalo Calf Woman gave the Lakota the pipe."

"Who?"

Adam pushed away the cookies, knowing that he was going to have to take some time to explain this to his new friend. He licked the crumbs off his lips. "White Buffalo Calf Woman, *Ptesan Wi*, zoomed out of the sky to earth. Two hunters were the first to meet her. The people were real hungry, 'cuz they weren't doing things right and all the animals had gone away. These guys saw her. She was the most beautiful girl they ever saw and one of them ran toward her, which wasn't right. 'Cuz when something's sacred, you gotta act respectful. Anyway, she zapped him when he got too close. When the smoke cleared, he was just a skeleton at her feet. The old people say there was all kinds of evil stuff crawling and eating on him. Really gross. She called to the other guy. He was real scared, but he had to go to her."

Adam shifted around in his chair, pleased that Emily was listening so carefully. "She told him to go home to his village and get everybody together. Then she came and taught the people how to be respectful and how to pay attention and how to use the pipe. She gave them a pipe and told them to take it to all the other Indian people."

"What a wonderful storyteller you are," Emily enthused. "Did you just make up this story?"

Adam looked at her as if she was out of her mind. "No," he exclaimed. "It's for real. Honest to God, it really happened."

Emily gave him a condescending smile, the kind adults give children when they're humoring them. Adam could see that she didn't really believe him.

"I'm telling you, it's true," he protested. "There's a guy named Looking Horse who's still got the original pipe White Buffalo Calf Woman brought."

"Well, then," said Emily, "I stand corrected. I thought you were just spinning me a myth."

"A myth?" Adam didn't know the meaning of that word.

"Oh, that's a kind of story people tell that's true but not factual. Truth comes in many forms and beliefs," Emily explained.

Adam looked more confused than ever.

Emily laughed and changed the topic. "So, do you have a girlfriend at school?"

Adam nodded.

"What's her name?"

"June Tubbs," he answered.

Emily leaned forward in interest. "Tell me about her, Adam."

"She was in a terrible accident last year. Almost died. Her face has still got scars. But I like her a lot."

"Poor thing," commiserated Emily. "It must have been really scary and painful for her. Tell me more about her."

Adam liked the way Emily paid attention to what he had to say. She asked him lots of questions and made him feel all grown up.

* * * *

Meggie scanned the intrigued faces of clinicians who had been listening to her presentation, "Therapeutic Stories for Children and Adults." She knew she had hooked their interest with case descriptions, followed by stories braiding in the clients' unique symbol systems with their behavioral symptoms. Every time Meggie began one of her stories, the therapists sank back into their chairs like children awaiting a delightful feast of words.

Meggie concluded, "Stories speak directly to one's heart. Your clients' metaphors are containers of partial truths. They are like the end-of-winter buds on the trees, not daring to fully open lest the frost return to kill them. In the safe and warm therapy environment these metaphors, so long nurtured in the soil of hidden pain, can blossom and display astonishing color and form. From symbol to metaphor to story, you can help your clients construct a narrative map along the journey of life. And if you do this skillfully," Meggie concluded, "the client's story will bring healing to you as well."

Applause spontaneously rippled across the room. Meggie opened up the floor to questions.

All eyes shifted to the wheelchair occupant in the front row: A tiny woman in her mid-seventies, her thinning hair tinted a light orange, frail in appearance with shoulders hunched against chronic pain. A woman of piercing, fiery eyes, it was the renowned Dr. Gertrude Gold.

The elderly psychologist punctuated the air with her sharp chin. "Thank you, Dr. O'Connor, for your most interesting talk." An eastern European accent heavily weighted her pronunciation.

The audience, hanging upon her every word, hardly breathed. A psychologist well known for terrorizing generations of younger therapists in her supervision sessions, Gertrude Gold held little patience for either professional stupidity or negligence toward clients.

Dr. Gold leveled a penetrating gaze at Meggie and tapped the fingers of both hands together, as if in impatient prayer. "In your talk, you suggested that therapists pay close attention to client metaphors and work those images into a healing story. But the clients you described all suffered from neurotic symptoms or personality disorders. I wonder if you would apply the same techniques to the patient who has been severely traumatized?"

All heads swiveled toward Meggie as if a professional boxing match was about to begin. Meggie sensed, however, that Dr. Gold was neither trying to snare her nor display one-upmanship. There was something about this topic dear to Dr. Gold's interests.

Meggie paused to frame her answer carefully. "There are times in psychotherapy with such individuals when a therapeutic story can work miracles in working through resistance. But when you're struggling with the problem of a client's fuzzy or repressed memories, you have to be extremely careful not to suggest stories that contaminate the memory retrieval of the traumatic events."

Dr. Gold turned her head toward the audience, many of them her current or former students. "Dr. O'Connor is right to confront the crucial difference between a therapist creating a healing story and the client who needs to tell his or her own story. A therapist must never place his or her agenda upon the client. When you are working with the severely traumatized individual, story takes on quite a different meaning. Healing cannot occur without the act of witness. To witness is to give voice to what happened. Only the client can legitimately do that."

A paunchy, middle-aged man addressed Dr. Gold. "The biggest question I face with my patients who are trying to recover memories of childhood trauma is: How do you know when enough is enough? How do you know when the client has retrieved all the memories? Sometimes it seems that you can go on for years and years of therapy recovering these stories."

Gertrude snapped back, "Years and years of therapy can be crucial when extreme damage has been done to an individual. On the other hand, client and therapist can also indulge in stories of victimization ad nauseam that leave both of them feeling angry, bitter, and disempowered. The healing story traumatized clients have to tell for themselves is one that accounts for what they remember, what they experience now, and what will sustain them into the future. And that is when you'll know enough is enough."

The man persisted, "But what about the truth of the stories? If the person doesn't recall *everything* that happened, how can that person know that his or her partial account is accurate?"

Gertrude shook her head. "Truth and fact are not identical. Truth is the meaning we make out of a bundle of facts. Truth is what helps us live from day to day. If the facts are wrong, the truth will eventually falter. But the truth of an event changes over time because we human beings change over time. What we need to make sense out of our existence changes over time. When Dr. O'Connor talks of creating stories out of client metaphors, she is not discussing facts. She is working with truth."

Meggie appreciated Dr. Gold returning the subject matter to the focus of the lecture. For about fifteen minutes thereafter, she answered technical questions about story construction, trance induction, and follow-up work.

As the therapists began to drift out of the conference room, several shook Meggie's hand, expressing the simple pleasure of hearing oral stories again. Meggie felt a slight dismay at how many commented, "It's a wonderful technique, but I could never write stories" or "I wish I had the talent that you do, but . . ."

Slipping her notebook into her cloth bag, Meggie was ready to leave when she noticed that Dr. Gold still sat in the front row, quietly waiting. Gertrude beckoned for Meggie to come closer.

Meggie sat down on an uncomfortable metal chair beside the old woman.

Licking her dry lips and arching formidable eyebrows, Gertrude cautioned Meggie, "A story is like a wild animal. I have seen powerful stories consume people, like a dragon's tongue flicking out and in, swallowing whomever comes across its path. A beautiful story can even seduce a whole nation and bewitch the people into the dragon's lair. Stories are powerful magic."

Meggie nodded and waited. More was coming.

Rubbing her deeply veined hands together, Dr. Gold continued. "Like all magic, it can go either way. Much evil is done to the human being through the faculty of the imagination. So, too, healing must also traverse that same pathway. It's clear to me that you are one of those few therapists who understands the sheer, awesome power of story. Use that power wisely, Dr. O'Connor. And if you ever need help in taming the beast, I am here."

Contemptuously, Gertrude looked down at her wheelchair. "As you can see, I am trapped where I am. But up here, in the mind, I am not imprisoned by any infirmity." She reached out to shake Meggie's hand, a gesture that was both a welcome and a dismissal.

What a extraordinary woman, Meggie thought.

*   *   *   *

"So, you believe in Spirits then?" Emily asked.

Adam solemnly nodded. "My grandmother told me that there are Good Spirits, Trickster Spirits, and Evil Spirits in this world."

"She sounds like a wise woman, Adam. Are you afraid of the Evil Spirits?"

His eyes widened. "I don't want nothing to do with Them."

"Because?"

"'Cuz They can hurt you. They can hurt people around you."

"So, They're real powerful, aren't They?"

Adam glanced at Emily to make sure she was serious. "Don't you believe in Them?"

Emily scratched her second chin. "Will you promise to keep a secret?"

Adam smiled. "Yeah." He liked the intimacy of secrets.

"I don't tell many people about my beliefs, because they'd laugh at me and say I was ignorant," confided Emily. "But I *know* that there are Evil Spirits and that They are really powerful. You have to be super careful around Them." She stopped and slowly stared around the room, as if suspecting that someone might overhear them.

She whispered, "You know what I think?"

"What?" Adam replied in a hushed voice.

Emily licked her lips. "I think that sometimes They are a lot more powerful than other kinds of Spirits. Not that there's anything wrong with power, but you've got to know how to use it, how to control it."

"You mean, to do good?"

"Yes, but . . ." Emily paused. "But what is good? What one person says is good, another says is bad."

She added, "Sometimes bad is good. You know what I mean?

The boy wrinkled his forehead.

Emily explained, "Adam, you remember how your cousin told you that the Christian missionaries passed laws on the reservations prohibiting Indian ceremonies? The white ministers proclaimed that those native ceremonies were 'bad,' but to your people they were 'good.' So, sometimes bad is good and good is bad."

Adam could follow that argument.

Emily continued. "So, you have to do what you feel like doing, what feels good to you, despite what others tell you." She pointed to a framed quotation on the wall: DO WHAT THOU WILT SHALL BE THE WHOLE OF THE LAW.

"Sometimes, Adam, when people try so hard to do what is 'good,' they just end up being weak and beaten. For many years, the Christian missionaries set out to destroy your people's religious traditions saying that to 'be good' meant to be only Christian."

Adam's face furrowed into angry lines as he thought of the white people trying to keep the Lakotas from performing inipi and sun dance ceremonies. Emily was right.

"Sometimes you have to do that which others see as bad. And," Emily warned, "you often have to pay the piper for that decision. People can get really angry at you. They arrested your great-grand-parents when they crept into the hills to do the old ceremonies in secret. Sometimes people can hurt you in other ways and make you feel all kinds of pain." Emily spoke as if she knew what she was talking about.

"Nobody likes to experience pain." She sighed and heaved her mighty frame off the kitchen chair. "But pain can be a pretty powerful teacher. If you can endure it, you can learn a lot about personal power. A lot of high and mighty people in this world go around spouting about how good they are. But as for me, I always look to see who has the power. Words are just words, Adam. Go with the power."

EIGHT

PREPARING

*Ritual is the soul's journey through images,
images which, while partaking of both spirit
and matter, belong to neither, are possessed by neither.*

—MARION WOODMAN
The Pregnant Virgin

whereas February teased and made false promises of spring to
the residents of the Leelanau Peninsula, the gray clouds of March swept
in and wept copious tears. Winter was washing away into the muck of
spring and the people began to reminisce poignantly of its snow-white
beauty. As if in answer to their prayers, a northern Plains blizzard blew
in with fierce, uncompromising fury and dumped nineteen inches of
snow. Enough is enough, the people said.

Meggie worried that the snow would disrupt their wedding plans.
Hawk had insisted that they marry outside, standing on Grandmother
Earth. She imagined the two of them, waist-high in a chilly snowdrift,
teeth chattering as they uttered their vows of love, the guests peering out
the windows from the warm house.

"Wouldn't it be easier to marry in an Episcopalian ceremony?"

Hawk paid her no mind.

The two of them had worked steadily for the past two months making giveaway gifts. Meggie's hands were tender from accidental jabs of

the leather and beading needles into her fingers. "I was not cut out for this kind of work," she protested. "That's one of the reasons I got a Ph.D."

"A Phooey on Domesticity?" he quipped. Hawk proved to be much more skillful with craft work.

One early March night, he proudly announced, "I'm done" and led Meggie by the hand to the off-limits bedroom. From the closet he pulled out a fringed elk skin dress, decorated in the front with elk skin teeth attached to small squares of red cloth. Raising it over her head and wiggling into it, Meggie was amazed by the heft of the material. He handed her two knee-high, matching elk skin moccasins. Even if they had to marry in a snow drift, it was clear she would stay warm.

"Oh Hawk," she glowed. She knew it had taken him weeks to make the old style, Lakota wedding dress.

"You're beautiful." He whistled while stepping back to admire her.

"And what will you wear?" she asked.

He shrugged his shoulders. "A new pair of jeans and a ribbon shirt, most likely."

Meggie shook her head. "Hardly."

From the tone of her voice, Hawk knew she was up to something.

"Stay here." Meggie exited the bedroom only to return a minute later with a white buckskin outfit, fringed pants, and over shirt. Spectacular woven bands of blue, red, and yellow beadwork adorned the legs, arms, and chest. Dangling on the wire hanger were two white beaded moccasins.

Hawk's eyes widened in delight. "But where? Did you . . .?"

"Are you kidding, Hawk? There isn't a chance in hell that I could ever have made such an outfit. In my hands, a beading needle is a lethal weapon. But Lucy has a talent you never knew."

"My cousin?" Hawk couldn't believe that the very modern Lucy would have had the patience, much less the skill, to make such an outfit.

Meggie explained, "Once I knew why you were spending so much time in this room, I went to her. I asked her if she could find me someone to make you a Lakota wedding suit. Lucy wanted to know if I were willing to pay the thousand dollars it would cost to do it right. When I said yes, she immediately told me for that kind of money, she'd do it herself."

Before trying it on, Hawk examined the fine detail in the beadwork, whistling in appreciation. "Whether you believe it or not, Meggie, she gave you a good deal." He stripped off his shirt and jeans and slipped on the buckskin pants and the heavy buckskin shirt.

He looked at himself in the full length mirror. "Ain't I pretty?" He stuck out his chest.

Meggie shook her head and commented, "The only thing more vain than an Indian woman is an Indian man."

He looped his arm around her and pulled her into the mirror's reflection. Meggie noted how her fair-skinned face paled in comparison to his darker flesh, how her dress glowed with the warmth of the reddish brown earth while his outfit reflected the white heavens dappled with beaded strips of sky-blue, fire-red, and sun-yellow.

A long time they stood there, white and brown, brown and white, staring at the glass image in which everything was reversed. Then out of Meggie's mouth issued a remark that was both strange and comforting:

"Hawk, I would love you even if you weren't Indian."

*   *   *   *

A week before the wedding, preparations intensified. Meggie cleaned house for the arrival of her parents and her sister's family. Katja Tubbs and Bev Paterson offered to put up Meggie's curious city friends. The medicine man, Laughing Bear, would stay at Lucy's house. He had called and stated he was bringing along his Polish-American fiancé, Dee Dee.

After conducting two inipi ceremonies, one for the women, one for the men, Hawk sealed himself up in the sweat lodge overnight, praying about the approaching marriage. The temperature dropped to thirteen degrees and the darkness seemed to go on forever. Morning fluttered in on the chirping notes of the chickadee.

Having spent the previous evening in Hawk's trailer, Meggie awoke at seven a.m. and quickly threw on a pair of jeans, a shirt, and boots. Crunching over the white snowpack, she headed to the lodge. Hoisting the door blankets, she peered inside. In the back of the lodge crouched Hawk, facing west.

"Good morning," she greeted him. Her breath spiraled white into the frozen air.

His teeth were chattering as he hunched over the cold rocks, still holding onto his Chanunpa.

"You look like a white man this morning," Meggie observed, helping him to gather up his paraphernalia—tobacco ties, stone-man, medicine bag, and Pipe.

"Don't you worry," he replied. "Soon it will be your time to spend the night in the sweat lodge. So I wouldn't get too feisty if I were you."

* * * *

Three days later, March turned fickle and a hot air stream blew up from the south. The temperature zoomed to a record seventy-three degrees. Meggie's turn for the night in the sweat lodge had arrived.

"I don't know why I should have to freeze my butt in the lodge and here you get the softness of a warm spring evening," Hawk protested. "The Spirits took pity on you."

That night, he poured the waters for the men's inipi ceremony first. After two hours in the sweat lodge, the men crawled out of the lodge, gasping for air and weak from the intense heat. As there was no woman who knew how to lead the women's sweat lodge ceremony, it was up to Hawk to conduct their sweat lodge ceremony.

Upon Meggie's request, Hawk filled her Pipe, the one with the beaded lightning design, and then his own. The women crept on all fours into the lodge, the pit stacked high with the rocks from the men's ceremony. New hot rocks were added. The door keeper lowered the blankets and darkness enveloped the women of the sweat lodge community. Hawk launched into his Spirit-calling song. The water sizzled onto the rocks.

In the first wave of steam, serenity flowed into Meggie. *I feel at home in this place*, she reflected. As Hawk had previously taught her, she sang the Four Directions song when he began the prayers.

The Grandfather of the West is looking at us. The Grandfather of the North is hearing our prayer. The Grandfather of the East is bending over to see what we are doing. The Grandfather of the South is pleased by this ceremony. Grandfather Sky, Grandmother Earth—all of Creation is paying attention to what we are doing here.

Meggie knew it wasn't that the Creator thought the human beings were anything special. Rather the inipi ceremony, the songs, and the prayers were the way the two-leggeds had of putting themselves back into balance with the rest of Creation.

Hawk prayed for everything that contributed to the sweat lodge ceremony—the trees, the fire, the stone nation, the water of life. He gave thanks to All His Relations for helping to make it possible for the two-leggeds to bring themselves back into the web of their sister and brother nations.

Meggie burst into a sun dance song to celebrate the strength of the people and this simple but profound way to make connection to all that is sacred. Hawk offered the last waters to the old ones who had kept the ceremonies, even when the whites had outlawed the inipi in favor of Christian traditions. "It wasn't until Jimmy Carter's day that our people were able to pray in the old ways without the fear of being arrested," Hawk said.

"Mitakuye oyas'in," the women shouted. The door of blankets peeled upwards, expelling the hot, steamy breath of *mni* and *inyan*, the water and stone nations.

In the second round of the ceremony with the door blanketed shut, everyone prayed in turn. Not lofty prayers for world peace or global understanding but down-home prayers about the petty quarrels that hang heavy on the human heart, about the losses that chip away at one's hope, about the need to get back into balance.

In the third round, the Pipe round, someone asked to know more about the Red Face of North, *Wazi*, the Giant. "Sing the Pipe-filling song," Hawk commanded while ladling water onto the hot stones. The heat intensified, prickling and stinging the skin. Meggie and the other women croaked out the song, gasping for air as waves of steam assaulted them. Most of them dove to the Grandmother for cooler air to shield their faces.

Hawk grunted and conversed with the Spirits. The women waited to hear the answer to the question.

"They say," he began, "that toward the pines, Waziyata, there is the harsh Face of Death and there is the Face of Life; in the keen edge between them is the Face of Healing. That is why we pray to the Grand-father of the North, Waziya, for healing. In the time of winter, there is always the struggle between life and death. And without death, you cannot have life. Ah hau!"

Hawk paused, then shouted, "Mitakuye oyas'in," the signal for the doorkeeper to fling up the blankets. The steamy air boiled high out the door as the cooler air tunneled low into the lodge. He passed around a ladle of water to each woman.

The last round was mild in comparison. Hawk made his personal prayers for Meggie's night alone in the sweat lodge. "Do not give her more than she can withstand," he asked the Spirits.

At the end, the women smoked Hawk's Pipe and then crawled out of the lodge, leaving Meggie behind. Hawk made sure she had the blankets she needed. Meggie positioned herself in the back of the lodge, planting her pipe tamper by the edge of the stone pit. In the pitch black-ness of the lodge, when the door had been lowered, the tamper would always orient her to the west. Hawk handed her the lightning Pipe, given to her fifteen months before by her deceased teacher, Winona. The last time she had spent sealed up in the sweat lodge for the night, the Spirits had come and smoked that Pipe and made it sacred, Wakan.

When she was ready, Hawk lowered the door, saying, "Have a good time, darling." She listened to his retreating footsteps.

The dark evening stretched out before her, periods of prayer bracketed by long silences. She noted the cars rumbling out of the driveway as the community departed after the typical post-inipi feast. Meggie could hear her stomach growl in protest. The rocks continued to suffuse a gentle heat.

One by one, the birds sang themselves asleep, until only an owl kept the lonely vigil. At one point, Meggie heard a snuffling sound outside the lodge. It could have been Adam's dog, Shunka, or a coyote; it soon abandoned her to the sound of her own voice and the echoes of enclosed black space.

Meggie prayed frequently about the upcoming blanket ceremony and marriage to Hawk. She asked what she needed to know to be a good wife to him, how to keep her feet on the ground and live in both the white and Native American worlds. Meggie repeated these prayers over and over, resigned to an evening of soliloquy, until suddenly she became aware of another energy in the lodge.

On the north side swirled a dim, diffuse light, like a distant constellation in the heavens, barely visible to the human eye.

"If you are from Wakan Tanka, please smoke with me." Meggie offered her Pipe but no one took it.

Meggie adjusted the sage twig over her left ear and kept her eyes wide open. She wanted to be alert to any response to her prayers.

The voice, when it came, sounded like Winona. Meggie wondered if that were a wish, fashioned by her imagination. But the words were no auditory hallucination:

"You are to be married by the Pipe. Forever. This life and the next and the one after that. Both of you are strong and proud people. But strength can become a weakness when it is relied on too much. He will push you to venture beyond your wildest expectations. You will ground him when he is pulled out of balance by forces bearing down on him. There will be great joy between you. But, remember, there will be times when the people, yours and his, will pull you apart into different worlds. Do not forget that at the center of your marriage dwells the Pipe. The Pipe will always show you the way home. Mitakuye oyas'in."

The light vanished. The voice spoke no more.

"Mitakuye oyas'in," Meggie softly answered.

* * * *

Meggie and Hawk grew exhausted as the wedding day approached. Family and guests had started to arrive. Meggie pulverized the corn by mortar and pestle; Hawk smoked and ground the buffalo meat, adding dried raisins and bacon fat to create the traditional *wasna*, pemmican. They bought a large jug of cherry juice for the ceremony.

The day before the ceremony, Hawk and Meggie stored the giveaway gifts in Hawk's trailer and started to put away all the craft supplies.

"I've still got to gift your father a horse," Hawk obsessed.

"Hawk, he's in his mid-eighties. He lives in the suburbs with a postage stamp yard. What's he going to do with a horse?" Meggie was adamant. Tradition must yield to practicality.

"But," Hawk persevered, "it doesn't have to be a really good horse. A sway-backed, broken-down nag will do."

"And why is that?" Meggie demanded to know, hands on her hips.

"Because," he grinned, "you've already been married once before."

She threw some leather scraps at him.

He ducked and laughed. "You wait and see. I plan to give your father a horse."

*　*　*　*

Laughing Bear and Dee Dee pulled into Lucy's driveway around dinner time. Hawk had never seen his teacher look so happy. Between entertaining everyone with reservation stories, the older man flirted outrageously with his blond fiancé.

Meggie teased him, "I thought you didn't believe in mixed marriages, that Native Americans ought to marry only Native Americans."

"I don't believe in mixed marriages," he snorted.

"But look at the two of you." She nodded toward Dee Dee. "You're planning to marry a white woman and a Polish-American at that."

"Well, she's one of the last good white women," Laughing Bear rationalized.

Meggie waited for the contradiction to sink in.

"What can I say about the human heart? It doesn't seem to give a hoot for my beliefs," Laughing Bear added.

Dee Dee sauntered over to the table and grabbed Laughing Bear's head in her hands, tousling his thinning hair in a flirtatious manner. "And how is my Snookums doing tonight?"

Laughing Bear threw up his hands to demonstrate his helplessness.

Dee Dee reached down and kissed him in front of everyone. Mischievously she looked up at Meggie and winked, "He calls me his 'chick.' That's shorthand for chick-a-dee-dee."

"Marry me?" he peered up into Dee Dee's brown eyes.

"Listen, you handsome hunk, you've gotta get divorced first before I'll marry you."

"Yeah, I know," Laughing Bear acknowledged. "You're going to have to learn about Indian time, Dee Dee." He turned toward Meggie and Hawk. "I'm not going to let this woman get away from me. If

I've learned one thing about marriage, it's this: A good marriage requires only one thing."

Dee Dee asked, "And what's that?"

"Obedience," the older man replied.

Meggie rose to the bait and challenged him, "What do you mean, 'obedience'?"

Laughing Bear grinned. "Obedience in a marriage can be summed up in two words: 'Yes, Ma'am.'"

*   *   *   *

Morning light had not yet edged the horizon when Meggie and Hawk rose early on their wedding day to light the sweat lodge fire at Lucy's place. By dawn, the rocks were glowing red hot. They woke up Laughing Bear and the three of them headed toward the sweat lodge.

"Now you will each make flesh offerings," announced Laughing Bear.

"What's that?" Meggie asked, not liking the sound of it at all.

"I take a razor blade and cut out little squares of flesh from both of your arms." Laughing Bear turned absent-mindedly toward Hawk and inquired, "Did you bring my glasses?"

Hawk shook his head.

"Surely you're joking, aren't you?" Meggie interrupted. She scrutinized Laughing Bear's face but he showed no signs of levity. *An ominous development*, she thought.

"What can you offer Wakan Tanka who has everything? A bit of your flesh. It's a small offering."

Not so small. I like my arms just as they are, Meggie inwardly protested. Upon seeing the razor blade, Meggie felt a lurching in her stomach.

Hawk jogged back to the house to retrieve the medicine man's glasses.

"Fill his Pipe," Laughing Bear commanded.

Meggie unwrapped Hawk's pipe bundle and did as he said.

Hawk returned without the glasses. "I couldn't find them." He knelt down on the ground and filled Meggie's Pipe with tobacco and prayer.

Laughing Bear said, "I'm going to take four pieces off your left arm and then four pieces off your right arm. Then, I'll do the same with Hawk."

Meggie didn't feel the least bit reassured. The realization that her parents were asleep at Chrysalis and thus not able to witness the cutting of the flesh gave her only slight comfort.

"If only I had remembered where I put my glasses," Laughing Bear muttered.

"You didn't tell me about this part of the ceremony." Meggie scowled at Hawk.

He shrugged his shoulders. "Sorry. I forgot. It doesn't hurt for too long. Laughing Bear will insert a small needle to raise your skin before he cuts it with the razor. Only I wish I could have found his glasses. It helps to see what you are doing."

Meggie glared at him. Goose bumps raised on her skin. "Maybe we could find a Lutheran pastor to marry us?"

"Oh, it won't be so bad, Meggie." He reached down and kissed her on the forehead.

Meggie was not comforted.

Laughing Bear spread a medicine quilt on the ground and directed Meggie to pick up her loaded Pipe. She knelt down on the quilt and held her Pipe.

"Pray," the medicine man commanded.

While Laughing Bear smudged the three of them with sage smoke, Meggie prayed.

Starting with her left upper arm, Laughing Bear poked around with a needle, all the while complaining of fuzzy vision.

Meggie tried to concentrate on her Chanunpa. The needle jabbed into her skin four times, followed by the cut of a razor blade. Blood streamed down her arm. Laughing Bear placed the scraps of flesh into a square of red cloth. He then shuffled to the other side and repeated the procedure on her right arm. Laughing Bear spat on the cuts and sopped up the blood with sage leaves.

He called for Hawk to come offer his flesh. Meggie leaned her Pipe against the buffalo head altar.

Solicitous, Hawk asked her, "How are you doing?"

Meggie gritted her teeth and answered, "It's not too late to find a Unitarian church."

"I promise you," Hawk whispered into her ear, "the rest is easy."

After the flesh offering, the three of them crawled into the sweat lodge. As the sun began to rise in the east, the heat of the inipi ceremony swirled around them, purifying them, renewing them for the wedding. The medicine man kept ladling the water onto the stones. Hawk and Meggie offered long prayers about their upcoming marriage and asked for help in the times ahead to bridge their separate cultures.

"I'm so happy to be marrying this woman," Hawk cried out.

"Ah hau," answered Laughing Bear.

"Help me to be a good human being alongside this man," Meggie prayed.

The medicine man poured more water on the stones until the rocks sang and sizzled with the heat. Hawk broke into song. With his rattles, Laughing Bear underscored the heartbeat of the Grandmother.

We are making a home in here with our hearts, thought Meggie. Gratitude flooded her—not just for the love of a good man and the teachings of an old woman but for the Sacred Pipe, the red road, and the inipi ceremony.

Drenched from the heat and profuse sweating, they staggered out of the lodge. Hawk looked over at the bedraggled bride, her hair hanging down in limp ringlets, steam rising off her sweat-soaked towel dress.

"Are you okay?" he asked.

Meggie looked up at the cloudy sky. "I've run out of denominations. I guess I'll have to marry you in the old way." She reached out both hands toward him, her damp hands curling into his strong fingers.

Just then, the sun escaped the prison of clouds, sprinkling magic gold dust onto the ground, gilding their flushed faces with the gentle light of the new day.

NINE

WEDDING MARCH

My true love hath my heart, and I have his,
By just exchange, one for the other given;
I hold his dear, and mine he cannot miss:
There never was a better bargain driven.

—SIR PHILIP SIDNEY
Arcadia

The temperature was perfect for an outside wedding, better than Meggie could have ever imagined for March. After taking a cramped shower in Hawk's trailer, she gathered up her damp towels and headed out toward her car. She was going to drive home to partake breakfast with her parents and sister's family. Hawk stayed to converse with Laughing Bear, eat pancakes at Lucy and Larry's table, and load up his truck with the giveaway gifts.

"When I next see you, you will become my bride," Hawk whispered into her ear.

Meggie crinkled her wet hair and scrutinized the thin scars forming on her upper arms. "The more I get to know you, Hawk, the less I can predict what marriage to you will entail."

"Does that worry you?" He didn't know if she were serious or joking.

"No. It simply means I'll never get bored living with you." She kissed him on the tip of his nose, climbed into her car, and drove off singing, "Oh, you'll take the high road, and I'll take the low road. . . ."

Meggie's mother had insisted on formal wedding invitations. "It's only proper." The invitations had said to come at noon. Since Hawk and Meggie were counting on Indian time for their Native American guests, the actual ceremony would not take place until two o'clock.

After breakfast, Meggie, family, and friends labored in the kitchen cooking up fry bread, buffalo stew, fried chicken, Jell-O concoctions, lettuce salads, pies, and cakes. Meggie set out card tables, paper plates, napkins, paper cups, and cutlery. Hawk was in charge of the giveaway gifts. The invitations had instructed everyone that, in the traditional Lakota blanket ceremony, it was the wedding couple who would offer gifts, not the guests. In this manner, Meggie and Hawk could share a portion of their happiness with others.

Meggie's mother stashed bottles of bubbly cider into the refrigerator. Hawk had requested that they not serve liquor. "Alcohol has devastated my people," he explained.

Meggie's father took a great deal of pleasure in having devised the parking arrangements and a system to shuttle guests up the mile-long driveway. "Not enough space up on the hill," he had declared.

When the guests began arriving, those who had never before visited Chrysalis marveled at the unspoiled acreage stretching northward toward Suttons Bay and a view of Lake Michigan, westward toward a deep and mysterious hardwood forest, and southward and eastward toward sensuous hills of cherry orchards, apple trees, and rectangular hay fields. The vista from Chrysalis encompassed a panoply of images: Impenetrable green cedar stands, wild stubbled meadow, agricultural fields, and always the distant, rolling, restless water of the Great Lake. Meggie's New York guests finally understood why she had left behind the gray grime of the big city for the lush, pastoral beauty of the Lee-lanau Peninsula.

It seemed only fitting to Meggie that she should marry Hawk at Chrysalis. Not only was it her home, her maternal grandmother had designed the house, built on grounds originally owned by Meggie's great-grandmother. At this very house, her father had courted and married her mother sixty-two years before.

Ancestral paintings and ancient photographs lined the living room walls, rooting Meggie to a sense of personal history. Chrysalis breathed *family* into her. Many times in the inipi ceremonies Hawk had spoken of doing things "in the name of the seven generations before you and the seven generations after you." On the walls of the house, the portraits took Meggie back to the time of the Civil War. In her bones, she knew the meaning of Hawk's admonition.

Many a night alone, she had talked to the oil paintings and the grainy, black and white photographs, trying to fathom her ancestors' dreams and hopes for the future. How many physical gestures, how many pet phrases, how many stubborn habits, how many personal philosophies had filtered down to her from these stern, two-dimensional faces on the wall?

In front of a full-length mirror, Meggie pulled on her elk skin dress and studied her reflection, looking for the ancestral tattoos in her expression. Was she the first one to marry an Indian or had there been others in her family who, migrating west, had been drawn to this continent's original pioneers?

She slipped her feet into the knee-high moccasins and tied a beaded hawk feather to her hair. A touch of lipstick, a slight shading of an eyebrow pencil, a dab of baby powder on her shiny nose, and Meggie was ready.

The guests had gathered on the eastern lawn by the spot where her parents had wed. From the bedroom window she spied Hawk, resplendent in his white beaded buckskin outfit, greeting the Peshawbestown contingent. He headed toward the house to join Laughing Bear. Love surged through her like a tidal wave, drowning her, tumbling her heart, and breaching the ducts of her eyes.

No man has ever shaken me to the core like this, she reflected. *He's my life, my best friend, my soul mate. Wiyohiyanpata, Grandfather of the East, You placed this man in the center of my journey. Thank You a million times over. In this second half of my life, I know the joy of living each day in celebration.*

Meggie wiped away her ecstatic tears and hurried down the stairs. Laughing Bear and Hawk stood patiently at the bottom of the stairway. The medicine man, noting the moist eyes, joked, "Any second thoughts?"

"Are you kidding?" Meggie answered, wrapping her gaze around Hawk. "I'm going to love this man for the rest of my life."

Laughing Bear corrected her. "It's going to be for much longer than that. You two are marrying by the Pipe."

"Amen to that," rejoined the groom. Hawk's eyes gleamed shiny, dark, and bright. He could barely contain the grin that spanned from one side of his face to the other. He reached for Meggie's hand.

Laughing Bear walked around the two of them, smudging them with sage smoke. "A great wedding dress," he exclaimed. "Now you look like a proper Lakota woman."

"Yes, but underneath I'm wearing Kelly green underwear." She knew who she was at the core.

In mock dismay, the medicine man shrugged his shoulders, muttering, "Crazy white woman" to no one in particular.

"Be careful what you say," Meggie warned. "One of these days you'll be marrying a white woman too." From what Meggie had already seen of Dee Dee, she didn't think that woman would take too much of Laughing Bear's gruff either.

"You two are as stubborn as mules, which is probably why I love you both," Hawk intervened. "But we've got a wedding and I'm anxious to marry this woman." Hawk picked up the bowl of ground corn and thrust it into Meggie's hands. He carried the bowl of wasna; a folded blanket hung over his arm.

Laughing Bear opened the door and headed up the processional, his Chanunpa leading the way. Hawk cut into a Lakota Spirit-calling song, asking the Grandfathers, the Grandmother, and all Beings of Creation to come, bend over, and witness the coming together of the two lovers.

Past the semi-circle of seated elders and standing guests, the three of them made their way to the spot where a medicine quilt had been placed on the ground. When they arrived, Hawk and Meggie set down the bowls of food and the blanket.

Laughing Bear encircled the couple, his eagle wing stirring the purifying smoke of sage over them. He asked Eva Arbre to come forth. He handed her the smudge bowl. With a saucy bounce to her step, Eva strutted over to the guests, wafting the smoke onto their faces and bodies.

Laughing Bear next held out his Sacred Pipe to Hawk. In his left hand, Hawk cradled the bowl while the stem pointed upward and outward toward the Sky Beings. Laughing Bear circled the medicine quilt four times, stirring the air with his eagle wing and calling upon the Grandfathers, the Grandmother, and the Good Spirits to see what was happening, to bless the union of Hawk and Meggie.

The medicine man reached for his Chanunpa and lit it, offering it to All the Directions. With his eagle wing he fanned the smoke onto the couple. Next, Laughing Bear handed the Pipe to Hawk who smoked it. With his right hand, he stroked the smoke back onto his face then passed the Chanunpa over to Meggie, saying, "Mitakuye oyas'in."

Her eyes gleaming, Meggie drafted deep on the Pipe, exhaled, and stirred the smoke back onto her face. "Mitakuye oyas'in." She offered the Pipe back to the medicine man.

"With this Chanunpa Wakan, these two people are now bound together, forever, as man and woman," Laughing Bear declared.

Meggie squatted and picked up the bowl of ground corn, straightened, and placed a pinch of corn on Hawk's tongue.

"With the corn, the woman shows that she will grow food and feed her man," explained Laughing Bear.

Hawk bent over, lifted the bowl of wasna, and fed Meggie a small amount. It was sweet and chewy.

"With the meat, the man shows that he will hunt game and take care of his woman." Laughing Bear wanted everyone to understand the significance of the vows.

The medicine man signaled for Adam Arbre and June Tubbs to come forth and take the two bowls of food. The two youngsters smiled shyly at each other. Meggie gave the corn to June, noting that the scars on the child's face made her look older than her eight years. June adopted a very grave expression as her delicate hands cupped the bowl.

In contrast to the girl, Adam was chunky and awkward. He tightly gripped the bowl of wasna. The children moved through the crowd of guests, offering everyone a pinch of the ceremonial food. Lucy signaled for her daughter, Eva, to hand Meggie the gallon container of cherry juice.

Meggie and Hawk then presented each other with the jug of cherry juice so they could each take a sip. Adam collected the bottle and passed it around to each guest to partake of its liquid. To the elders, June gave cups from which to drink.

"When two people marry this way," explained Laughing Bear, "they are marrying into community. They offer you this food and this drink, which they have prepared. You must remember that they gave you this food, for if they ever come to your door hungry and thirsty, you are to welcome them and feed them. By eating their food, you are making them this promise. They stand before you now as husband and wife. They are your brother and sister. Do not forget them. They are your relations. Mitakuye oyas'in."

Laughing Bear and Larry Arbre plucked the folded blanket off the medicine quilt, shook it open, and placed it over the shoulders of Meggie and Hawk.

"With this blanket, they will make a home for each other," explained the medicine man.

Turning back toward the couple, Laughing Bear whispered, "Well, you're married. Now and forever."

Hawk gathered Meggie into his arms, his eyes brimming with tears of gratitude, their faces protected from public view by the blanket. "I will always love you, Meggie O'Connor," he swore, bending his lips to her.

"Forever, Hawk. Forever," she promised.

The guests broke out in applause and laughter as the jumbled folds of the blanket danced atop the kissing couple.

Inside the house, each guest found a spot to sit. Servants to the community, Hawk and Meggie ladled out the soup and waited on everyone. First fed were the children and the elders. Meggie and Hawk did not eat until everyone had a plate piled high with chicken, fry bread, soup, and salad. Their appetite, however, was not for the food but for the presence of each other. In and out of the kitchen, Hawk and Meggie passed each other, touching briefly as they moved, searching each other out with smiling eyes.

Everyone ate until they were full and then they ate even more. Bellies bulged to bursting. Fritzie, Meggie's terrier, wandered through the dark, crowded corridors under the tables, snacking on everything that fell to the floor. The best pickings could be found under the children's table but he had to pay attention to hyperactive feet. When the pace of eating slowed down, the overstuffed Fritzie waddled toward Meggie's mother, slumped down upon his haunches, and sat up shamelessly in a begging position.

"Oh, Baby, are you hungry?" the old woman cooed.

But Fritzie had eaten too much; his ballast had shifted. He tilted first to the left, then to the right, his front feet pawing the air, before keeling over backwards onto the floor.

Even in the downed position, Fritzie managed to open his cavernous jaws as Meggie's mother offered him a tidbit to ease his humiliation.

Meggie arrived on the scene. "Oh, God, Mom. Fritzie's going to be sick if you give him any more to eat. And since you've agreed to take care of him while we're gone the next two weeks, you're going to have to be the one to clean up his mess."

"But he's so cute," Meggie's mother protested.

Meggie shook her head. What kind of bulging shape would Fritzie have developed by the time she returned from her honeymoon?

After clearing up the dishes from the table, it was time for the give-away. Hawk's friends crowded in, curious about the pile of gifts. They knew that the giveaway promised to be abundant.

Hawk gave a simple but genuine speech, thanking Meggie's parents for the gift of their wonderful daughter and for welcoming him into their family. He called Meggie's mother to come forth and presented her with a deer-bone necklace at the base of which hung a carved eagle. The old woman immediately put it on and proudly displayed it to the others. Meggie handed her a large framed piece of four photographs, each depicting the entrance to Chrysalis in a different season.

"I will always cherish this place, Mom. Now, no matter where you live, you will always have a part of Chrysalis with you."

Meggie's mother smiled and placed both hands upon her daughter's cheeks. "The photographs are beautiful, Meggie."

Hawk asked Meggie's father to come forth.

The old man smiled but appeared ill at ease with center stage. He stood before Hawk, not knowing what to expect.

"I owe you horses," Hawk explained.

Meggie's father shook his head.

"It's the custom for a man to give horses to the bride's father as a form of respect," Hawk continued.

Meggie's father chuckled, then said, "You're kidding, of course."

Hawk replied, "I've never been more serious in my life. I must give you horses. Your daughter is a fine woman."

"But I have no use for horses," he protested.

"I understand that so I made sure to give you horses that you could stable." Hawk reached around and pulled a blanket off two handmade sawhorses.

The crowd laughed and Meggie's father nodded. "Well, I can certainly put those to good use."

Meggie sighed with relief at Hawk's solution. She handed her father a framed poem written in calligraphy. The poem described a time when she was a child, no older than June, sailing in a tiny boat with her Dad off the coast of Maine. They had been lost and both had been afraid. He glanced at the verses and nodded knowingly. Despite her protestations, he insisted on reading her poem to the guests:

"Unknown Currents"

The island dissolves
*   into a speck's distance.*
No breeze luffs the sail,
*   and only the ocean's*
Lapping cuts this stillness.

A fog edges the horizon
*   creeping closer,*
And we are caught adrift
*   in the unknown current*
With no push homeward.

We tack. We tarry.
We try not to worry.
Our words are of other images.

Slightly and finally she picks up
  the wind's scent,
  and billows out
Like a pregnant woman
  to catch the invisible.

Our humility renewed,
  we follow her lead,
  No longer Masters of Fate
But servants to her journey.

Meggie blushed at the ensuing applause because the experience and the poem's mood had been private, shared only by her father and herself. *Besides,* she thought, *I am no longer afraid of the journey. I have Hawk by my side.*

Her new husband presented Laughing Bear with a buffalo robe. Meggie gave the medicine man a tape of polka music. "You're going to need it." She nodded, smiling at Dee Dee.

Everyone, from the oldest person to the youngest, received a special gift.

Hawk gave Lucy a new tape recorder with a microphone so that she could record stories for her children. Meggie thrust a large container of skin cream into her hand, saying, "Your fingers must be sore from having made Hawk's outfit."

A Chief Joseph blanket and a bottle labeled *Magic Indian Love Potion* went to Bev, a Native American cookbook to Katja, a beaded tamper to Adam, beaded hair ties to Eva, a deer-bone choker to Larry, a leather bear amulet stuffed with sage to June, a beaded bolo tie featuring a green lizard to Sam. Even Fritzie was given a present—a can of yellow tennis balls.

When everyone had a gift in front of them, Hawk and Meggie pulled out a laundry basket filled with small items: Gum, sample bottles of shampoo, candy, pencils, combs, pens, and toys. Upon a signal, everyone dove into the basket, grabbing the small articles until the basket was totally emptied. The giveaway was a great success.

As guests gathered their children and belongings, Meggie and Hawk packaged the left-over food and placed it on the table for everyone to take. They were tired but it had been a fine day.

When the last guest had departed and the clean-up was finished, Meggie's family finally staggered off to bed.

Bleary-eyed, Meggie looked at her beloved. The clock sounded midnight. They would leave for their honeymoon on the next day.

"It was a wonderful wedding, Hawk."

He wrapped his arms around his tired bride.

"It will be a wonderful life," he promised.

TEN

OF MISTS AND MYSTERIES

The holy centaurs of the hills are vanished;
I have nothing but the embittered sun;
Banished heroic mother moon and vanished,
And now that I have come for fifty years
I must endure the timid sun.

—W.B. YEATS
Lines Written in Dejection

The newlyweds flew to New York City where they stayed in an over-priced hotel for two days. Hawk was amazed by the canyons of sky-scrapers, the stampede of taxi cabs, the thrum of noise and the shake of ground, the press of bodies upon the street, and the constant motion of people, like flies around dead carrion. His muscles tightened against the crowd. He felt dizzy. It was no place for him. He was glad that Meggie had no desire to leave the Leelanau Peninsula and return to city life.

Even their love-making revved into high-pitch: Frantic moments of consuming passion and consummating release. It was oddly dissatisfying, dislocating to both of them.

At a trendy restaurant in the Village, he met several of Meggie's old friends. Self-confidence and personal power radiated from the women in the group. Two of the men linked arms and openly displayed their pride in being gay; no one seemed offended, men or women. Clearly Hawk was in a place different than Pine Ridge Reservation, where a gay man served as just another excuse to do battle. He had to admit to himself, he liked it when people stood up for themselves.

His large silver, turquoise watch band flashed in the noonday sun. A white bone choker around his neck set off the sheen of his black unbound hair. Over a western shirt, he wore a light brown leather vest, beaded in a feather design. Dark and ruggedly handsome, Hawk obviously fascinated Meggie's friends.

His difference of dress and feature endowed him with an aura of mystery which made him sexually intriguing to the women and an anthropological oddity to the men. Tempted to grunt "Ugh" and adopt a stern visage, Hawk remembered Meggie begging him that morning to keep his trickster jokes to himself. "They will take you at face value," she warned.

"And that's what worries me," she added.

"I'll try to be good," he promised.

"That worries me too," she said.

Hawk did his best. He feigned interest in whatever her friends had to say about Native Americans, whether it be about crystals, past lives, the genocidal history of the government, the politics of casinos and fishing rights, or the ecology of primitive man.

"I hear that some Indians still take several wives," said one bearded fellow, an unlit cigar dangling from his mouth.

Hawk replied, "Yes, a man might take one wife or three wives, but never two wives. You won't find any bigamists among Indians."

"Oh?" The man leaned forward, elbows on the table. "And why is that?"

Hawk smiled. "A man who marries two women risks having them gang up on him and making his life miserable. But since three women can never agree to anything, he'll always have one wife to take care of him."

The cigar inclined upward. Meggie's friend sat back, roaring with laughter. His wife nudged his ribs, loudly complaining, "Sexist humor."

Meggie shrugged her shoulders. There would be no stopping Hawk now.

"Is Meggie going to be your only wife?" The feminist took aim at Hawk.

"Oh, that's her choice." With the most solemn facial expression, he explained, "She's my Sleeps-Beside-Me-Wife and whether I am allowed to have any more is up to her."

The woman contracted her eyebrows and looked to Meggie for clarification.

"It's true," Meggie said, "that in some tribes there was the practice of polygamy, but that tradition has pretty well died out."

Hawk elongated his chin into a sad, downcast countenance. "I don't think she's going to let me have other wives."

"Not if you know what's good for you," Meggie replied. She knew her friends were no match for Hawk's humor. They would think him serious when he was really having the most fun with them. As she watched him answer their questions, she thought, *Heaven knows what he is going to say next.*

Later that afternoon, Meggie led Hawk on a tour of downtown Manhattan, Harlem, and the Bronx, pointing out hospitals where she had worked, apartment buildings in which she had once resided.

"I don't know how one could ever live in such a place," Hawk exclaimed. The congested traffic, the stacked, concrete boxes in which people resided, the constriction of vista made him hunger for the rolling hills and winding beaches of Northwest Michigan. He could see why so many Native Americans felt overpowered in cities, out of balance, lost. There didn't seem to be any place for a person to discover the stillness and gather strength from the Grandmother. In every place he looked was a restless seething. Even the birds didn't dare squat too long on the tree branches. Only grizzled men and gray pigeons slowed down to stake out corners and beg from the moving waves of human beings. *A lonely town*, observed Hawk.

He was glad when they boarded a plane, left behind the tarred and tired city, and headed eastward across the Atlantic Ocean to the Emerald Isles. In contrast to New York City, the lush green vegetation and deep blue fjords of Ireland refreshed his spirit and nourished his soul. Every morning for the next twelve days, the two of them set out in a rented car, driving on the wrong side of the road. They followed a path from the ring of Kerry up the western, wild coast. They angled over mountains, around deep lakes, through sudden rains and shrouded mists, into the blessings of bright sunlight and pulsating rainbows. Every night they stopped at bed and breakfast inns and were warmed by peat fires, friendly conversation, and the sweet intimacy of each other's love.

"You're an Indian," commented one innkeeper.

"Yes," replied Hawk, adding, "I'm Native American."

The woman looked perplexed.

"I'm not from India," he explained.

"Oh," the woman answered. She turned toward Meggie. "Aren't you supposed to be wearing a dot in the middle of your forehead?"

Meggie winked at Hawk.

He was grinning from ear to ear. "It's a sari tale," he quipped.

In the northern part of Ireland, County Donegal, the two of them parked by a cow pasture in the middle of which stood a stone structure. The top had caved in, spilling the stones into the center pit. They climbed over the stone fence to inspect it closer.

Meggie read from the guide book. "It says that this is an ancient sweat bath, used in previous centuries for curing arthritis and temporary insanity."

"Meggie," Hawk said, "this is a sweat lodge. It's built like ours, only out of stone. Who were the people who used it?"

In search of answers, they turned back toward the western town of Sligo where they had discovered a butcher's shop whose front window displayed carvings of mythological Celtic figures standing next to prime cuts of meat. Hawk and Meggie entered the store; a man in his forties was trimming fat, his apron speckled with blood.

"You're Indian," the butcher observed. "We've had several native visitors from North America here."

Hawk simply nodded, giving the man room to say more.

Meggie's curiosity got the best of her. "Do you worship in the old ways?" she asked.

"This is a strongly Catholic community," the man answered, slicing the gristle off a slab of beef.

Hawk shot her a look of warning and inquired about the carvings in the window. The man referred to old legends then turned back to Meggie.

"Many Native American customs are similar to those of Celtic ritual. If you follow your travel book to the sacred well around here, you'll note that the Catholics have cleverly placed the Stations of the Cross on an ancient Celtic site. The old Irish used to say the surrounding two hills were the breasts and the well was the vagina of the Great Mother. Follow the path by the well to the end. You'll discover a black thorn bush and some offerings on it. There are still some who practice the old ways. . . ."

At the sacred well they discovered the black thorn bush laden with bits of cloth, a baby pacifier, some tied pieces of paper. "Like our tobacco offerings," observed Hawk, "these are the prayers of the people."

Driving east, Hawk and Meggie arrived at New Grange, a giant megalithic tomb of white quartz and granite stone, reconstructed out of the original material. It was an awesome sight.

"New Grange was built long before Stonehenge." A man lectured a group of school children nearby. Hawk and Meggie drifted into the group's periphery. "The archeologists estimate that New Grange was erected around 3200 B.C. by pre-Celtic engineers. They were interested in tracking the movement of the sun. On the winter solstice, at dawn, the sun's rays will snake deep into the interior through a special window above the main portal."

"Where do the stones come from?" asked a young man.

The guide smiled. "The quartz came from the Wicklow Mountains, several days journey to the south, and the granite from the Mourne Mountains, several days journey to the north. It must have been a wealthy class of people to have brought these stones such a great distance."

Hawk and Meggie wandered away from the group and entered the tomb. The narrow stone corridor led to the interior chambers where geometric spirals decorated the walls.

"Can you sense the energy of this place, Meggie? It's vibrating through my feet," Hawk said.

Meggie tried to feel something other than the tired toes of a tourist but it was useless.

Upon leaving the tomb's interior, Hawk pulled out a pouch of tobacco and walked around the large structure, sprinkling tobacco on the ground, offering a prayer of thanksgiving to the people who had created it. Meggie could tell he had been stunned by New Grange's ancient secrets and modern beauty.

As they drove away, heading south toward Dublin, Hawk grew increasingly pensive.

"A penny for your thoughts?" Meggie asked.

"I've always been taught of the vast gulf between my people and the whites, the way we think, the way we worship. Yet here in Ireland is an ancient sweat lodge, a thorn bush covered with prayer offerings, and a monument built to track the movement of the sun. There seem to be a lot more similarities between our people than differences."

He looked into the rear view mirror to see if he could catch one last glimpse of New Grange high atop the hill but already the monument had slipped out of sight.

Dublin was a gray disappointment. A stone city, it seemed indistinguishable from other gray cities, everybody hustling to make a living.

The next morning, Meggie and Hawk retreated to the countryside, found an isolated inn, and spent the day hiking in the green hills. "I'm no city person, Meggie," Hawk said.

That evening they stretched out in bed, arms around each other, noses almost touching, lips in pecking distance, Meggie's cold bare toes seeking the warmth of Hawk's long legs.

"Thank you for being my wife," he murmured, pulling the wool blankets over the two of them.

"The pleasure is all mine," she whispered back. She rolled even closer. "I don't ever want this happiness to end." Melancholy crept into her voice.

"Are you getting superstitious on me?" Hawk asked.

"It's been my experience that great joy is often followed by a plunge into darkness, as if life is a giant roller-coaster. I want time to stop, to savor moments like these."

He ran his thumbs over the arches of her eyebrows, tracing and committing her face to tactile memory. He wanted to remember everything from this time in his life, the happiness of finding love again when he had despaired of it, the fiery passion and the tender romance between them, the ancient ceremony of their wedding, the magical time together in Ireland.

"You can see why the red road calls to me," she added.

It was not what he had expected her to say.

"The Celts once talked to the Spirits of this land," she continued, "but most of the Irish have forgotten what their ancestors once knew."

"It's true of my people as well, Meggie."

"But I want to remember, Hawk." Meggie yawned with sleepiness in her voice. "What happens if a people walk away from the old traditions and the ancestral knowledge? Do the Spirits of the land abandon them and disappear when they take up with newer religions?"

Hawk's index fingers lowered Meggie's eyelids like soft shades to a window. "The Spirits don't leave the land. We do. Out of fear we grow blind, Meggie."

He kissed her eyelids and felt her slowly release into the sweet breath of sleep.

The Irish night wrapped around them. Off the seas, several wind storms crossed high overhead. Rain sparkled down through scudding clouds and emerging shafts of moonlight. Mist swirled around the low hills and blanketed the deep lakes. It would have been a perfect night for the little people to issue forth under rock and mushroom, to play their tricks on the sleeping Irish, to refresh the old sacred sites, to give thanks to the dark at dusk and to the sun at dawn, to dance and play under moon beams, to celebrate the ancient rhythms of the land without upsetting the modern cadence of the people.

Holding Meggie in his arms, Hawk listened intently to the garbled night sounds floating through his opened window. He didn't know if it were simply his imagination or the whispering of the wind against the inn but he could swear that he heard high-pitched voices floating off the dark hills. He cupped his ear to listen more closely.

The voices were faint, firm, and repetitive.

"We are still here. We are still here," they whispered into the lonely night.

ELEVEN

HOME SAFE

There are those who prefer terra firma.
The firma the ground, the lessa the terra.

— ANONYMOUS

Palm Sunday marked the return home. The flight over the Atlantic was smooth but as soon as they arrived back in the States, en route to Detroit, all hell broke loose. A storm system was blowing over the Midwest. Turbulence rocked the upper skies.

"I'd feel better if I were on the ground right now," Hawk muttered. His palm was moist as he gripped Meggie's hand. The steady drone of the jet engines gave him slight comfort.

"Don't put all your weight down on the floor," she admonished him.

Again the plane bucked the air currants. The seat belt sign flashed overhead.

"You're not being helpful." He gritted his teeth. The plane dropped. His stomach lurched. Against his better judgement, he released the pressure of his feet grinding into the floor.

"You need to become more spiritual, Hawk." Meggie adopted a Buddha-like smile.

The plane jerked side to side; rain sheeted against their window.

Meggie grinned. "In moments like these, you must repeat the Lakota saying: 'Today is a good day to die.'"

The plane shuddered.

Hawk groaned.

The flight from Detroit to Traverse City was hardly better. It was to his great relief that they finally landed in the early evening. Karl and Bev stood expectantly at the gate.

After looking at Hawk's face, Bev couldn't help commenting, "A little green under the gills, are you?"

"A bit of Ireland rubbed off on him," Meggie said.

Hawk added, "Truth is, Meggie wore me out on the honeymoon. I'm glad to be home."

"Too much passion?" Bev raised her eyebrows but Karl gripped her by the elbow and whisked her off toward the escalator before she could utter another word.

When they arrived at Chrysalis, Fritzie waddled to the door to greet them.

"Good grief, you're a blimp," Meggie exclaimed, her hands rounding over his distended belly.

Fritzie sat back on his haunches, begging, two front paws lifted into the air.

"You're shameless too," Meggie scolded.

Fritzie lowered his ears but did not give up hope.

Meggie's mother appeared in the kitchen attired in a red terry cloth bathrobe. "Welcome home," she said, giving everyone a big hug. As if on automatic pilot, the old woman reached for a doggie treat and popped one into the gaping jaws of the terrier.

"Mom," Meggie complained.

"Yes, Dear?"

"You're teaching him bad manners. Besides, he's become a fuzzy butterball while I was away." Meggie scowled.

"Oh, Meggie." Her mother bent down and looked Fritzie straight in the eyes while rubbing his ears. "Baby's so adorable when he begs. I simply can't resist."

Meggie picked up the dog treat box and pushed it way back into a bottom cupboard.

"We have to go," Bev announced.

Karl agreed. "High Holy week is coming up. I've got to get my rest."

"Welcome home." Bev kissed Meggie one last time.

Meggie had to admit that while the honeymoon had been heaven, it was good to get back to more earthly surroundings.

The next morning, Meggie's parents promptly departed for the east coast. Two weeks of babysitting Fritzie had stretched the limit of her father's tolerance for being away from his medical laboratory. Meggie, too, was anxious to get back to work, to discover how her clients, especially the children, had fared during her absence.

* * * *

Later that evening, Meggie cuddled up next to Hawk on their double bed. "It would be nice to have a little baby girl with you." He was reading about the dispute over tribal fishing rights in The Leelanau Enterprise.

He lowered the newspaper and angled his arm over her. "A little girl? What about a little boy?" He kissed the crown of her head.

Meggie thought a moment and answered, "Boys are okay until they reach puberty. Then they go into an awful funk where they lose the power of speech and retreat to their rooms for several years. When they finally emerge from their cocoons of silence, they've changed form. They fly away and never look back."

Hawk stared at her as if she'd lost her mind. "You think girls are different?"

"Yes, I do. They're more like blossoming flowers rooted to the family garden."

Hawk shook his head. "Believe me, boys are easier. Everyone says so."

"I doubt that any kind of parenting is ever easy," Meggie allowed. She shrugged her shoulders. Sadness lightly etched the lines in her face. "I'm probably too old to get pregnant quickly. Still . . ."

"Nothing's certain, Meggie. But you'll make a wonderful mother to our baby, no matter if it's a boy or a girl." Hawk wrapped both arms around her in both a protective and affirming manner.

But what if I can't get pregnant? What if I have another miscarriage? What if our child is born with Downs Syndrome? Meggie didn't like the vagaries of chance. Yet she stubbornly refused to give voice to her fears because to speak them aloud was to give them power over her. To make Hawk a witness to all her *what ifs* would only solidify their strangling grip upon her dreams.

Silence keeps its own company, Meggie concluded.

T W E L V E

TO PAY THE PIPER

When, lo, as they reached the mountain-side,
A wondrous portal opened wide,
As if a cavern was suddenly hollowed;
And the Piper advanced and the children followed,
And when all were in to the very last,
The door in the mountain-side shut fast.

—ROBERT BROWNING
The Pied Piper of Hamelin

AS Katja hurried back along M22 from Traverse City and grocery shopping, she braked suddenly. The car in front of her was moving at a snail's pace but there was no way she could risk passing. She was going to be late, very late in picking up June at the school playground. Her fingers drummed on the steering wheel.

During the pre-tax days, it seemed to Katja that she was always running behind the clock. On April 16, Paul would resume his normal schedule and paternal duties but right now he was practically living at the office. Katja had to serve as father, mother, and chauffeur.

Robert had agreed to remain at soccer practice until six o'clock but June had been a problem. Katja knew she couldn't juggle picking June up after school, driving to Traverse City, shopping, and still get back home in time to pick up Robert.

"I'll stay at school, Mom," June had offered.

The eight-year-old girl liked to help her teachers. It would give her time to finish up her homework. But there was about a forty-five minute span when the school would be locked and the teachers gone home.

"I'll wait for you on the playground," June had suggested.

If it had been anywhere else but Suttons Bay, Katja wouldn't have even considered that plan. But nothing bad ever happened there, a town where people normally left their doors unlocked. Reluctantly she agreed. "Don't leave the playground," she warned June. "I'll get there as soon as possible."

"I won't, Mom," she promised.

And here Katja was, already fifteen minutes late, moving slower than a snail behind some old geezer who probably couldn't see the road if he tried.

"I'll be there real soon, honey," Katja whispered out the window, looking for the passing lane.

She roared past the poky car and tore down the highway to the turnoff for the elementary school, slowing to just ten miles above the speed limit. When she saw the school she heaved a sigh of relief. Parking the car, she grabbed her keys and headed toward the playground.

June wasn't there.

"I told you to stay here," she said aloud, exasperation rippling through her voice. *June must have returned to the classroom*, she thought.

Katja tried the main school door. It was locked. She walked all around the school. Nothing was open. She pounded on the doors. No answer. Nor were there any cars in the parking lot. The school was deserted.

"Damn," Katja exclaimed. Where could June have gone? It was unlike her to wander off. Maybe the youngster had decided to explore the surrounding area. "June. June, where are you?" Katja called out several times.

But only a chickadee answered.

Katja tried not to let panic surface. *Come on, think. Where might she have gone?* Back in her car, she drove in widening circles around the streets bordering the school, then down by the bay, calling out her daughter's name.

She checked her watch. Still a good half hour before she needed to pick up Robert. Quickly she drove home to check if a neighbor or parent had dropped off her little girl. *But June promised she would stay at the playground*, Katja thought.

Nobody was at home.

Opening the back door, Katja ran to the telephone and started calling all of June's friends. To a one, they said she had stayed at school after class. Katja called June's teacher, Mrs. Howard.

"But where could she be, Mrs. Tubbs? I was one of the last staff to leave the building. June was sitting on the swings. She even waved goodbye at me."

Katja dialed her husband at his office. "Paul," she said, "I can't find June anywhere. Is she there with you?"

"Katja, I'm at work. Why would June be here? Weren't you supposed to pick her up at school?"

"Yes, but I was late and she wasn't there." Katja could see she would have to leave soon to pick up Robert. *Oh why did I have to be late?* The self-recriminations began.

Paul apparently could sense that Katja was on the verge of hysteria. "Look, honey, she's got to be around. Maybe she had to go to the bathroom and is at the playground right now waiting for you. Or a friend invited her home. Don't worry. We'll find her. I'll leave work in about ten minutes. After we retrieve her, I need to come back to the office. I've got a lot of returns to finish."

Katja took a deep breath. "Okay. I'm going to pick up Robert. I'll swing by the school again. If she's not there, what are we going to do?" Desperately, Katja hoped her husband would have a plan.

"We'll talk about it when I see you at the house in about thirty minutes, okay? Don't worry. We'll find her." He sounded confident, as if Katja were getting all worked up over nothing.

Katja slipped into her car and drove back toward the school. *Paul's right. June's okay and I'm simply a worrywart. She'll be there, waiting for me.* Katja slowed her rapid breathing and told herself to get a grip on her anxiety. She turned the corner of the street by the school.

The playground was empty.

At the soccer field, she asked Robert, "Where is your sister? I can't find her."

"She's waiting for you at school, like you told her," the boy answered. Dirty at the knees and smelling of sweat, he clambered into the front seat of the car.

Doubting herself once again, Katja drove by the school playground, expecting to see June's relieved face. She imagined June asking, "Where were you, Mommy? I stayed here as long as I could, waiting for you."

The car swung around the school's corner. Darkness was already crowding out the light of day and shadows stretched ominously across the silent swings.

Eight-year-old June had vanished without even an echo.

The town of Suttons Bay, where most everyone is known by their first names, turned itself inside out looking for June Tubbs. News spread as fast as fear could travel. What was worse—a little girl lost or a mother whose daughter has simply disappeared without a trace?

First the local police conducted the search; then the state police were called in, speaking the dreaded words of "child abduction." The Federal Bureau of Investigation was notified.

The disappearance had happened so quickly, in an instant. But the hard hours of waiting stretched sluggish and slow afterwards. Every minute, every hour ate away at the hope of recovery. News broadcasts featured the parents' tortured faces and pleas for their daughter's safe return.

Before the camera, Paul tried to maintain a stoic facade. "We would ask that anyone who has knowledge of our daughter's whereabouts, please contact the police. Please." His voice cracked. Light bulbs flashed in his face. "I beg you," he whispered.

The next morning, it was Katja's turn. A lack of sleep and deep wells of dark fear in her eyes had aged her. "If you saw my little girl, you would not forget her. She's only eight years old, but she has scars on her cheeks from a previous accident. If you're the ones who have her, please return her to us safe and sound. If it's money you want, we'll give you whatever we have. But please, please don't hurt my baby." Katja started to collapse on the lawn and many hands reached out to support her.

The camera wheeled to focus on the young blond broadcaster speaking into the microphone. "As you can see, the mother is absolutely distraught."

A recent photograph of June scrolled across the scene. "Last seen on Monday afternoon, eight-year-old June Tubbs has not been heard from since. Authorities are baffled and time is running out. According to FBI statistics, the probability of finding the child decreases significantly if the youngster is not located within the first twenty-four hours. We promise to keep you up to date on this breaking story. . . ."

While news broadcasters and photographers camped outside the Tubbs household, inside a buzz of law enforcement people kept up a steady vigil. The police had tapped the telephone and the parents waited, hoping that a kidnapper might call. But no call came. Nor were there any letters in the mail demanding ransom money. Despite a countywide search, no child's body surfaced in the woods or swamps.

Up to a point, the details were clear. As June had promised, the little girl had finished her homework and had gone out to the playground to await her mother. Eyewitness accounts of school personnel put her there in the swings. After that, no one knew what happened next. There were no sightings of strange cars, no evidence of any struggle, nothing to tell the parents where their little girl had gone.

Katja cursed herself for being late. While Paul secretly agreed with his wife's self-blame, he agonized over his own neglect of the children for work. Daily their son, Robert, convicted himself for not having protected his little sister.

And despite all their cumulative guilt, June never ever returned home.

*   *   *   *

Like most parents on the Leelanau Peninsula, Lucy's reaction was to become especially vigilant. "Now I don't want you kids going anywhere without my permission," she lectured her children.

Eva was not a problem but Adam was a different matter. He was growing increasingly independent. And he had special feelings for June.

"I don't want you wandering off into the woods looking for her, you hear?" Lucy wagged a finger at her son but the boy looked away. *A bad sign*, thought Lucy.

Forcefully, she took his chin in her hand. "I want you to promise me that you won't go searching for her unless an adult is present with you."

"She might be hurt. She might have broken an ankle or something," the boy protested.

"If that's the case, the search party will find her. There are a lot of people out looking for the girl. I don't want you to get lost too. Then everybody would have to spend time searching for you and June might never be found." *A little guilt induction won't hurt*, Lucy reasoned.

"Besides," she digressed, "you need to set up the rat traps. I saw two rats in the basement last night."

"They're just field mice, Mom."

"Rats, field mice. I don't care what they are. Unless we get rid of them, they'll soon swarm all over this house. Now promise me that you won't go off alone," Lucy commanded.

The boy cast down his eyes and nodded his head.

"And no staying behind at the playground after school lets out. Adam, I hold you responsible to watch over your sister. I wouldn't know what I'd do if anything bad were to happen to either one of you." In light of June's disappearance, Lucy wanted to bundle her children in her arms and keep them safe with her all day. But the kids needed to continue with school and Lucy had her nursing job. Life had to go on.

On the Thursday before Easter, Adam accompanied his sister to her after-school gymnastics class. The teacher offered to drive Eva home when the ninety-minute class was over. For Adam, that ninety minutes represented freedom. He took off on foot towards home.

Ninety minutes in which to do whatever he wanted.

He could briefly search for June who had been gone now a full three days. But he had promised his mother he wouldn't look for June unless an adult were present. He thought his mother was being silly and over-protective, but he had made a promise to her.

He could take the shortcut through the woods to Emily's house and ask her advice. Maybe even persuade Emily to check the old apple orchards with him. He consulted his watch and realized that time was against him.

What to do?

He could take out his pipe and pray for June's return. Even better, he could ask his cousin Hawk if it would be possible to find June in the old way, through the eyes of the Spirits. That thought gave him comfort.

Adam wished he had an article of June's clothing to show his dog. Shunka might be able to pick up the scent of the girl.

Ninety short minutes. Adam sprinted down the street, determined to make good use of his limited freedom.

Ninety short minutes.

In that small frame of time, hardly enough to accomplish anything of significance, Lucy's fear congealed from idea to reality.

Nine-year-old Adam disappeared.

THIRTEEN

MAUNDY THURSDAY

. . . betrayal is at the heart of the Christian mystery. The sorrow at the supper, the agony in the garden, and the cry on the cross seem repetitious of a same pattern, restatements of a same theme, each on a higher key, that a destiny is being realized, that a transformation is being brought home to Jesus.

—JAMES HILLMAN
Betrayal

Karl stepped up to the pulpit. Reverend Atherton had asked him to conduct the Maundy Thursday service as the senior minister was not feeling well. Karl cleared his throat.

"Tonight is the night of the Last Supper, when Jesus celebrated the feast of the unleavened bread. In the readings of the Scriptures, you heard how Jesus broke the bread, blessed it, and said to his twelve disciples, 'Take, eat, this is my body.' He then took the cup of wine and gave thanks, saying, 'This is my blood of the new testament, which is shed for many.' It was the first Communion." Karl leaned over the pulpit to better see the small group of parishioners scattered throughout the church pews.

Bev Paterson sat all by herself in the second row, intently listening to Karl's sermon. He spoke as if trying to help her understand the passion of the Easter story.

"The long night was the culmination of Jesus's ministry. Everything was cresting to a crisis point. The Romans wanted to make sure that

Jesus wouldn't lead a revolt against them. Many of the Jews, the Pharisees in particular, were unhappy with Jesus and his declaration that he was the 'Son of God.' Others wanted Jesus to manifest himself as the conquering Messiah. But his message of humility, the portrayal of himself as the Lamb of God, not the soldier, was a radical notion, politically unpopular. Everyone was scared of this man and what he might or might not do."

Karl paused and scanned the sparse evening congregation. His voice became solemn. "It was also the night of betrayal and Jesus knew it. Many think that Judas sold Jesus out for money, the infamous thirty pieces of silver, but the truth may be that Judas was simply trying to force Jesus to become the kind of Messiah that the people wanted. We human beings have our own agenda when it comes to the Sacred. We're always trying to force God into our own images."

Karl nodded. "I am as guilty of that as the next person."

Bev sat up straight.

Karl continued, "Even Jesus had his moments when he asked God to do it differently. He said, 'Oh my Father, if it be possible, let this cup pass from me.' He did not want to die. He was still a young man. No sooner did he utter those very human words then he added, 'Nevertheless not as I will, but as Thou wilt.'"

Karl leaned over the pulpit and asked the congregation, "Is that not how each one of us should approach the Sacred? As Thou wilt, not as *I want*? We are always telling God what we want from Him. But the more important question is what does God want of us?"

Karl looked down at his sermon outline. He sighed, sorrow sifting through his words. "Tonight is the first communion, the time in the garden, the betrayal by Judas. Tomorrow would be the trial and the crucifixion, Saturday the quiet wait in the tomb, and Sunday the glorious resurrection. But tonight, tonight is the time of celebration and the last meal between Jesus and his disciples, a time of fear and aloneness when Jesus, in the garden, has to face his harsh destiny. A time of anger at the people who misunderstood his mission. A time of sadness when the disciples came up against their own human limitations and could no longer protect the man they loved."

Karl stepped down from the pulpit and held out his arms to the congregation, saying, "In the spirit of this special night, we will now celebrate the Eucharist together."

Later, after Karl had shaken hands with everyone, he turned to Bev and asked her, "Well, what did you think of the service?"

"You don't want to know, Karl."

"Sure I do. I want to know everything that goes on in that head of yours." Karl took her elbow and guided her back to the vestry.

"I don't believe it," Bev said.

"What don't you believe?" Karl pulled the vestments over his head.

"The whole communion thing. Bread turning into flesh, wine transforming into blood. It's cannibalistic. Do you really believe that happens?" Doubt riddled and wrinkled Bev's face.

"It's complicated. Some of my ministerial colleagues will tell you that communion is symbolic, representing the sacrifice of Jesus. Others will tell you it's a mystery not to be ever fully understood. The Catholics will tell you that it does indeed happen."

"But what do you believe, Karl?"

Karl shook out his rumpled corduroy jacket. "I think those people who come to the altar for the purely symbolic act of communion are profoundly moved by that act. I also believe that for those who come to the altar with the faith that bread and wine convert to body and blood, that does indeed happen for them, inside of them. And I'm not sure that it makes much of a difference whether it is the literal or symbolic truth. Either way, the person links himself or herself with Jesus and enters into the story of Christ."

"Well, I liked the sermon," Bev said.

Karl smiled at her, bemused. "The sermon is simply a sideshow and a minor one at that."

"What's in the main ring then?" She looked confused.

"The ritual of communion. It's the gateway to God."

* * * *

Meggie couldn't believe all that was happening. First June, now Adam. Still, Adam had been missing only a few hours and might suddenly reappear. Hawk responded quickly to Lucy's call of alarm and organized a search party fanning out in all directions from the Arbre household. Already, night had drawn down the shades and people were reduced to flashlights and shouting out the boy's name.

The police cautioned everyone from panicking. "It's too early to say that he's a missing child." That didn't prevent them from mobilizing on and off the reservation.

All night long and well into the morning of the next day, Hawk, Larry, Karl, and other men trampled through the cherry orchards, back woods, swamp, and forest areas. Exhausted, they turned the search over to others for a few hours of restless sleep. Hawk retreated to his old trailer by Lucy's house; it would save time. He didn't even notice the dust rise as he slumped down onto the lumpy mattress.

Meggie canceled her Friday clients and tried to divide her time between an anxious Lucy and a despairing Katja. The two mothers had not reached out to each other. Lucy wasn't willing yet to place Adam into the limbo of the missing girl nor was Katja wanting to relive the first hours of sheer panic. But all over the Peninsula, children were being locked into their houses and closely guarded by frightened parents.

Who was going to be next? reverberated in the shadows of everyone's imagination.

With the boy's disappearance, the news media again descended upon the quiet little town of Suttons Bay, interviewing children and adults alike. An inspired national broadcaster had the genius or the perversity to dub the village of missing children "Hamelin town."

The headlines of a local newspaper screamed, "WHO IS THE PIED PIPER?"

Everyone in Suttons Bay agreed. It was a hell of a way to have begun Easter weekend.

FOURTEEN

DARKNESS

It's dark and I'm scared. I'm really really scared. I don't know what's going to happen. Why are they doing this to me? Oh please, I want to be anywhere else but here.

Where's my father? Why hasn't he come to help me? Oh please, I need help.

I thought you were my friend. I trusted you. When my Dad finds out, he'll make you wish you'd never been born. Yes, he will. I hope he tears your eyes out.

You're going to hurt me. I know that.

It's already started. And you're taking me so far away.

Oh, won't somebody please help me?

FIFTEEN

GOOD FRIDAY

No worst, there is none. Pitched past pitch of grief,
More pangs will, schooled at forepangs, wilder wring.
Comforter, where, where is your comforting?
Mary, mother of us, where is your relief?
My cries heave, herds-long; huddle in a main, a chief
Woe, world-sorrow; on an age-old anvil wince and sing—
Then lull, then leave off. Fury had shrieked 'No ling-
ering! Let me be fell; force I must be brief.

—GERARD MANLEY HOPKINS
No Worse, There Is None

"When I find out who did this, I will kill the sonuvabitch who took my son." Larry glared into the bright morning air. "I swear I will, Lucy."

"Maybe he's just lost." Lucy still clung to the hope that her son might emerge out of the dark woods, walking and tired and full of boyish apologies.

"No." Larry shook his head. "You have to face facts. Adam knows the woods around here like the back of his hand. He isn't lost." Grim lines tightened his face; his coal black eyes narrowed into an expression of quiet fury.

"Why would anyone . . ." Lucy stopped herself as soon as the answer became clear to her.

"Oh God," she uttered. Sinking down on the front stoop, she wrapped her arms around her knees. Larry stood apart, scanning the sky as if looking for a clue.

"I'm going to kill that sonuvabitch," he promised.

* * * *

Paul Tubbs organized. He copied June's photograph onto hundreds of posters and distributed them to an army of people. He called broadcasting stations across the country to see if they would run a brief birthday video of his little girl on national television. "Somebody will have seen her. I'm almost glad now she had that accident last year."

"Paul, how can you say such a terrible thing?" Katja's sharp voice jabbed at him.

"Because the scars on her face will help people recognize her from the photographs." He placed both hands on his wife's shoulders and looked her straight in the eye. "We're going to get her back. You've got to have faith and not give up."

"This is the fifth day, Paul." Despair haunted Katja's sunken eyes.

"Our baby is going to be found. She's going to come home. I just know it. And if she's hurt in any way, we'll make it better. I promise you, honey." Paul didn't even realize that he was shaking Katja's shoulders.

"Then come to church with me tonight, Paul," Katja pleaded.

Paul stepped back and dropped his hands. "I can't. I've got too much to do here."

"I need you there with me, Paul."

"I'm sorry. I'm sorry. I can't."

But Paul knew the lie did not fool his wife. *How can I forgive a God who would do this to me?*

* * * *

"I told you," said Daisy, sweeping up dog poop, "that human beings are not to be trusted."

"Oh posh, you're too young to be thinking that way," Jillian responded. "Haven't I been extra good to you?"

"Yeah, but you're different." Daisy was appreciative of Jillian for letting her stay at her house while Daisy's mother and sisters were off visiting relatives downstate. She didn't want to miss a single day at work. Nor did she want to stay home with a father who would be drinking and . . .

"I'm not all that different from other people." Jillian interrupted the girl's thoughts. "The truth is, Daisy, I wouldn't have given you a second's notice if it hadn't been for Sam."

Jillian didn't see Daisy flinch.

She don't mean no harm by that, Daisy reminded herself.

"Sam knows I'm good with animals. Didn't I get that dog a home?" Daisy was learning to stand up for herself in positive ways.

Jillian bent over her desk, arranging the stacks of paperwork. "Nobody's complaining. Sam's very happy with your performance. So am I. You've worked hard and complained little."

Daisy smiled. Even if Daisy did have to prime the pump, praise from Jillian didn't come too often.

"There are bad people in this world. That's why kidnaping and rape and murder happen, but that doesn't mean most of us are that way," Jillian continued.

Daisy turned away, thinking, *Jillian's a nice lady, but when it comes to people, she don't know shit.*

* * * *

Sick with a full-blown virus, Rev. Atherton asked Karl to take over the Good Friday evening service. Karl scrambled all afternoon to write a sermon for the solemn occasion. Minutes before the service, he peeked through the vestry door to gauge the number of parishioners. A goodly number of people had already filed into the pews while others stood out in the vestibule greeting each other.

He grinned at seeing Bev Paterson and then noticed Katja Tubbs sliding into the pew beside her. *Oh, that poor woman*, he sorrowed, *what sermon could possibly give her comfort and ease her mind?*

Karl reviewed his notes, seeking some words of consolation for Katja in this service of lamentation. On his way into the sanctuary, it warmed his heart to see the two women sitting close together in the fourth row. Bev was holding Katja's hand.

As the congregation rose, hymnals in hands and voices soaring to the lofty ceiling, Karl looked upward toward Heaven and asked a silent question of God. *Who suffered most at the crucifixion—was it Jesus or was it his mother?*

* * * *

By the sweat lodge, Hawk took out his Sacred Pipe. The moon was rising full into the night but low scudding clouds threatened to blanket it with impending darkness. He cleansed himself and the Chanunpa in the smoke of the sage. Slowly and surely, in the ways taught to him through seven generations of his Lakota people, Hawk began the Pipe ceremony. After filling and offering the Pipe to all the Grandfathers and Grandmother, Hawk made his prayers.

"Grandfathers, I ask that you protect those two children—Adam, grandson of Winona, son of Lucy, and the little girl, June Tubbs. Tunkasila, Grandfather, help me do whatever is in my ability to find them, whether they are apart or together. Let these youngsters return to us as the healthy children we have always known them to be."

Hawk kept his words short because it was not what he had to say that was important. Rather, it was the answer that *Wakan Tanka* and His Spirit Helpers might give him that focused his attention. He made his mind a blank screen and purged himself of everything, even the fear about what might have already happened to the two children.

He waited as the moon slipped in and out of the dark cloud banks.

* * * *

After the lay readings from both the Old and New Testament, Karl slowly rose to his feet to address the congregation. He began the sermon with a question. "Are you the King of the Jews?"

"That's what everybody wanted to know. And what did Jesus reply when Pontius Pilate asked him that very question, 'Are you the King of the Jews?'

"Jesus answered, 'Thou sayest.' To say 'yes' meant certain death. But to say 'no' would have denied the hopes of all those who believed in him as the Messiah. Jesus didn't harbor any secret death wish. But he understood what was happening. Perhaps he also wanted to slow down the process, to taste life a little bit longer."

Karl perused his notes as if consulting them for answers. He looked toward the parishioners. "So when they badgered Jesus with more questions, he simply refused to reply. He chose silence as his refuge."

Karl paused, giving silence its due.

"His refusal to answer their accusations made the crowd demand his blood, because Jesus would neither declare himself King of the Jews nor deny it. Their fury spilled over into the vacuum of his silence. They dressed him in scarlet robes, pushed a crown of thorns upon his head, and placed a reed scepter in his right hand. They ridiculed him as the captive, powerless king. They beat him; they spat on him; they taunted him with mocking words. And then they crucified him in the company of two thieves."

Karl flapped his hands in the air as if they were on fire. "You can imagine the intense physical pain Jesus must have felt when they nailed his hands and skewered his feet to the cross. Think of the emotional pain as they hung a sign over his head proclaiming THIS IS JESUS THE KING OF THE JEWS. The crowd mingled below and scoffed at him. 'If you are strong as it is said, then save yourself. If you really are the Son of God, then come off the cross.'" Karl gesticulated with his fist, as if part of the unruly crowd.

"These are not the words of simple bullies. These are the words of despair from an oppressed people who had lost hope. Many in the jeering crowd half-wished, half-expected a miracle to happen, that Jesus would break the bonds of his captivity and climb down off that cross. And when he didn't save himself, wrath exploded out of their dream denied."

Karl cautioned the congregation, "Don't hold yourself above that crowd. We all have the ability to become enraged when what we want most doesn't happen, when hope disappears and we are left trapped within unchanging misery."

Karl peered meaningfully at Katja, then returned his eyes to his sermon.

"How did Jesus feel with all that anger and rage swirling around him, when his hands and feet burned with pain, his throat grew parched, and his life-force was ebbing away? The last Gospel, St. John, states that Jesus said at the point of death, 'It is finished.' As if Jesus had grown battle-weary with his role in history and was ready for death.

"In the Gospel of St. Luke, Jesus said, 'Father, forgive them; for they know not what they do.' In the midst of pain and suffering, his concerns were with others. And when he died, he said, 'Father, into thy hands

I commend my spirit.' Here is the message of both compassion and anticipation. He was going home to paradise."

Karl's voice softened. "But in the Gospel of St. Mark, written closer in time to the actual event, Jesus had something quite different to say. Up there on that cross, hurting from the punctured flesh, bleeding, reviled by the crowd below, mocked by the sign over his head, Jesus cried out, 'My God, my God, why hast thou forsaken me?'"

Karl paused, his cheek muscles trembling with checked emotion. He shouted out into the church, "My God, my God, why hast thou forsaken me?"

Karl spread his arms wide as if hanging from a cross.

"These are perhaps the most human words of all that Jesus spoke in his whole journey. Here he is, the Son of God, assailed by doubt as to God's intentions. Hadn't he spent his whole life preaching God's new covenant with man? Hadn't he been the most faithful of God's servants? And yet, what happens to him? His is the most painful of deaths—the physical suffering of being nailed to a cross, the jeering degradation of a crowd throwing his reputation back up at him. Hadn't his good works and his constant faith earned him a better end?"

Karl looked out at the parishioners, questioning each one of them. Several of them nodded their heads in agreement. Jesus had deserved better treatment from God.

"'My God, my God, why has thou forsaken me?' It is these words alone that tell us of the magnitude of Jesus's sacrifice. He did what he had to do *and* he suffered for it. Each one of us will find ourselves in times when we, too, will feel abandoned by God. We'll ask the question: How could God let such terrible things happen when we try so hard to be good Christians? When we encounter and struggle with the worst perversities in human nature, we'll say to ourselves, 'God can't exist in a world where such things happen.' And we will grow as enraged as that crowd on Calvary who wanted a miracle. We will mock and revile all the things we have previously held sacred and dear."

Karl could see Katja burying her head into her hands and Bev leaning over to comfort her

He spoke with compassion, his eyes on the grieving mother. "If this were the end of the story, then Jesus' life would have been in vain, his message meaning nothing. But these last words bleed into our hearts with their honesty, their doubt, their fear, their cry of pain,and we know it is not the end of the story. For Jesus or for us. It is that knowledge which gives us hope. Even in the darkest moments of our lives, when there seems to be no future and there is only grief, we must each remember Jesus' humanity. We must make his sacrifice count for something. We must not abandon him in our time of fear. Our despair holds no surprises for him. He's been there before us."

Karl drew back from the pulpit and stood taller. "On Sunday, we will gather together to rejoice in the resurrection and the possibility of eternal life. We will dress in our fancy clothes. Our faces will reflect the hope of new life. But tonight, on Good Friday, it is the time for us to remember what Jesus said and how the dying was difficult for him. It is the time for us to gather up our individual sorrows, our secret fears, our insidious despair, and enter into this story of Jesus, making his story our own.

"Only then can we truly know the promise of Easter morn."

*   *   *   *

The Thunder Beings roared and shook the ozone-laced air. Lightning snaked to the ground and all the little night animals scurried for cover. Hawk didn't move. *Let it pour. I need an answer to my prayers and I will not budge,* he vowed.

Holding out his Sacred Pipe, Hawk waited for the Spirits to tell him what to do. The full moon vanished into the sweep of the black storm clouds and rain pelted his face. Kneeling on two bent legs, Hawk could feel the sharp ache of his left hip—an old rodeo injury. From the west the storm was still bulking up in mass, cast in relief by the lunar back light; the winds were picking up and lashing at the trees.

Once again, Hawk forced all thoughts out of his mind but no images came to him, no animal spoke to him, no cloud shaped a message to him, no words whispered into his left ear. He took seven deep breaths, a prayer made with each exhalation, as raindrops ran into the creases of his mouth. Each time his chest expanded, the Stone-man banged against an upper rib. Encased in a deerskin pouch, hung round his neck, the Stone-man had been a gift to Hawk from his father, the man who had deserted him when he was a child.

He reached into the damp pouch and extracted the small gray rock, hollow in its center. The stone grew warm in his hand and began to vibrate. Nothing more happened but Hawk understood that the Stone-man would tell him more as Hawk awakened its power.

Three Legs, his Spirit teacher, had once lectured him: "The Stone-man will help you. All his life, your father carried that Stone-man, but he was unable to be hollow at the center; he wasn't strong enough to withstand the emptiness. When you ask Wakan Tanka and Unci Maka to work through you, They will use you, but you must stay balanced, grounded when that happens. That's where the Pipe will help you."

As the Stone-man rocked in his hand, Hawk understood that on the next day he would put up an inipi ceremony. The sweat lodge, the Chanunpa, and the Stone-man would help him find the children.

Wakan Tanka works in mysterious ways, he thought.

SIXTEEN

DEEPER INTO DARKNESS

I promised I'd remember his name. *Jay, Jeff, Jesse. What's his name?*

I'm so tired, dizzy, thirsty. What was that green drink? Makes me puke.

John? No. I promised. . . .

My hands, my feet they hurt so. My head. Why can't I remember? What's wrong with me? I just want to curl up and die.

Name, he said remember my name, and I can't, oh god, I can't remember. I didn't know him. Remember me, he said but no, they said I'd forget him.

Sleep, they said, and I'll forget everything.

I promised.

Fire. Everything becomes smoke and I can't remember.

Fire. Everything becomes smoke and I can't forget.

They lay me down into darkness, a box, and it's all black and things are sucking on me.

SEVENTEEN

SATURDAY

He who asks questions cannot avoid the answers.

—CAMEROONIAN PROVERB

$\mathcal{M}orning$ broke bright and clear over the Leelanau Peninsula. The media had shifted their interest and location toward Lucy Arbre's house. The missing Tubbs girl was now old news whereas the disappearance of Adam was fresh in the public mind. No one knew whether the two children had been abducted by the same person or persons but much was made of the fact that June and Adam had a "special" relationship. Only the tabloids, though, suggested that the nine-year-old boy had eloped with his eight-year-old girlfriend.

Lucy wanted to evict the media camping out in her front yard. The mounted tribal police were certainly willing but Larry insisted that the publicity would only help Adam in the long run. "They're like a bunch of bottom feeders," she protested. "You know what they asked me?" She banged the coffee cup down on the kitchen table.

Larry could only imagine.

"Those goddamn piranhas wanted to know if Adam was a physically abused child. They actually asked me if we beat our son."

"You tell me which one asked that and I'll get rid of him. But the others, Lucy, they're a necessary evil right now. We've got to stay focused on getting Adam back."

Lucy peered out the kitchen window at the media trucks, the satellites, and the cameras, ready and waiting for the family to step outside for interviews. She shook her head. "Bloodsuckers. And to think that white people have the nerve to label us as savages."

*   *   *   *

Katja pushed away the tranquilizers that the family physician had prescribed for her. She poured orange juice for Paul and her son, seated across from her. The boy was scarfing down a large bowl of Wheaties.

"Robert, you've got a soccer game this morning," Katja announced.

The boy looked up, surprised.

"Hon, there's work we have to do on the posters. We don't have time for a soccer game," Paul interrupted.

Robert glanced back and forth between his parents.

"I'll work on the posters after his game. Hurry up, Robert, we've got to get to the field in thirty minutes." Katja began cleaning up the kitchen.

"Okay, Mom." The boy excused himself and tore up the stairs.

"Katja, what are you doing?" Paul asked.

Katja spun on her heels and leaned over the table, her hands supporting her. She stared at her husband with ferocious determination. "I've lost one child. I am not about to lose another. We'll do what we can to find June, but life also has to go on. And Robert is our son. He has a soccer game this morning."

Paul retorted, "You've given up, haven't you? Well, I haven't. June is out there, needing our help and our protection. I, at least, will not abandon her."

"I can't believe you said that, Paul."

But he didn't apologize.

In a grim, foreboding silence, she gathered up her car keys and hollered to Robert to hurry up. The front door slammed shut as mother and son made their way to the car. Paul stood at the kitchen window, coffee cup in hand, as he watched the remnants of his small family disappear.

* * * *

Paul heard a gentle tap on the kitchen door. He knew it was too early for Katja to be returning from Robert's soccer game. Probably just another reporter wanting "an exclusive interview" with a family member. But, no, it was Meggie O'Connor's husband alone and obviously ill at ease.

"Come in," Paul said, stepping aside.

"Is your wife here?" Hawk asked, looking around the room. Scattered posters covered every available surface.

"She's at a soccer game with our son. Did you want to talk to her?"

Hawk shrugged his shoulders. "Have you heard anything new about your little girl?"

Paul turned away. *Good grief, was the man here as a curiosity seeker?* Seized by a sudden flash of anger, Paul resented that he had nothing new to say about his daughter.

Hawk took off his Western hat, ran his fingers around the rim. "It's not a good time for you, I know that. I want to help. There are ways I might be able to find out something."

Paul pivoted around to stare at him. *What was the man talking about?*

Awkwardly Hawk plunged on. "Tonight I am going to do an inipi ceremony and ask about the missing boy. Adam Arbre's my cousin."

"I'm sorry, I should have realized that you were related to the boy."

"It's okay. But I got to thinking that I could also try to find out what happened to your little girl."

Paul slumped down on a kitchen chair. Hawk continued to stand, nervously fingering his hat. Paul leaned forward, "How would you, how could you . . .?

"I'll call in the Spirits and ask Them to locate the children."

"You can do that?"

Hawk nodded.

"And They'll tell you where June is and what's happened to her?" Paul's voice wavered high and incredulous.

"Maybe." Hawk sighed. "It's not exactly like picking up a telephone and calling information. There's a lot more static on the line, caused by my own limitations. And when the Spirits do choose to speak, They often do so in words or images which are hard to understand. And sometimes I simply ask the wrong question."

"The boy's been gone two days. Why didn't you consult these spirits immediately?" *My daughter's been gone six days.* The thought turned bitter inside of him.

"Because it doesn't make sense to ask the Spirits to help us when we don't need Their help. I thought that Adam would have turned up by now."

He didn't mention June, Paul noted. *What does he want from us?*

"I came here with three questions."

"What are they?" *Is he going to ask me for money?* Paul wondered.

"First, do you want me to ask about June in ceremony?" Hawk's eyes scanned the man's face.

"Sure. I mean, what harm would it do? Maybe you can find out something from these spirits that the police have overlooked. I'm willing to do anything, try every pathway. Do you want me there?"

"No. I need to do this alone." Hawk was adamant about this. "Secondly, do you have an item of June's clothing? The Spirits don't need it to find her but I do. It will help me concentrate better."

Paul rose and left the room, returning with an unwashed jersey belonging to his daughter. "Katja will be angry at me for giving you a dirty blouse."

But Hawk put up his hand to signal that it wasn't a problem. He gripped the jersey in his right hand, holding the hat brim in his left.

"What else do you want to know?"

"I'd like to know how you would ask the question." Hawk said this slowly, thoughtfully.

Where is my little girl? Is she hurt? Is she nearby or far away? Who kidnaped her? Is she dead? A barrage of questions assailed Paul's mind.

Hawk stood there quietly as Paul sorted out what was most important for him to know.

At first Paul's lips silently mouthed the questions until finally he said, "Where can we find June?"

"Okay, I'll ask that question." Hawk turned to go.

"Wait," Paul exclaimed. "I want to know who did this to her."

Hawk's face fell. "I was afraid you were going to ask that." Without saying another word, he replaced the black felt hat on his head, opened the door, and left.

Alone by the kitchen window, Paul sat there cradling his head in his hands. His child's happy, trusting face peered up at him from the posters and circulars scattered all over the table. Paul slammed his fist down and shouted, "I have a right to know." His daughter's face crumpled under the force of his hand.

"Damn it all, I have a right to know," he said softly.

EIGHTEEN

OR NOT TO BE

I can't see anything.
I can't hear anything.
I can't smell anything.
I can't know anything.
I can't remember anything.

I must be dead.

NINETEEN

Two Visions

The smoke of sweetgrass is pleasant to the good spirits.
They come to the smoke. They are pleased with one who
makes this smoke. They will listen to what such a one asks.
But the bad spirits come also to enjoy the smoke. So sage
must be burned to make them sick.

—TAKES THE GUN
Lakota Belief and Ritual

After Hawk lit the fire, night pulled up a blanket of darkness from the east. For two hours, the flames burned brightly then banked into hot coals; the stones glowed red on the surface, white in the center. Hawk changed into his towel and crawled into the lodge. He had been fasting all day in preparation for this inipi ceremony. His Chanunpa leaned against the buffalo skull, alongside the short chanunpa that belonged to Adam. Hung in the rafters of the lodge were his prayer ties and the blouse that belonged to little June. On the outside, standing next to Lucy, Meggie passed in the cedar, sweet grass, sage, antlers, rattles, and tobacco.

Larry had intended to sweat but the police had called him to review photographs of young boys. Lucy asked if Hawk needed her presence in the sweat lodge. "You'll be of more help on the outside," he gently replied. Her disbelief in the old ways might interfere with what the Spirits had to say to him.

With a pitchfork, Meggie transferred twenty-one hefty rocks from the fire to the center pit of the lodge. She then covered up the remaining seven stones with fresh wood. Fingers of flame curled around the new logs.

"Mni," ordered Hawk.

Meggie hoisted the metal bucket of water. The dipper clanged loudly against the rim.

Hawk touched the pail to the pile of glowing stones and placed it on a platform of sage. The smoke and aroma of burning cedar, sage, tobacco, and sweet grass saturated the lodge and stung his eyes. Throwing out the tobacco and antlers, he nodded to Meggie that he was ready.

Both women reached up and lowered three dark blankets and a star quilt over the lodge opening. They tamped in the blankets at the bottom so no light would penetrate. Hawk had asked them to sit by the fire. He didn't know if things would be said that were meant for his ears only.

Lucy retreated to the house, returning with an extra cup of coffee for Meggie, generously laced with sugar and cream. Together, the two women watched the flames devour the new wood.

"God, I hope this works," Lucy said. She reached into her pocket for a pack of cigarettes.

Meggie didn't reply. Instead she reached over and placed a hand upon Lucy's arm. That simple gesture spoke more forcefully than any words.

* * * *

Hawk sang his Spirit-calling song. Then, instead of moving directly into prayer, he sat quietly, studying the stones, centering himself, letting go of the busy chit-chat of the brain, his fear for the two children, his concerns about Lucy, anything that might divert him from his purpose for being there.

"Inyan," he addressed the Stone People, "thank you for letting me come into your lodge."

The stones glowed red, shimmering and vibrating with intense heat. Faces and figures pulsated across their surfaces until the hot cores banked into flickering shadows. From a cross-legged position Hawk bent over close, watching. The warmth of the stones radiated onto him, into him, through him, until every muscle fiber, every nerve cell resonated in the power and the gift of their presence.

He burst into a sun dance song, ladling cold water onto the rocks. The heat boiled up, spat, and spluttered across the stones.

"Tunkasila, Wakan Tanka, Unci Maka, Grandfathers in All the Directions, I come before You asking for help. I give thanks for the power of the lightnings, for the trees who have given their life so that I can do this thing, for the water without which we cannot live, for the help of Inyan. I come into this lodge, an *Ikcewicasta, a* simple earth man, asking for your help. Grandfathers, bend down so that you can hear these prayers. Mitakuye oyas'in."

Hawk poured on more water until the heat rippled down his back and smarted on his bare chest. Sweat dappled his face, his arms, his legs.

And still he kept adding water, sinking into quietness. Except for the sizzle and crackle of water on hot stones, the silence, darkness, and nettling heat simultaneously settled him down while heightening, honing all his senses. He was coming alive to other realities.

Something caught his attention. At first he thought that it was Lucy and Meggie on the outside. A small, tinny sound of voices singing. He bent closer to the darkening stones. It was Them. The Stone People were singing *Heya, heya* over and over and over again, a rising, falling quatrain full of strength and hope, sadness and endurance.

Tentatively at first, he began singing along with Them, *heya heya*, then with fervor and fire burning in his voice.

Heya, heya, his voice kindled the words and ignited the music. The notes broke free, *heya heya*, spiraling up from the rocks, dancing off the ceiling and sides, *heya heya* boomeranging back into his mouth, *heya heya* until Hawk swallowed into the song of the Stone People, rising, falling, getting up again. Over and over he intoned the lines *heya heya* knowing that the song was singing him. The words, the music burrowed down into the lodgings of his heart. Then and only then did the Stone People hush.

Hawk cried out, "Wopila, wopila, Grandfathers. Mitakuye oyas'in!"

Meggie flung open the door. White billowing steam cascaded out into the dark blue night air. A brief respite.

The door came down again. The second round of the ceremony began.

Hawk's prayers were of gratitude and respect.

"For the gifts and the wisdom of the winged ones who know how to resist the pull of the Grandmother, to soar into the heavens, to travel to other worlds." In his hand the eagle fan fluttered and stirred the steamy currents in the lodge.

"For the fins who roam the depths of the oceans, the lakes, and the streams, the whales who stroke along the ocean floors singing, the dolphins who delight in play—all flowing through the veins of the Grandmother, all sensing the tidal rhythms of Her heart.

"For the creeping, crawling things that populate the surfaces, casting out their webs into the air, digging, dragging, cleansing the Grandmother of death and decay, loosening the soil so that the plants might live and the trees might grow.

"For those nations of being, the trees and the plants, rooted into the Grandmother but stretching toward the sun and sky, breathing air back into the world, giving shade to the hot and food to the hungry.

"For the four-leggeds, the ones deep in shadow and rare to human sight, raising their young and keeping the world in balance. The wary ones at the edges, watching us, flicking their ears with curiosity, lifting their noses to catch the scent of our presence. The ones that have made a pact of domesticity with us, caught between their instincts and their wish to please, always teaching, showing, telling us what is important."

Finally Hawk prayed for "the two-leggeds of all colors. Help us learn to live in balance with this Creation."

Ladling the water to the stones, the steam rolled over him and flickered down his back. He gave thanks for the ancestors who had kept the ceremonies for seven generations. He remembered his feverish vision.

"I see now, at what cost, Tunkasila, it must have been for the old ones who kept the traditions. Outlawed by the white missionaries, ridiculed by our own people, arrested by the tribal police for setting up sweat lodges and sun dances, enduring the suffering and despair of their own hearts. But they still held onto what they knew to be true. Grandfather, if the old ones had not done that, I could not be here pouring the waters of the inipi, talking to You like this in the ways of my ancestors.

"These prayers I make are for All My Relations. They surround me through time and in space. Without them I could not live. Hau. Mitakuye oyas'in!"

Meggie threw up the door covering. Rolling out of the lodge, white, hot steam whooshed into the night air and dissipated into the darkness. Hawk's face glowed from the intense heat.

"Inyan," Hawk grimly commanded.

Meggie took the pitchfork and uncovered the seven large stones in the fire. One by one, she carried them over to the sweat lodge where Hawk, seated inside, positioned them atop the others, using the antlers. This was the third round, the Pipe round. Hawk would ask the Spirits about the children. Once he applied water to the new stones, the heat of the lodge would soar, sear the throat, and choke his words. Through prayer and song, he would find the strength to endure the stinging, burning nettles upon his skin.

After filling the bucket with water, Meggie lowered the door and moved back towards the fire.

Ladling the water onto the fresh red stones, Hawk burst into the White Buffalo Calf Woman song, the same song he had sung many times before, the one that had helped Meggie heal after the miscarriage, the one that had prefaced his marriage proposal to her. A pipe-filling song, the words of Ptesan Wi promised, *If you do this, what you wish will come true*. To the last note, his voice croaking against the waves of withering heat, Hawk powered the song with conviction.

"Tunkasila, Wakan Tanka, Unci Maka, Grandfathers in All The Directions, Wanbli Gleska, my medicine helpers, Three Legs—I ask You all to bend over to hear my prayers, to see those two Chanunpas on the buffalo altar. The Chanunpa Wakan is mine; the small chanunpa belongs to my cousin, my nephew Adam. Grandfather, he's been gone two days now and we don't know where. I ask You to help me see him, to know whether he is still alive and where we can find him.

"Grandfather, above me is a blouse belonging to a young girl, June Tubbs. She too has disappeared and has been gone many days. Grandfather, we don't even know if the two children are together or apart. Her father wants to know where he can find her and if she is alive and well."

Hawk paused and spoke in a soft, sorrowful voice. "Grandfathers, he also wants You to tell him who has taken his little girl."

Having ended his prayers with a soft "Mitakuye oyas'in," Hawk sat back in the suffocating heat. It was easy enough to ask the questions but it was much harder to receive the answers. He knew the Spirits might speak to him in his left ear or They might show him an image of the children. Hawk kept his eyes open and scanned the darkness. They might even come and sit down beside him and talk to him. Or They might choose to say nothing at all.

Hawk's worst fear was that They would answer his questions and he would be blind or deaf to what They had to say. It was easy enough to get into one's own way through mental preoccupation, fear, or wanting to shape an answer. Hawk had to hollow himself, like the pipe, to empty himself of anything but attention. Only in that way could he serve as a true messenger.

At first all he saw was the swirling of thick air in the blackness that surrounded him. An itchy feeling of bugs crept along his skin. Then suddenly, as if a remote channel had been switched on, the face of Adam appeared before him, shiny but distant, a glassy image. The muscles of Adam's cheeks were tightly clenched, the mouth shut. His pudgy hands squeezed against both ears and his eyes, while open, did not appear to be seeing anything. *Oh God, he's dead.* Hawk's face fell but then he noticed a rising and falling of the boy's chest.

He's alive. Hawk reached into the air as if to touch the boy.

The image, like a mirror, fell forward and soundlessly shattered into many pieces on the sweat lodge floor, each shard reflecting a part of Adam—an eye, a nose, a hand, jumbled and mixed up with no apparent coherence.

The next image superseded the fractured mirror. A tearful Lucy was bent over, hugging her son. Adam stood there, arms down by his side, his left hand bandaged, his eyes still seeing nothing, a dazed, lifeless expression frozen to his face.

Then Hawk knew two things: The boy would be coming home, but something terrible had happened to his soul.

The image vanished into the swirling thick darkness of the sweat lodge. Hawk waited to see what the Spirits would show him about June, what had happened to her. He ladled more water to the groaning rocks. The steam poured over him and it hurt to breathe. He kept his eyes open.

For a long time there was nothing but silence and blackness until finally a weak specter emerged out of the darkness. The face of June

Tubbs wavered before him. In her eyes she carried the sadness of the whole world. Her tears were like two mighty rivers streaming down the sides of her wavering face. Slowly the rest of her body came into focus and the image shifted.

She was stretched out on a stone table, eyes shut. Hawk studied the figure closely and his heart sank in grief. There was no chest movement, no breathing in, no breathing out.

Even worse—where her little heart used to beat, there was only a gaping, bloody hole.

"Aaiii," cried Hawk.

The thick swirling blackness in the lodge swallowed back the image of June. Hawk waited for more information but there was none forthcoming.

"Grandfather, her father wants to know who has done this to his little girl," Hawk pushed.

It seemed like a long time before his Spirit teacher, Three Legs, spoke. "If we answer that question, it will destroy that man's life. He will see nothing but revenge before him. There will be no healing for him. He will tear out his own heart."

The silence that followed was deafening.

TWENTY

EASTER

We are what we tell and we tell what we are.

—JANE YOLEN

Meggie studied Hawk's ashen face as he emerged from the sweat lodge. He looked as if he had aged twenty years in two hours. When she asked him what he had seen, he could only shake his head. Lucy stood by, waiting for him to tell her the news, good or bad.

"Adam will come back," he said.

Lucy threw her arms around him in a fierce hug. "Thank God," she exhaled, tears at the corners of her eyes. She took off for the house before completely losing emotional control.

But Meggie looked at this man whom she loved, at the grim lines that spidered around his mouth. She knew the news was not good.

"June?" She wanted to be able to tell Paul and Katya something, to give them an image of hope.

But Hawk only shook his head and turned away from her. He took the child's blouse over to the glowing embers of the fire, murmured a prayer, and dropped it onto the coals. The blouse flared up in flames and disappeared.

It was then that Meggie decided to go to church next morning, to join her friends Bev and Katja.

On Easter morning, Karl rose to the pulpit and looked over the congregation, the pews bulging with people, many of whom only showed up in church once a year—at Easter. The air was redolent with the sweet, cloying smell of white lilies. All over the church, the women's flower guild had positioned the flowers as if the church itself were some grande dame who had doused herself with French perfume.

"Welcome," he said to the people, then sneezed. Little girls wiggled in their seats against the itch of new dresses while their mothers shushed them. Boys with wet, slicked back hair sat stiffly at attention. Women swiveled around to catch sight of their neighbors and the men looked bored, as if they would rather go outside to smoke a good cigar. Karl knew he would have to work hard to focus their attention and draw them into the passion of Easter.

"Welcome to the House of God," Karl said again, opening up his arms to include the whole flock. "We have now come to the end of Holy Week, to the beginning of the new covenant God has made with man. After all the hopes, all the fears, the sadness, the cruelty of death's dominion, we now break free to everlasting life. Placed within his rock-sealed tomb, Jesus arises today in the flesh. The first person he encounters is a woman, Mary Magdalene. That is fitting, because women are the source of all new life.

"In the gospel according to John, Jesus tells her not to touch him 'for I am not yet ascended to my Father.' Jesus is still earth-bound, not a ghost or a spirit without substance. In this state He appears before his disciples three times, eating and drinking with them. He wants his followers to recognize Him first in flesh, then in faith, because without their conviction and testifying to what happened, He knows He will be forgotten."

Karl leaned forward over the pulpit. "Unless you and I spread the words about His life and His message, then Jesus the man and Christ the Son of God will be forgotten over time. For you and I are the tellers of His story."

Wearing a clip-on microphone, Karl stepped down from the pulpit and strolled the central aisle, speaking directly to the people who turned and watched him as he moved past. "Three times, Jesus asks Simon, son of Jonas, 'Do you love me?'

"Three times, Simon answers, 'Yes, Lord; you know that I love thee.'"

Karl swung around and started back down the aisle, again making eye contact with each of his parishioners. "Do you know what Jesus says in response to Simon's declarations of love? He doesn't reply, 'Hey that feels good. Tell me more about how you love me.' No, Jesus wants us to know what it means to *really* love him.

"So Jesus answers Simon the first time, 'Feed my lambs.'" Karl smiled at a little girl who was clattering her new shoes against the back of the pew.

"The second time and the third time, Jesus says, 'Feed my sheep.'" Karl reached over and patted the arm of an elderly white-haired woman and shook the hand of a prominent deacon.

Returning to the front of the church, Karl paused and spoke softly, forcing the congregation to lean forward to hear his words. "We must pay attention to what Jesus is telling us. Words of love are not enough. Like shepherds, we must care for the young and those in need of help. We must reach out to our elders, make them part of our community. Your flock, my flock, are your fellow human beings. He gave up His life so that you and I might live.

"And that is not the same as saying *so that you and I might have an easy life*. All we have to do is look around and see what has happened this past week to our neighboring community of Suttons Bay, to the children and the families there. What can be worse than losing a child?" Karl stared at the mothers in the congregation and finally at Katja. He turned pained eyes away from her grieving face back to the congregation.

"What can be worse than to have all your hopes pinned on a messiah who was going to come and free your people from their suffering and to witness, instead, his being nailed to two wooden beams, humiliated and mocked, then killed?"

Karl ascended the remaining steps to the pulpit. "Death is a fact of life. Jesus came, not to rule on earth as a king but to proclaim a triumph against the final despair of death. In the gospel of Matthew, he says, 'I am with you always, even unto the end of the world.' Not even death can snuff out His presence in our lives."

Karl again scanned the faces in the church, lowering his voice. "But if we refuse to live his message, if we do not tell his story in action as well as words, then his death is all for naught. We will be telling a false story. We will be *masquerading* as Christians."

Karl smiled. "I have not seen some of you in this church for some time. Perhaps it is because you didn't find the inspiration here that you needed to live your life. Maybe your spouse or parents dragged you here today. Maybe it was guilt, spiritual insurance, or family reunions that pulled you to church on this holiday. But I suspect the real reason you came today is because you *want to believe* the story of Jesus Christ. And Easter is the day Jesus fulfills the promise of His story."

Karl looked up toward the highest point in the modest church and spread his arms high in praise. "Today, He is arisen. Hallelujah. God be praised!"

And then, Karl dropped his arms dramatically and thundered out to the congregation, "With gladness, take Jesus into your hearts. 'I am with you always,' he promises us. Jesus will ask each one of you, 'Do you love me?'"

Reviewing the attentive faces staring up at him, Karl repeated the question: "'Do you love me?' Feed my lambs. Feed my sheep," he echoed.

Pausing a long time for emphasis, knowing that the congregation expected a rousing finish, he surprised them instead with paradox, his gentle voice sternly commanding: "It is up to you to tell His story well. Amen."

* * * *

While Meggie and her friends attended the church service, Hawk knew he had no choice but to drive to the Tubbs house and report to June's father. The driveway was empty. *Perhaps nobody is at home.* He recognized the wish.

But when he knocked on the kitchen door, he heard a man's footsteps approach. The door swung opened and Paul stood there, hope and fear glittering in his eyes.

"Come on in." The two men entered the kitchen area. Hawk stayed standing. Paul sat down on a wooden chair.

"What did your spirits tell you?" Paul asked.

Hawk couldn't look at him. *How can I take hope away from this man? Maybe I didn't really understand what the Spirits showed me. He wants to know. He doesn't want to know.*

"They didn't tell me where she was, but they showed me. . . ." Hawk stammered.

"What?" Paul sat on the edge of his chair, studying Hawk's tormented face.

"She was crying and her face was very sad."

"That means she is still alive." Paul grabbed onto a thread of hope.

Was alive, thought Hawk.

"Then They showed her on a stone table," he continued.

"On a table? What does that mean?" Paul's voice surged with anger and urgency.

"Her heart." Hawk could barely utter the words. "It was missing."

"Goddamnit, what are you telling me?" Paul rose to his feet, his fists clenched by his side. He thrust his face toward Hawk.

Hawk backed up a step. "I don't know what it means."

"Who's taken her? What did you find out about the boy?"

"I don't know who has taken her. The boy will be found, but . . ." Hawk wished he could be anywhere but in Paul Tubbs' kitchen. He had wanted to help the man; all he was doing was shredding the man's heart and a father's hope.

"But what?" Paul demanded to know.

"Adam will be coming home in pieces. He won't be the same."

"And nothing more about June?" Paul's voice was getting angrier.

Hawk shook his head.

Paul scoffed, "Some help those spirits of yours have given. Mystery messages. I'm sorry." He waved his arm in a dismissive gesture. "I should never have agreed to ask those questions. It's not my religion and it doesn't have anything to do with me or my little girl. I apologize for my impatience, my anger. I truly hope the boy comes back to your family. I want you to know that I'll find my little girl and I'll bring her back home, safe. Of course, her heart is broken. She's been gone from us too long, but she's coming home. I know it."

Hawk nodded. It was time to leave. He didn't say what he was thinking: *June's heart wasn't broken. It had been ripped out of her body.*

Meggie dropped her keys onto the dining room table, as she greeted Fritzie. "I'm home," she yelled up the stairs.

Shoe-less, Hawk pattered to the top of the steps and looked down, relieved to see Meggie back from church.

"How was the service?"

"For Katja, healing. It gave Bev a lot to think about. Karl's pretty serious about his profession."

"How about you? How was church for you, Meggie?" It was not a disinterested question.

She looked up at him. "I was distracted, thinking about you, last night's sweat lodge, your meeting with Paul this morning. Karl's a good speaker, but . . ."

"But what, Meggie?"

"Truth is, I'm more at home in the sweat lodge than I ever was in a church. Does that surprise you?"

Hawk shook his head.

"Well, it surprises me. I'm not Indian." Meggie looked up to her dark-haired lover with his high cheekbones, his flat nose, his strong, determined jaw—a face of the Plains.

Hawk descended the stairs and eased himself down on the last step. Extending a hand, he invited her to sit beside him. "The heart has its own wisdom, Meggie."

Lowering herself to the step, tucking in the edges of her skirt, Meggie grasped his hand and stroked it with her thumb. Softly, she said, "I bet it was hard talking to Paul. What did you say to him about what you saw last night?"

"Oh Meggie," he sighed. "I didn't tell the story well."

TWENTY-ONE

SLENDER THREAD

Hopes, what are they?—Beads of morning
Strung on slender blades of grass;
Or a spider's web adorning
In a strait and treacherous pass.

—WILLIAM WORDSWORTH
Inscriptions.

Monday morning, Meggie and Hawk drove over to Lucy's place to join reservation folk addressing mailers with Adam's photograph. The house spilled over with people. Buoyant and full of energy, Lucy organized everyone. Larry supplied the volunteers with ashtrays and hot cups of coffee.

He invited Hawk outside for a short breather. The air was brisk and bright, the day full of promise.

"Lucy said that our son is coming home. Did the Spirits give you any time line?"

Hawk shook his head.

Larry probed. "I get the feeling, Bro', that there were some things you didn't tell my wife. Things you saw in the inipi ceremony."

Hawk wandered over to a large, cut stump and sat down. He rubbed his eyes with calloused hands.

"I want to know what they showed you, Hawk." Larry squatted down on the ground, putting himself at eye level.

Hawk spoke. "The boy's coming home. I saw Lucy greeting him. But he's different. He's not the same kid that left here."

Larry didn't say anything. He waited to hear more.

Hawk's brow furrowed. "I don't really understand all that They showed me. Physically, Adam seemed okay but his left hand was bandaged. I saw his reflection on glass. And then the mirror broke and Adam was shattered into pieces." Hawk stared straight ahead as if trying to bring the world into focus.

"I guess we'll find out what They meant soon enough, won't we? Was that all?"

Hawk raked over his memory from Saturday night. The only thing that popped into his mind was the image of the three monkeys: *Hear no evil, see no evil, speak no evil.* But he couldn't see the relevance of that image to Larry's question. "That about covers it," he said.

Larry nodded, stood up, and wandered back toward the house.

Hawk continued to stare out into the countryside, trying to clear himself of all internal distractions, hoping that something new, something helpful would break through to his consciousness. Perversely, a childhood rhyme surged into his thoughts, demanding attention:

> *Humpty Dumpty sat on a wall.*
> *Humpty Dumpty had a great fall.*
> *All the King's horses and all the King's men*
> *Couldn't put Humpty together again.*

* * * *

Later that night, long after Hawk and Meggie had settled into bed and were drifting into the place of dreams, the telephone rang and rudely yanked them back to consciousness.

Hawk's hand groped for the phone and knocked the alarm clock off the stand.

"Yeah," he said, too asleep to be more articulate.

"You were right, Hawk," the man's voice said.

"They've found him; they've found him," Lucy interrupted, her voice fluttering with excitement and relief.

"Where?" Hawk sat upright in the bed and switched on the light.

"Illinois, alongside a rural highway. We're calling you because we wondered if we could drop off Eva? Lucy and I are about to head downstate and pick him up."

"Sure." Hawk cupped his hand over the receiver and whispered to Meggie, "They found Adam in Illinois. Eva's coming over tonight. Alright?"

Meggie nodded. "Is the boy okay?" she whispered.

Larry continued talking to Hawk. "We don't know much. He's in the hospital, in shock. That's all the police would tell us."

Hawk asked, "Was the girl with him?"

Larry hesitated, as if unsure. "I don't think so. We'll be right over."

Meggie and Hawk jumped out of bed and turned on the outside lights. Meggie checked the guest bedroom and turned down the blankets. She plugged in a small night light.

Fritzie barked at the sound of a car graveling up the long driveway in the middle of the night.

Eva was half asleep, slumped in her father's arms. Her mother quickly put her to bed, promising, "We'll be home before you even know it, and your brother will be safely with us." She shut the bedroom door.

Larry murmured to Hawk, "Sorry to rush off."

"Go," said Hawk. "Your son is waiting for you."

Like statues, Hawk and Meggie stood there, hand in hand, as the bright glow of the car's headlights raked across them, stabbing at their eyes, then swept down the hill, scattering back the night shadows. Long after the long beam of car lights had departed from Chrysalis, the two of them remained there, waiting for their eyes to adjust to the deepening darkness.

What am I ever going to say to Katja tomorrow? Meggie worried.

Hawk listened to the metallic sounds of a car fading in the distance until all that he could hear were the echoes of a poem pinging in his brain:

> *All the King's horses*
> *And all the King's men*
> *Couldn't put Humpty together again.*

TWENTY-TWO

DISCORD

Home is the place where, when you have to go there,
They have to take you in.

—ROBERT FROST
The Death of The Hired Man

"Sam, I've got a problem," Jillian said, peering into his office.

He swiveled around in his chair. It was unlike Jillian to bring up issues that she couldn't solve all by herself. He pulled up a wooden chair and peeled off the veterinary magazines, stacking them into a neat pile on the floor. "Is it with the clinic?"

They both knew that there wouldn't be any customers arriving for another half hour. The first hour of every morning was devoted to setting up the day's schedules and getting organized. Daisy had already departed for her classes to return later in the afternoon. It was a good time for Jillian and Sam to talk without interruption.

"Daisy?" Sam was guessing.

"Bingo!" answered Jillian.

"But you told me she was making real progress here. I've been impressed with her performance and I must say, Jillian, it's been mainly due to your efforts with the young lady."

"That's the problem," Jillian said.

Sam pulled out his briar pipe. He knew he had time for a quick smoke. He thumbed cherry-flavored tobacco into the bowl, lit the pipe with a match, and took a couple of deep, satisfying puffs. Jillian got up from her chair to close the door and open the window so that the smoke wouldn't spread to the rest of the clinic. Besides, it would set the wrong example for Daisy.

"You two seem to be on good terms with each other," Sam commented.

"We are and that's the issue. She wants to move in with me and with my husband."

Sam sat back. "Well, that's a surprise."

"Come on, Sam. You and I both know what her family's like. Her father is the town drunk."

Sam nodded. Only too well did he know of Clyde Bassett's reputation, the drinking and the suspicion of incest. He had hoped that by working in the clinic, Daisy might begin to develop a more benign view of people as well as a sense of social responsibility.

Jillian continued, "Her mother took off with the other kids for Easter and apparently has just sent word saying that she isn't coming back. She's given Daisy the choice to stay here in Suttons Bay or to join them."

"And Daisy doesn't want to leave her classmates and friends," Sam conjectured.

"No, that's not it," countered Jillian. "She doesn't want to leave us."

"Us?" Sam didn't understand.

"Sam, we're the first people who have ever really treated this girl with respect. And we've now got a problem on our hands. She doesn't want to leave and she sure as heck doesn't want to live alone with her father."

"Well," Sam was trying to think it through. "I could clean out the back storage area in my house."

Jillian shook her head. "It won't work, Sam. You'd just be putting your reputation in jeopardy. All that would need to happen is for Clyde Bassett to start spreading rumors that you were after his daughter and you know how people love anything that hints of scandal. He'd be demanding money from you for the *loan* of his daughter."

"Jillian!" Sam was truly shocked.

"Sam, let's face it. You're a great veterinarian but you're naive as all get out when it comes to people. It's probably why you were willing to employ Daisy when other people in town shut their doors. No, there are only two choices here: She goes to live with her mother or she comes to stay with me."

Sam could see Jillian's point. He puffed on his briar pipe and waited to see how his office manager would work it out.

"If she joins her mother, she's going to drop out of school. I know that's what'll happen." Jillian paused.

"She's got only one more year to go," Sam said.

"It's not the money. I know Clyde Bassett wouldn't contribute a cent for her upkeep. Since my kids have grown up and flown the coop, it's not like we don't have room in our house. It's just that . . ." Jillian didn't quite know how to phrase it.

"Sam, you've lived alone most of your adult life and so time alone is nothing unusual or special. But Dave and I, we've spent years raising our kids, devoting our time to their activities, and now that they're gone, we finally have time for ourselves. Even more important than the time is the privacy. When raising kids, you forget how much fun it is walking around your own house, totally in the buff."

Sam grinned. "Why Jillian, I learn something new about you every day."

She thumped him on the arm to let him know he'd better not pursue that line of teasing.

He drew himself up in the chair and tried to be serious. "Well, you can't promise to take her for a whole year unless you can keep that commitment. It's something you're going to need to talk about with that fine husband of yours."

"Oh, you know Dave," she sputtered. "He'll tell me that anything I want is okay with him."

"So, what do you want?" Sam asked.

"I want my privacy," she replied.

"Well, I guess that about decides it." Sam rose and knocked out the pipe's ashes into a metal wastebasket.

"And I also want Daisy to finish high school," Jillian added.

* * * *

"Can't I stay with you today?" Eva inquired.

Meggie tousled her hair. "You have to go to school and I have to go to work."

"What about Hawk?" The girl continued to look hopeful.

"What about me?" Hawk entered the kitchen nook where Eva was dangling her spoon into a bowl of cold cereal and Meggie was nursing her second cup of coffee.

"Can I stay with you today?" It was an old routine with Eva. If one parent said no, the other parent might say yes.

Hawk caught on to the manipulation but to her surprise he answered, "Only if you'll help me."

Eva warily looked at Meggie to note her reaction. A puzzled expression wrinkled across Meggie's face.

Hawk continued, "First, I need to go buy some grass seed and fertilizer. You'll have to help me carry the heavy bags from the store. Then I need to stop over at Oleson's supermarket and pick up a buffalo head."

"A buffalo head?" Eva was curious.

"Yes, I'm building a sweat lodge here at Chrysalis and it needs a buffalo head altar."

"Oh," Eva replied, stuffing her mouth with cereal.

"But," Hawk added, "it won't look like the old one at your place because that old buffalo head has been bleached by the rain and the wind. No, this new one will be frozen and kind of bloody. It'll still have a lot of tissue on it: Hair, nostrils, eyes."

"Eyes? Gross." Eva scrunched up her face.

"And I'll definitely need your help in carrying it to the car. We'll take the buffalo head and put it on the biggest ant hill that we can find."

Eva wiggled her nose in disgust. "Why an ant hill?"

Hawk smiled. "Because there are only a few ways you can clean a buffalo head. You can bury it, but it would have to be a really deep hole. You can boil the meat off of it, but I don't have a pot big enough. So that leaves the ants and the maggots, the crows and the buzzards to do the job thoroughly."

"Maggots?" Eva looked as if she was about to get sick.

Meggie grinned.

"Oh, yes," said Hawk. "I really could use your help, Eva. It was thoughtful of you to ask."

"I better get ready for school," the child said, pushing away her half-eaten breakfast and avoiding her cousin's smiling eyes.

After dropping Eva off, Meggie drove over to Katja's house.

"I thought you ought to know that Adam Arbre was found last night in Illinois," she told her friend.

"Oh my gosh." Katja's eyes grew wide. "Was June . . .?"

Meggie held up her hand. "I don't think so. The police would have called you as well if they'd any new information. I suspect that right now, they're interrogating Adam and trying to find out if June was with him."

"If he can reappear, then maybe . . ." Hope surfaced but then had nowhere to go.

"Anything is possible, Katja," Meggie said, putting more reassurance in her voice than she truly felt.

*   *   *   *

Toward evening, Larry called from Illinois.

Meggie answered the phone.

"How's Adam?" she asked.

"When we talk to him, all we get back are glassy stares. It's obvious that he recognizes us but he's not there. Meggie, you're a psychologist. What does it mean?"

Meggie prodded. "Tell me more. What do the police know? What do the hospital doctors say?"

Lucy butted into the conversation. "Somebody cut off the first joint of the left little finger. Who would be perverse enough to do that?"

Larry added, "His hand is going to be okay but it's missing the tip of that finger."

"Tell her what else the doctors found," Lucy interrupted, disgust and anger in her voice.

"He's got tearing around the asshole," Larry continued, his voice tightening into a suppressed rage. "The police said that it looks like somebody sodomized our son. When I get my hands on that pervert, he'll wish he had never been born."

Meggie's heart sank. *Oh Adam. You're only nine years old.*

"Why isn't my son talking?" Larry persisted. "Why doesn't Adam tell us what happened and who did it to him?" Impatience surged in his voice.

"I don't know," Meggie began. "Maybe the pedophile threatened to kill him if he talks. Maybe he's ashamed about what happened. Maybe he's simply in shock. It will be absolutely crucial that he see a therapist when you return home with him."

"A mind shrinker?" Larry scoffed at the suggestion. "What he needs most is to tell us who did it and watch his father beat the holy shit out of him."

"No!" Meggie's tone was sharp. "What the boy needs most is time and understanding and to learn how to forgive himself."

"Forgive himself? What kind of psychological mumbo-jumbo is that?" Larry's voice sharpened with exasperation.

"I don't understand," interjected Lucy.

Larry barked into the receiver, "Somebody hurt my son. Somebody is going to pay. But the boy has no reason to forgive himself for whatever happened."

Meggie took a deep breath, knowing how overwrought the two parents were. They had hoped and expected to find their son scared but whole. She said, "You know and I know that Adam does not have to feel ashamed about what happened. But you have to realize Adam does not know it."

TWENTY-THREE

I Spoke

Something terrible happened, because . . .
I spoke.
I can't remember anymore.

I promise
I will never speak again.

TWENTY-FOUR

THE WOUND OF SILENCE

*The conflict between the will to deny horrible events
and the will to proclaim them aloud is the central
dialectic of psychological trauma.*

—JUDITH LEWIS HERMAN
Trauma and Recovery

Eva stayed at Chrysalis a whole week.

The Illinois state police kept hoping that Adam would tell them something, anything. But the boy just stared at his interrogators with unfocused eyes while drinking one cup of water after another. They asked him about June and got no answers. They showed him photographs of known pedophiles and he looked away. Adam scratched and picked at his skin until he raised bloody sores.

"The boy needs help," a trooper told Lucy.

"He's in a state of psychological shock," pronounced the hospital psychiatrist.

"He just needs to get home, back to his dog and friends, where he can feel safe. Isn't that right, son?" Larry's question bore into Adam.

The boy looked down at the floor.

"It's like he's somewhere else," Lucy whispered to no one in particular.

They arrived back in Peshawbestown in the middle of the night, wanting to avoid the media, the crowd of friends, the curiosity seekers.

"Meggie, please come over," Lucy begged the next morning.

"Of course I will." She could hear the desperation in Lucy's voice.

Hawk drove with Meggie to his cousin's place. Out by the vegetable garden, Adam sat listlessly on a stump, Shunka at his feet. Hawk turned to Meggie. "I'm going to go talk with him. You coming?"

Meggie shook her head. "Something tells me Adam can only deal with one person at a time. Lucy's probably up at the house."

Hawk moved slowly, purposefully snapping twigs underfoot to give the boy warning of his approach.

The boy jerked around, his eyes wide with fear.

"Just me, Nephew," Hawk spoke softly. He came up to the boy and lowered himself, eye level, into a sitting position. Shunka took that as an immediate invitation to jump up and slather Hawk's face with a raspy canine tongue until Hawk gently eased him down.

"It sure is good to see you," Hawk said, looking off toward the woods in the direction of Adam's gaze. "I know it's been a hard time."

And that was all that was said, acknowledgment neither given nor demanded, man and boy sitting side by side, staring at no particular point, simply occupying the same space of nearness, one to the other.

Lucy peered out the window. "It's going to be a long hot summer. What am I going to do with Adam? I can't send him to school in this condition. Larry refuses to let me take him to the mental health clinic. He tells me to leave the boy alone, that he'll come around in time. That the sweat lodge will put him right."

"That's wishful thinking," Meggie commented.

Lucy nodded and nervously rummaged in the kitchen cabinet for her pack of cigarettes.

Meggie continued, "Adam's been through hell, you and I both know that. And unless he can talk about it, he's going to stay in hell. Larry's denial won't change that fact one bit."

Lucy's hand shook as she lit a cigarette, then inhaled deeply. "I'd be going against my husband's wishes if I took him to a psychiatrist."

Meggie reiterated, "The boy needs to start talking about what happened."

Lucy walked to the screen door and looked toward the garden, sprouting with weeds. "I'll give Larry one week. If Adam hasn't pulled out of this silence, then I promise you I'll take him wherever you suggest. One week's waiting can't hurt."

One week is an eternity, thought Meggie.

"Someone stole the boy's spirit," Hawk said to Meggie, "and left behind the body."

Meggie didn't really know what Hawk meant by that statement. How can anyone steal a soul? It was obvious that the boy was suffering from Acute Post-Traumatic Stress Disorder.

While Hawk talked to Lucy, Meggie strolled out to the garden.

Adam was leaning back against the garden fence, hugging his knees and staring into the dirt. He didn't look up when she came into view but only squeezed himself smaller into the dirt.

"Hi Adam," Meggie squatted down beside him. She didn't touch him or look directly at him.

The soil to the front of his right shoe began to shift slightly and, from the subterranean depths, a worm poked up, easing itself out of the loose dirt to the surface. Adam's eyes tracked its movements. His head shifted to catch more of the worm's journey, studying the muscular rippling of elongation, then contraction.

Adam's right hand reached back, fishing into his pocket. He pulled out a small jackknife and opened the blade. A little spittle formed at the side of his mouth but he paid it no mind. Adam leaned forward from his perch against the fence, bending toward the traveling worm with his knife. In calculated, slow motion, Adam sliced the worm in half. His face took on a terrible intensity as he watched the two halves convulse in separate directions.

Meggie knew she should say something to the boy about his bottled-up rage but it wouldn't help until he was ready to share his feelings. She chose the lesser road, the interpretation that would do no harm and might stir up a desire to talk.

"You saw that worm. He was all alone," she said. "Then you cut him in half. Perhaps you thought the worm needed a friend."

Adam's only response was to click shut the knife, return it to his pocket, wrap his arms around his knees, drop his head onto his chest, and close his eyes. Meggie knew that he was telling her to get the hell away from him.

Later that morning, Meggie dropped over at Katja's place to see how her friend was faring. There had been no new developments in the June Tubbs' case except for the dwindling hope of false leads and dead ends.

Katja insisted, "I've got to talk to Adam Arbre. He may know something about June."

Meggie answered, "Lucy's not letting anyone badger the boy. He's in too fragile a state and he's simply not telling anyone anything."

"Meggie, if it were your daughter who was missing, you wouldn't take no for an answer. I'm going over there today. The boy must tell me about my daughter, whether she was with him or not. I don't give a damn that the police couldn't get him to talk or that you or that his parents couldn't either. What's important is that he tells me about June. Don't you understand?" Katja's voice rose in agitation, her jaw jutted forth in determination, and there was fire in her eyes.

"I will get him to talk," she vowed.

Lucy declined to let Katja into the house. "He's asleep in his bedroom."

"Then wake him up," Katja demanded.

But Lucy refused. She had to protect her son.

Something snapped. Sweet, gentle Katja, lover of children, pacifist in her beliefs, threw her body against the screen door and Lucy's obstructive presence. "Adam, Adam," Katja screamed. "Tell me where my daughter is."

Lucy pushed her backward onto the porch.

"Adam, wake up!" Katja yelled, balling up her fists, backpedaling from Lucy's forceful hands.

"Leave. Now. Before I call the cops," Lucy threatened, her face fierce and angry.

Katja tried to run around her but Lucy grabbed her by the elbows and with one heave, flung Katja to the ground. "Don't mess with me," she swore, hovering over the fallen woman. There was not a single doubt in Lucy's mind that if Katja tried to pull that stunt again, she would deck the white woman.

Katja stayed on the ground but burst into tears. "My daughter," she cried out piteously.

"My son," Lucy answered, glowering.

And up in his dark bedroom, Adam lay on the bed staring at the blank wall, willing himself, surging himself into the unfeeling wall and the welcoming blankness, only to be spat back, kicked back into the quivering, shivering flesh of the human body.

TWENTY-FIVE

ECHOES

For echo is the soul of the voice exciting itself in hollow places.

—MICHAEL ONDAATJE
The English Patient

The first full day home, Adam slept and drank a copious amount of water. At night, he kept the bedside lamp lit. When his mother woke him up the next morning, she could smell the acrid drift of ammonia on the sheets. She checked the bed; the sheets were wet. She didn't say anything to him but put on fresh sheets and threw the others into the laundry. It puzzled her. Adam hadn't wet the bed since he was three years old.

The second day, Lucy discovered the family Bible was missing from the living room bookcase. She looked everywhere for it. It was only when she opened the large barrel on the porch to deposit kitchen trash that she found a heap of torn and mutilated, scriptural pages. She questioned Adam about whether he had taken the Bible. He ignored her and looked away.

The boy ate dinner with them but seemed disinterested in his food. *My son has become a robot*, Lucy thought. Larry continued to reassure her that all the boy needed was time, the knowledge that he was safe, and immersion in traditional healing ceremonies when he was ready. So, over and over, Lucy spoke the word *safe*, as if by magical incantation, she could envelop her son in the protective bubble of a word.

"You are safe here with us," she said.

But it's a lie, she thought. *He was kidnaped from this place.*

The third day, the police returned to question her son. He said nothing. He hadn't uttered a word since he had been found. The cops asked him to write down information; they grew hopeful when he picked up a pen. But he sat there as if paralyzed, the pen loose in his fingers, the paper untouched, the vision unfocused. The police left, shaking their heads, saying to Lucy, "Be sure to call us the first time he speaks."

And, strangest of all, Lucy noted that Shunka began to avoid Adam's company. Every time her son came into a room, Shunka would scratch a door to be let outside.

The fourth day, Eva ran to her mother sporting a red splotch on her cheek. "He hit me," she cried. "I hate him." She claimed that she had done nothing to provoke her brother. She had simply entered his room without asking. Surprised, he had turned around and socked her with his fist. Lucy heard herself trot out feeble explanations about why Adam was acting so strangely when Eva blurted out, "And he pushed me against the wall and he . . .he touched me. Yuck!"

"Touched you? What are you saying, Eva? Touched you how?" Alarm bells began jangling in Lucy's mind.

"You know," Eva pouted, tears forming at the edges of her eyes.

"No, I don't know. What did he do?" Lucy couldn't keep her voice from sounding harsh and urgent.

"He touched my titties and then down there." Eva stretched out the elastic band of her shorts and pointed. "I hate him. I wish he'd never come back."

Lucy squatted and folded her arms around her daughter. "Your brother was hurt by a very bad person, and I guess he's trying to show us what happened. But that doesn't give him the right to touch you that way or to hit you. I think it better that you stay away from him right now. Can you do that?"

Eva nodded and wiped away her tears with the back of her hand. No way was she going to let her brother get near her again, not if she could prevent it. Besides, her mother would keep an eagle eye on him now that her brother had turned mean as a snake.

Lucy was more bothered by this last action from Adam than she wanted to admit. Even Larry was shook up by it. He barged into his son's room that evening and said, "I better never catch you groping your sister again or I'll beat your hide bloody."

On the fifth day, the tool shed caught fire and burned to the ground. Gasolene cans near Larry's power equipment exploded, fueling the combustion. The fire department roared into Lucy's place but it was too late. Noting the pattern of the burn, the fire inspector pronounced that it looked "of suspicious origin." Lucy remembered that Adam seemed excited when all the fire equipment had arrived, a small grin affixed to his face, his hands clapping, his gaze intent.

On the sixth day, Lucy heard the dog screaming. She ran outside and found Shunka attached to a chain. A kerchief was tied around his nose as a muzzle and there were two long brass tacks inserted into his front paws, now spotted with blood. Adam was nowhere to be found. Lucy yanked out the tacks and hauled the dog to the Suttons Bay Veterinary Clinic.

Sam Walters asked, "What happened? It's not like the dog stepped onto nails. These entry wounds are from the top."

Lucy shook her head, confounded. "Could it have been an accident?" She momentarily dismissed the make-shift muzzle she had found on Shunka.

Sam shook his head, dabbing the wounds with an antiseptic ointment and bandaging the two paws. He would have to report it to the Sheriff's Department as a clear-cut case of animal abuse. "Do you know who did this?" Sam asked.

"No, I don't," proclaimed Lucy.

But I have my suspicions, she thought.

On the seventh day, a foul odor drifted from the upstairs bathroom. Lucy entered. At first she saw nothing out of the ordinary. The stench, however, was putrid, overwhelming. Lucy pulled back the shower curtain. Up on the white, tiled wall, written in excrement, were the letters *N A T A S*.

The fecal smell, the utter recognition of her son's madness, the fear that had been building in her heart for days, exploded. "Adam, Adam, where are you?" Lucy cried out.

But the only answer that returned was the foul odor and a word, scrawled upon the bathroom wall:

NATAS

TWENTY-SIX

SPARKS

Love's primal moments are his best,
While yet a new and modest guest;
The first fleeting touch of finger tips,
The first soft pressure of the lips.

Too oft, amidst his full possession,
Begins a rapid retrogression.

—FRANCIS BROOKS
Margins

"So, what happened after the resurrection?" Bev asked, curled up at one end of her couch. Karl had hooked her interest.

Karl sat at the other end, pleased that she was asking the question. "After the trial and crucifixion, the disciples went home, back to their jobs as fishermen, to take care of their families. Before ascending to Heaven, Jesus appeared to them several times to remind them to continue preaching His message to the world. The action shifted to the synagogues in Jerusalem where His story was told and retold. Then Paul appeared on the scene and spread the story of Jesus to the Gentiles. From then on, Christianity began to blossom."

"I want to ask a strange question, Karl." Bev wasn't quite sure how to phrase it without appearing hostile. From the side table, she plucked a small, colored bottle, uncapped it, and began applying toenail polish.

"Go ahead." Karl leaned back, lacing his fingers behind his head.

"You tell me that Jesus had a new message for the world, one of love and compassion, different from the Old Testament message of 'an eye for an eye, a tooth for a tooth.'" Bev took another bottle and dabbed a different color on her big toenail.

"That's right."

"Well, why does Christianity then have such a bloody history? I mean, think about all the wars, the Crusades, the Inquisition, the attempts to exterminate the Indians in this country because they were considered 'heathens.'"

Karl waited, knowing that Bev had more to say.

"How can you trust a religion that preaches compassion yet tells people that homosexuals are sinners and not to be tolerated? Especially when research suggests that true homosexuals are born that way and don't have much choice in the matter?"

Karl played the devil's advocate. "Because, in the Bible, it says that homosexuality is a sin."

"It also says that God created the world in seven days. Come on, Karl!" Impatient skepticism underscored her words.

Shifting to the middle cushion, Karl answered, "I could tell you that those who practiced fundamentalist Christianity are not *true* Christians, that they follow the letter rather than the spirit of the Law. But the fundamentalists argue that they are the only *real* Christians because they take the Bible at face value. Who is *real*? Who isn't *real*? Who makes the definitions?"

Karl inched closer to Bev. "There's a difference between the message and the messengers. There's a difference between the freedom of the human spirit and the conformations of a religion. One is the divine spark, the other an oily motor. Politics, preachers in search of status, theologians in love with their own voices, the edifice complex, slavery to budgets, and the intrusions of the Zeitgeist—all these things clog us up, keep us from soaring, distort our visions, and deafen us to the Jesus story. It's the power of that single story, not the institution of the church, that has touched the hearts and minds of so many people and made them want to live better lives."

He stopped in his slow, snail-like progress across the couch. "And the worst thing," Karl added, "the very worst thing in human nature that drives intolerance and creates divisions across race, gender, culture, and religions is a simple thing."

"What?" Bev interrupted.

"The fear of difference," he answered. Karl stopped, waiting for Bev to make the next move.

"It's not easy for either one of us, is it?" she reflected. "I sit in one corner, thinking there's no way I could ever subscribe to a religion or philosophy that claims to be the one and only way to live. I don't even know if God exists, Karl. And you sit in your corner, trying to live out a faith that goes haywire from time to time, massacring people and killing unbelievers. It wasn't so long ago that in the name of Christianity the Klu Klux Klan lynched black people. Now we have the Aryan nation preaching the same kind of garbage. I can't trust any religion, Karl."

He moved close enough to pick up her free hand, cold to the touch, and warmed it to his cheek. "Do you believe in love?"

He kissed her fingers.

Bev nodded, not sure where Karl was going to take the argument.

He simply said, "With a single spark, then everything becomes possible."

* * * *

"I told her she could live with us, Sam." Jillian shuffled the papers on his desk and approximated orderly piles. She flung open the window in his office and fanned the smoky air. Seated, Sam rolled back his desk chair to get out of her way.

"I knew you would." He puffed his pipe and blew smoke in her direction when she wasn't looking.

"Didn't bother Dave any. Now that kind of concerned me. Wouldn't you think a man would want to have his wife to himself after years of raising children? But, no, he said that he would love to have Daisy come live with us next year." Jillian shook her head and properly aligned Sam's framed animal pictures on the wall.

"Dave's a good man," Sam commented.

"Sometimes goodness is not what a menopausal woman needs from a man." Jillian lifted up Sam's rug, yanked it out from under his feet, and gave it a couple of solid flaps into the air. Dust motes rose and drifted in the shafts of sunlight before settling on Sam's black and freshly laundered trousers. He brushed them aside.

"It's going to take some adjustment, Sam, having a teenager living with us," Jillian continued, replacing the rug on the floor and evening it out with the toe of her shoe.

"No running around naked in the kitchen for sure." His eyes twinkled.

Jillian cut him a frosty look.

He quickly added, "I haven't the slightest doubt that you will take Daisy in hand and set her straight on the path of life." *With military precision*, he thought.

Appearing somewhat mollified, Jillian nodded affirmatively, "Well, you're right. I do have a lot to teach that young woman."

"I'm positively sure of it." Sam cheerfully exhaled as Jillian exited his office. Once she was gone, he rolled his chair onto the circular rug, rumpled it at the corner, and then, for good measure, puffed his briar pipe in all directions.

* * * *

Bev wandered into her colleague's office as Meggie was writing her session notes. "You had a call from Lucy Arbre on the answering machine. It sounded pretty urgent."

Meggie peeked out into the waiting room. Her next client, a procrastinator, hadn't yet shown. Meggie decided to risk making a quick call.

Luckily, Lucy was at home. Her voice was frantic with worry.

"Meggie, I need your help. It's not working out with Adam. I can't go to work when he's at home. I'm afraid he'll burn down the house. I can't leave him alone with his sister. He's already attempted to molest her. I'm also sure that he was the one to abuse the dog. He still hasn't uttered a word, so I don't know what's going on inside of him. I am at my wit's end. I love him, but he's . . ."

"A danger to self or others?" Meggie interrupted. Lucy was a nurse and knew the dreaded words of institutional commitment.

"Oh God, Meggie. He can't stay here. And I don't want to send him over to the Medicine Lodge. I work there. I don't want all my colleagues on the reservation knowing the family troubles. Do you understand? Can you see him?" Lucy pleaded.

"Lucy, I'm family. It wouldn't be appropriate for me to diagnose or treat Adam, but I'll make some calls. I want him seen by a psychiatrist who has understanding of trauma. The physician will probably recommend both medication and hospitalization if what you say is true."

Meggie could hear the outside door open. Her next client would just have to wait. "What about Larry?" Meggie asked.

"I'll deal with him later. He's at work. If you can get me an appointment to see someone right away, I'd be grateful."

Meggie hung up, searched through her Rolodex, and dialed Dr. Shawn Volarik. He agreed to see the boy and his mother immediately if they could drive to Traverse City. "But I warn you," he said, "there are no good facilities in the area for children. If he needs hospitalization, we'll have to send him downstate to Grand Rapids or to St. John's."

"That's a good four hours away, Shawn," Meggie protested.

"Hey, since the state politicians closed the children's unit here in Traverse City, that's all we've got to offer."

With a sigh, Meggie hung up the phone and called Lucy. She knew that Shawn would have no choice but to report the sexual molestation of Eva by her brother and that Social Services would now descend upon the Arbre family for an investigation. The boy needed help, that was for sure. Meggie wished she could be more confident in the ability of the mental health system to reach out to a hurting, traumatized child.

Other thoughts plagued her mind as she headed to greet her next client:

First, Adam was kidnaped.

Then he was raped.

Now he'll be medicated and placed downstate.

He'll think he's being kidnaped all over again.

TWENTY-SEVEN

TWO CANOES

Voyager upon life's sea,
To yourself be true,
And whate'er your lot may be,
Paddle your own canoe.

—ANONYMOUS

Larry was furious.

He had left work at the casino as soon as possible. By the time he'd arrived home, Lucy had already driven their son to the psychiatric appointment in Traverse City. She called him from Dr. Volarik's office.

"It's out of our hands now." Over the telephone, her voice sagged with resignation.

"He's our son, Lucy. Why didn't you wait for me? Why didn't you, at least, take him to the Medicine Lodge on the reservation? There are traditional healers there." A quarrelsome tone threaded his words.

Lucy sighed. "I work there, Larry. I know everyone at the Medicine Lodge. I don't want my friends, colleagues, and busybodies on the reservation knowing our business. It's a basic conflict of interest. It's better this way. Besides, Meggie highly recommended Dr. Volarik."

"What does Meggie O'Connor know? Did Hawk go along with this plan?" Larry's voice was souring into sarcasm and suspicion.

Lucy held herself in check. She knew that his anger was simply the way her husband masked his anxiety. But, over the past seven days, she had been suffering too.

"Dr. Volarik says it's too dangerous to keep Adam near Eva." Steady and calm, Lucy spoke into the receiver.

"You just need to watch him better," Larry interrupted.

Unfettered by that careless remark, her anger and fear bolted out of the gates, ready to trample anyone who stood in her way. Her words bucked and flashed at him: "Goddamnit, I have a job too, Larry. This is not about maternal negligence. Whether you want to believe it or not, our son is going crazy, falling apart at the seams. He molested his sister, he burnt down the tool shed, he jammed tacks into Shunka's paws, he's peed in the bed every night, and if you haven't happened to notice, he hasn't said a damn word to either one of us since he's been home. So don't give me all this crap about my not being a good mother. All your denial isn't doing shit to help our son. Stop this blaming and grow up, Larry. It's not helping either one of us or your son."

The phone shouted into his ears. He knew better than to continue questioning her judgement. Better wait until later.

"Pack his bags," Lucy ordered. "He's going to a children's facility in St. John's area. We're to take him there tonight."

"But that's way down by Lansing," Larry began to protest then thought better of it.

"It's the nearest place without a waiting list. Our son needs professional help, Larry."

In a tentative manner, Larry floated another idea. "What about a temporary foster home in this area, one without other kids?"

"Maybe later. Right now Dr. Volarik says that Adam's going to hurt someone else or himself. Adam needs to be in a hospital." The anger and defensiveness in her voice began to subside, submerging to just below the surface.

Lucy needed to jab her husband awake to reality. "Look, I agree with Dr. Volarik about Adam requiring medication and hospitalization. You also need to know that Social Services has been informed of the molestation. They plan to monitor the situation."

Larry said nothing. In the ensuing silence, Lucy could hear him smouldering over the telephone.

He feels he's lost control over his family, she reckoned.

* * * *

Hawk was confused. He slumped down onto a kitchen chair.

While making supper, Meggie recounted all that had happened. After his session with Dr. Volarik, Adam Arbre had been transported by his parents to the St. John's children's facility.

"Larry agreed to this?" Hawk's voice registered dismay.

Meggie was surprised by his reaction. She put down the spatula she had been using to turn over the pork chops. "What choice did he have? The boy is severely regressing."

"Meggie, the boy's soul has been stolen. What do you think all the mental health professionals are going to do about that? They don't even believe in such things." Hawk's hands twisted in the air, a gesture of incredulity, his eyebrows furrowing into lines of consternation.

Meggie confessed, "That's the same thing you said the other day and I didn't understand it then either. What do you mean when you say the boy's soul was stolen? How can one take something so deep and wrench it from its moorings? Hawk, the boy has been traumatized. He was kidnaped. He was sodomized. He's flooded by feelings inside that he doesn't know what to do with and so he sits on those feelings and they drive him crazy inside. It's called Post Traumatic Stress Disorder. It's bad enough. Don't make something else of it."

Hawk sat there listening. He rubbed his temple with the fingers of both hands. He lowered his hands, letting them drop to the table.

"I know what I'm talking about, Meggie. The boy's eyes were dead. Somebody put a spell on him. You're being naive."

Meggie grew hot. The grease from the pork chops began to spatter in the pan and the meat curled black at the edges. She turned away for a second to lower the stove's heat, then back again toward him. She hadn't spent years of psychological training in her work with children and adolescents to be told that she was an ignoramus. Her eyes bored into him. "As long as you put all your energies into looking for the spell-caster, the boy will never do the work that he needs to do to finally come home. I don't give any credence to spells, Hawk. That's all hocus-pocus to me."

"Do you believe in the Spirits?" He picked up a ribbed glass salt shaker and peered into the angles of reflection.

"Yes, I do." She'd had too many paranormal experiences over the past year and a half to discount Their reality.

"Do you believe in the Evil Spirits?"

"Yes," she answered, "but I don't know much about Them." Winona had taught her that there were Good Spirits, Trickster Spirits, and Evil Spirits aplenty in the universe.

"Do you believe in the Chanunpa Wakan and the power of the Pipe to change your life?" he pushed. He tipped the shaker slightly; the salt shifted then cascaded into new directions.

"Of course I do. The Chanunpa has already changed my life." Meggie thrust her hands down upon her hips in a stance of strength. She didn't know where Hawk was taking this argument.

"Then what is so hard to understand about someone being able to summon those Evil Spirits and work a spell on another person's soul?" He brought her to the brink.

But Meggie backed away. It was not a world in which she wanted to dwell. She chose her words thoughtfully:

"For Evil to enter into people, they have to say *yes* to it. You can't simply cast a spell on someone, steal his or her soul, and infect him or her with Evil without that person agreeing to the process." Meggie was a firm believer in the Faustian bargain.

Hawk looked at her, this woman he had come to love and cherish over the past two years. Gently, he placed the salt shaker down on the table. "Meggie, you're a fine psychologist, a good person. But you know nothing about the world of Evil Spirits, about what one human being can do to another in the name of power or greed or jealousy. And that may be partly why I love you so much."

Meggie cocked her head, puzzled by his last statement and the paradox of being simultaneously told she was both cherished and stupid.

He continued, "You still have faith in the innate goodness of people. That's why you are so strong a therapist. You radiate both a hope and an optimism about the world that I don't share. What happened to Adam's body was terrible. But what has happened to his soul is far worse."

Meggie wanted to counter Hawk's arguments, tell him that he was being a fool, but too many other opposing thoughts kept bombarding her:

There is no word for soul in psychiatry.

There is no word for evil.
Neither, therefore, exist except in the realm of the imagination.
Meggie sighed.

"What are you thinking?" Hawk asked.

She shook her head as if to discredit her own conclusions. "We're caught betwixt and between, Hawk. Winona would say our feet are firmly placed in our own two canoes heading downstream. You live in a world of supernatural occurrences and I live in a world of psychological constructs. Somewhere, in between, the truth about reality lies. I do know some things, Hawk."

He looked up at her, curious about what she was going to say and wondering if she were still smarting from his blunt comment.

She chose her words carefully. "The imagination can both inflict hurt and invoke healing, whether it be psychological or supernatural. You and I often journey in different canoes, but there's common ground in the imagination, in its capacity to go beyond what seems logical or traditional. Perhaps Adam will find his way home by meeting us in the middle of the river."

"I apologize, Meggie," Hawk said. He rose from his chair to help her with the dinner preparations.

"What for?" She looked at the burnt chops and sighed.

"It was wrong to call you naive. Sometimes we straddle each other's world. Sometimes we paddle along different currents. Sometimes you lead and I follow. Sometimes I'm the one in front. Yet we want the same thing. And unless we honor our own traditions and teachings, the journey will only take us into stagnant waters. But make no mistake about one thing, Meggie."

"What's that?" she asked.

Hawk's mouth compressed into a somber expression. "Our efforts to help Adam find his way back home will not be a journey downstream. It's going to be upstream the whole way. And taking the boy to a hospital was a turn in the wrong direction."

TWENTY-EIGHT

CONVICTION

They said it would happen.
Inside, the badness is eating on me.
Please, please don't leave me alone.

Soon, I'll be all gone.

TWENTY-NINE

STORM TOSSED

Still as they run they look behind,
They hear a voice in every wind,
And snatch a fearful joy.

—THOMAS GRAY
Ode on a Distinct Prospect of Eton College

May arrived, not with a garland of flowers in her mossy hair, but with a dark and foreboding sky. The morning's steady gray-blue ceiling roiled into a fickle slate green by late afternoon. The waves of Lake Michigan frothed white against the sandy beaches, heralding a spring storm. The tree tops began to dance as fingers of wind first tickled, then grabbed and chastened the tender branches. Lightning flashed across the Manitou and Fox islands to the west and shuddered groundward to the sound of ripping skies and kettle drums. *Boom, Boom!* The Leelanau Peninsula shook and vibrated as if the Thunder Beings were carrying out a celestial war of canon fire. *Boom, Boom!* The rain began to fall hard, shooting bullets of hail at any creature who dared to venture out into the storm.

Daisy looked out the door of the veterinary clinic as the wind battered and howled around the building. "Ain't nobody coming to the clinic, if they be in their right mind."

Jillian had turned off all the computers to save them from being fried by any burst of lightning. Without looking at Daisy, she said, "You used a double negative so they canceled each other out."

"Huh?"

Jillian stopped and turned toward the girl. "You said that 'nobody ain't coming' and, because 'ain't' contradicts 'nobody,' that means somebody is coming."

"No way. Not in this storm," Daisy persisted.

Jillian shrugged her shoulders at the futility of trying to teach a teenager the elements of grammar.

But Daisy got to thinking. "Whaddya mean when you say two negatives cancel each other out?"

Jillian once again looked up from the task of sorting her desk. "In language, two negatives produce a positive. 'Ain't nobody coming' means somebody is about to arrive."

"What about in families?"

Now it was Jillian's turn to be confused. "What do you mean, Daisy?"

"My parents." Daisy didn't need to say any more about negatives: One alcoholic and abusive parent and the other who ran away. Daisy's mother didn't even have the decency to leave behind an address where she could be reached. And as for the father, Clyde Bassett, he couldn't have cared less that his daughter had chosen to live with Jillian. No more mouths to feed.

Daisy looked expectantly at her.

Jillian nodded. *Some questions are more important than others*, she thought. She answered, "Two negatives can, indeed, produce a positive. I think it's going to be a good year for both of us, Daisy."

* * * *

Paul packed his bags. "I'm going to Illinois. This waiting and not knowing is driving me crazy."

"But we want you here. Your son needs a father," Katja protested.

Paul stuffed his hiking boots into a separate bag. No telling where he might have to go. "A man's got to do what a man's got to do. Our daughter may still be around the same area where that boy Adam was found. Sometimes, Katja, you act as if you've given up hope."

"It's been over three and a half weeks. The police . . ."

"I don't care what the police say," Paul shouted. "She's not their daughter. She's our baby and while I still have breath in me, I'm her father and I will find her. I will *not* give up, do you hear?" His face set into grim lines of determination.

Then he made the cruelest cut of all. "And if you are worried about the money, the firm has agreed to continue paying my salary during the time I'm away."

"Oh Paul." Her heart sunk as she felt the last shred of respect between them tear loose from its mooring. "That's not it and you know it." Katja shook her head. How could she share what she knew to be true, the thoughts and feelings that frequently surged through her now:

June is dead.

Where once my heart was filled with the knowledge of her curiosity, the constant barrage of questions—why, Mommy, why?—her delight in all things new, the sound of high-pitched shrieks and giggles, the sharp angles of hyperactive legs and arms, the soft graze of her fingers upon my cheeks, the tangy sweetness of her breath, the steady rise and fall of her chest as she slept, and now . . .

Now there is simply a hole, widening ever deeper into the cavity of my heart. And my heart, perversely, keeps on pumping.

Why, Junie, why?

THIRTY

DIFFERENT POINTS OF VIEW

I am the daughter of Earth and Water,
And the nursling of the Sky;
I pass through the pores, of the ocean and shores;
I change, but I cannot die—
For after the rain, when with never a stain
The pavillion of Heaven is bare,
And the winds and sunbeams with their convex gleams,
Build up the blue dome of Air—
I silently laugh at my own cenotaph,
And out of the caverns of rain,
Like a child from the womb, like a ghost from the tomb,
I arise, and unbuild it again.

—PERCY BYSSHE SHELLEY
The Cloud

Alternating warm afternoon blushes of spring with recurrent night chills of winter, May breezed across the cherry orchards, sprinkling white bridal blossoms over the newly greened landscape before finally banking into the dependable heat of summer. Locals scurried about to open up the lake cabins, turn on the water, clean out dead mice and cobwebs, install docks, mow lawns, and stock the grocery shelves with exotic fare. A stream of tourists trickled into the Leelanau Peninsula to bask on the sandy beaches, tour the wine country, sample the native wares, fish for perch, bass, and trout, swim the smaller lakes, squander money at the casino, and toast the spectacular sunsets with fizzy gin and tonics.

Smiling and sweet, the June sun meandered down the crowded sidewalks of Traverse City, dappling shoppers with irregular patches of light and sparkling across the rolling surface of Lake Michigan. Slowly, the wintry lake stretched its watery, cold limbs and eased into summer's warmth. Sailboats, motor craft, and jet skis skimmed across its elastic skin; hardy children dove beneath the chilly wind-topped waves.

On summer break, Daisy worked full-time at the animal clinic. During the evenings, she waitressed at Hattie's, the posh Suttons Bay restaurant where the food was gourmet, the cost extravagant, and the tips outrageous. "I'm going to buy a car with my summer money," she boasted.

Meanwhile, Paul Tubbs continued to return home every weekend from his search in Illinois. The accounting firm put pressure on him to resume work but he delayed and said that he would be back on board after Independence Day. There had been no trace of June except for a pair of generic brand sneakers that could have been hers. Still, he refused to give up. Worried, Katja found a part-time job at a roadside stand, selling farm produce, setting aside a little emergency money in case Paul chose not to honor his commitments.

During the times he reappeared, Paul seemed preoccupied and distant. Katja was too weighted down by grief to really notice or care. She moved through her days like a robot, cooking, driving Robert to environmental day camp in Omena, going to her job, returning home, and trying desperately to sleep at night. In her restless dreams, June would call out to her but Katya could never find or reach her little girl in time.

Meggie worried about her friend, even suggesting that she might take some anti-depressant medication. But Katja refused. Mid-western stoicism was bred into her bones; depression had always been its side-kick. She began to lose weight. To eat meant to affirm life.

When Robert spent overnights with friends, Meggie made sure to invite Katja to the movies or for dinner. When they talked to each other, Katja would frequently lose the trail of the conversation and wander off into spaces where Meggie couldn't follow. "I'm sorry, what were we just talking about? I must be getting old to be so forgetful."

Meggie knew that it wasn't age but grief that gripped her friend, like a buzzard plucking the marrow from her bones and feasting on the vital parts. Mourning clawed and clutched at Katja's heart, refusing to budge or release her. To let go of the grief meant to let go of June; it was as simple as that. So it was easier, better this way, to keep June alive in her memory even though it required Katja to live in the past, in the heavy drag of time pulling her backwards, with sorrow as its yoke.

It wasn't sadness but fear that ricocheted inside of Lucy Arbre. On her days off from work, she regularly drove the four hours to the St. John's children's facility to visit Adam. Clearly, her son wasn't getting any better. The ward staff reported an increasing number of violent outbursts and required time-outs in the padded isolation room. The escalating response by the resident psychiatrist was to increase the dosage of sedating medication until Adam could hardly keep his eyes open. Not a word had crossed his lips.

"We haven't found the right psychotropic drugs yet," the staff advised Lucy. The somnolent quality to her son's movements disturbed her even more than the reports of his sporadic violence.

"How can he get better if he sleeps all the time?" she asked. Nobody at the mental hospital could give her a satisfactory answer.

The insurance company pressured the facility to move Adam out of the intensive unit to a less restricted, less expensive setting. "They'll only pay for short term hospitalizations," the social worker apologized.

The psychiatrist duly complained, then upped the medication and transferred Adam to a cottage on the grounds. In the more permissive setting, Adam discovered a trove of sharp blades—a razor, a pen, a sewing needle. Systematically he began to carve deep, crisscross hatches on his arms, his legs, and his belly, tattooing his body with his own blood.

"It's like a goddamn winter count," Larry whispered to his wife.

To Hawk, Larry spoke forcefully. "This can't continue. My son's dying right before my eyes. Surely there is something we can do?"

Hawk understood. "I'll go up on the hill and ask the Spirits again for Their help."

Meggie was surprised. "A vision quest? Is this going to be a four-day, four-night hanbleciya, when the Spirits let you know what They want you to do with the rest of your life?"

Hawk shook his head. "This is different, Meggie. I'm going up on that hill with my Chanunpa, crying for a vision about Adam, not about me. I'm going to ask the Spirits to tell me how to heal the boy. This isn't the time for me to contemplate taking a medicine altar. I'll stay up there until They give me an answer."

Hawk made preparations. He gathered together the blankets, the eagle feathers, the cloth. Larry, Meggie, Lucy, and Hawk fashioned four hundred tobacco ties to secure the boundaries of his vision quest altar. Four days, he prayed with his Chanunpa, readying himself on the inside. Four nights, he purified himself in the inipi ceremony.

At last he was ready.

Larry added more wood to the fire for the two-round sweat with Hawk. Meggie had worked all morning, constructing the vision quest altar with Hawk, cooking with Lucy, serving a lunch of kidney soup, fried buffalo heart, slices of raw kidney and heart, and then keeping the door for the inipi ceremony.

It was just the four of them working to put Hawk on his vision quest. Hawk didn't want the needs of the larger sweat lodge community to distract him. After the inipi ceremony, Hawk led the way up the hill, holding out his Chanunpa and eagle-wing fan before him, singing the prayer songs that pulled the old medicine knowledge back into being. Behind him trooped Meggie, Hawk's medicine bundle cradled in her arms. Behind her walked Larry, carrying blankets, sweet grass braids, sage sprigs, and eagle feathers. Lucy brought up the rear of the procession, a quart jar of cool water firmly held in her hands.

Atop the knoll, they helped him get settled, gave him his last drink of water from the quart jar, wished him well, then started to peel off, heading back down the hill. A bluish white fog had begun to seep through the woods, rolling in from the west. Meggie was the last one to leave. As Hawk stood outside his altar he kissed her, reluctant to let her go. He resisted watching Meggie slip away into the mist for fear that image would pull him off the hill.

Hawk could barely make out the spreading fingers of the cedar trees. Eager to start the conversation with the Spirits, Hawk was also scared that They would ask more of him than he could bear.

Meggie knew better than to turn around and glance back at him lest she pull him off the hill and what he had to do there. When the three of them reached the bottom and Hawk was safely out of sight, they looked up, surprised to discover that the hill had disappeared into a cloud bank.

Meggie and Larry threw themselves into preparations for the women's inipi ceremony, piling up cold rocks on hot coals and new wood. Meggie would spend the night in the sweat lodge, praying to give Hawk strength during his hanbleciya.

Hawk had already begun to teach Meggie how to pour the waters for the sweat lodge ceremony. He knew that the Spirits would take pity on her clumsiness for the solo sweat.

But then Lucy asked if she could join Meggie.

She doesn't practice the old ways, Meggie thought. But she kept her reaction to herself. Although uncomfortable and unprepared to pour the waters with anyone else in the lodge, Meggie knew she couldn't refuse. *What if I do something wrong? What if Lucy gets hurt in the ceremony? Hawk's not here to tell me what to do.*

"I've never been inside the sweat lodge before, but I'll do anything if it will help my son," Lucy pushed.

"Of course," answered Meggie. *I will ask the Grandfathers to protect Lucy from my ignorance*, she vowed.

*   *   *   *

A white, diffuse light glowed over the altar area, demarcated by the four hundred tobacco ties. After arranging his blankets and medicine bundle, Hawk began the round of prayers to each pole, each Grandfather. The old ways of moving his feet through the grass, the dance of prayer, the quietness which entered and curled up inside of him, the excited flapping of the flags on his poles that signaled a breeze, the steady hum of grasshoppers around him, the sharp crackling of brush as unseen deer edged closer, curious about his presence on the hill—all these sights and sounds and smells brought him sharply back to other vision quests. It was almost like he had never been away.

Tendrils of fog draped themselves over the fir trees. To Hawk, the woods looked like an audience of ghostly white giants with peaked caps, bending over in respectful silence to hear what the pitiful two-legged had to say. He had done his previous vision quests in the hot sun, the cold rain, and the dark doubts of nighttime, but never had he done a hanbleciya in the blinding obliterations of fog.

Hawk held out his Chanunpa and began singing the old Lakota prayer songs. His voice reverberated throughout the damp woods. He sang until the notes cracked in the back of his throat, until he knew that the Spirits had heard him summoning Them to the hill.

He prayed for Adam, then for Lucy, Larry, and Eva. He prayed for June Tubbs and her family. He asked the Grandfathers to watch over his woman while she poured the waters for her first solo inipi ceremony. He prayed for everyone in the community, for his people and all Native Americans, for the nations of whites, blacks, and Asians. He beseeched the Grandfathers to have pity. "We know so little. We are but two-leggeds. We forget what it means to be human beings."

He gave thanks for his teachers, for Three Legs who came to him from the Spirit World, for Davis and Winona Pathfinder who had served as his first guides before completing their earthwalk, and for Laughing Bear on Pine Ridge Reservation, South Dakota. "Grandfathers, I ask you to surround that man with a fierce and sweet love. He does a lot for the people and they don't take good care of him. I pray that you help his new woman learn to guard him well and keep him strong and grounded in what he does."

Hawk prayed until his mind went blank and then he sat down with the Chanunpa in his hands to let the silence surround and enter into him. He knew he would spend the first hours dissociating himself from the clutter of work and worries, slowly letting himself unfold, peeling away the crusty layers of identity that, while protecting the soul from over-exposure, keep it from being nourished by the Sacred.

Above him the sun sailed high, distant and invisible above the impenetrable blanket of clouds. Below him, the ants tunneled and the worms churned the soil. Around him, the fog drifted, thickening and thinning, shifting the images. Before him stood a patch of tall purple flowers, the blossoms shaped like bells in descending order. They too faded into the vast whiteness.

The raucous cry of the pileated woodpecker scratched across his eardrums. He turned, Pipe in hand, but could not make out the giant bird. He knew the woodpecker hovered nearby; the harsh drilling of its beak against a dead tree resounded like machine gun fire.

Time passed and the fog backed off from the altar area. Trees and plants emerged into his sight. Hawk's left eye started to water. When he closed it, the view was limited, ordinary. Yet when he opened his left eye the images jumbled into confusion.

Hawk experimented. He shut his right eye and peered outside the altar area. A greenish blue light, several inches thick, outlined each tree, each branch, as if ethereal blue flames were flaring off the new foliage. Left eye closed, right eye open; his vision once again cleared to normal.

Left eye open, right eye closed; a different world again revealed itself, one with auras and vibrating bands of energy. When he tried to keep both eyes opened at the same time it was a miserable competition of viewpoints that offered neither the clarity of vision nor the insight into a different way of seeing. Hawk pulled the bandanna down over his forehead and slanted it over his right eye.

Pay attention, he told himself, *the Spirits are trying to teach you something.*

THIRTY-ONE

PRAYERS

An old, old man lived alone in the middle of the forest. One day, he left his cabin to gather wood in a terrible blizzard. His knees gave out and he collapsed. He was too weak to rise to his feet. "Oh God," he cried out. "I am so old. Come take me Home."

A young man suddenly appeared and announced, "God has heard your prayer, and I have come to take you Home."

"Oh," said the old man. "I am very grateful, but now my prayer has changed. Could you help me carry the wood back to the cabin?"

—ANONYMOUS

A hole opened up in the clouds; the blue iris of sky and the yellow pupil of sun peered down at the man. "Grandfather," Hawk shouted and held aloft his Pipe.

Sunbeams pierced the remaining clouds and shredded the lace curtain of lingering fog. To the west dense cedar woods, to the north stalwart rectangles of cherry orchards, to the south broken patches of vineyards, to the east the rolling blue-black of Lake Michigan. Small white specks of sailboats scratched lines across its glassy surface, traces soon rippling away in the slight breeze.

A bee zoomed by Hawk's nose, seemingly indifferent to his presence. Sporting striped feathers, a downy woodpecker fluttered onto a branch in front of him but paid him no mind. The rustle of whispering leaves alerted Hawk to movement. He turned to look. Springing from the bushes, swinging his tail from side to side, galumphed Shunka. It was the first time Adam's dog had ever visited Hawk on a vision quest.

He trotted over the tobacco ties, slurped on Hawk's bare leg a second, then flopped down near the altar, panting. It looked as if he were settling down for a long wait.

He loves Adam too, thought Hawk. The man had learned not to challenge the wisdom of the Spirits and whom They sent to him.

Between long stretches of prayer, Hawk sat in his altar area and waited. The grasshoppers thrummed and scratched the air with a steady *eeeee*. In late afternoon, the June sun blew hot and humid. Sweat trickled down his bare chest. Eyes closed, Shunka stretched out beyond the pipe rack and snuffled in his sleep. Hawk's mind wandered to the political troubles on Pine Ridge, the fights over who are the *real* Native Americans, whether non-Indians should be allowed in ceremony, and family wars that stretched across generations. *My Lakota people are always tearing each other apart*, Hawk thought.

A mosquito jerked him back to attention. *Zee, zee* the insect sang, then bit his ear for good measure. *Pay attention*, it was telling him. *Stay focused on what is important.*

Chanting the sacred songs, Hawk rose and danced to the poles before another long round of prayers. His sentences repeated and tumbled over themselves. Under the sun's glare, he watched the words melt as soon as he gave them utterance. He gave up praying the man prayer. With each breath, each inspiration, a cleansing hollowness tracked down his spine from head to toes through his stomach and heart until he stood there, Pipe in hand, utterly quiet, open. Woman prayer.

Ka-thump, ka-thump. A heartbeat pulsed in his left hand, the hand that cradled the bowl of his Chanunpa. He could not tell if it was his heartbeat or that of the Pipe. No matter. He was becoming one with his Chanunpa.

"Wopila," he cried out to the Grandfathers. "Thank you for my life. Thank you for the Pipe."

A red-tailed hawk swooped overhead, dropped a feather near the center of his altar, then settled onto a branch and studied the man a few moments before wheeling off toward the west. In rapid succession, a raucous crow besieged by harassing sparrows flew over his western boundary of tobacco ties, a cardinal winged over the northern boundary, a goldfinch alighted on the eastern pole, and a flock of squawking gulls flapped southward toward Suttons Bay.

"Help me, Tunkasila," Hawk said. "Adam is lost, Grandfather. Without his soul, without his center. How can he survive, Grandfather, if there is no fire within him? The boy exists in an empty prison. Tell me what to do."

Hawk reached down and picked up the feather of the red-tailed hawk with his right hand and stroked the stem of his Pipe with it.

From the West, a Voice resonated deep and gruff. "Bring the boy home."

Hawk looked up but could see no one.

"Grandfather?" he asked. He held out his Pipe. "If you are a Good Spirit from Wakan Tanka, please come and smoke the Pipe with me."

"Bring the boy home."

Hawk had never heard this voice before.

"Bring the boy home? You mean to Lucy's place?" he asked. No one answered. Hawk knew he hadn't yet understood the command.

"To Pine Ridge?" Adam had kinfolk on his mother's side there.
But still no response.

Hawk swallowed hard, knowing that for every question asked of the Spirits, a person had to take responsibility for the answer given. You don't go up on the hill, call the Spirits, ask for guidance, and then say, "No thanks, that just doesn't fit into my plans."

His heart sinking, he questioned the Spirits one more time: "To Chrysalis?"

"Bring the boy home," the Voice ordered.

*　*　*　*

Adam, Adam, wherefore art thou? The biblical phrase buzzed around Meggie's head in the silence of the sweat lodge. The stones glowed red and hot but Meggie had not yet anointed them with *mni*, water. "Look at their faces," she suggested to Lucy, who was sitting by the closed door. "This is the lodge of *Inyan*, the Stone Nation."

Checking to make sure that the water bucket was where she had last placed it, Meggie's eyes began to adjust to the darkness. In the reflecting light of the stones, she could barely see Lucy's feet and one hand. Solicitous, she asked, "Are you ready?"

"Yes," came the quick reply.

"If it gets too hot, lay down on the Grandmother," Meggie cautioned. "She will cool you off. If you think you can't stand it a moment longer, call out 'Mitakuye oyas'in' and Larry will open the door. Okay?"

Lucy grunted assent. Meggie knew that Lucy was probably scared and that only the fierce love for her son dragged her into a ceremony for which she had previously held private scorn.

"This first round I will sing a Spirit-Calling Song, then pray. Take time to let yourself center and grow quiet inside. Keep your eyes open and watchful," Meggie said.

Meggie launched into a prayer song, her voice strong. *I'm at home in the inipi*, she thought, forgetting that Winona had once spoken the very same words to her. The smoky aromas of sage, sweet grass, and cedar commingled in the lodge and settled Meggie's initial anxiety. *The Spirits will take care of both of us.*

Lucy coughed, unaccustomed to the initial smokiness.

Meggie dipped the ladle into the cool water and poured a judicious amount to the stones. They hissed and crackled, sputtered and blinked, driving the first wave of steam up to the ceiling and down upon the women's backs. To each direction, Meggie applied the dipper of water. "Tunkasila, Wakan Tanka, Grandfathers in All the Directions, Wakan Tanka—Sky Beings, Unci Maka—Grandmother on whom we sit, Wanbli Gleska, the spotted eagle who takes our prayers to the Grandfathers—I ask that you look upon us pitiful two-leggeds as we come once again before you, looking for help, trying to get back into balance with this Creation. We give thanks for the trees that gave their lives so that we could do this thing, for the lightnings that fueled the fire, for Inyan who come into this lodge time and time again, singing to us, helping us. Without the water of life, we could not live. Without the steam, we could not do this ceremony."

The heat rose and shimmered hot and stinging, forcing what was toxic in the body to rise to the surface and squeeze out the pores. Lucy began to cough in earnest.

"Lie down," Meggie commanded. "Grandfather, we ask you to look at that man on the hill. Help him, Grandfather. He wants to know how he can bring healing to Adam Arbre. See that boy there, in the children's facility. He won't talk. He can't talk. He is hurting inside. Grandfather, none of us knows what to do. See his mother in the lodge here with me. Have pity on her."

Meggie poured more water on the stones. "This is for the ancestors, the Lakota elders who kept the ceremonies alive even when they were persecuted by the whites and the missionaries. Without them, we could not know what they knew seven generations back."

When Meggie knew the heat had grown too intense for Lucy, she yelled out, "Mitakuye oyas'in."

Larry flung up the door and the steam billowed out into the night air.

"Phew." Lucy looked cooked. She pushed herself up into a sitting position.

Meggie gave her a dipper of water to drink, then a second dipper to Larry. She peered out the lodge door and could see that the fog had not lifted.

"It never let up, did it? He's doing the whole hanbleciya in the clouds."

Larry grunted and handed her back the empty dipper. "Could be that he sees just fine up there."

"You okay?" Meggie checked on Lucy.

She grimly nodded.

"This next round I want you to pray as long as you need to, Lucy."

Lucy blinked but kept quiet.

Larry lowered the door blankets and once more the two women were encased in darkness. Meggie waited while Lucy got her bearings.

"Grandfathers," Meggie began, "We come in here, into the lodge of our Grandmother. We come naked and pitiful, human beings. We give thanks for our sister and brother nations. For the feathered ones who fly before the sun. For the fins who sweep the ocean floors and swim the arteries of the Grandmother. For the crawling things who most abundantly inherit this earth. For the four-leggeds who offer their life so that we may live. For those who watch us from afar. For those nearby who try to teach us about love and for those who are simply curious about the behavior of the two-leggeds. For the plant nations and the tree nations who feed us and shelter us. For the two-leggeds of all races who are trying to figure out what it means to be a human being. For all these nations, we give thanks. We ask you to see that man up on the hill, praying to you, needing your help. Grandfathers, Grandmother, I ask you now to listen to the prayers of my friend and sister, Lucy. Her little boy is in very deep trouble. Tell her what she needs to know and do not ask more of her than she can bear. Mitakuye oyas'in."

Meggie poured water on the stones; waves of heat assaulted their faces and rolled over them.

Lucy's voice was tentative, apologetic in tone. "Wakan Tanka, I don't know how to pray. I haven't done it since I was a little girl. And it's crazy, because I don't really believe in You. Or at least I didn't think I did. But my son. My son, Grandfather, needs help. Oh God, he needs help. . . ." Lucy's voice cascaded into sobbing cries.

Small pinpoint lights danced in the throbbing darkness. *Spirit lights,* Winona had called them. *"That's the way the Spirits show that they are pleased with what is happening."* Meggie applied more water to the stones.

"My son was kidnaped," Lucy resumed praying, "and when he returned he had become someone else. He wouldn't say anything. He hurt his dog whom he loved more than himself. He touched his sister and threatened to hurt her. He set the shed on fire and smeared his own feces all over the bathroom wall. Grandfather, I want my boy back. What has returned to us is more like a monster, a demon child with my son's name. And I don't believe in devils anymore than I believe in You."

Lucy broke again into tears.

Meggie poured more water on the stones, so that the steam could cleanse and give Lucy strength.

"My cousin up there on the hill . . ." Lucy caught her breath. "He's gone up on the hill to pray. Show him the path of healing for my son. Help him bring my son back to himself so that Adam can stand up whole and proud. So that he can tell us what happened to him when he was kidnaped. Help us become a family once again."

"Tell her to pray about what is eating her heart," a Voice hissed into Meggie's left ear. It sounded suspiciously like Winona.

No, I won't, resolved Meggie. *These have to be my own thoughts. I'll not burden Lucy with them.*

"Tell her." The Voice grew louder, insistent.

Lucy kept praying, obviously deaf to the interruptions.

No, Meggie replied silently. *I can't do that. What right do I have to do that?*

"Tell her she is forgetting something." The Voice pushed at Meggie.

No. Meggie started to repeat herself, then changed. *Show me a sign. Then I can know it's You and not my own foolishness.*

Lucy stopped praying. No "Mitakuye oyas'in" to indicate that she was finished with her prayers.

Meggie waited for Lucy to continue but there was only silence, punctuated by the sound of their breathing and the sizzling of water on the rocks.

"Tell her now," the Voice ordered.

This time, Meggie did not resist. "Spirits want you to pray for what is eating at your heart."

"Aaiii," Lucy wailed from deep down to the bone, her cry splitting across the darkness, the sound of utter despair and loathsome shame. "Aaiii," Lucy shrieked, as if the wound had pierced the flesh and all was pain.

"What kind of mother am I?" she howled.

"Ask for Their help," Meggie urged.

"How can I do that?" Lucy cried, "Adam, oh Adam, I love you."

Meggie put more water to the stones. The heat relentlessly rose, washing over them like a tidal wave, smothering them and sending both women crashing to the ground.

"Adam, Adam," his mother yelled. "Where have you gone? What kind of monster has taken your place? You hurt your sister, your baby sister. You drove nails into Shunka's paws. Shunka, who has always loved you, watched over you. You don't talk to us. You don't seem to care about us anymore. You don't care about yourself. Where have you gone? You scare me, Adam. What are we to do with you? How can I love you so much, Adam, and then hate whom you've become?"

Oh my God, that's it, thought Meggie, struggling to regain her breath in the oppressive heat. *Love and hate are tearing her apart.*

"Grandfathers," Lucy begged in between wrenching sobs, "Bring back my son to me, the way he used to be. Bring back the old Adam and send whatever lives in him now far far away. Mitakuye oyas'in."

Oh, Lucy, thought Meggie, *don't you know that your son will never be the same again?*

The door came up. Anxiously, Larry peered in. "Honey, are you all right?"

Lucy covered her face with her hands and didn't answer.

Meggie was at a loss for words before the tormented woman and a husband who wanted everything returned to normal. No matter what happened in the near future, Adam couldn't go home.

Larry placed fresh hot rocks in the lodge for the third round. Meggie asked Lucy if she had any more questions.

"No," she answered. The shame of her confession squelched any more entreaties.

She is afraid of what the Spirits might tell her, guessed Meggie.

The door came down and the two women were once more plunged into the silent darkness. Meggie prayed long and hard for Adam's healing, for Hawk's hanbleciya, for June's reappearance, for Katya, Paul, Robert, Eva, and Larry. "Have pity on this woman here whom I've grown to love as family," Meggie asked. "It is hard for her to come into the lodge tonight, when all her beliefs tell her that this is a foolish thing to do. She prays for her son. She loves him, but she hates what he has become. Help her cherish the parts of her son that she recognizes. Let her see the strength in him as he struggles on the journey toward wholeness. We will not keep the vision of his sickness close to us but rather see him as well and happy. Help us. Help that man who is standing up on the hill. Speak to him. Tell him what he needs to know. Tell us what we need to know. Mitakuye oyas'in."

Outside the lodge, Larry burst into a Pipe-filling song.

The Voice whispered again into Meggie's left ear. "Tell him what is home."

Winona? Meggie's mind inquired. *Is that you?*

No answer.

"Tell whom? Hawk? Adam?" Meggie asked aloud.

But no one answered.

THIRTY-TWO

COMING DOWN

Vision is the art of seeing things invisible.

—JONATHAN SWIFT
Thoughts on Various Subjects

IN the middle of the night, Hawk strode off the hill, carrying his pipe and medicine bundle. He headed down a path through the cedar woods to the sweat lodge, Shunka loping behind him. Leaning the Pipe against the buffalo altar, he hoisted the lodge door, knowing that he would find Meggie sealed inside. She had been praying all night long, adding her strength to Hawk's hanbleciya.

"You're back?" She was startled and confused, having anticipated that he might be up on the hill for several days and nights.

"It is finished," he croaked, his voice raspy from all the singing and praying. He picked up his Chanunpa.

As Hawk was still a sacred Being, Meggie knew not to talk to him any further or to touch him. She scrambled out of the lodge, placed her own Pipe on the buffalo altar, and tore off toward the house to awaken Larry and Lucy. She knocked on their bedroom door. "He's come down."

She could hear Larry jump out of bed. Retrieving her clothes, she changed from her towel dress into a tee shirt, jeans, and sneakers.

"I'll make some coffee." Yawning and hair all akimbo, Lucy scuffed out of the bedroom toward the kitchen.

Larry and Meggie hit the front door at about the same time, running toward the sweat lodge. Their immediate task was to construct the fire, heat the rocks, and not disturb the man in the lodge.

"Is he okay?" Larry whispered.

"I think so. All he said was: 'It is finished.'"

The two of them scrambled; it wasn't long before flames were licking up along the logs surrounding a mound of rocks. They perched on the large stumps around the fire pit. Lucy brought out two steaming mugs of coffee.

Night was still pitch black but the fog had finally cleared. Meggie estimated that it was about three a.m. From her vantage point, she could see Hawk in her peripheral vision. Her husband was seated, cross-legged, bent over, holding onto his Pipe, bowl toward his heart, stem toward the ceiling of the lodge. She guessed he was deep in prayer.

The coffee warmed her insides. Meggie hoped it had been a good time for Hawk on the hill, that he had learned what he needed to know. Relief flooded into her. She knew that anytime a person went up on the hill for hanbleciya, the Spirits might choose to take that person away forever. She had to be prepared for the possibility that he might never return. "Wopila, Grandfather," she whispered toward the west.

After drinking coffee and stoking the fire with more wood, Larry filled the water bucket and gathered together sweet grass, sage, tobacco, and the deer antlers for handling the stones in the lodge. Hawk handed out his Chanunpa which Larry gently positioned against the buffalo skull next to Adam's pipe.

From the house, Meggie retrieved fresh towels, a quart of water, and a small bowl of strawberries with which Hawk would break his fast when the inipi ceremony was finished.

Larry passed deer antlers to Hawk's hands. "Want me in the sweat, Bro'?"

Hawk shook his head no. He took the braid of sweet grass, the pouch of tobacco, the sprigs of sage and cedar, and arranged them in front of him.

After a couple of hours, the rocks glowed red and hot in the velvety darkness. Larry hefted them onto the pitchfork and, one by one, slid them into the lodge stone pit. Each time the pitchfork entered the lodge, Larry called out, "Mitakuye oyas'in."

With the deer antlers, Hawk maneuvered the stones into the pit until there were sixteen large stones piled up high in the center of the lodge.

Larry next handed in the bucket of water which Hawk touched to the stones and placed on a bed of sage. He threw out the antlers and sprinkled a path of tobacco from the door to the lodge pit, then around the hot and glowing stones. Hawk signaled to Larry to pull down the soft door of blankets and star quilt.

Once Larry had stomped in the door to make sure no crack of light would penetrate the lodge, he stepped back, away from the lodge. What Hawk had to say to the Spirits, what They had to tell him in return, might be meant for his ears only. Larry retreated to the stumps nearby where Meggie patiently waited.

They could hear Hawk break into a Spirit-calling song followed by the indistinct, mumbling sounds of his voice talking, telling what had happened up there on the hill. He was sharing his account, giving witness in words to what he had seen, what he had heard on the hanbleciya, so that the Spirits could know that he had paid attention. If Laughing Bear had been around, he would have conducted the vision quest and poured the waters for this inipi, but as it was, the Spirits were Hawk's only audience. It was a long round.

Meggie knew that in other times, in other circumstances, Hawk might have included Larry in this particular sweat lodge ceremony but as he was Adam's father, it only complicated matters. Hawk needed to hear what the Spirits had to say about the hanbleciya without the confusion of an anguished parent.

"Aaiii, aaiii," Hawk yelled from inside the lodge.

Larry looked at her, concern etched on his face.

Meggie didn't know whether Hawk was suffering from the heat or from recounting what had happened to him. *What had the Spirits told him about Adam?*

"Aaiii," he yelled, consternation in his voice. Then all was quiet in the lodge, until Hawk finally sang out, "Mitakuye oyas'in!"

Larry and Meggie hurried to the lodge and flung up the blankets. A blast of hot steam rolled in waves over their faces and out into the night's darkness.

"Mni," Hawk ordered. The bucket of water was totally empty. Meggie realized it must have been a blistering round. Sweat poured off his face, down his chest. He smiled at her to let her know he was alright but his eyes betrayed the smile; they gleamed dark and serious.

What happened up there on the hill? Meggie fretted.

Water slopped over the bucket as Larry handed it back into the lodge.

After resting a few minutes and catching his breath, Hawk gestured at Larry to lower the door.

The hanbleciya began with the first two rounds of the inipi ceremony and ended with the last two rounds. In the fourth round, Meggie knew that the Spirits would interpret the visions and respond to his questions about Adam.

Over by the coals of the fire Meggie, Larry, and Lucy sat, waiting, each one deep in his or her own ruminations. They could hear Hawk praying but not the words. Silence, then more words. Meggie knew it was not a monologue. Hawk was engaged in conversation with his Spirit helpers, probably Three Legs. They were telling him, instructing him, prodding him.

It was a long conversation and the three outside the lodge could only hear the inflections of Hawk's voice followed by silences and grunts and expressions of acknowledgment.

"Aaiii," he shouted several times as he applied more water to the stones.

Finally Meggie heard him sing the last song, the one he always sang when he asked the Spirits to go back where They came from, to come again when They were called.

It was finished. The hanbleciya was over.

"Mitakuye oyas'in," he shouted.

Meggie looked up as Larry rushed over to the lodge to fling up the blankets. The faint light of dawn was easing up over the horizon. The birds began to sing their welcoming songs for the new day.

THIRTY-THREE

THE WIDENING GULF

Love may be blind but marriage is a great eye-opener.

—IRISH SAYING

"Absolutely not, Hawk. It's a crazy idea." Meggie stood there, hands on her hips, astonishment written all over her face.

"But Meggie, that's what the Spirits told me to do. I'm to bring the boy home. I went up on the hill and asked Them about Adam. I can't turn around and say, 'Sorry, it doesn't fit my life right now. Too inconvenient.'" Hawk threw up his hands as if addressing the heavens.

Meggie rolled her eyes.

"Besides," he continued, "you yourself told me that there's no way the boy can return to live with his family."

"Yes, but . . ."

"Larry has already signed over to me the temporary guardianship of Adam." Hawk decided it was better to tell her now rather than later. He knew it wasn't going to be a popular decision.

"You did all this without consulting me?" Controlled anger rippled through her words.

Hawk blindly pushed ahead. "And I want to go retrieve the boy from the hospital and bring him to Chrysalis to heal."

"When?" She eyed him suspiciously.

"Today."

"Today? Wait a minute, Hawk. What in the hell do you think you're doing? The hospital is not about to discharge Adam. He isn't talking yet. He's violent and self-mutilating. They haven't even found the right medication for him." Meggie looked askance at him as if Hawk had gone suddenly mad on her or turned into a doddering old fool.

Two days had passed from the time of the vision quest. Hawk knew he was moving too fast for Meggie, much too fast, but the boy was dying inside. The Spirits had spoken. Larry was right. Something had to be done. And quick.

"Did Lucy agree to this?" Meggie's voice continued to be incredulous.

Unhappy about the discord, Hawk took a deep breath and plunged ahead. "Lucy respects you as a therapist. She thinks that maybe you're the one person who can break through the boy's silence and turn him around. She's signed the papers as well."

"But I'm family, Hawk. I can't treat Adam as a patient. It's unethical as well as impractical. No, there's just no way this is going to work out. He'll have to stay at the hospital until he gets better." Meggie was wildly shaking her head back and forth. She held out one hand as if to say *stop*.

"I wouldn't ask this of you if I didn't think we could do it." Hawk put his hand over his heart. "Besides, the Spirits said . . ."

"To bring him home," interjected Meggie. "But whose home? Why ours?" Meggie's eyes swept across the room.

"Why here?" she repeated, her voice deadly calm. "Adam jammed tacks into his dog's paws. What about Fritzie? What's going to happen to my old terrier? How can I protect him?"

A smile started to creep into Hawk's face. He tried hard to clamp down with his cheek muscles. It was not a wise time to express humor. Any man of wisdom knows that you don't make light of a woman's anger.

"Of all dogs, I think Fritzie can take care of himself," he answered. Fritzie possessed an outstanding set of long, fearsome canine teeth.

Meggie's voice rose a notch, indignation revving up her motor. "Shunka was defenseless. He was found chained with a make-shift muzzle around his jaws."

From the fierce concentration on her face, Hawk knew she had more to say on the matter.

"Adam set the shed on fire. His mother's afraid to take him back because next time he might light a fire in some corner of their house and burn them up alive. What's to stop him from doing that here? This is the house my grandmother built, Hawk. I love this place. I don't want it burned to the ground. Why be stupid enough to take the risk?" Her head shook a definitive no.

Hawk waited, certain that Meggie would come around one way or another. The plan made perfect sense. The hospital was doing the boy no good. Being at Chrysalis put the boy under his direction, his healing rituals, and it didn't hurt that Meggie was a psychologist who knew how to treat disturbed children. The more he thought about it, the more convinced he became of the Spirits' wisdom.

"Come with me," he said. An invitation.

"Where?" Meggie was wary, arms crossed, eyes narrowed.

He could feel the air between them shiver with unspoken misunderstandings. He was asking her to make major changes in her life without having talked it through in advance.

"To the hospital." *Help me*, Hawk silently whispered. A prayer directed toward the Spirits. A wish aimed towards his wife.

"What are you planning to do?" Meggie scrutinized Hawk's face, trying to read his intentions. *Are you going to bring Adam to Chrysalis despite my protests*? hung there between them. Both understood that new marriages can crack under the weight of such questions.

"To see the boy, to talk with him. Come with me." He extended a hand to her but she did not take it. He pulled his hand back. "That's all I ask. Make up your own mind, Meggie. After you see him, if you decide that there's no way he can come live with us, then I'll . . ." Hawk didn't have the slightest idea what he would do if Meggie refused the boy.

"I'll figure out something else," he promised. *Help me*, his eyes begged.

Meggie budged a little. "Okay, we'll go see him together. But it would be crazy to bring him here. For many reasons, Hawk. Don't expect me to change my mind. He's better off at the hospital."

* * * *

Tell him what is home. The intrusive thought kept nagging at her as Hawk drove toward St. John.

It made her uneasy that Hawk was not the only one with instructions from the Spirits. *But he's more comfortable with it. How can I be sure that it wasn't simply my own unconscious speaking?* Meggie had great respect for the unconscious.

At the fluid edges of Lake Michigan, the land had buckled and contorted into unusual shapes but as the car headed southeast and inland, the landscape flattened out into orderly fields. *Home for Adam is where he can be safely supervised*, she reassured herself.

But Meggie also recognized that she often rationalized paranormal occurrences which didn't make sense to her twenty-first century sensibilities. She liked to fit everything into a logical pattern.

Pay attention was what Winona had taught her.

Meanwhile, Hawk fiddled with the radio dial searching for a country music station, something to soothe and relax the stiff atmosphere between them. The Interlochen station was playing Copland's *Appalachian Spring*.

Immediately, the familiar notes and the echoes of old hymns surfed waves of nostalgia through Meggie's heart. When Meggie was young, her mother had bought a radio, placed it by her daughter's bed, and tuned into a classical station. Every night, her mother would come into her bedroom, read a story from a book of mythology, kiss Meggie goodnight, switch on the radio, and turn off the light. Every night, the preadolescent Meggie would fall asleep on the soaring wings of violins, the deep vibratos of cellos, the definitive pronouncement of trumpets, the lilting speculation of flutes, the sad invitation of clarinets, and the somberness of soft percussion. Certain symphonies became like old friends to her, speaking a secret language of joy and sorrow. She thought of Copland like a lovely old uncle who, time and time again, came to visit her and share his love for the mountains and countryside.

Hawk moved to switch the stations but Meggie lightly touched his hand and indicated that he should turn up the volume. She wanted the notes to fill up the car and transport her back in time. She marveled at how her parents had made her feel safe at home while always stimulating her mind to outer exploration. How they encouraged independence yet nurtured in her a sense of belonging.

Pay attention, the notes sang to her.

Tell him what is home.

*   *   *   *

The car pulled up into the visitors parking lot. Meggie's heart sank at the sight of the institutionalized setting. The brick walls of the hospital spoke of society's need to protect themselves from children who were out of control. Off to the right were situated several cottages. "I guess he's in one of them," ventured Hawk.

They walked up to the entrance to register. At the front desk, a white-haired woman sat reading the Lansing newspaper. She stood up as they approached. "May I help you?"

"We're here to see Adam Arbre. His parents gave permission. He's in a cottage on the grounds." In his hand, Hawk clutched the guardianship papers. Just in case they were needed.

"Your names?"

Meggie answered. "Dr. Meggie O'Connor and Slade Spelman." She knew she had to use Hawk's Anglo name in case proof of identity were required. She thought it wouldn't hurt to establish from the very start that she was a health-care professional.

The woman didn't ask any more questions. Her eyes scrolled down the list of patient names. "He's back in the main hospital, third floor, ward C-3."

"Do you know why?" Hawk asked.

She shook her head. "I'll buzz you in. Take the first staircase to the left. Third floor. I'll tell them you're coming." She pushed a button on the wall. Meggie opened the unlocked door.

They headed up the stairs, their footsteps loud and hollow in the echoing staircase. At the third floor, they stopped and peered through a heavy glass window set into a metal door. They could see adolescent boys aimlessly roaming the hallway, shadow-boxing at each other, gabbing, or watching television in a side room. One chubby boy sat in a chair opposite the nursing station rocking back and forth, his eyes unfocused, his arms dangling by his side. A male aide ambled down the hallway to let Meggie and Hawk in the ward.

The heavy door clanged shut behind them. The competing sounds of the boys' conversations and the television blared at them. "You'll need to sign in at the nurses' station," the aide said before heading off in the opposite direction, a set of keys jangling from his belt.

The boys in the hallway eyed the visitors. "Got a smoke, Cochise?" one asked Hawk.

He shook his head.

Another gave a wolf whistle at Meggie.

She smiled self-consciously.

Inside the nurses' station, beyond the open dutch door, two people were filling out charts. One of them, a middle-aged woman, looked up at Meggie and Hawk. "Yes?"

"We're here to see Adam Arbre. Family," Hawk explained.

"Gavin, show them to the visitors room. Then wake up Adam and tell him there are folks here to see him," the head nurse ordered.

Hawk followed behind Gavin but Meggie stayed at the nurses' station and introduced herself. "I'm Dr. Meggie O'Connor, a psychologist up in the Traverse City area. How is the boy doing?"

The nurse looked up from her notes. "You want the truth or do you want to hear what the doctors will tell you?"

Meggie smiled. She understood that this tough-talking nurse probably knew a lot more about Adam's daily functioning than did his doctor. "Why don't you give me the party line first and then tell me what's really happening."

"Adam is suffering from PTSD—Post Traumatic Stress Disorder. None of us disagree with that diagnosis. But what we can't understand is why a kid with such a good premorbid history would deteriorate so fast. Dr. Wright suggests that the boy had a genetic predisposition for Bipolar Disorder and that, under the stress of the kidnaping and sexual abuse, the psychosis popped out."

"Bipolar Disorder?" Meggie was confused. "What genetic predisposition?"

The nurse shook her head and thumbed through Adam's file. "Something here about an alcoholic grandmother who committed suicide last year."

"Maternal or paternal grandmother?"

"Maternal grandmother," the nurse read from the sheet.

Meggie shook her head. *Winona's death a suicide? Hardly.* But Meggie knew that modern medicine had no other way of describing the conscious act of crossing over. There was no place in the medical history of Adam Arbre for the action of the Spirits.

"It wasn't a suicide," Meggie commented. "And the maternal grandmother had been sober many years before she had died."

The nurse looked at her, a curious expression on her face. "Do you want me to add that to the record?"

"I certainly do." It was the least Meggie could do in respect for her former mentor.

The nurse noted the correction.

"Now, would you be so kind as to tell me how you, not Dr. Wright, sees the situation with Adam?" Meggie asked.

The two of them looked into each other eyes, an understanding passing between them that this conversation was collegial, off-the-record, and not to be repeated.

"The psychiatrists keep switching medications and upping the dose, and all the kid does is sleep and pick at his sores. Every day that goes by without this kid being able to talk about what happened is a day lost. In my humble opinion, he's getting sicker. I'm afraid he's going to get used to being crazy. You know what I think?"

"I very much want to know," answered Meggie.

The nurse looked around to make sure that nobody else was listening in on their conversation. She spoke sotto voce. "That somehow being crazy, violent, and silent seems safer to him than the alternative."

"The alternative?"

"To kill himself." The nurse sat back, having said her piece.

Meggie nodded, thinking that the head nurse was a woman of uncommon insight.

Unspoken between them hung the simple question:

During Easter week, what had happened to Adam?

THIRTY-FOUR

WINDOWS OF THE SOUL

As all looks' yellow to the jaundic'd eye.

—ALEXANDER POPE
Essay on Criticism

Meggie joined Hawk on the white plastic chairs in the visitors room. The fresh paint on the yellow walls barely concealed a history of scrawled graffiti. "Fuck you!" in orange had been recently washed over but still asserted its paling message.

"Hey, I thought you were right behind me."

Meggie sat down. "I was doing a little schmoozing."

Hawk looked puzzled.

Meggie explained. "In every mental health facility, people make the mistake of thinking that the doctors know what is going on. In the hospitals, it's the nurses and the aides. In the outpatient clinics, it's often the secretaries. You just have to know who's the one with the most accurate, up-to-date information."

"So, what did you find out? Why did they switch him from the cottages to the locked ward?"

Meggie shook her head. She had her own hypothesis about that.

Adam was too great a challenge, too much of a risk for the cottage program.

"We need to get him out of this place," Hawk groused.

Meggie looked at him, thinking, *He doesn't yet understand what he is asking of himself or of me. The boy is severely disturbed. Hawk, Lucy, Larry all want Adam to come live with us. One big happy family. Sure. Whom are we kidding?*

Hawk must have noticed a grimace cross her face. He leaned over. "Hey hon, don't worry. It's going to be okay."

His pat reassurances didn't quell the roiling protest in her mind. *Ethically, I can't treat Adam in psychotherapy. He's family. Have they all forgotten that I'm a working woman? Who is going to supervise the boy during the day hours?*

Meggie didn't even like the fact that she was mulling over these questions. She knew that by so doing, she was opening the door. *It won't work. I'll just have to say no louder.*

Then Adam entered the room.

Meggie looked into his eyes. Despite what Hawk had said about the theft of the boy's soul, there was nothing dead about the child's eyes that bored into her.

While the rest of Adam's face remained frozen and he spoke not a word, the eyes that looked upon Meggie's face were wild eyes, tormented eyes, eyes that tried to hide and speak to her at one and the same time.

*   *   *   *

Hawk didn't press her as they drove homeward.

After Adam had entered the visitors' room, he'd slouched down in a chair opposite them. Hawk had spoken in a bravado voice. "Hey, Nephew, good to see you! How are you?"

But the boy hadn't answer him. Instead, he'd looked at Meggie.

Meggie had bent toward Adam. She'd reached out, touched the back of his hand, and softly said, "Adam, I don't want you to say anything to me. Not now. I just want you to know that Hawk and I are going to find a way to bring you back."

For a flicker of a moment, Meggie had thought she'd seen a blink of hope cross his eyes and then it was gone, disappeared. And in that moment, the word *home*, a word she had meant to say, vanished into her own doubts, her own confusion.

I need time to think. Time to plan. What am I doing? Questions had crowded into her mind and both she and the boy sat back in their respective chairs.

Hawk had filled up their wordlessness with descriptions of what Eva was doing, how Shunka was healing, brief details on Adam's friends, but it was all hollow talk and the silence had been deafening. Every once in a while, Hawk had interjected a question: "Have you made any friends here? Do you like any of the aides? How is the food?"

The answer was always the same. The boy had said nothing. He'd looked at the floor. He'd stared at his feet. He'd studied the orange "Fuck you!" crayoned on the yellow wall.

Much to their relief, Gavin had soon come to collect Adam for his daily group session.

Meggie had deposited her business card at the nurses' station and requested that Dr. Wright call her. She'd handed over a signed release from Adam's parents for the physician to communicate with her.

"I'll give him the message," the nurse had replied, her attention already back on the daily charts.

On the way home, Meggie stewed. *Absolutely a crazy idea. But there was that momentary flicker in Adam's eyes.* Meggie had great faith in tiny windows to a child's inner world.

As they passed Mount Pleasant, Meggie spoke. "I'll only agree to your plan under certain conditions."

Hawk was startled. From the silence, he'd assumed that persuading Meggie was a lost cause, that he was going to have to come up with another idea.

"What conditions?" He stared ahead at the road, trying not to smile.

"First condition is that another counselor will have to be responsible for intensive psychotherapy with Adam, somebody who is really knowledgeable about PTSD with children. That way I won't be seen as violating the ethics of my profession by treating him as a formal client."

"Okay, I think we can arrange that. But what if he doesn't talk to that therapist?" Hawk had great faith in Meggie's abilities but not in other therapists.

Meggie wanted to say *That's not my problem.* She knew it wasn't true. "They will have to work it out between them," she said. "Secondly, I'm going to ask Dr. Gertrude Gold to supervise both the therapist and myself so that we can coordinate what happens to Adam. I can't be undermining the therapist's treatment of the boy."

Hawk nodded. It was a sensible idea.

"Third, I can't be responsible for him," said Meggie.

Hawk stiffened, confused by that remark. "What do you mean?"

"I know you have great faith in me. But sometimes you look at me as if I'm the earth mother who can heal all manner of children. This boy needs supervision and I don't want you or Lucy or Larry to hold any expectations that I am about to quit my career and become a nanny. I will help him as much as I can but you or somebody else is going to have to take the responsibility of supervising him. Adam can't be left alone. At any time. Is that clear?" Meggie was putting it to him. Her voice was deadly serious.

"Well, I'll watch him," Hawk interjected.

"Don't be so quick or easy with an answer. Don't say you'll do it and then secretly expect that the woman is going to be the one to take over."

Hawk looked hurt, as if Meggie didn't trust him.

Already, the pain of Adam is working its way into our household, thought Meggie. *And it's only beginning.*

"It's not you, Hawk," Meggie explained. "It's men in general. Over and over, I've listened to fathers in my practice make facile promises with regard to their children. But when their own interests come to the fore, the children take a back seat. Again and again, they expect the woman to pick up the slack. I wish that weren't the case, but that's what happens too many times. So I want us to be perfectly clear with each other. Adam Arbre is not my responsibility."

Meggie closed her eyes. She knew it was a lie as soon as she uttered it. If she took the boy into her home, he would become like a son to her. But it was better this way. Better that Hawk take seriously his commitment to the youngster.

For the rest of the journey home, they traveled mostly in silence. Meggie's words had given them both a jolt.

"Meggie, you can't do it. I'm telling you, it's all wrong. Wrong for the boy. Wrong for you. If the Board of Psychology ever got the notion that you were trying to treat Adam Arbre in your own home, they could lift your license and ruin your career based on a conflict of dual relationships." Bev wasn't mincing any words.

"But . . ."

"But nothing. You don't fool me a moment with your requirement of another psychotherapist. If the people down at St. John's couldn't get through to the boy, what makes you think that another therapist can?" Bev stood in the living room shaking her head. She had come over as soon as Meggie had called and told her of the plan.

Karl sat off-center in an easy chair, watching the confrontation between the two friends, the two psychologists. He said nothing for a long time.

"I saw something in his eye. . . ." Meggie began.

"You saw the boy blink. Don't project your own wishes onto Adam Arbre. He has enough trouble as it is. Meggie, the kid is dangerous. To you, to this place, to himself. Don't put your career into jeopardy over something that is not going to work." Bev started to pace up and down the room. She kept pushing. "I can't believe you're acting so dumb. It's Hawk, isn't it? You love him and you want to please him?"

"No!" Meggie emphatically rejected that suggestion.

"Well then, what makes you throw away all the years of your professional training to consider this asinine idea?"

Tell him what home is. Meggie knew there was no way she could talk about the Spirits to Bev. It would be like speaking another language. Bev would deem her certifiably psychotic. Meggie began laughing.

"What's so funny?" Bev asked.

"I just got this image of you asking me if I heard voices," Meggie replied.

"Yeah?"

"Well, I guess I would have to truthfully answer 'Yes.'"

Bev looked confused.

Karl intervened. "I think what Meggie is trying to tell you, Bev, is that sometimes in one's profession there comes a moment of choice, when to be 'legally ethical' is to ignore what is important. There are rules meant to be followed most of the time, and then there are those extraordinary circumstances which require risk, something different."

Bev turned and glared at him. "Karl, with all due respect, you don't know much about transference, counter-transference, and the projections that occur within the process of psychotherapy. If you had understood these processes better, you wouldn't have almost ruined your own career with your sexual behavior."

At that very moment Hawk entered bearing a tray of coffee. The atmosphere in the room had honed razor sharp. Meggie's hand was up by her mouth, her eyes wide open. Bev had turned the full force of her gritty, piercing look upon Karl. A slight blush crept into Karl's face.

"More sugar?" Hawk handed a mug of coffee to Bev.

Karl's eyes softened. "I'll take mine black."

"I shouldn't have said that," Bev apologized.

Karl shook his head and sipped the coffee. "You'll never make a conventional minister's wife, that's for sure."

"Why?" Bev didn't understand. His remark had caught her off guard. *Was Karl hinting at marriage or what?*

"Because you always say exactly what you're thinking," Karl answered.

Bev cocked her head, obviously undecided whether his comment was a compliment, a criticism, or an implicit marriage proposal. She scrutinized her three friends, "Why do I get the feeling that you're all out in La La Land and that I'm the only one here with a lick of sense?"

Hawk answered, "To bring the boy here is the right thing to do."

"But how do you know it's the right thing to do?" Bev demanded an explanation.

"I went up on the hill. . . ."

Meggie interrupted him because Bev was not going to understand that argument either. "We've given the traditional treatment a chance and Adam is getting worse. If he doesn't talk soon, Bev, his only choice is to go completely crazy. There is a horrendous pressure building up inside of him. He vents it from time to time with his violent episodes but it's like a volcano, always building and boiling. Adam picks at his skin, seeking release. Unless he tells someone what happened, he can't transform the pain. It stays inside of him, a grenade loaded with shrapnel and nails. Underneath that grenade is another and another. And what

I fear is that he'll weaken, collapse into the silence. If that happens, eventually one of those grenades will kill him."

"But your career, Meggie. . . ." Bev's eyes shone with concern for her friend.

"To save a child? It's worth the risk," Meggie answered.

The following day, Dr. Gertrude Gold graciously agreed to see Meggie for immediate consultation. The older woman with her carrot-colored, wispy hair sat up straight in her wheelchair. "Let me understand your proposal. You want me to set up psychotherapy with one of my clinicians for this traumatized youngster. The boy will be living with you. And you are asking that I supervise both you and the psychotherapist in conjoint sessions?"

Meggie nodded. She had done as thorough a job as she knew how in presenting the case of Adam Arbre to Dr. Gold—the boy's premorbid history, the kidnaping, and the subsequent deterioration of behavior. She omitted any mention of instruction from the Spirits. "I will need help in avoiding dual relationship problems."

"Meaning that you doubt your ability to stop acting like a therapist when at home with the boy." Gertrude was quick and to the point. There would be no ambiguities with her.

Meggie nodded.

"What if he needs a mother instead of a second therapist?" Gertrude looked over her bifocals.

"He's got a mother already. Lucy Arbre lives nearby and will see her son almost daily." But as soon as she said it, Meggie knew it was a facile answer to an important question.

Gertrude let it pass. "What is your hypothesis about what happened to the boy?"

"Medical evidence shows tearing around the rectum. It would suggest that the boy had been sodomized not just once but several times. He may think that he is now homosexual or dirty or to blame somehow for the violation of his body. It could have been a serial pedophilic rapist or a group of people."

"So you think the boy is reacting to the sexual abuse?" Gertrude took off her glasses and began wiping them with the hem of her dress.

"Yes," Meggie first answered. "No," she amended. "Something else happened. I don't know what. But I've worked with a lot of children who have been abused sexually and they didn't show this level of disturbance. There was something else I forgot to mention."

"Yes?"

"The tip of Adam's little finger on his left hand was cut off." Meggie grimaced in disgust.

Gertrude's eyes narrowed in anger. "Sadists. What do you think is the meaning of this barbaric act?"

"I honestly don't know." Meggie shrugged her shoulders. "What kind of person would get gratification in mutilating a child?"

Gertrude started to answer, then folded her hands on her lap. Always the teacher, Dr. Gold wanted Meggie to form her own conclusions without prejudice. "Is there any other detail you have forgotten?"

Meggie nodded. "There was a Suttons Bay child, June Tubbs, who was kidnaped days before Adam. She hasn't been found yet. Maybe there is some connection there. Adam was sweet on her."

"Are you suggesting that they were abducted by the same person? Or that there was an organized group of pedophiles?"

Meggie shook her head. "I don't know. But the police don't think so. June was taken from a public place but they think Adam was at home. Right now, the law enforcement people are treating the children's disappearances as separate occurrences and Adam isn't saying a word."

Meggie lifted up her hands. "What is really bizarre is that I was one of the few people, outside of the school system, who knew both children, both families. For a while there, I thought the police might think I was a suspect."

Gertrude dismissed that idea with a singular wave of her hand. "Tell me about Adam. Tell me everything you know about his likes and dislikes, the family dynamics, his culture. If I can develop a sense of Adam, then perhaps I can help you, Dr. O'Connor." Her voice was reassuring, inviting.

"Well, I think I have to begin first by describing his maternal grandmother, Winona. Almost two years ago, she became a a client of mine. A reluctant client. Her daughter dragged her in to see me after Winona had announced that she was going to die in two moons. But there was nothing physically or emotionally wrong with her. . . ."

Gertrude Gold sat forward in an attentive fashion, aware that Dr. Meggie O'Connor was not simply launching into a description of Adam Arbre's family. The psychologist was also telling the story of her own journey.

* * * *

Upon her return to Chrysalis that night, Meggie called out to Fritzie but her old fox terrier didn't respond.

"Have you seen him?' she asked Hawk, giving him a quick peck on the cheek. He was standing over the stove, a large spoon in his hand, stirring and sampling the supper fare.

"He was in the living room an hour ago."

A luscious homemade split pea soup was bubbling on the back burner; fresh olive bread and a salad of mixed greens had already been placed on a tray. "Where do you want to eat?" he asked.

The kitchen table, the dining room, the living room in front of the television, the east porch near the bird feeders, and the south screened porch were all possibilities.

"I want to find Fritzie first," she obsessed. "Why didn't he come when I drove up the driveway?"

But Hawk had been too busy cooking supper to notice.

Meggie descended into the living room. "Fritzie?" she called out in a soft voice. Then she heard a low snuffling sound behind the couch. Dead asleep, the terrier only twitched his paws to the sound of her voice. His eyes remained close.

"Fritzie!" she yelled.

His boxy head jerked up. When he saw her, his body levitated. He jumped all over her in glee, licking her face, her legs, her arms.

"He's getting deaf," Meggie said later, watching her dog chase the chipmunks by the bird feeder. Hawk had set the table out on the east porch.

"He's getting old, Meggie. Do you like my soup?"

It really was delicious. Much to the surprise of both of them, Hawk's repayment of his medical debt had unleashed a culinary fanatic. He had discovered the joy of cooking and the adventure of new recipes.

"I don't want him to get old," Meggie said. It was terrible, but the image of her dog becoming increasingly infirm and eventually dying filled her with as much sadness as did the thought of her parents' advancing mortality. For a single moment, Meggie felt nostalgia pull her back toward the comforting past, away from the dread of the awakening future.

Adam would arrive tomorrow.

THIRTY-FIVE

THE SOUND OF SILENCE

. . . where I am, I don't know, I'll never know,
in the silence you don't know, you must go on, I
can't go on, I'll go on.

—SAMUEL BECKETT
The Unnameable

Tourists and cars clogged the streets of Suttons Bay in July. Sometimes a local could zip into town to buy some groceries and see nary a neighbor or friend. A yuppie crowd competed with the sunburned boat people for specialty coffee drinks and baked cherry goods.

"Sure is crowded these days" would be as close to a complaint as the locals would utter. The summer tourists were good for the economy, sustaining many a family during the winter season.

"You betcha," another would answer. "Had to go up the road some to find a parking spot."

The other talk of the town was of the rapid economic expansion of the Grand Traverse Band of Ottawa and Chippewa Indians. "Their casinos must be racking up a pile of money." Admiration and a trace of envy underscored the observations of the townspeople. Not too long ago, it had been advisable to downplay one's Indian heritage due to the animosity between the native fishermen with their gill nets and the sports fishing industry.

Every other day now, the Band seemed to be in the public news—purchasing real estate, diversifying their economic base, and giving generous, politically well-placed contributions back into the surrounding communities.

Lucy couldn't help comparing the astute financial planning of the Grand Traverse Band to the impoverished world of her Oglala Lakota people on Pine Ridge Reservation. The money from the Leelanau Sands Casino and the Turtle Creek Casino had enabled the Grand Traverse Band to set up superior medical facilities and educational opportunities for their people.

But when Lucy returned home to Pine Ridge every year, her old friends would tease her, saying, "But is it a good thing? Where that money comes from, you know."

Lucy would point out all the benefits enjoyed by her family. "Besides," she'd crow, "the whites took our land. Gambling is the red man's revenge."

The insurance from the Band paid for Adam's medical treatment in town. Dr. Gold had set up Stanley Schwartz, M.S.W. as the boy's therapist. "I think," she told Meggie, "he would do better with a male therapist."

"Why?" She was curious.

Gertrude answered, "Partially due to his age. At nine, a young man tends to ally himself with other males and wean himself from the seductive, comforting world of the mother. But for other reasons, I think Stanley is the right choice. The boy was probably penetrated by a penis. He'll experience his own maleness with a lot of confusion now as well as distrust and perhaps disgust. If he can form a safe and loving bond with an adult male, then he can learn that most men will treat him with kindness and not abuse him. And he can learn to love himself as a man."

"Why not a psychologist or psychiatrist?" Meggie didn't know anything about Stanley except that he was a social worker.

"Oh," said Gertrude Gold caustically, "are we now to play professional status games?" She had a way of cutting off discussion when she thought the topic was irrelevant.

Chastened, Meggie backed off.

"Besides, Stanley is one of the best therapists we have in our clinic. And he's a Jew." Gertrude threw in that last comment.

Meggie almost missed its significance. "Is it important that Adam's therapist be Jewish?'

"No," Gertrude replied. She tapped her fingers together as if impatient with Meggie's questions. The telephone rang and Gertrude answered it. "I'll be right there," she said.

As she wheeled out of the room, she looked back at Meggie, adding, "It's only important that Adam's therapist not be a proselytizing Christian."

That comment left Meggie thoroughly puzzled. *What was Dr. Gold telling her?*

* * * *

Meggie had previously called the St. Johns facility and faxed them the guardianship papers. As to be expected, the hospital staff refused to give Adam's leaving their blessing. "Against Medical Advice" was written all over the discharge summary.

"The boy is not well yet," warned Dr. Wright on the telephone. "We can't predict whether he can safely survive outside in the community. You're making a serious mistake in judgement."

"Nevertheless, we'll be down in the afternoon to pick him up," she replied. "Please have all the papers completed and send the treatment summaries and prescriptions to the Gertrude Gold Clinic in Traverse City. Also, the nursing staff needs to make sure his clothes are packed and that the boy is informed that we're coming to get him."

On the drive down to St. Johns, Meggie talked to Hawk, emphasizing the need for clear expectations with regard to each other. "Whatever happens, Hawk, we have to back each other up. If we split in decision-making, the boy will play off both of us."

Hawk outlined the summer schedule of continuous supervision of Adam, with Larry and Lucy filling in when he had to be working elsewhere. "I'm going to rebuild the barbed wire fence around the lower field," he added.

Meggie looked at him, astonished. "But that fence was falling down even in my Grandfather's day. It will take you weeks to dig the posts and string the wire. The field is a full thirteen acres."

Hawk nodded. "Several weeks at least. All summer, maybe."

"But why?" A local farmer had occasionally leased the land to plant corn or hay but now it had been lying fallow in rye for a couple of years. There was no immediate requirement for a fence.

Hawk gave her a mysterious grin. "Who knows? Maybe we'll run a couple of buffalo in there next year. Besides, your grandfather would appreciate my efforts."

"He's been dead now for thirty-four years, Hawk."

"I want to do it. It will make a good project for us."

"Us? Oh," Meggie realized. "You and Adam."

"The boy needs to do this. The hard work will give him a sense of accomplishment. A job with a clear beginning and a definite end."

It also has a middle, thought Meggie. Out loud, she said, "You know, Hawk, you're a lot smarter than people might think."

Hawk eyed her with a questioning look.

Meggie added, "How will Adam ever find a gate if he hasn't built himself a strong fence?"

They pulled up to the hospital. At the front office, Hawk signed the papers, taking over charge of Adam Arbre, followed by a brief meeting with Dr. Wright who did his best to dissuade them from their course of action. But when the psychiatrist could see that his words were having no impact, he gave up the argument. "Good luck," he said, shaking his head in disapprobation.

Dr. Wright buzzed Hawk and Meggie into the main section of the hospital and pointed them in the direction of Adam's ward. The nursing staff lined up to say goodby. Adam was holding onto a duffel bag of clothing. A couple of the kids shouted out affectionate obscenities to which he responded with a weak, shy smile.

The same head nurse was on duty. "I wish we could have helped him more," she said in an aside to Meggie. "Will there be a psychiatrist following him for medication?"

Meggie nodded. The Gertrude Gold Clinic had a consulting psychiatrist on staff. She knew that there would be an initial move to decrease the psychotropic medication. In addition, Dr. Gold had scheduled Adam for twice-a-week individual psychotherapy. Family therapy would most likely commence a month later.

That and a lot of hard work with Hawk, thought Meggie.

Adam was respectful, stiff in his movements around them. He sat quietly in the back seat of Meggie's car. Casually, Hawk activated the child locks so that the boy couldn't open the door and fling himself out onto the highway. With some interest, Adam looked back upon the hospital and the cottages where he had spent the last two and a half months.

In the front seat, Meggie jabbed Hawk lightly in the side as a reminder.

"Sure is going to be good to have you living with us, Nephew," Hawk said, turning onto the highway. "But like all places, Chrysalis has its own set of rules. Are you ready to hear them?"

Adam nodded. He was paying attention.

"It can all be summed up one way. You're not to hurt yourself, us, or the property on purpose. That means no fires, no violence, no running away. Do you understand?" Hawk looked in the rear view mirror.

The boy was studying the scenery as it whizzed by the car. No answer.

"Adam," Hawk spoke loudly.

The boy turned his head.

"Did you understand what I just said?"

The boy stared ahead, right through the mirror's reflection and beyond. He neither said a word nor acknowledged Hawk's words. He leaned his head back against the seat. His eyes blinked shut. After a couple of minutes, the boy's mouth dropped open.

Adam Arbre had fallen asleep.

Meggie turned around. The boy was breathing deeply.

"Must be tired." Hawk shrugged his shoulders.

"He's building the best fence he knows how," said Meggie.

Adam opened his eyes again halfway through the four-hour trip. He watched with fascination as the flat inland landscape slowly gave way to the heaves and hills of northwest Michigan. A smile broke out on his face when the car crested the long hill that finally gave view to the distant Grand Traverse Bay and the blue waters of Lake Michigan.

But instead of traveling M22 to Peshawbestown, they turned off toward Chrysalis in Suttons Bay. Meggie knew that Fritzie would be stationed in the front yard, waiting patiently for their return. Hawk pulled into the long driveway. Trees, planted by her grandmother, laced their upper limbs to form a bower over the mile-long road winding up the hill. "Home at last," Meggie announced.

Fritzie barked and pirouetted with joy upon their arrival. First he jumped all over Meggie, because she was Alpha dog, then he turned his attentions to Hawk, Beta dog. When the fox terrier noticed the boy, he ran over to him and sniffed the pant legs.

Adam didn't pay him any mind but pulled out his duffel bag from the back seat.

His nose still upon the boy's trousers, Fritzie started to hoist a back leg.

"No!" yelled Meggie.

Surprised by her outburst, the old dog looked up, promptly dropped his raised leg, and cocked his head to better hear what else Alpha dog might have to say.

"What do you think you are doing?" She crossly shook her finger at him. Turning to Adam, she apologized. "I don't know what came into him. Thank heaven, I caught him before he did anything."

Fritzie backed away from the group and followed them at a safe distance. Alpha dog was angry.

"You'll have the east room on the third floor," Meggie informed Adam. "It used to be my room when I was your age. You'll discover that the built-in bookcase is filled with wonderful novels for kids."

Unfortunately, during the summer, it was also the hottest room in the house. But she and Hawk wanted the boy close to their second floor bedroom in order to keep an eye on him. Lucy had already been over and judiciously positioned several familiar items in the room. Adam's NFL clock sat on the night table, a night light protruded from a wall plug, two scruffy baseball caps dangled from the truncated bed post, new leather work gloves leaned against the bureau's mirror, a frayed but beloved blanket curled up at the end of the bed, and a colored photograph of the smiling Arbre family in happier times stood sentinel on a bookcase shelf.

Adam peered around the strange room and unshouldered his bag of clothes upon the bed. He looked to Meggie for instruction.

Like a new recruit in the Army, thought Meggie.

Like a zombie, reckoned Hawk.

* * * *

"Why don't you two give Fritzie some exercise while I make us some dinner?" Meggie had planned to serve homemade pizza, something she knew every kid liked. She figured she'd take it slow in introducing Adam to gourmet food.

Hawk took his cue. "Come, Nephew. I want to walk the edge of the field with you."

Adam had changed down into jeans and tee shirt. Hawk told him to put on socks and shoes due to the sea of poison ivy that bracketed the meadow.

With Fritzie charging ahead of them, they descended the driveway and veered off toward the field, stepping over downed barbed wire attached to rotten posts. Some of the posts had fallen and sprawled upon the ground, slowly disintegrating over time. Others tilted precariously from their upright positions like drunken sentries.

"They used to grow potatoes in this field and tap the surrounding maple trees for syrup. Maybe you didn't know it, Adam, but Suttons Bay was a big potato producer in the 1800s and early 1900s. Several schooners a week would sail into the bay to pick up the bags of potatoes from the farmers hereabouts and take them south to Chicago." Hawk enjoyed steeping himself in a place's history, to learn about where he was walking, among what ancestors he was living, and whose forgotten voices continued to whisper at the edges of human consciousness.

Adam looked bored, disinterested in the past, distracted from the present conversation, unable to project himself into any future, the silence reflecting his state of tight containment.

He's like a house with all the windows shut, the doors locked, where nothing moves, no breeze, no fresh air, Hawk concluded. *But I will keep talking, spinning my web of images, and tangling him with my words. I will not join him in the land of the dead. I will pull him back.*

"Over there," Hawk pointed toward the encroaching woods, "was once a wonderful forest of hemlock trees. But one winter during the First World War, when Meggie's grandparents had departed south, a local farmer brought in a team of horses, cut down all the hemlocks, and sold the lumber to ship builders. Never paid Meggie's grandfather a damn cent for it either. Everybody knew who had done it but there wasn't any proof. What do you think about that?"

Adam said nothing but he did look over toward the trees.

Drawn by their absence, Hawk observed.

As twilight began dimming their view, Hawk plucked a blade of grass and blew on it, a last trumpet blast before nightfall. The piercing, squawking sound shivered across the darkening meadow.

THIRTY-SIX

THE CLOSING OF THE EYES

The difference between Despair
And Fear—is like the One
Between the instant of a Wreck—
And when the Wreck has been—"

—EMILY DICKINSON
The difference between Despair

The first night, Adam wet the bed. His tears fell on the pillow; he peed in his sleep.

Meggie heard him get up and then there was silence. She eased herself off the mattress so as not to awaken Hawk. The clock read ten after three. Meggie yawned, threw on a cotton shift, and tiptoed up to Adam's bedroom.

Adam was on the floor, curled up on a rug and covered by a thin blanket. Meggie could smell ammonia and immediately deduced what had happened.

"Adam, wake up." She touched his shoulder.

He was pretending to be asleep, obviously embarrassed. His head turned and he opened his eyes. He had put on fresh underwear. Over in the far corner were stashed his wet pajamas.

"Let's strip the bed and throw the sheets into the washing machine," Meggie suggested.

Together they pulled off the damp sheets and the mattress cover, balled them up with the soiled pajamas. Carrying the awkward bundle, Adam followed her downstairs to the laundry room. Meggie pointed out the settings on the machine. "Use hot water with the sheets." She had him measure the soap and water softener, add them to the sheets, and start the machine.

"It's real simple." Meggie smiled.

Adam bit his lip and looked away.

Next, she opened the linen closet and showed him the difference between the straight and fitted sheets. They took one of each and a mattress cover and went back upstairs.

Together, they made the bed. "You did well, Adam," she said. "Accidents happen to all of us. And rather than sit around and feel bad about it or try to go to sleep on a hard floor, it's better to get up and take care of the matter. Now, if you ever again have an accident, you won't need my help, will you?"

Adam wouldn't look at her.

"You're still upset," she added. "Do you want me to help you so it won't happen again?"

He shifted his eyes up to her face.

Bingo! That's it, she thought.

"Okay, I will." Meggie set up Adam's NFL alarm clock within reach of the bed.

"You had the accident around three o'clock because that's when I heard you get out of bed. Tomorrow night, I want you to set the alarm for two-thirty. When it goes off, get up and head to the bathroom. Now if you're already wet, you'll know that you have to set the alarm even earlier for the following night. Okay?" She showed him how to set the alarm.

"Now it's time for both of us to go back to sleep." Already, it was past four o'clock. Meggie knew she'd be dragging tail in the morning.

Adam climbed into bed and snuggled down in the fresh sheets.

Spontaneously, Meggie leaned over and kissed him good night on the cheek.

Adam graced her with a smile.

Hawk groaned as she came back to their bedroom. "What time is it? What was that all about?" He half-opened his eyes and made room for her under the bed coverings.

"Adam had a bad dream and wet the bed." She pulled off her shift and nestled down next to him, spoon-fashion. Hawk curled up behind her.

"Did you psychoanalyze the dream?" Hawk nibbled on her ear lobe.

"I wish. But he's not telling. Instead, I taught him something every man should know."

"What?" Hawk blew on the back of her neck. "How to avoid making women angry in the middle of the night?"

"No, silly. I taught him how to change his bed."

And though Meggie wanted nothing more than to fall asleep at that moment, Hawk's hands softly teased her awake. His fingers stroked a sensual path from her shoulders to her belly to her thighs, exploring the landscape of her body, his breath upon her neck and her hair, his feet wedging apart her legs as he gently rocked against her hips. It was a fight between the wish to sleep and her awakening desire to make love with him.

"I'll leave you alone if that's what you want, my sleepy goddess," he whispered into her ear.

Rolling onto her back, she laughed and stretched like a preening cat, elongating her body, pleasure rippling through her whole being. Sleep would simply have to bide its time.

Hawk hovered over her body as if it were a temple of worship. With reverence, delight, and the ancient prayers of kisses and touch, he sought passageway into the mysteries of the flesh.

＊　＊　＊　＊

Next morning, Stanley Schwartz pushed open his office door and headed straight to the clinic waiting room. He had been briefed by Dr. Gertrude Gold, Dr. Meggie O'Connor, Dr. Wright, and Dr. Volarik about Adam Arbre. The day before, he had met the parents and gathered a developmental history on the boy. Dr. Gold had agreed to supervise him and Dr. O'Connor.

"Mr. Slade Spelman, the guardian?" Stanley proffered his hand. The handshake by the dark muscular Native American was surprisingly light, barely making contact.

"Call me Hawk."

"And this must be Adam Arbre. Am I right?" Stanley smiled at the nine-year-old boy but did not offer his hand.

The boy shifted uneasily from one foot to another.

"Adam, would it be all right with you if I met with Mr. Hawk for a few moments?"

Adam nodded and promptly plopped down on the waiting room couch. Stanley handed him a sports magazine from the wall rack. "Something for you to read."

"The boy needs supervision," Hawk warned.

"Linda will watch him." Stanley spoke to the clinic receptionist.

Taking off his large felt hat, Hawk followed the short, dark-haired therapist back into the office area.

"Do sit down," said Stanley, noticing that the man seemed as ill at ease as the boy.

Hawk perched on the edge of the couch.

"You're married to Dr. O'Connor?"

"Yes."

"Dr. Gold speaks very highly of her. You understand that what we are going to do is highly unusual. Typically a child like this would remain in the institution, so it'll be a real challenge for you and Dr. O'Connor. And for me, as well."

Hawk nodded respectfully, listening and taking his measure of the man before him.

Stanley instinctively liked the long-haired fellow before him. He knew that he was being studied. "What are your ideas about what happened?" Stanley didn't want to prejudice the man with his own hypotheses.

"His kidnapper knew about Evil Spirits."

Stanley sat back in his leather chair and tented his fingers. "Tell me more."

Hawk's fingers worried the brim of his hat. "His soul's been stolen. Somebody put a spell on him."

"Like a curse?"

Hawk nodded.

For what reason?"

"Power."

Stanley pushed. "So you think some evil person tried to hurt Adam for reasons of power."

Hawk nodded. "When you call the Evil Spirits, They will come. If you know how, you can use Them to work a spell on another human being. Some people believe that if you capture the soul of another, you will grow in power."

"Do you believe in that?"

Hawk nodded, then added, "But there's a catch."

"Oh?"

"When you work evil spells on other human beings, they'll eventually come back on you or your family."

"A high price to pay for power." Stanley arched his eyebrows. "Does your wife also believe that an evil spell has been cast on the boy?"

Hawk shook his head. "She's an Anglo. She's got the notion that evil can't enter people without their agreement, that a soul can only be given away, not stolen."

"But your opinion is different," encouraged Stanley.

Hawk passed his eyes over Stanley's face and said, "I tell her it is like a fever that takes over the body. Things begin to die inside. Slowly the soul is eaten away."

"And how far gone is the boy?" Stanley asked.

"To the edges of the darkening lands," Hawk answered.

Stanley brought Adam into his office, leaving Hawk behind in the waiting room. Upright, in the center of the room, sprawled an easel with paints, charcoal, pastels, and large sheets of paper. "This is where we'll be meeting twice a week, Adam. I hope you'll let me get to know you. Do you know why you're here?"

Adam nodded and looked at his feet. He sat down on Mr. Schwartz's stuffed chair.

"Can you tell me?"

The boy didn't say anything.

Stanley didn't let the silence go on too long. He wanted Adam to feel comfortable with him. "You're here because your parents and your cousin, Mr. Hawk, and Dr. O'Connor are all concerned about you. I understand that a few months ago you were kidnaped for over a week. That when you came back, you were missing the tip of your little finger."

Adam tucked his truncated finger into the palm of his hand, out of sight.

Stanley continued, "What I have also been told is that you were sexually abused at that time and that you've not said a word since."

Stanley waited to see if there were any reaction. Beyond blinking, the boy remained still, listening.

"Your parents reported to me that you had been a pretty good student. That you were the kind of son that made them proud. They told me that you were a dancer in the Peshawbestown Pow-wow."

A sliver of a smile. It was the first indication of any positive reaction from the boy.

"I also learned that just before you were kidnaped, you lost a good friend, June Tubbs."

Adam's face shut down. The smile vanished. His eyes closed, his mouth grimaced tight, his cheek muscles clenched, and he buried his face into the back cushion of the chair.

"And that pretty well sums up what I know about you, Adam. Anything else, you're going to have to tell me."

The boy kept his face hidden.

*   *   *   *

Paul Tubbs had finally turned his face back homeward, defeated, unable to locate his daughter. But he was restless at home, at work, anywhere. At least four times a week, he telephoned the investigators in Michigan, Illinois, and Indiana.

He wanted to talk about his little girl to anyone who would listen. Katja, on the other hand, closed the door to June's room and pulled down the shades. She took down the photographs of June in their bedroom and stacked them, face down, on the girl's bed. She concentrated all her energy on Robert.

Paul collected the photos and hung them up in his office so that everywhere he turned, he could see the face of his daughter.

When he would bring up her name at home, Katja would sigh heavily and soon find something else to distract him.

"It's not healthy to shut her out this way," he told his wife.

"She's dead, Paul."

"I refuse to believe that."

Katja would then walk away, her body concave against the forces of depression, her shoulders hunched against grief denied, her mind plotting escape from the image of her daughter calling out to her.

No, she vowed. *I will not give into the despair of hope.*

THIRTY-SEVEN

WHAT IS NOT SAID

We have scotch'd the snake, not kill'd it;
She'll close and be herself, whilst our poor malice
Remains in danger of her former tooth.

—WILLIAM SHAKESPEARE
Macbeth

The second day, Hawk took Adam to the field and demonstrated the posthole digger. They sweated through a morning's hard labor. As the sun began to rise hotter in the sky, both pulled off their tee shirts, letting the sun bake into their muscles. Thirsty and tired, they finally quit for lunch. Together, they devoured bologna sandwiches and cold lemonade. Hawk was pleased that the boy had worked steadily, without complaint. *Meggie worries too much*, he thought.

"By the time you're ready for school, Adam, you'll have muscles like a construction worker."

Adam slathered peanut butter and jelly on another slab of bread and drank his fourth glass of lemonade.

"Okay, I'm going to take a shower, clean up, and then we'll head off to Northern Lumber for the posts. Okay?"

Adam's tongue was working furiously to free his upper gums of peanut butter.

As there was no else one around but he and Fritzie, Hawk felt safe
in leaving the boy alone for a few minutes. The shower eased some of
the shoulder pain, exacerbated by the hoisting and ramming of the post-
hole digger. Hawk knew it would be a helluva lot easier to get a
mechanical digger but he wanted Adam to know the discipline of hard
work and the sense of accomplishment. The slippery fingers of water
massaging his tired limbs made him relax longer than usual. Finally, he
turned off the faucet and climbed out of the stall, dripping wet. Rubbing
himself dry with a large fluffy towel, he heard the snarl then the snap
of Fritzie's jaws.

Hawk tracked wet footprints over to the window, above the east
porch. "Fritzie?" he shouted. The dog was backing off the porch, across
the lawn, limping and favoring his left shoulder.

Damn! Hawk immediately guessed what had happened. He wrapped
the towel around his waist and ran downstairs, yelling "Adam, where
are you?"

The boy wasn't out on the east porch.

Hawk could hear water running in the kitchen. He turned and
headed in that direction. The boy's arm was bleeding. Teeth marks
punctuated the wound. Not bad enough for stitches but the boy
needed a tight bandage. Hawk retrieved a bottle of rubbing alcohol and
bandages from the downstairs medicine cabinet.

With Adam's arm still slung over the sink, Hawk dabbed it dry with
a paper towel then poured rubbing alcohol on the wound. Adam
flinched when it burned but he didn't make a sound. Hawk applied a
bandage to the arm. "Fritzie?" he asked.

The boy nodded.

"Now Adam, I want you to be honest with me. Did you try to hurt
Meggie's dog?"

Adam looked away, propping up his hurt arm with the other hand.

Hawk grabbed the boy's chin and forced it back towards him.

"Did you?"

And then Adam faded, drew back from his eyes, and disappeared.
His body stood there, his eyes remained open, but Hawk knew that the
boy was no longer there.

Hawk dropped his hand from Adam's chin. He wanted to reach in
through those eyes into the boy's brain, his heart, his departing soul and

yank him back into the kitchen. He wished Meggie were there to witness how the light in Adam's eyes had vanished.

He spun on his bare feet and walked outside. Fritzie was waiting for him, wagging his tail, sitting on his hind legs with his left paw in the air. Hawk could see the hurt in the dog's eyes. He picked up the terrier and cradled him in his arms and took him back upstairs.

Hawk pulled on a pair of jeans and a tee shirt, socks and sneakers while talking to Fritzie. "We're going to see Sam, old guy. To check you out."

Then he carried Fritzie out to his pick-up truck, placing him in the front seat. He came back to the house and yelled for Adam.

The boy appeared. He wouldn't look at Hawk.

"You're coming with me to the vet," Hawk said grimly.

The boy shook his head. He didn't want to go.

"No choice about it, son." Hawk shut the back door behind them.

Apprehension flooded the boy's face when he realized he was going to have to sit next to Fritzie. He held his hurting arm away from the dog.

Fritzie paid him no mind.

It was clear to Hawk that they had come to some kind of mutual understanding.

Soon, they pulled up to the veterinary clinic in Suttons Bay. This time, Hawk insisted that Adam carry the dog. He watched to make sure that the boy was gentle with the terrier.

Sam Waters was examining a sick cat so Jillian instructed Hawk and Adam to sit down in the waiting room. She slipped into the back room where Daisy was cleaning the cages.

"You remember that Indian kid that got kidnaped?"

Daisy rested her chin on the broom handle. "Yeah."

"Well, he's out in the waiting room, sitting there with Dr. O'Connor's husband."

"Really?" Daisy was curious, as Jillian knew she would be.

Jillian returned to her desk. It wasn't long before the broom came sweeping out into the waiting room, Daisy attached. The teenager looked up and glanced at the Indian boy. Her brow furrowed. She took one more quick look then retreated to the back room.

Nothing much escaped Jillian. She'd ask Daisy about her strange reaction later. But meanwhile, Sam had emerged from the examining room and was ready for Fritzie.

"What's the problem?" he asked.

"He's favoring his left leg." Hawk indicated that Adam should carry the dog into the Sam's room.

"We'll take a look. Um . . ." With Fritzie secure on the table, Sam felt along the leg and slowly rotated the shoulder joint.

Fritzie pulled back in pain.

"I'd say he's got a very sore joint up on the shoulder area. Did he fall?" Sam looked at Hawk.

Hawk looked at Adam.

Adam stared at the linoleum floor.

"You're the owner of Shunka, aren't you?" Sam addressed the boy, noticing the bandage on the boy's arm.

Adam nodded but avoided eye contact.

Sam switched his attention back to Hawk, "Well, it could be due to a fall, or yank, or kick, or beginning arthritis. The dog needs to stay off his feet for awhile. Put him in a closed room for a day or so and only let him out to pee. He should get better quickly. But can you tell me anything more?"

Hawk answered, "Fritzie wasn't limping earlier. Adam here got dog bit."

"Fritzie bit you? What did you do to provoke the attack?" It was suddenly clear to Sam that the joint pain was due to an inflicted injury.

The boy scraped his bottom lip with his own teeth.

"Well, let me say this." Sam spoke in his most authoritative voice. "If you ever try to hurt Fritzie again, he will go for your throat. You were lucky this time. This is the second dog around you that has been hurt. If I hear of any more incidents, I promise you that I will turn you over to the police. Do you understand, boy?"

Adam nodded, miserable.

Hawk reached out and shook Sam's hand, saying. "Thank you for your help."

* * * *

The police in Indiana telephoned Paul at his office. In a field, a farmer had uncovered the shallow grave of a child's torso. It was a female, about the same age as June. Based on hospital records from Traverse City, they thought it was very likely the Tubbs girl. Would he come and take a look at the body? It was missing the head, but there were features on the body that might be able to identify her.

It was also missing the heart.

Paul caught the next plane out of Traverse City, convinced that the police had made a dreadful mistake. June was alive. He knew it to be true.

But Katja and he agreed that he should go to Indiana to discount the probability. June had a small mole on the upper right back and a chest scar from the accident last year with the horse. He was confident on the basis of those two distinguishing marks that he could rule out the death of his daughter.

The sight of the child's torso and the violence done to it set Paul to gagging in the sterile atmosphere of the Indiana morgue. Holding his nose and mouth against the stench of decay, he indicated to the coroner's aide to turn the body over onto the stomach. There, nestled on the upper right, was the distinguishing mole. *No*, his mind said. *It can't be. This is somebody's else's child.*

He asked that the torso be rotated again so that he could inspect the torn chest area. And there, he saw what he had first refused to see— the scar where June had hit the ground, flying through the air from the stallion's back.

Where were her arms, her legs, her head? Where was her heart?

"Aaaaa," he moaned, clutching his stomach and turning away from the remains.

Who could do this to a child? My child.

Roils of rage uncoiled within him, pushing aside the nausea. *I will hunt him down and kill him if it is the last thing I do*, he swore to himself. Fists clenched, he nodded to the police inspector who stood outside the door.

Eight years old. Oh Junie, what have they done to you? My precious little girl.

He pulled out a photograph of her, a goofy kind of picture where she was rolling her eyes and sticking out her tongue, laughing at her own antics. Anything to replace the sight of that tortured body lying on the cold steel table. But the two dimensional picture mocked him, compressed and bent into the shape of the wallet. *It's all I have left of her.*

And the image of her small mutilated body.

* * * *

"There's a bee under your bonnet," said Jillian.

"Huh?" Daisy was about to leave for her evening job at Hattie's.

"Come on, 'fess up. Something about that Indian boy today."

"What boy?"

Jillian confronted her. "Daisy, don't play dumb with me."

Daisy let out a big sigh, hung up the white coat, and fluffed out her hair. "He reminded me of someone."

"Who?" Jillian pressed.

"One time, a few months ago, you sent me home early. Said that I looked green at the gills and I did feel kind of sick. I saw a kid leaving our house. Don't think he noticed me, 'cuz I was back on the road. But I asked Mom about him. She said that sometimes the kid would come to our place in the afternoon for cookies and milk. She felt sorry for him or something. That Indian boy today sure looked like that kid."

"What are you saying, Daisy?"

"I dunno. It's not important." Daisy shook her head and headed out the door, not wanting to discuss the matter.

But Jillian began looking at the calender.

Sam came out of the examining room, yawning and stretching his arms after a long day of appointments. He caught Jillian scrutinizing the month of April.

"Wrong month. It's July, Jillian."

She shook her head. "Do you remember the exact date when that Indian boy was kidnaped?"

"No, but it was right before Easter." Sam remembered in detail how the community had mobilized around the disappearance of the two children. He, too, had gone out into the countryside searching for them.

"And wasn't it just around that time that Daisy came to live with me?" Jillian was onto something like a hound dog that had picked up the scent of the prey.

"Yes."

"I thought so," she bayed triumphantly.

Sam patiently waited for more.

Jillian stabbed her finger at the month of April. "Emily Bassett left town with her own children around the same time that Adam Arbre disappeared."

"Probably just a coincidence." Sam knew that Jillian was a devout fan of detective mysteries.

"A very interesting coincidence, if you ask me." She picked up the phone and dialed the sheriff's department.

* * * *

Meggie was not happy upon seeing Fritzie limping. She noticed how both boy and dog appeared to give each other respectful distance. On the one hand, it made her angry enough that she wanted to call it quits with this insane idea of playing foster home to a disturbed child. On the other hand, she had to hand it to her terrier for teaching Adam a very quick lesson about the consequence of cruelty. No one could arrest Fritzie for child abuse.

That night, she entered Adam's bedroom. "Did you set the alarm clock?"

He nodded.

She wondered what to say to him. The behavior toward Fritzie was unacceptable. Hawk believed that by making Adam carry the dog, going to the veterinarian, and hearing the explicit threat from Sam, the crisis had been resolved. "Besides, Fritzie will stay on the alert now around him."

But Meggie didn't think that was sufficient. She struggled on how best to approach Adam. Just as she was about to confront him, the telephone rang. She left Adam's room to answer it.

It was her mother.

Oh, my God, Meggie remembered. Her parents were due for a month-long visit in less than two weeks. *How could I have forgotten?*

"Meggie," her mother said, "your Dad's not been feeling well this past week so I forced him to see a doctor."

There's something else she's not saying, Meggie worried.

"What kind of symptoms?" Meggie asked.

"He's not digesting food well. There's blood in his stools. They want him to stay for more tests. I think we're going to have to cancel our trip."

It must be serious, thought Meggie. She couldn't remember a year when her mother hadn't spent at least part of her summer in Suttons Bay.

"What do they think is the problem?" Meggie pushed.

"Hard to say. But they want to rule out cancer."

"What does he think?" Meggie knew her father, also a physician, detested medical procedures and complained bitterly when he had to wait long past the appointment hour for consultation.

"You know your Dad. He says they're making mountains out of mole hills, that it's silly to undergo all these tests."

"What do you think?"

A brief moment of silence. Meggie wondered if they had gotten disconnected; then she heard her mother sigh.

"I think it's serious, Meggie."

"Do you want me to fly out there?" Meggie could hear the anxiety nibbling on her mother's voice, chewing away her self-confidence.

"Not yet, honey. I think you'll be coming soon enough."

Her mother's words sent a small trickle of sadness slipping down subterranean trenches of grief. Meggie knew the shape and texture of death. Over the past two years, she had felt almost haunted by the experiences of mortality around her beginning with the death of Winona, her elderly teacher, and ending with the loss of the baby, her baby.

But not my Dad, oh please not my Dad, she prayed. *I'm not ready to have my parents die.*

Once again for Meggie, life slipped on its fragile apparel.

Winona had told her, "You're in that middle generation whose job is to take care of the old ones and the young ones. For the old ones hold the wisdom of the past and the young ones carry the future."

Meggie summoned up the energy of those words to help with the healing of Winona's grandson. *If I can't save my Dad from death, then surely I can do something to help this young boy.*

"Adam," said Meggie, returning to Adam's room after the telephone call, "I want to tell you a story."

The boy had been stiff, tensed against the expected rebuke over Fritzie. But Meggie's words and tone of voice relaxed him and he loosened his grip upon the blanket.

"Long before I knew you," she began, "I knew your grandmother, Winona. Tough lady she was. I think she took one look at me and said 'That white woman sure needs help.' Your grandmother thought I was living out of balance. She was right, Adam. So, one day she decided she was going to do some healing on me. Only I didn't know it."

Adam unconsciously nodded his head. Clearly, he could see his grandmother in Meggie's words.

"Through the gift of story, she taught me in the manner of your people. That's why, tonight, I'm going to tell you a story. I want you to listen, pay attention, the way I did to your grandmother."

Adam smiled. A story was better than a reprimand.

"Once upon a time," began Meggie in the way of all storytellers, "there was a village in India. At the edge of the town, there lived a large cobra. At first, the cobra used to go about his business being a cobra and not bothering a soul but something happened. We don't know what happened, but it must have been pretty terrible. So terrible that the cobra's personality changed for the worse.

"The cobra would coil up near the village's well and when the children would come for water, the cobra would dart out and strike at them. The kids would run screaming back to their mothers, terrified. When the women and the men came to the well to fetch water, the cobra did the same thing. He hurt a lot of people and nobody knew why.

"Finally one day a swami came to the village to help the people. They told him about how mean the snake had become. Could he help them? The swami was a wise and respected man so he went to the well to talk to the cobra.

"'What are you doing?' the holy man asked the snake. 'You are biting people and hurting them. This is not the right way for you to act.' The cobra became ashamed in front of such a wise and holy man. He promised the swami he would try to do better.

"With that promise, the swami left the villagers and promised to come back in another six months to check up on the cobra's behavior.

When he returned, the swami headed to the well. There he found a group of children gathered in a circle, kicking and throwing rocks at the cobra. The snake was barely alive, its skin ragged and torn. The swami shooed away the children.

"'What happened to you?' the swami cried.

"'I did as you told me and look how the human beings treat me,' the cobra complained.

"The swami admonished him, 'I told you to stop biting them. I never told you to give up your hiss.'"

The boy looked puzzled.

"Good night, Adam." Meggie rose from the side of the bed and touched the boy's forehead, sweeping aside a lock of hair. "Treat my dog with respect and he won't bite you."

The boy lifted his bandaged arm and, for a second, let his hand graze Meggie's arm—a moment of brief but real contact.

A window inching open, thought Meggie.

THIRTY-EIGHT

FROM ICE TO FIRE

For everything hidden must be revealed,
each secret longs to be disclosed . . .

—ISAAC BASHEVIS SINGER

On the third morning, two neatly attired FBI agents arrived at Chrysalis to question Adam. They positioned themselves across the dining room table from the boy and Hawk.

"We're investigating the disappearance of Mrs. Emily Bassett," the younger one said. Without letting his back touch the chair, he sat rigidly attired in a perfectly knotted tie, spotless white shirt, creased dark pants, and expensive sun glasses.

Adam shifted in his seat.

"Did you know her?" the agent pushed.

Adam looked at Hawk.

"Yes, you have to answer them," Hawk ordered.

The boy bit his lower lip and nodded.

"Did you see her the day you were kidnaped?"

Adam's eyes restlessly scanned the wall, growing wider and more fearful by the minute.

Again he nodded, swallowing hard.

The older of the two officers leaned forward, his face friendly, his hair graying, a slight paunch to his middle. He looked straight at the boy and spoke gently. "Did Emily Bassett have anything to do with your kidnaping?"

Wildly, Adam looked around the room but the walls offered him no escape.

"Tell them, Adam," Hawk urged.

And for the third time, the boy nodded yes.

Then, in the dash of a second, Adam disappeared. The light blinked out of his eyes.

"That's enough questioning for now," Hawk advised the officers. He rose to his feet.

A furrow of frustration plowed across the younger officer's forehead. "But why stop now?"

The older agent tapped him on the shoulder. "It's time to go. We'll come back. Thanks for your help."

Hawk left the boy and accompanied the men outside.

"I appreciate your understanding," he said to the older man.

"Hell, I've seen that look in my mother-in-law's eyes. Boom, she's there. Then she's gone. Course, she's got Alzheimer's, and I don't reckon that's the boy's problem."

"No, it's not," said Hawk.

The two agents climbed into their car. The younger one, the driver, leaned out the window and reiterated, "Here's my card. If he says anything at all about Emily Bassett or about June Tubbs or about the kidnaping . . ."

"I'll be sure to give you a call." Hawk accepted the card then turned back toward the house. Fritzie limped alongside him, still favoring his left leg.

Hawk entered the house, expecting to find Adam frozen to the chair, eyes dead. But instead the boy had descended to the living room and was leaning over the fire grate, lighting matches one by one, flicking them into the stone fireplace.

Hawk cleared his throat. "Looks to me like you and I need to burn some paper trash today."

He didn't notice the goose bumps sprouting on Adam's arms.

* * * *

I can feel
the wind blowing through me
the house is shaking

I forgot to shut the doors,
lock the windows
the cold wind is blowing

Waziyata.

* * * *

The coffee was tepid and weak at the clinic as Meggie, Stanley Schwartz, and Gertrude Gold gathered for an early morning meeting. Dr. Gold was attired in a light dress with a purple silk scarf at the neck, stockings, and sandals on her feet. Stanley's rumpled clothes looked as if they had never encountered an iron. In his early thirties, Stanley could have passed for an assistant professor, his bright studious face warm and inviting.

"Sorry about the coffee," he said. "It's brewed by a secretary who doesn't drink coffee. I've got my own percolator pot. Would you like some? Ethiopian brand."

Meggie nodded and held out her cup. Stanley briefly absented himself.

The two women waited for his return before beginning the supervision session.

Upon his return, Dr. Gold said, "Why don't you go first, Stanley?" As he was the formal therapist, it was a matter of respect.

The social worker first blew on his hot coffee before lifting his mug. "It is hard to know where to start with a mute, traumatized child. Like most young clients, Adam initially inspected my office but didn't make eye contact or say anything. I decided I needed to establish a base of information by sharing with him what I knew and what I didn't know. Not that it made much of an impression on him. When I touched into more difficult matters, he retreated."

"How?" asked Gertrude.

"He burrowed into the back of the chair."

"How far did he get?" A wry question from Meggie.

"To Iceland, I think." Stanley smiled. "Because after that, he didn't budge, blink, or boogie. Just stayed frozen until I finally suggested the session was over."

"What specifically caused him to dissociate?" inquired Gertrude.

Stanley consulted his notes. "He tolerated my statements about being kidnaped and the sexual abuse. No hiding there. I mentioned his dancing in the Peshawbestown pow-wow and got a positive facial response. But when I followed it up with a probe into the loss of his friend June Tubbs, the boy completely shut down."

Gertrude asked, "Tell us why you chose an aggressive strategy instead of letting Adam make his own discoveries in the session."

Stanley appeared unfazed by the implied criticism. "Because the world is too unstable for Adam right now. Here you have a boy who suffered the loss of a beloved grandmother in one year then in the next year loses his best friend. A few days later he's abducted from home, thrust into strange territory, and raped and abandoned along a highway where he's found mute and disoriented. As he struggles to understand these experiences, he is then removed from his home, hospitalized, and drugged."

Meggie winced.

Stanley continued. "He's finally allowed to come back to his community but not to the family home. His violent and sexually assaultive behavior tells us that he had a horrific set of experiences during the week he was kidnaped. Whom and what can he trust? I think that's the question behind his stance of silence. For me to place him into an open-ended therapy session and to allow him to set the rules, expectations, and boundaries would be an act of cruelty. The boy needs to know who I am and what I know. Then he can make his own choices about what is safe to share with me."

"What do you think?" Gertrude turned toward Meggie.

"I agree. One of the very first things we did with Adam was to set up house rules. We told him he was not allowed to hurt himself, us, or our property."

"And has that worked?" Gertrude was sitting back in her wheelchair, listening intently.

"No." Meggie answered. "Adam assaulted my dog."

Gertrude leaned forward, curious. "And your reaction to this violence?"

Meggie glanced at Stanley. She knew that Gertrude was asking about her emotional, not behavioral, response. The older woman's eyes bored into her. "I got angry. Very angry," Meggie confessed.

"And?"

"I wanted to send the boy away."

Stanley threw her a look of concern.

"Ja, go on," said Gertrude.

"But I couldn't," Meggie added.

"Why not? He had just hurt your dog."

Gertrude wasn't going to let her escape. And for some unbidden reasons, tears came welling up from the back of Meggie's throat. "I was going to confront Adam, but my mother called. She said that my father probably has cancer."

"Ja." Gertrude waited for Meggie to work out the issues of counter-transference, the hidden unconscious conflicts that Meggie was bringing to the situation.

"And I got to thinking about how I wasn't ready for either of my parents to die. How they had always given me a sense of deep belonging. I owe them a debt that I can never repay. Perhaps, in some small way, I can pass on that sense of belonging to Adam."

"And you understand, Dr. O'Connor, that as you try to welcome Adam to your home, he pushes you away. He lets you know that he doesn't want to belong to you, to his parents, to anyone."

"But I think he does," Meggie protested.

"No. You *wish* that is how he felt," insisted Gertrude Gold. "It's not safe for anyone to get too close to him. And when you get too close, he runs away, does he not?" She looked at Stanley.

"Okay," reasoned Stanley. "If it's not safe for him to let us in, then when we approach him directly he'll find a way to leave, whether it be burrowing into a chair or dissociating."

"Precisely," Gertrude agreed.

"But he's not catatonic or passive," Meggie argued.

"Precisely," Gertrude reiterated. "The boy is trying not to say any-thing. Words are too dangerous. Yet the story presses on him and so he tries, in other ways, to tell us what happened. He hurts the dog, yet he has always loved animals." She veered into another direction, "What part of the dog did he hurt?"

The question surprised both therapists.

"The left leg," Meggie answered.

"And which hand of the boy is missing the finger tip?"

"His left hand," Stanley said.

"Precisely," said Gertrude, leaning back in her chair.

*   *   *   *

"The first fire we make will be a small one." Hawk had driven the boy and himself to the water's edge on the western side of the Peninsula. Carrying his medicine bundle, he walked to a secluded spot.

"This is good place to pray," he said to the boy, orienting toward the Fox islands. He knelt on the sand and unwrapped his bundle. The boy stood apart but looked over Hawk's shoulders.

Loosening the rawhide thongs, the small blanket fell open revealing an assortment of objects: Hawk parts, two braids of sweet grass, sprigs of sage, a turtle shell, tobacco, cedar, stones, small medicine bags, and Hawk's pipe bag. Opening up his denim jacket, Hawk pulled out the pipe bag that contained Adam's small chanunpa. He placed that bag down by Adam's feet.

With three sticks, Hawk fashioned a crude pipe stand. Stripping several of the sage sticks, he rolled up a large ball of the gray leaves, placed them in the turtle shell, and lit the leaves with a match. Immediately, the ball of sage flamed and smouldered. With an eagle wing, Hawk wafted the smoke over himself and the contents of his bundle. Stiffly, he rose to his feet and circled the boy, stroking the small plumes of smoke onto the youngster. Adam's nostrils twitched.

"I am purifying both of us," Hawk said, aware that Adam Arbre already knew this.

Returning to the kneeling position, he retrieved Adam's pipe bag. Pulling out the bowl and stem, he assembled Adam's chanunpa and placed it against the pipe rack. He smudged the small chanunpa with the sage smoke. "You must always treat the pipe with respect, whether it is a Sacred Pipe or a social pipe. Once purified with the sage smoke, all these red stone pipes will carry our prayers and protect us."

Hawk assembled his own Chanunpa and smudged it as well.

"Come Nephew, sit down beside me on the sand." It was more of an order than an invitation.

The boy complied but said nothing, slumping down cross-legged to the right of Hawk.

Holding the bowl toward his heart, the stem toward the west, Hawk began the ancient ritual of filling his Pipe with prayer and tobacco.

"Tunkasila, Wakan Tanka," he began, "Grandfathers in All the Directions, Grandfather Sky, Unci Maka, Grandmother Earth, Wanbli Gleska, the Spotted Eagle, Three Legs, my medicine Helpers, I ask you all to bend over and listen to our prayers. I ask you to recognize this Chanunpa Wakan and the chanunpa that belongs to my nephew here. We come before You this morning to pray about what is in our hearts."

Hawk's eyes raked the western skyline, the rolling surf of Lake Michigan, the Fox islands to the northwest, the Manitous to the southwest.

To each of the seven Directions, he offered tobacco, asking for help.

"Wakan Tanka, Great Mystery, Adam and I come before You. My nephew has come back to us. We ask that you help make him whole again. Grandfather, there is a part of him that is missing."

Adam cast his eyes down.

"We give thanks for his return."

Hawk oriented the Pipe to the west. "Wiyohpeyata, up on that hill, a vision came to me. I am to take my nephew here to the waters, pray with him, show him his chanunpa. Let him find his way home. He is still lost, Grandfather, though his body is here. I ask you to send Wanbli on the West Wind to find what is missing and bring it back to him."

Adam peered sideways at his cousin, his face puzzled. He was listening intently to Hawk's prayers.

To the north, Hawk offered the tobacco. "Tunkasila, Waziyata. We come to you with this Chanunpa in hopes that your wolves, the sungmanitu, will chase the boy's spirit away from the land of the ghosts. It is not yet time for the spirit of the boy to go beyond the pines to the edge of the world. Let it return to the boy's body."

"Wiyohiyanpata," Hawk called out, facing east. "Send out the night hawks to find him and guide him home, back to his body, back to his people, back to his family." He circled the tobacco before placing it in the bowl of his Chanunpa.

"Itokagata, Grandfather of the noonday sun, my nephew here needs your kindness and the warmth of your breath because it is cold inside him now. He has to make a nest inside, to welcome back that part of him that has gone wandering. He has to open his eyes, look, and call out for that part of himself. Blow your south winds gently into that hole."

"Wakan Tanka, who wraps the night sky around us at the day's end and reveals the distant lights, you teach us that not all is darkness. Hanhepi wi rises high, shining trails upon the ground, stirring up the oceans with Her power. Then, at her time of the month, she disappears, only to return to us once again. Grandfather, we ask that you help Adam here come back again from the darkness, like Hanhepi wi.

"Unci Maka, give this grandson of Yours, Adam Stands-By-Dog, strong footing. Let Your power surge up through his legs to his heart. Let him know that You surround him with Your gifts and Your love. He is but a pitiful human being, Grandmother, trying to find his way home."

"Wanbli Gleska, I ask you to carry these prayers. And now, I hand my Chanunpa over to my nephew, so that he can send you his prayers. Mitakuye oyas'in." Hawk finished inserting the last smidgins of tobacco into the bowl. He offered the Pipe and handed it to the boy, seated next to him.

Adam squirmed nervously as if the Pipe were burning his hands. He swallowed hard and closed his eyes but he could not deny the heft of the Chanunpa.

Hawk could see the boy clenching his jaw. He waited, not knowing if the boy were going to pray with the Sacred Pipe, drop it onto the sand, or simply return it to Hawk.

Adam opened his eyes, scanned westward and heavenward. The eyes were not dead but beseeching.

Yes, thought Hawk, *the old ways are returning to him, calling him back. The Pipe summons him home, just as You said it would on my hanblecya. A little piece of him is coming home.*

Then, as if the Pipe had suddenly transformed into a snake or hot coal, the boy jerked and thrust it back into Hawk's hands, fear and revulsion criss-crossing his face.

"Mitakuye oyas'in," Hawk spoke the words of respect.

The boy closed his eyes to shut out the light.

THIRTY-NINE

AFFIRMATIONS

'Yes,' I answered you last night;
'No,' this morning, sir, I say.
Colours seen by candle-light
Will not look the same by day.

—ELIZABETH BARRETT BROWNING
The Lady's Yes

Stanley Schwartz did something which he realized would provoke a disapproving comment from Gertrude Gold: He took Adam out of the clinic building to walk along the Boardman river. The confined space of Stanley's office had squeezed the boy into a frantic restlessness.

Shading his eyes against the bright sun, Stanley announced, "It's almost August."

They strolled past boys of Adam's age fishing off the pedestrian bridges, young lovers seeking the brief shade of a maple tree, teenage girls whispering into each other's ears, an old man on a bench reading the Traverse City Record Eagle. They climbed the stairs to the street and were greeted by throngs of tourists strolling down Front Street. Adam's eyes were alert, watching the flow of traffic.

Suddenly his muscles tightened; he stopped to stare, his eyes frowning with questions. Stanley followed the direction of Adam's intent. All he could see was a young man in his early twenties, a knapsack on his back, one foot on the sidewalk, one on the street, thumb out, angling for a ride.

"Do you know him?"

But the boy didn't answer.

As the current of traffic heedlessly glided by, the slope of the hitch-hiker's shoulders drifted downward.

"Come on, we need to be heading back," Stanley urged, but Adam would not budge or shift focus.

Time to go with the flow, Stanley silently conceded. "Would you like to meet him?"

Just then a red car slowed down at the light; the driver leaned over and thrust open the passenger door. The hitchhiker smiled, adjusted his pack, and jumped into the vehicle.

As fast as his two pudgy legs could move, Adam ran toward the red car and the hitchhiker. He flailed his arms as if to take flight. "No-o-o-o," he howled. The light turned green and the car growled in response, speeding away from the boy in the rear view mirror.

Out of breath, his heart pounding in his chest, Stanley gave chase. He caught up to Adam, standing in the middle of the street, indifferent to the honking cars that diverted around him, his eyes fixed on the vanishing red car and the disappearing hitchhiker. Stanley grabbed Adam's arm and yanked him back to the sidewalk.

"You almost got us both killed back there," panted Stanley, bending over to catch his breath. "You could have been hit by a car. As for me, I'm still likely to have a heart attack."

Only then did the boy turn his gaze away from the street to look at his therapist.

"So, you said something, didn't you? It's a beginning." Stanley rapped the boy's arm. He reckoned to himself, *I'll accept whatever the boy has to offer, even a simple no.*

* * * *

"Yes, that's what Paul said. He wants a divorce. Can you believe it, Meggie?" Katya's astonishment was already souring into anger.

But Meggie knew only too well how a child's death can rip a family into many pieces. She had seen it happen again and again in her practice.

"You know, it's crazy. He blames me for June's death. If I had just gotten to the playground on time. . . ." Katja's voice trailed off.

"A lot of 'what ifs,' Katja, and they don't solve a damn thing. Guilt is simply the backward face of perfection. So, what's your immediate plan?" Meggie knew that it would help Katja to focus more on the details of living than the indulgences of self-blame.

"I don't know what to do. The house and car are all paid for and there are no outstanding debts. Paul says that I'm not to worry about finances, that he's selling his stake in the accounting agency and will leave me enough money for the immediate future. What am I going to do, Meggie? How can I stop him from going? He said he feels really badly about all this."

"He should." Outrage surged in Meggie but she stifled her own feelings. Katja didn't need to hear others spout their opinions. She was doing her best to cope one day at a time.

"How's Robert doing?" Meggie worried about the impact of all this on the boy.

"He doesn't know yet. Paul's in Illinois right now, getting himself an apartment. He said he'd be back up here next week and explain everything to Robert. But what can he say to me, Meggie, that will make any sense of this decision? It's so sudden. We've been married forever. What can he ever say to me?" Katja's voice wavered between anxiety and confusion.

"How are you coping?" Meggie treaded softly.

"Me? Not well, Meggie. When he said I want a divorce, it was like a hot wire zapped me with a zillion volts. I said, you're joking, aren't you and he said no, he wasn't, that the time away from me has put things in perspective. You're joking, I said, and he accused me of not listening to him, but there it was, Meggie, all that jangling going on inside my brain, and I couldn't listen to him. Whatever am I going to do?"

"Take one day at a time, Katya."

"I'm scared. What does the future hold for me? A dumpy middle-aged woman who hasn't held down a real job for God knows how long.

Why is he leaving us when we need him the most? Where has Paul gone, Meggie?"

As far away as he can from his own pain, thought Meggie.

*   *   *   *

"No, I don't know where she is," Daisy repeated. The questions of the older investigator kept pushing at her. Daisy looked at Jillian for relief and a friendly smile. Her eyes turned back, soft and dewy, toward the younger fellow.

"Nice duds," she said.

The man smiled back at her. "You're being really helpful, Miss Bassett. I know you must be worried that you haven't heard from your mother for a long time."

Daisy gave a disinterested shrug of her shoulders.

"There's been no contact since before Easter?" The pot-bellied man tapped the table with his ball-point pen.

"No. No. No. No." Daisy could feel irritation scratch at the surface of her words.

"But, before Easter, you saw the Indian boy, Adam Arbre, up at your house?" The younger man fingered his tie; his gray-blue eyes crinkled.

Daisy cut her eyes accusingly at Jillian for revealing their earlier conversation.

"Answer his question," Jillian ordered.

Daisy bit her lip, wanting to prolong her interaction with the cool cop. "Yes."

"But your father, Clyde Bassett, denies ever seeing the boy there." It was not a challenge, just a statement of fact from the handsome one.

"My Dad don't know shit," Daisy blurted out then blushed. She looked at Jillian, expecting a reproof.

But Jillian said, "What Daisy means is that her father is drunk most of the time or out hunting with his dogs."

"He didn't hang 'round the house much, 'cuz he don't like all the noise. It don't mean nuthin' that he didn't see the kid."

"But you saw him. How many times?" The young man flipped back his suit jacket in a gesture of disclosure.

"Only that one time, but he came other times to see my mom."

"How do you know that?" the older man interrupted.

Daisy sighed impatiently. "'Cuz who do you think had to clean up after their little parties? Geez, she treated him better than her own kids." She turned her eyes back to the friendlier face.

"Why did your mother encourage Adam's visits?" The older man kept clicking his pen on, off, on, off.

"How in the hell do I know? Why don't you ask him?"

The younger man leaned toward Daisy. "Because we're more interested in your ideas."

"Well, I've found it much safer in my family not to have ideas. Ya know what I mean?"

"No," said the older man, "I don't know what you mean."

"Yes," answered the younger investigator. "You thought that what you didn't know wouldn't hurt you."

Daisy sat up straight and announced, "I ain't talking no more." Then she hesitated. "But when I do, I want to talk only to you. Nobody else in the room. Okay?"

"Okay," the younger man replied.

* * * *

"Yes and no," Bev answered. Once again, ambivalence reared its ugly head in her love life.

"Yes what?" Karl asked.

"Yes, I love you. Yes, I want to live with you. Yes, I would like to spend a lifetime with you."

"Sounds good to me," he observed. "So what's the problem? Did I not propose in an acceptable fashion? Would you like me down on my knees, begging? I can do that, Bev. It's not hard for me to humble myself." With exaggerated gestures, Karl sank down onto both knees before the couch where Bev sat.

She reached out and pulled on his shirt sleeve. "Get up."

But Karl didn't budge.

"No, I can't become a minister's wife when I don't believe in what you do." Bev frowned.

"No, that's not what I mean. I can't support your beliefs when I doubt the very existence of God." In a gesture of dismissal, Bev waved her hands toward the heavens.

"No, I can't belong to a church and pretend that I am someone whom I am not." She placed a hand over her heart.

On his knees, Karl crawled closer toward her, gripping her waist by both hands and sliding her toward him.

"No, We can't. . . ." She tried to push him away but his hands were strong and her resistance was weak.

"No, no." She began laughing as he buried his head into her lap. "No, no, no, no," she said, tumbling off the couch onto the carpet, pulled by his arms and the tidal forces of love.

"Yes. I want you to say yes, Bev," he answered before swamping her with kisses.

"Yes," she murmured, coming up for air.

∗　∗　∗　∗

"Yes, the word was 'no,'" Stanley reported, much to the pleasure of both Meggie and Gertrude Gold.

"Now we make some progress. He opens the door once, then it will be soon again, yes?" Gertrude looked to Meggie for confirmation.

But before Meggie could even nod, Gertrude turned her attention back to Stanley. "So, what was it that brought out that single most important word?"

"It was either the red car or . . ."

"The hitchhiker, yes?" Gertrude was excited. "You said that he was interested in that man before the car even came into view."

Stanley nodded.

"So, Dr. O'Connor, what would you recommend we do with this piece of information? If you had a traumatized child in therapy who was mute . . ." Gertrude let the suggestion dangle before her.

Meggie rubbed her forehead, deep in thought, then looked up at Stanley. "Do you have any plastic or metal cars for younger children?"

"In the play therapy room." Stanley obviously didn't know where she was going with this idea.

"And I know you have plastic doll figurines that bend. I've seen them in your office."

"Yes."

"If Adam were a client of mine, I think I would take a male figurine, like that hitchhiker, and act out the scene of his trying to thumb a ride. I'd start telling a story but not take it beyond the hitchhiker starting to get into the car."

A light began to dawn in Stanley's eyes. "You're suggesting that I try to involve Adam in the creation of a story."

Meggie's eyes shown with increasing enthusiasm. "And I'd have him demonstrate how the story should end. He's probably not going to say anything."

"And what if Adam shows no reaction, Dr. O'Connor? What then?" Gertrude asked.

"Then, I would push the boy harder," answered Meggie.

"How?" The hawk-eyed, red-haired old woman leaned forward in her wheelchair.

Meggie turned to Stanley. "I would yell out, long and strong, "'N-o-o-o.'"

Returning her gaze to the formidable Dr. Gertrude Gold, Meggie added, "And, in the silence, I would listen for the echoes of the boy's pain."

FORTY

SEPARATE CURRENTS

An unlearned carpenter of my acquaintance once said in my hearing: 'There is very little difference between one man and another; but what little there is, is very important.' This distinction seems to me to go to the root of the matter.

—WILLIAM JAMES
The Importance of Individuals

Neither as subtle as June nor as coy as July, the month of August wantonly, brazenly advertised her charms on the Leelanau Peninsula. The sun sparkled gleaming white teeth on the rolling surf of Lake Michigan, the sailing ships swayed suggestively in the seductive waters, the winds tickled the soft earlobes of sunbathing lovers, the enchanting trill of forest birds caressed the human ear, the mid-day heat unbuckled all clothing to a bare minimum, the hammock, the porch, and the shady tree offered sweet bedding, and the pastel skies blushed before the fiery embrace of orange-red sunsets and black diamond nights.

The tourists more than anyone else could enjoy the slow languid days of full summer and the freedom to do everything. Or nothing.

The year-round residents glanced out their office windows during daytime, bemoaning the rush of activity that kept them disciplined, faithful to their work. Only on the weekends could they escape into the loving arms of summer and even then, Fridays and Mondays were like nagging spouses, consuming precious moments of liberation. The residents smiled indulgently at the fudgies who exclaimed how wonderful it must be to live on the Peninsula year round. While nodding their heads, they were reckoning, in sun-dappled hours, how fast the warm season was slipping away. Fall would soon enough be nipping at the ankles of summer.

As much as the human heart might bend to wishing, time relentlessly keeps its appointments. Illness catches up to old age, families dissolve and reform, young men nurture secret dreams, love blossoms beyond all reason, middle age softens and tempers the rebellious spirit, a child begins to remember, and the dead refuse to be forgotten.

A telephone call jangled the serenity of a beguiling summer day. It was Meggie's mother bearing the unwanted news. "Our worst fear: He has cancer and it has metastasized to other organs. Your father doesn't have long to live."

From the sagging tone in her mother's voice, Meggie knew the deathwatch had begun. "I'll fly out tomorrow, Mom." *Oh, please, God, don't let him die before I get there*, Meggie prayed.

Outside Hawk was bent over, repairing an owl kite for Adam. As Meggie approached, he muttered, "Damn thing keeps breaking up on us. When the spine goes, so does everything else. There, I think that patch might do it." He handed the kite to the boy.

Adam ran down the hill, unraveling the line behind him. The plastic owl hovered in the air, as if uncertain, then caught the upward drift and shuddered into the breeze, bending and swooping; the yellow black-rimmed eyes and hooked beak danced in the drafts above Meggie's head.

"Dad's dying," she whispered to Hawk. "I've got to fly home tomorrow. I don't know how long I'll be gone."

"Meggie, do you want me to come?" Hawk peered into her eyes, his face a mirrored reflection of her own sadness.

Meggie shook her head. "You need to stay here with him." The owl kite whistled overhead, steadied by the tension of Adam's grip on the string.

"I've called the airport and reserved a morning flight. Bev promised to inform my clients and to handle any emergencies," Meggie said. "But can you take care of Adam all by yourself?"

Hawk glanced at the boy who kept a tight grip on the string, balancing the kite between shifting currents of air. "I think the two of us can manage."

"There's a pot pie and a couple of soups in the freezer. . . ." In her distraction, Meggie couldn't remember what else she had to tell him.

Hawk pulled her into his arms and held her. His voice offered reassurance. "Honey, you need to go be with your Mom. We'll be just fine."

That night, she sat by the boy's bed. "I'm leaving tomorrow for the east coast." She swallowed hard, choking back her rising feelings of sadness. She smoothed down the boy's cowlick. "My Dad is dying and I want to go say goodbye to him. Remember how you were there when your grandmother died?"

Adam nodded. His gaze roamed over her face as if by studying each wrinkle of emotion he would know what to feel.

A tear trickled down her left check. With the softest stroke, Adam's finger reached out, touched her cheek, and gathered up her tear as if it were a pearl of great treasure. Curling the rest of his hand to protect the quivering tear, he brought it toward his heart and looked back into her face.

"Thank you, Adam." Meggie leaned over and kissed his cheek.

*   *   *   *

Into the vacuum of one departure often comes another.

Paul Tubbs reappeared. At night, he entered into his twelve-year-old son's bedroom for a "heart to heart talk."

"Your mother and I seem to be going in different directions," he explained.

"North and south, you mean?" Robert asked.

Paul didn't know if his son were being cleverly facetious or simply literal.

"We need separate space from each other," Paul said.

"But what about me, Dad?"

"I will always love you." Paul spoke the lie of reassurance.

He left the next morning.

"Just as I suspected," groaned Katya on a long distance call to Meggie. "He's found a younger woman. With her, he can create a brand new family. Ours contains too many dark shadows and wandering ghosts."

* * * *

By the first week of August, the fence at Chrysalis was already three-quarters finished. Digging, inserting, and hammering post holes into the ground had added muscles to the frames of both man and boy. Adam was beginning to sprout height and lose the flab of childhood. Hawk was pleased how the boy took to hard work.

"Meggie will be delighted to see the fence up when she gets back. Then comes the big question." Hawk pulled off the bandana around his head and wiped the sweat off his face.

The boy looked at him and leaned on the post-hole digger.

"Well," said Hawk, "the three of us have to decide what should go into the meadow. Any suggestions?"

The boy dropped the post hole digger. He mimicked a rider, grabbing up the reins and hoisting himself onto a saddled horse, then cantered in a circle around Hawk.

Hawk pretended to be dumb. He replaced the bandanna back on his forehead. "Time to get back to work instead of horsing around," he ordered.

The boy's shoulders drooped. His message hadn't gotten through.

"One of these days, you'll tell me your ideas," Hawk said, bending over to pick up the maul. Adam couldn't see the shit-eating grin that tracked across Hawk's face.

* * * *

Despite all protestations to the contrary, Bev found herself agreeing to an engagement to Karl Young. "Am I crazy or what?" Before anyone could give serious answer to her question, Bev replied, "Yes, crazy in love."

Karl had slipped a diamond ring on her finger. An itty-bitty diamond. "Better get used to it," he'd explained. "Ministers are God's servants and not expected to reap large salaries."

She hadn't dared tell him her yearly income as a psychologist. It might have ruined his romantic image of a humble future.

* * * *

Lucy Arbre announced that she was going to regularly attend the inipi ceremonies. "It's not that I believe in the old ways," she informed her husband, "but it makes me feel closer to my mother."

The accuracy of communications from the Spirits about her missing son and the little girl had shaken her to the core. All her advanced education and professional training was for naught when it came to bringing her son home.

"Your mother warned me you'd never be really happy until you came back to the ways of your people," Larry said.

In knee-jerk fashion, Lucy griped, "What did she know?"

"A helluva lot," he countered.

In truth, Winona had evaporated from Lucy's dreams, from Adam's entreaties, from Meggie's loneliness. She was now among The Dead for them, brought forth only in the slippery medium of memory. Lucy had finally settled the painful issues from the past but only after Winona had crossed over to the Other Side. These days, when Lucy studied her own face in the mirror, more and more she observed the comforting physical imprint of her mother's expression.

Adam, on the other hand, had given up on his grandmother. Winona had vanished from his inner landscape. He decided that she had abandoned him because he was bad, not worthy of her presence. His world was dark, limited, full of sharp pain, and numbing disregard. There was no site in him for the appearance of Winona.

Meggie did not forget her first teacher along the Red Road, but Hawk was a wonderful husband and a patient ceremonial leader. Meggie knew that with him and her Chanunpa, she had found her spiritual home. By releasing Winona from her own needs, Meggie had truly bid her goodbye.

No one called to Winona.

No one asked for her help.

* * * *

At first, Adam refused to enter into the story set up by Stanley. He turned away his face and stared into the office wall.

But the plastic hitchhiker waited patiently as the toy car slid across the carpet, guided by the therapist's hand. Finally, Adam could stand it no longer; he swept his arm, knocking the car out of Stanley's grasp, and sent it careening across the room. He grabbed the hitchhiker figure and stuffed it under the seat cushion of a chair.

"The car crashed?" Stanley asked.

The boy shook his head.

Wrong guess. Stanley tried again. "The man wants a ride, but he doesn't get into the car."

Adam nodded his head vigorously.

Stanley pushed, "Is that what really happened?"

The boy looked away, his eyes scrunched into sadness.

"Oh," said Stanley in the rush of insight. "The hitchhiker, he got into the car, didn't he? But you didn't want him to do that. You wanted to warn him to stay away from the car?"

The boy's eyes looked at Stanley, full of confirmation and hopelessness.

Stanley had a choice: He could leave off and give the boy a recess or he could take the therapy a step farther. The boy was fully engaged in the conversation. He decided to chance it. Stanley retrieved the plastic car. He dug out the plastic man. He began again, saying, "The man needs a ride. He is going somewhere. He has a destination in mind but no transportation. He decides to thumb a ride. Maybe somebody will pick him up." Stanley advanced the car toward the toy man.

Adam's eyes grew wider.

"Here comes the car. The door is opening. See, the man is getting into the car." Stanley insisted that Adam look.

Adam bit his lower lip with his upper teeth. His body began to tremble.

"The car is now driving away with the young man inside," continued Stanley.

Adam flung himself down on the office carpet and began to beat his fists against the floor. "No-o-o-o," he screamed. "Don't, don't, don't," he shrieked.

"N-o-o-o," the boy moaned, clutching himself in agony.

*   *   *   *

Adam was a wreck after seeing Stanley.

"The session was rugged," the therapist told Hawk.

Adam said nothing about what had happened but his eyes had turned glassy, unfocused. He was as unresponsive as when he had first arrived at Chrysalis. Hawk was worried, afraid that the boy was moving backwards, away from life. Meggie wasn't there to reassure him about this whole therapy business.

"I'm taking him into the sweat lodge tonight," he announced to Lucy. "I need you to be there on the outside in case anything happens."

Lucy agreed. Larry would join Hawk and Adam for the inipi. In the spring when the sap was running, Hawk had constructed a family sweat lodge at Chrysalis, smaller than the one at Lucy's place. In a small clearing hidden by trees, the lodge did not attract attention from casual visitors.

Lucy cooked food on Meggie's stove and spent time talking to her listless son. Larry gathered hefty rocks. The two men built the sweat lodge fire, piling the stones high on a wooden foundation.

"I don't like the idea of my son seeing a head shrinker. He looks worse off to me," grumbled Larry. He thrust dry sticks around the pile of stones.

Hawk didn't say anything.

"I mean, what does this Schwartz guy know about my son? He's Jewish, not Indian. The boy needs to see a traditional healer."

"There's a Lakota ceremony."

"Yes?" Larry was interested.

"To help bring back a soul that has been stolen. . . ."

"Can you do it?" Larry interrupted him.

Hawk added more wood to the fire. "I don't know how to do it. I've never seen this ceremony. But there are men at Pine Ridge who know how. . . ."

"Forget it, Hawk. Lucy wouldn't allow it. She's committed to trying the white man's way." Larry threw up his hands.

Hawk began to chuckle.

"What's so funny?" Larry was surprised by Hawk's reaction.

"Irish-American, Lakota, Jewish—it's all the same."

"What do you mean?"

Hawk grinned. "At home man protests, but woman rules."

* * * *

Stanley Schwartz met alone with Gertrude Gold. "The boy is making progress," he reported. "I don't yet understand who this hitchhiker is."

"Could it be Adam?" Gertrude smiled. "Could this be how the kidnaping began?"

"You mean, did the boy innocently thumb a ride toward home and end up in hell?"

Gertrude let Stanley work out his own ideas.

Stanley shrugged his shoulders. "Why did he fixate on an adult male when we were outside? How can I find out the identity of the hitchhiker, whether it's Adam or someone else?"

"It's simple," answered Gertrude. "Ask."

"But he still won't talk to me."

"Ach, Stanley, you know better than that. The boy is talking all the time. It's just that you don't listen. It's not safe for him to speak aloud, but perhaps it is okay for him to write."

Of course, thought Stanley.

"In the world of magic, one must maneuver around the literal truth," Gertrude said.

"I don't understand," said Stanley, feeling quite stupid. "Magic?"

"Stanley, you've forgotten. What did that boy write on the bathroom wall with his own excrement?"

"Some letters."

"But what letters, Stanley?"

He bowed his head a moment, trying to recall. "N-A-T-A-S, I think."

Gertrude tossed him a pen and blank piece of paper. "Write those letters down in that order."

Stanley did as he was told.

"Now go to the mirror over there on the wall and hold up the paper."

Stanley ambled to the wall and read the words in the mirror. "Oh, my God," he uttered.

"Precisely," Gertrude answered.

* * * *

The first round of the sweat lodge ceremony had been hot and fast. Hawk had situated Adam in the back of the lodge while he and Larry sat by the door. The boy had not resisted their instructions to sweat with them; they hadn't given him any choice about the matter. During the first round he kept his silence but the two men could hear his physical restlessness. When the door came up and the steam had escaped, long red welts emerged upon the boy's forearm.

"Did you scratch yourself?" Larry asked.

The answer was obvious as the boy continued to dig his fingernails into the palms of his hands.

During the second round Larry prayed long and hard for the recovery and well-being of his son. When it came time for Adam to pray, not a word ushered forth. After a long interval, Hawk said, "Mitakuye oyas'in." He then prayed for the young man to open himself to the healing energies of the Grandfathers and the Grandmother. "The Good Spirits are all around you, Adam, and you are safe in here."

"Errrr, rrrrr, arrrr, urrr." The growling of a wild animal rose from the boy's throat; anger, torment, hate, and threat issued forth as if the boy were transforming into something that wasn't human.

"Larry, sing," Hawk commanded, throwing more water upon the stones. "Grandfathers, look at this child. Help him."

The heat rose, prickled, and stung their faces and bodies. They could hear the boy scrabbling on the ground, hiding under his towel.

"Errrrrrrrrrr." Muffled, the pitch wobbled from fierce to fearful until it resembled the whine of a frightened puppy.

And still Hawk applied water to the stones, letting the Stone People reach into the boy and purify him in the excruciatingly hot steam. Only when the sounds had turned to silence did Hawk finally release into "Mitakuye oyas'in." The door opened and the heat tumbled out into the night air.

Under the tent of his towel, Adam whimpered ever so lightly. When the water jug was passed to him, he poured the cool water all over his head and body; little clouds of steam lifted off his bare chest.

"Phew, I didn't know if I were going to survive the heat," exclaimed Larry.

But Hawk didn't answer. Already, he was somewhere else. In the lodge, yes. But in the world of his Spirit Helpers too. The third round, the Pipe round, was when he would summon all the medicine help he could get for his little cousin.

He knew that the Evil Spirits could not enter the lodge because he had taken precautions. But the sounds that had come from the boy had shaken him deeply, as if the boy were possessed by an inhuman force that had entangled the boy's spirit and was slowly strangling what was left. Behind all the ferocity of the growl he also heard the desperate voice of a trapped child.

Hawk didn't know what was going to happen in the third round. When the door came down, he gave thanks for the Pipes on the buffalo altar.

Hawk was surprised that, when he looked up in the dark of the lodge, he could see a young man sitting next to the boy. Neither Larry nor Adam had the sight to pierce the darkness; they were unaware of any such visitor.

"Ah hau," said Hawk in greeting. He did not recognize the young man.

The dark-haired visitor was about twenty, clean shaven, and dressed in jeans and an old shirt. He looked like a Mexican. His face was relaxed, peaceful.

"Tell him," the young man addressed Hawk, while nodding at Adam, "that I finally arrived. Tell him it wasn't his fault."

Hawk waited for more but the young man sat there, quietly expectant.

"Adam Stands-By-Dog, there is a man here who has a message for you."

Adam's head jerked up.

Hawk continued, "The man says that he has arrived. That it wasn't your fault."

Adam cocked his head and looked all around him but could see no one in the enveloping darkness of the sweat lodge. He began to shake his head no, in disbelief, in disavowal.

"You must give him a sign," said Hawk to the Mexican.

"Tell him to remember my name." The man began to fade at the edges and then totally disappeared.

"He says that you must remember his name."

Adam sat up straight, gulped air, and frantically searched the darkness.

"He's arrived, Stands-By-Dog. It's not your fault and you will remember his name," repeated Hawk. Knowing that strength flows from a positive vision, Hawk had altered the "must" to "will."

The boy exhaled deeply.

When the inipi ceremony was over and the Pipes had been smoked, the three of them exited the lodge. Adam emerged looking all about him in awe as if seeing the world fresh and new. Despite being wrapped in a dripping wet towel, he approached his mother, threw his arms around her, and gave her a big hug.

The dim amber light of the outside fire flared, briefly illuminating the boy's chest. The word "*LIVE*" descended in red bloody scratches from his neck to the navel.

∗   ∗   ∗   ∗

"He's dead, Hawk." Meggie's voice sounded flat, devoid of emotion, on the telephone.

"I should be there with you." Hawk experienced a rare moment of guilt.

"No, there are too many people here as it is."

"How's your Mom doing?" Hawk hated being away from Meggie.

"As expected. Tearful, lonely. She wants Dad back. He went so fast. How can you ever be ready for that to happen? For him, it was quick and soon over; he wouldn't have done well suffering a long-term illness. At the end, he was surrounded by family and love. He didn't die in a sterile hospital room."

"Was it a peaceful death?' Hawk asked.

The fierce old man had always denounced the idea of life after death, saying, "After death comes nothingness. Make the most out of this life, because that's all there is. Anything else is conjured out of superstition."

Meggie began to cry. "Right before Dad died, he told me that he wasn't scared to go, but he didn't want to leave Mom. They'd been together for such a long time. I promised him I would look after her."

"Tell her to come live with us, Meggie. I mean it." It would require an adjustment, but Hawk loved the old woman. "It would be an honor for us to have her."

"I'll tell her, but she's pretty independent. She wants you to do the burial ceremony. After a memorial service here, we'll bring his ashes to Chrysalis. Mom said she'll stay for the week, then it's back home for her. She's got to figure out what to do for the rest of her life."

"Of course I'll do the ceremony. Will your father be offended if I mention the Creator?"

Meggie sopped up her tears and started laughing. "If you say 'Wakan Tanka' instead of 'God,' it'll be okay. He doesn't know Lakota."

Hawk paused. "Adam sweated tonight." He thought Meggie would like to know.

"Did you clear that with Schwartz?" She sounded anxious.

Hawk felt a rising irritation. "No. He does his thing, but this is my territory."

Momentarily Meggie deflected away from his annoyance. "How did Adam respond to close confinement?"

"Real good." Hawk decided not to go into any detail. It was hard enough to bridge two separate cultures without the gaps of long distance communication.

"Hawk, promise me one thing."

"What?"

"Tell Stanley Schwartz what happened in the sweat lodge."

At first hesitant, Hawk waffled. "He may not understand."

Meggie insisted. "If we don't try to paddle in the same direction, how can we expect Adam ever to find his way home?"

Hawk laughed. "Okay, Two-Canoes. You win."

FORTY-ONE

POWERFUL STORIES

Brother! Our seats were once large, and yours were very small. You have now become a great people, and we have scarcely a place left to spread our blankets. You have got our country, but you are not satisfied. You want to force your religion upon us. . . .

Brother! The Great Spirit has made us all. But he has made a great difference between his white and red children. He has given us a different complexion and different customs. . . .

Brother! We do not wish to destroy your religion, or to take it from you. We only want to enjoy our own.

—RED JACKET, 1792
Brother, the Great Spirit Has Made Us All

"I *need* to talk to you, alone, for a few minutes," Hawk informed Stanley in the waiting room of the clinic. He stood there fingering the brim of his hat, obviously uncomfortable.

Seemingly disinterested, Adam plopped himself down on a couch and picked up a sports magazine.

Stanley closed his office door. "How was it after our last session?"

Hawk shook his head. "Not good."

"I thought it might be rough. But I want you to understand something about the nature of psychotherapy, Mr. Spelman. Therapy isn't a smooth process. More like two steps forward and then one step back."

"Meggie told me to speak to you."

"It's good to consult with each other. I can't share the details of what happens in the session. That's confidential."

"No, that's not it. She said you needed to know about the inipi ceremony."

"What?"

"Sweat lodge," Hawk explained. "I put the boy into the sweat lodge the other night."

Stanley sat down and gestured for Hawk to do the same. "Go on," he urged.

"The inipi is the oldest religious ceremony on this continent. It's our way of purifying ourselves." Hawk looked briefly at the therapist who was intently listening.

Hawk continued. "When the water pourer knows how, he can travel between the worlds. He can see things others can't see. He can hear the voices of the Spirits. He can use himself so that the healing energies of the Grandfather and the Grandmother can flow through him, like a pipe, like a hollow bone."

"Yes," encouraged Stanley, leaning forward.

"The other night, a man appeared in the sweat lodge, a young Latino."

"Appeared?" Stanley asked.

"He was a Spirit," Hawk explained. "Adam and his father could not see him."

"But you could?"

Hawk nodded.

"What did he have to say?" Stanley suspended his disbelief.

"That he had arrived. That Adam was not to blame."

"Arrived where? Blamed for what?"

Hawk shrugged his shoulders. "Many times the Spirits tell me things I don't understand. But it makes sense to the intended person."

"Was there anything else that the man said?"

Hawk nodded. "That Adam needed to remember his name."

"Whose name? The boy's own name?" Stanley pushed.

"No," answered Hawk. "Adam should remember the man's name."

"And who was he?" Stanley asked.

Once again, Hawk shrugged his shoulders, then stood up to leave. "I don't know," he said.

But I have an idea, thought Stanley.

"Ask" was what Gertrude Gold had suggested. And now, Mr. Slade Spelman had given Stanley Schwartz an unexpected opportunity. On the way back to the waiting room, Hawk had mentioned the writing on Adam's belly.

"I'm ready for you, Adam," Stanley announced, already plotting out the session.

No sooner was Adam inside Stanley's office than the therapist thrust a yellow legal pad and ballpoint pen into his hands. "Your guardian told me that you were in a sweat lodge ceremony the other night."

The boy's eyes were clear and bright, a distinct difference from last time.

Stanley continued. "A young man came into the lodge, a spirit, and he wanted you to know that he was okay and that whatever happened, between you, around you both, that it wasn't your fault." Stanley hoped that his elaborations would fuel some associations for the boy.

So far, he could tell from the boy's responsive gaze that he was on track. Stanley added, "But there is always a price to pay for such reassurance. You are to remember his name, yes?"

The boy briefly looked away.

"You owe him that," Stanley pushed.

Adam looked sideways at the therapist.

"He has a name, but I don't want you to tell me his name," Stanley instructed.

Puzzled, Adam cocked his head.

Stanley knew that he had to allow for the expression of the boy's defenses. So be it: The name would not be spoken.

"Instead, I want you to *write* his name," Stanley said, "on that pad of paper."

The boy studied the yellow sheet but the hand that held the pen did not move. Frustration buckled his eyebrows and tightened his lips.

"Do you remember the man?" Stanley probed.

Adam nodded.

"Was he there with you during the week of Easter?"

Again, Adam nodded.

"Can you remember his name?"

Adam's face scrunched into fierce concentration until he let out a loud sigh, shaking his head *no*.

"I'll help you to remember then."

The boy looked at Stanley as if the therapist were a magician about to pull a rabbit from a hat.

"You know his name, Adam, but you've forgotten. So, it's simply a matter of my helping you to retrieve it. Now, close your eyes and lean back in the chair."

Adam did as he was told.

Good, thought Stanley, *the boy is fully cooperating.*

"I want you to visualize a place that is very soothing, safe for you. It may be inside a house. It may be outside, where you can hear the birds overhead, smell the pines and cedar, and feel the warm sun on your shoulders. And everything in you is beginning to relax. Slowly, I'm going to count down from twenty to one, and as I do so, you will find yourself growing more and more sleepy, more and more relaxed. Twenty. Re...lax. Going deeper down. Nineteen and re...lax..."

The lulling quality to Stanley's voice gently coaxed Adam into a more fluid state of mind. When Adam's eyes twitched behind closed eyelids, Stanley knew that the boy had slipped deep into hypnotic trance. The therapist's voice rhythmically rose and fell, paralleling the movement of the boy's chest.

"You will be able to indicate *yes* to me by lifting your right index finger and *no* by raising your left index finger." Stanley tapped the boy's two fingers. He put Adam through a quick series of discrimination tasks.

"Are you Adam Arbre?"

The right finger raised.

"Are you four years old?"

The left finger rose.

"And when you need to stop my questions and come back awake into the room, you can raise all the fingers on your right hand. Do you understand that?" Stanley had to give the boy an escape route.

The right finger raised.

"Good. Now I want you to see that young man who came into the sweat lodge, the one who was with you during Easter week. Take your time."

Stanley waited for a minute. "Do you see him?

The right finger raised.

"Good. Now he is going to lean over and whisper his name into your ear and I want you to pay special attention." Again, Stanley waited a minute. "Did he tell you his name?"

The right finger flashed.

"Good. You are doing what he asked you to do. Now, I want you to repeat that name, again and again, to yourself, so that you will not forget it."

With great agitation, Adam's right index finger began to jab the side of the chair. Stanley waited.

Suddenly the whole right hand jerked up and Stanley spoke in an authoritative voice. "Okay, you are ready to leave that scene. You now know the man's name and you will be able to write it down when your eyes open. Upon the count of five, you will come back into this room, *safe*, with that name in your mind. And you will write that name down on the paper. One, two, three—your eyes are beginning to open now." Stanley's voice grew louder. "Four, coming into this room, and five, your eyes are now fully open."

Adam looked around, dazed and disoriented. Then, without a word, he picked up the pen, closed his eyes, and scribbled in large letters:

S   U   S   E   J

Adam threw the pen and paper onto the floor. Stanley paid no attention to the paper or what was written on it. Instead, he concentrated on the boy.

"You're back in the therapy room with me. You're okay. You worked hard this hour, Adam."

The boy's eyes blinked open.

It wasn't until Adam had departed that Stanley picked up the paper and held it up to the mirror.

"Jesus," he said.

Jesus? he wondered. He didn't have the slightest idea what it meant.

∗   ∗   ∗   ∗

After the memorial service, Meggie flew back to Traverse City from the East Coast. In the two days before family members followed, she seized the opportunity to meet with Stanley Schwartz and Gertrude Gold.

"Catch me up on the therapy," was her first request.

Stanley laughed. "I told your husband that I couldn't share the therapy information with him, that it was confidential."

Meggie nodded. She knew that what the three of them were doing was not strictly ethical, as Hawk was the boy's guardian. But that was what Gertrude was for, to help set the boundaries, to let her know what she could share with Hawk and what she couldn't.

"Summarize, don't go into detail," Meggie suggested, but she was simply skating around the issue of confidentiality.

"What do you need to know?" asked Gertrude.

"What to expect from Adam. What issues to work on," Meggie answered.

"But Stanley is the therapist here," Gertrude gently chided her. "We must focus on what Stanley needs to know—about the boy, about how to approach the problems in the treatment."

Meggie chafed at being placed in an ancillary position. "Okay, I'll back off with my questions. But I have a question for you, Dr. Gold."

"Yes?"

"Why did you tell me that it was an advantage that Stanley wasn't a Christian?"

Stanley's ears perked up. He hadn't heard anything about this conversation.

Gertrude's eyes smiled, "I was wondering when you would ask me about that. I think it time that Stanley discuss the mirror writing." She backed her wheelchair away from the table and rolled it toward a large easel by the wall. On the top sheet of paper, Gertrude wrote NATAS, SUSEJ, LIVE.

"These are all words that Adam has written, in one medium or another," Stanley explained. "And if you read them backwards, you have SATAN, JESUS, and EVIL. Our thinking is that Adam was not abducted by a simple pedophile."

Meggie studied the backward words, trying to understand what Stanley was saying.

"Oh my God." It suddenly hit her full force.

"Yes," echoed Gertrude. "It is much worse than a simple kidnaping and rape."

"But why the backward writing?" Meggie was out of her league here.

"Because," said Gertrude, "the Black Mass is the reversal of the Christian Mass, the mirror image of it. And without a Christian God, you cannot have the Satanic ceremonies. Historically, Satanism began as a form of protest in response to persecution by the medieval Christian churches. Later, it developed into a true worship of evil forces."

"But why would anyone want to worship evil?" Meggie was confused.

Gertrude was growing impatient. She rolled back a long sleeve revealing a tattooed number on her arm. "For the very reason that evil exists in every generation, Dr. O'Connor. Sometimes you Americans like to pat yourself on the back and say that evil only flourished in Germany during the Holocaust, but evil is alive and well in this country today."

She held up her unsheathed arm. "When I was an adolescent, the Nazis prided themselves on being a cultured, superior race of human beings; they branded me with this number."

A concentration camp number. Meggie was speechless, stunned by Dr. Gold's revelation.

"They wanted something so badly that they were willing to slaughter family after family to get it. The wish for absolute power over others is at the root of all evil." Gertrude pulled down her sleeve and rolled back toward the table. "But the people who love power have to first tell the story—about how strong they are, how weak and defective are their enemies. And only when they win over the imagination of others can they begin to carry out their pursuit of evil. You see, Dr. O'Connor, I know the power of story well. It can be used for healing and it can be used for sheer destruction."

"But Adam isn't a Christian," Meggie observed.

"Lucky for him! With a Jewish therapist and an Indian healer, we have a real chance. But we don't know what he has been told."

"A chance?" Meggie wasn't quite sure what the old woman meant.

"An opportunity to retrieve the boy from the Satanic story." Gertrude's right hand mimicked a yanking motion.

Stanley smiled. "Your husband and I are the flanking forces."

"I don't understand," said Meggie.

Gertrude tried once more with Meggie. "Most likely, the story told to Adam by his kidnappers was of the great war between the Christian

God and Satan. These Satanic cults like to use confusion, pain, and terror as brainwashing methods to convince people that Satan will be victorious. To ally with Satan is to join the most powerful one. They're prepared for others to apply exorcisms and Christian teachings to their Satanic converts; that is the struggle they expect their converts to fight. But, you know, Yahweh and . . ." Gertrude searched for the right name.

"Wakan Tanka," Meggie interrupted.

"Are not part of their story. So, you see, Dr. O'Connor, we refuse to do battle on their territory."

"But he's safe now, no longer around those people," Meggie protested.

"No," Dr. Gold barked. "He'll never be safe as long as his brain believes what they've taught him. I worry more about the rape of his mind than that of his body. It is fear that has tied his tongue in knots."

"So we have to reeducate him and surround him with love." Meggie was trying to put it all together.

"Now you are beginning to understand," Gertrude said. "And what about the power of story?"

Meggie took her time, summarizing what she had learned: "Adam's got one story firmly in place: The story of Evil defeating Good. Because of what happened, what they did to him, he's terribly frightened. His sense of self is compromised, contaminated. He believes their Satanic teachings. And we don't know the details of the kidnappers' story or the particulars of Adam's experience. Only he can tell us."

Gertrude's face softened. "You can't simply put up one story against another without knowing Adam's experience. There are always booby traps when you wander about in an unknown landscape."

"And he has to describe that terrible week, what happened day by day," Meggie continued. "That will be very difficult for him, won't it?"

Gertrude nodded, compassion underlining her words. "He has to tell us of the pain, the terror, and of his sense of guilt. The Satanists use one of the oldest ploys in the world—involving people in the sacrificial ceremonies, making them accomplices to the deed, and convincing them that evil is really for the greater good. They turn logic upside down. Good is bad and bad is good."

Stanley spoke. "He has to tell us the whole story."

"That's where you come in," Meggie said. "But what do I then tell Adam, to give him hope, to promise him a world of compassion, meaning, laughter, and joy?"

Gertrude leaned forward over the table, her eyes dancing with fire. "Why, it is the very story your husband is already telling him."

The Chanunpa Wakan. Yes. Meggie now understood the supervisory direction of Dr. Gertrude Gold. Adam would spill out the bloody guts of the story to Stanley Schwartz, leaving behind the entrails in the therapist's office, and then, protected by the Sacred Pipe, stride out of the clinic into Hawk's story: The Lakota world of Good Spirits, Trickster Spirits, and Evil Spirits. One disgusting, perverted, power-hungry world-view shattering under the power of love and the promise of the Pipe.

Meggie studied the uncompromisingly sharp features of Gertrude Gold, her arms and upper body gesticulating and full of rapid fire energy, her lower body paralyzed and rooted to the metal wheelchair, her powdered face wrinkled like a dried apricot, her flaming orange-red hair expertly coifed, the elegant, long-sleeved blouse hiding the ugly stain of evil, a Jewish woman promoting a Lakota solution. Gertrude Gold was definitely a woman of contradictions.

An absolutely brilliant woman, judged Meggie.

FORTY-TWO

IN ABSENTIA

*I learned that night that love is never as ferocious as when you think
it is going to leave you. We are not always allowed this knowledge,
and so our love sometimes becomes retrospective."*

—ANITA SHREVE
The Weight of Water

Hawk circled the eagle wing above the grave of Meggie's father.
"Grandfathers, I ask that you watch over this man who has completed
his earthwalk. He now makes his way across to the Other Side. We wish
him a good journey."

The old woman, Meggie's mother, stood erect, bracing herself
against her grief. She firmly held the hands of her two granddaughters
but the muscles in her face drooped with fatigue, resignation, and sadness. The well of tears had gone dry from a week of crying.

Meggie had been too busy organizing the ceremony, making beds,
arranging for transportation and lodging for the arrival of family
relatives to grieve. She had only been able to squeeze in one day of psychotherapy for her most desperate clients. At the graveside, time suddenly lurched and slowed; her father's death could no longer be denied.

As much as she tried to stem the tide and dam the flow, the tears
began to trickle and then stream down her face. Her older sister moved

to her side, passed her a tissue, and grabbed her right hand. They cried together.

During the ceremony, Hawk recounted the man's life in the milestones of the heart—his devotion to his wife, his love for his children, the keen intellect that nurtured many a physician in training, the curiosity that drove his research, the sense of humor evidenced in his medical writings.

Meggie's mind protested. *Snapshot words. What can they say about a life long lived? About the joy of discovery in childhood, the shyness of adolescence, the disciplined years of education, the wonder of passion, the creation of marriage, the diversionary dreams and babies that rudely intruded, the years of solid collegiality and spontaneous family outings, the magical, summer visits to Chrysalis, the final launching of offspring, and the inevitable yielding to the forces of old age?*

Her tears refused to stop. Her sister's hand tightened its grip but Meggie felt that nothing would bring her comfort. Nothing would fill the hole of a parent's passing.

A sweaty palm picked up her free hand and held it. Her head turned. To her surprise, it was Adam.

*   *   *   *

"I'm ready to talk now," Daisy said. "But only to the young guy."

Jillian rolled her eyes. Nevertheless, she pulled out the investigator's card and dialed the number. A meeting was arranged for later that afternoon.

"Just answer his questions directly. Flirting isn't necessary," Jillian advised.

That afternoon, Daisy warned the officer, "It ain't really what I got to tell you. It's what I got to show you. But I'm not going back home without you being there."

"Why?" he asked.

"'Cuz my Dad might be there. And I don't mess none with him."

"Are you afraid of him?"

"Shit, yes! And you should be too. If he's there and takes a notion he don't like you none, and if he's been drinking, he'd just as soon shoot you as shake your hand."

Before easing into his car, the officer checked his revolver to make sure it was fully loaded. "I don't want any trouble with him but it's better to be prepared," he explained.

Daisy flopped down onto the passenger seat, her skirt riding up her thighs.

He couldn't help noticing that she was wearing make-up and smelled faintly of violets.

"You married?" she asked. There was no ring on his finger.

"Nope." He started up the car and pulled into the street.

"Engaged?'

He shook his head. "What are we looking for?" he asked.

But Daisy wouldn't be deterred. "Involved with someone special?"

"Hey, I'm supposed to be the one who does the interrogation." He turned his head and smiled at her. She was fingering a lock of hair. They locked eyes on each other.

"You do have something to show me, don't you?" A little hint of suspicion crept into his voice.

Daisy pointed a finger, "Take a left up there. The driveway is the third one on the right."

He swung the car onto Daisy's street then into the rutted dirt driveway. To his relief, there wasn't any car parked out front of the weathered gray house. "Doesn't appear that your Dad is at home."

Daisy checked her watch and snorted. "He's probably at Dick's Pour House, drinking. Come on." She jumped out of the car and mounted the porch steps. Daisy put her shoulder against the front door and shoved it open.

The house was filthy. Empty beer cans and loaded ash trays littered the small living room. A faint, cloying smell of decaying garbage hung in the air. Dirty dishes wallowed in kitchen sink water. "What a filthy pig," Daisy exclaimed, holding her nose.

The officer did a quick walk-through, making sure no one else was in the house. "Okay, he's definitely not here. What did you want to show me?"

Daisy led the way into her parents' bedroom. The bed sheets were in a tumble and they had to step over jumbled piles of clothing on the floor to reach the closet. "In there," Daisy pointed.

The officer peered into the dark closet. "What am I looking for?"

"A black box," Daisy said. "Underneath her dresses."

The man bent over and reached into the back of the closet, fumbling around for a box. "I can't feel anything," he said.

"I'll help you." She eased her body into the closet next to his and bent down, brushing against him. "There, I think I've got it," she exclaimed.

As she dragged the box out, he reached into the darkness to help her. They pulled out a black trunk.

"It's locked."

Daisy reached up onto the overhead rack, her fingers searching for the key. Her blouse rode up high, exposing a brief flash of white skin.

"It's warm in here," he said.

"I found it." She extracted a key from under a pile of clothing.

A large key for a large clasp.

"It'll open. It's just the right size," she reassured him. She handed him the key.

Sure enough, the old lock sprung on the first try. Slowly, he pried open the wooden lid and knelt down to examine the contents. "What is this stuff?" From the box, he pulled out a dented silver chalice and silver plate, a voluminous and dusty black robe adorned with red designs, a torn black cloth, ziplocked bags of white powder, two sharp daggers, some rusty razor blades, a chipped ornamental sword, a dog-eared book titled *Magick in Theory and Practice*, a broken crucifix, and stubby, melted black candles.

"Creepy, isn't it?" Daisy backed away from the trunk, her voice sounding almost childlike in pitched fear.

Puzzled, the officer looked up at her and ordered, "Tell me what this is all about."

"Do I have to spell it out for you?" Daisy sounded incredulous.

"Your Mom a witch?" he asked.

"No, she's a priestess."

"A priestess?" He turned back to examine the trunk's treasure.

"Look, I ain't getting any closer to all that stuff. You still don't get it, do you? I thought you FBI guys knew everything." Daisy was astonished.

He began to sound irritated. "Why don't you just tell me what you know."

Daisy threw up her hands. "My Mom is a priestess in a Satanic cult."

"Satanic cult? You've been watching too much television."

Suddenly, he didn't seem so cute anymore. "You don't believe me, do you?"

"Look," he said, "we're always getting reports about Satanic cults. We investigate them and not once have we ever been able to find evidence that they exist except in the imagination of unbalanced people. So, I suspect that your Mom is playing around with some of the wiccan earth religions. They're pretty harmless. But, hey, I'll look into it." He smiled condescendingly.

What an asshole, thought Daisy. "They kidnap children."

His head jerked up.

Now he's beginning to get the picture. "For their special ceremonies. Like on Halloween. Or Easter," she added.

"Do you know this for a fact?" The condescension in his voice vanished.

"Yes."

"Will you tell me more about it?" He was listening to her now.

"No." She smiled.

"But . . ." he started to protest.

She cut him off. "I'll talk only to your partner." *At least he'll pay attention.*

He shrugged his shoulders, acknowledging that he had blown it. "Okay. Help me carry this trunk to the car."

Together, they hauled the box outside. On the whole way back to town, they rode in silence. Daisy stared out the window, her skirt primly covering her knees, her mouth set into the quiet fury of a teenager scorned.

* * * *

Meggie marveled at how her mother set out to win over Adam's heart. From the back closet, she retrieved old and musty games that Meggie had not seen since childhood—a marbled mahjong set, a wooden maze with silver ball, puzzles of ancient castles, and a stereopticon with doubled postcards. They played games at night after Hawk and Adam had worked on stringing barbed wire to the fence.

"He's a good boy," the old woman observed.

Meggie was pleased that Adam was no longer self-mutilating or performing bizarre acts that would tarnish his image with her mother.

"When are you going to have your own children, Meggie? Time is working against you," her mother cautioned.

"Mom, don't," Meggie pleaded. "We want children, but so far it hasn't happened."

Ever the pragmatist, her mother added, "Well, you can always adopt."

Meggie smiled as Adam entered the room. "But I already have, Mom."

The old woman shook her head in consternation. "No, Meggie. Someday you have to give him back."

When her mother left the following week, a hole opened up in Meggie's heart. As long as both parents had been alive, Meggie was still able to claim a portion of childhood. Her mother was right. Adam was a temporary stopgap. She loved him dearly but he would never belong to her. And, since that miscarriage, there had been no pregnancies. She realized that maybe her body was simply moving into aging infertility. But she wasn't willing to call it quits yet on having her own child. The gynecologist had suggested that she and Hawk return for tests.

When her menstruation came cycling back in the month of August, Meggie took only the terrier with her to the south knoll at dusk to watch the sunset. She went alone, not because Hawk would be deaf to her grief, but because she was ashamed of her melancholy.

The dropping sun backlit the dark blue clouds and rimmed them with gold filament. Bringing her knees up to her chin, she hugged her legs, watching the colors of the western horizon transform from blue-bland to brilliant, from day-pastel to dusk-fire.

The grass rustled. Fritzie barked a warning.

Out in the clearing came Adam. After close examination of her face, he sat down beside her, cross-legged.

"I've been crying," Meggie confessed.

The boy picked up a blade of grass and held it into the light breeze. It swayed in a circle.

"I miss my dad," she said, looking off again at the dying sun.

"I miss my grandma," he whispered into the wind.

FORTY-THREE

GETTING READY

*If one looks at something evil, Plato once said, something evil
falls into one's own soul. One cannot look at evil without something
in oneself being aroused in response to it, because evil is an archetype
and every archetype has an infectious impact upon people.*

—MARIE-LOUISE VON FRANZ
Shadow and Evil in Fairytales

The next morning, Hawk took the boy out to the water's edge. Only
this time, he didn't bring his Chanunpa Wakan. Instead, he had wrapped
Adam's pipe in a blanket with sage, matches, turtle shell bowl, and
tobacco.

"We are going to pray with *your* pipe this morning," he announced.

Adam looked surprised.

"Once cleaned with the sage smoke, this pipe is as good as any
Chanunpa for praying." Hawk handed the bundle to the boy and sat
down on the ground.

Adam stood there as if confused, not knowing what next to do. Hawk
signaled with his hand that the boy should kneel down and open the
blanket.

Adam understood the seriousness of this occasion. Hawk was asking
him to be a full participant in the pipe ceremony. He knelt down, kicked
off his sneakers, and unwrapped his pipe. Hawk pointed to the sage and
the turtle bowl.

"First, we must cleanse ourselves before handling the pipe. Then you must put the pipe together and pass it through the sage smoke." Hawk began to strip the leaves and roll them into a tight ball. He placed the matches into Adam's hand.

Adam knew what to do next. He lit the ball of sage and fanned the smoke around himself. Holding the turtle shell, he smudged his cousin, Hawk. Then he reached into the pipe bag and pulled out the salmon-colored pipestone bowl and stem.

"The bowl is woman; its red stone is the color of our people. The stem is man. When you put the two of them together, you have all of Creation in your hands," Hawk said.

Adam assembled his pipe and wafted it through the smoke spiraling up from the turtle bowl. With his left hand clasping the bowl towards his heart, stem upward toward the heavens, Adam's right hand reached into a pouch for a pinch of tobacco.

"Offer the tobacco first to Wakan Tanka, the Great Mystery," ordered Hawk.

Adam's hand circled. His lips moved in prayer but Hawk could not hear any sound.

Next, Adam offered the tobacco to the Grandfathers of the west, the north, the east, and the south, each time holding up the tobacco with his hand and silently praying.

The sixth pinch of tobacco was for Wakan Tanka—the Sky Beings and all that made up the heavens. The seventh pinch was for Unci Maka—Grandmother Earth. Adam reached down and touched the ground with the tobacco before sprinkling it into the bowl.

"And the last tobacco is for Wanbli Gleska, the spotted eagle, who wings these prayers to Wakan Tanka," instructed Hawk.

At last, the pipe was loaded. Adam offered it to the sky and to the ground and handed it to his cousin.

"Mitakuye oyas'in," the boy murmured.

Hawk smiled, took the pipe, and held it up, his forehead briefly touching the bowl.

"Grandfather, we ask that you see this chanunpa and recognize it as the pipe of Adam Stands-By-Dog. My little cousin here is in need of Your help. Bad things were done to him by bad people. Grandfather, it has left him all confused about what is right, what is good. With this pipe, I ask you to look inside of him, help clear his head and his heart, so that he may know what is true and what is false."

Adam bowed his head but kept his eyes open.

Hawk continued. "The first one to teach him the way of our people was my teacher—Grandmother Winona. I will now tell Adam what his grandmother told me. I would not ordinarily do this for someone of such a young age, but he needs to hear it."

That piqued Adam's interest. His head jerked up.

Hawk held the pipe in a strong, steady grip, his eyes straight ahead. "There are Good Spirits who come to help us when we pray and do things right. We call out to Them with the Chanunpa, with our medicine, with our inipi ceremonies. We recognize and honor Them with our songs and ceremonies. They teach us what we need to know to live as human beings."

Hawk's eyes scanned the skies. "There are the Trickster Spirits. They are many. Sometimes They play cruel jokes on us when we get swollen up in our own importance. When we forget that we are just two-leggeds in a world of four-leggeds, fins, wings, and crawling things. They also come to instruct us, though their teachings are hard and humbling. When They laugh at us, They teach us to laugh at ourselves. Their tricks help bring us back into balance. *If* we pay attention."

Adam grinned, for he had heard many a story of Old Man Coyote, Rabbit, and Iktomi, the spider-like creature who even fools the Evil Ones.

Hawk's face turned somber and dark. "And then there are the Evil Spirits. There is an evil Wakan Tanka who was created out of the good Wakan Tanka."

Adam sat back on his heels. No one had ever mentioned such a Being before to him.

Hawk continued. "Wakan Tanka understood that the two-leggeds had to choose whether to serve Him or not. Therefore the two-leggeds needed the evil Wakan Tanka."

Adam looked puzzled.

In a softer voice, Hawk explained. "In the beginning was *Inyan* whose spirit is Wakan Tanka. Inyan had no shape; his blood was blue. He created a mass with no beyond and called it *Maka* and gave it a spirit, *Maka-akan*. But that effort took so much out of him that he became hard rock and his blood formed the oceans. There was a further division of energy and the heavens, *Skan*, formed above Maka. Of the two children of Inyan, one was very evil, called *Iya* because he made love with his mother, *Unk*. Iya is the chief of all evil beings. There are many stories of what happened at the beginning, a long time before the two-leggeds were ever created."

Adam paid close attention.

"What is important for you to know, Adam Stands-By-Dog, is that there is good and there is evil in this world. There is also something else; Anglos call it perversity. There are people who do things that hurt other people not because they intend to hurt others but because they want something. They are blind; they do not see what happens when they do these things. The perverse ones have forgotten how to be human beings."

Hawk swallowed. It was unlike him to give such a long speech. "But you also need to know, Adam Stands-By-Dog, that there are truly evil people and Evil Beings. Hurting others is part of their plan. It is the Pipe which helps to protect us from these people, these Beings, these influences. It is the Pipe you must hold when you find yourself getting hurt, out of balance. It is the Pipe which will protect you and bring you back home."

Hawk held up Adam's chanunpa. "I have spoken the words of my teacher, Winona Pathfinder. I ask you, the Grandfathers, to help my little cousin to take in these words and to find the truth in them. Mitakuye oyas'in." He offered the pipe to the sky and to the earth and passed it back to Adam.

Adam lifted the chanunpa and uttered four words: "Wakan Tanka, help me." He then lowered the pipe and brought the stem toward his mouth.

Hawk said, "Mitakuye oyas'in" and, lighting a match, reached over and touched the flame to the bowl's tobacco. Adam sucked on the pipe; the tobacco began to smoulder. Remembering the instructions from his grandmother and Hawk, Adam took four puffs and raised the pipe to Wakan Tanka. Then, with other puffs, he offered the pipe to All the Directions before passing it to Hawk.

When the pipe ceremony was over, the pipe smoked and back in its bag, the bundle rolled and secured with thongs, the two of them stood up and looked eastward.

Hawk placed his hand on the boy's shoulder. A sweet smile crossed the boy's face as the sun's rays anointed their faces with the gold dust of early morn.

*   *   *   *

"He talked to me. Then he spoke in front of my husband," Meggie exclaimed in her morning meeting with Stanley Schwartz and Gertrude Gold. Both were immensely pleased by the good news.

"We're on the right track," Dr. Gold enthused.

"What did he say?" Stanley was dying of curiosity.

"He told me that he missed his grandmother, Winona Pathfinder."

"The one who died in unusual circumstances?" Stanley was trying to be diplomatic.

"It wasn't a suicide, believe me," said Meggie. "Someday I'll tell you all about it. What's important is how much she meant to Adam, not only before she died but afterwards. She was the one to tell him the stories of her Lakota people. She gave him a sense of belonging, of pride in being Indian."

"Didn't Adam claim to have seen his grandmother on several occasions after she had died?" Stanley was picking his words carefully in front of Dr. Gold.

Meggie nodded. "He was the only one who could see her."

Dr. Gold interrupted. "She's the power person in his life."

"'Power person?'" Meggie didn't know what she meant.

"In everybody's life there are certain people who exert incredible influence on that person. It sounds like this Winona, the grandmother, is one such person in Adam Arbre's life."

"Was," corrected Stanley. "She's dead."

"Is," retorted Gertrude Gold. "That power extends long beyond the life of the mentor. We must respect that power and use it." She turned her attention toward Meggie and asked, "Do you have an old photograph of this Winona Pathfinder?"

Meggie shook her head, then added, "But Lucy Arbre would."

"Good. I want you to place a photograph of this grandmother by Adam's bed so that every night he will see her. When he thinks of her, that power will come again into him. His loneliness for her will create a space for her in his heart. She will help make him strong."

"What did Adam say to your husband?" Stanley was more interested in words than images.

"The two of them were doing a pipe ceremony with Adam's pipe. Adam prayed, 'Wakan Tanka, help me.'"

Gertrude clapped her hands together in glee. "Wonderful. The boy is reaching out for help."

Meggie added, "He also said, 'Mitakuye oyas'in' when passing the pipe."

"What does that mean?" asked Stanley.

"It's like 'Amen' at the end of a prayer, but it means the whole of Creation, not just mankind. 'All My Relations' includes the four-leggeds, the winged ones, the fins, the crawling things. In the Lakota world, the human beings are simply part of the universe. We don't stand above it. We're not the appointed masters of it. So, when we pray, it is in the name of all parts of the Creation."

"That was very helpful, Dr. O'Connor. Very soon now, Stanley, the boy will start telling you the story. Are you ready to hear it?" Gertrude pointedly asked.

"Sure," he replied.

"A quick answer, Stanley. Too quick, I think," the old woman cautioned.

Both Meggie and Stanley sat back, puzzled by Gertrude's comment.

"You think it is just a matter of listening? Oh no, the story he has to tell us will be like acid. It will eat away at you, at Dr. O'Connor, at me. It will tattoo your soul as surely as that hateful number has set black hooks into my flesh. You will not get away from this work so easily, I promise. So, think about getting ready, the two of you. It's not going to be easy. The story of evil is never neat or contained. It'll seep into you and suck away at the sap of you. It'll leave you feeling dirty, contaminated. You'll never look at the world the same way again."

FORTY-FOUR

THE TELLING BEGINS

> *. . . But that I am forbid*
> *To tell the secrets of my prison-house,*
> *I could a tale unfold whose lightest word*
> *Would harrow up thy soul. . . .*
>
> —WILLIAM SHAKESPEARE
> *Hamlet*

"I'm ready if you are," Stanley said.

Seated on the stuffed chair, the boy said nothing.

"Adam, you need to talk about what happened to you. It's the only way to break the spell."

The boy's body jerked to attention. Anxiety creased the edges of his mouth. His eyes wildly searched the room. He swung his legs up on the chair as if to form a shield in front of him.

Despite the appearance of marked fear on the boy's face, Stanley pushed the matter. "It's like an infection on your finger that has swollen up, full of puss and debris. It's painful and you can't ignore it any longer. You go to a doctor and what does he do, Adam? He lances it. The yellow-green puss oozes out. The relief is immediate. Only then can your finger heal. We need to lance the infection that has settled upon you, Adam."

The boy hugged his knees to his chest even tighter.

"You're scared and I can understand that," said Stanley. "I'll tell you what I think happened and you can lift your right finger for a *yes,* left finger for a *no,* and your whole hand if you need to stop. "

The boy promptly shut his eyes.

"No, Adam. Keep your eyes open. We don't need to do this work in hypnosis. I want you wide awake. Are you ready?"

The boy peered over the tops of his knees. A right digit raised.

"Good. On the Thursday before Easter, were you kidnaped by someone you knew?"

Right finger.

"A man or group of men?"

To Stanley's surprise, the boy's left finger raised.

A woman then. Stanley took a moment, then inquired, "Did you go willingly with her?"

Both fingers raised.

Yes and no. "I don't understand," Stanley said.

Adam looked at the puzzled therapist, then mimicked sipping from a cup.

"Ah, did she give you something to drink then?"

Right finger rose. Adam then blinked his eyes shut and exaggerated falling asleep.

She drugged him. Stanley knuckled the side of his head. He was beginning to get the picture.

"When you woke up, did you know where you were?"

Adam placed his hands over his eyes, then took his hands and imitated steering a car.

"At first you couldn't see anything and then you drove a car?"

Adam shook his head in exasperation, then acted out something being tied over his head.

"Oh I get it," said Stanley. "You woke up and you couldn't see anything due to a blindfold."

Adam's right finger lifted. Then he put his hand behind his back and his ankles together.

Stanley guessed. "You were tied up and couldn't move. But you could tell that you were in a car."

Both fingers raised.

"A truck?'

Left finger.

"A van?"

Right finger. A smile lit up his face.

A macabre game of charades, reflected Stanley. *But it works.*

"You were being driven somewhere. Do you know where you were taken?"

Left finger.

"When you were brought out of the van, did she take the blindfold off?"

Again the left finger. Adam mimicked untying of the legs but not the hands.

"Were you put in a room?"

Right finger. Adam took an imaginary key and twisted it in the air.

"In a locked room then. Were there any other prisoners in that room with you?"

Right finger.

"Show me with your fingers how many?"

One finger went up.

"A youngster such as yourself?" Stanley was afraid to mention June by name, lest it totally halt their progress.

Left finger.

"An adult then?"

Right finger.

"A man?"

Stanley chafed under the step-by-step question-and-answer inquiry but he couldn't think of any other way.

Right finger.

"Was it the hitchhiker?"

Adam's eyes grew large. He lifted up the right finger but then turned his head away from Stanley as if ashamed.

Stanley decided to make a giant leap. "And was this the same man who came into the sweat lodge the other night?"

Adam hid his face but the right finger raised.

Stanley knew they were getting close to the point when further pushing might create too much intense emotion and block the flow of information. *Better quit while I'm ahead*, he decided.

"That's enough for this session. You did really well, Adam. I'm proud of you. I admire your courage. Next time, will you talk to me out loud?"

Left finger up.

"Why not?" Then, Stanley realized that there was no way for Adam to answer the question. He rephrased his question. "Is it because you're too scared?"

Right finger.

"If you could feel safe enough, would you then be able to talk to me in words?"

Right digit.

"I want you to feel safe here with me, Adam. I won't let anyone hurt you. But you need something else to help you. Can you think of what would make you feel safer?"

To Stanley's surprise, the boy's right finger lifted.

The therapist thrust a pencil and sketch pad into the boy's hands. He ordered, "Draw me what you need." He half-expected the boy to outline a suit of armor, a phalanx of policemen, or a walled-off enclosure, but that's not what the boy sketched.

Adam handed back the pad, on which was crudely drawn:

* * * *

"It's the chanunpa, the Lakota pipe," said Meggie, examining the drawing.

"How can I get hold of one?" asked Stanley.

Meggie smiled. "Adam has his own little boy's pipe. All you have to do is to ask him to bring it to session."

Stanley seemed startled. "This kid has his own pipe?"

"It's for prayer and ceremony. Don't worry, we're not trying to addict him to tobacco or smoking. Actually, you don't inhale when you smoke the pipe." Meggie laughed. She knew, in the modern world, that it wasn't politically correct to give a child a pipe. "It's part of the old Lakota traditions. A learning pipe, not a Sacred Pipe. It teaches the boy how to handle a pipe with respect."

Stanley couldn't totally erase the disapproval on his face.

Gertrude barked, "Stanley, see the boy three times a week now. The time will go fast and hard for him now. We must lance this evil and let it flow. Call him, Stanley. Ask him to bring his pipe and whatever else will make him feel safer. Meanwhile, Dr. O'Connor, you must find out what the police know. We cannot tell them what is happening in the therapy yet but we must coordinate our efforts. It's a delicate matter."

Gertrude knew Meggie would be sensitive to the confidentiality of the psychotherapy process. If the police were to know that Adam was beginning to talk, they would insist on immediately interrogating him— before the boy had done the work needed in the therapy to shore up his defenses, to make meaning of what had happened. Premature inquiry could be devastating to the boy and to the therapeutic process.

Better that Meggie sniff around and see if she could uncover any corroborating evidence.

*　*　*　*

Daisy sat opposite to the older investigator. He offered her a cigarette but she shook her head. "That stuff will rot your lungs, you know."

He shrugged his shoulders as if he didn't care, but he replaced the pack in his shirt pocket. "My partner said you wanted to talk to me. He showed me the trunk in your mother's closet. You told him that your mother was some kind of priestess in a Satanic cult, that they kidnap children."

"You know my talking to you like this could get me killed?" Daisy warned.

"Then why you are doing it?" The older officer wasn't cutting her any slack.

Suddenly, Daisy realized that it didn't really matter to the officer why she had changed her mind and decided to talk, why she decided to betray her mother, maybe even send her mom to jail. What did the cop care about how Jillian had taken her in and how Sam had treated her with respect? How, for the first time in her life, she was learning to stand up for herself.

All the cop wanted was information. Well, she'd give it to him but only because Jillian had told her it was the right thing to do. She'd tell him about the creepy people who'd come calling for her mother at odd hours, about how her mother tried to involve her once in Satanic ceremonies. She'd seen enough to judge that most of these people were freaks and sex addicts. Unlike her siblings, Daisy would disappear around the time of Satanic holy days.

She didn't need any of that crazy shit in her life, not when her own drunken father would bang her every chance he got. What did hell have to offer her that wasn't already in her own home?

So, she didn't answer that officer's particular question. Instead she asked, "What do you need to know?"

Jillian would be proud of me, she thought. *Damn proud.*

FORTY-FIVE

SOMETHING OF THE ABYSMAL DARKNESS

The sight of evil kindles evil in the soul -
there is no getting away from this fact . . .
Something of the abysmal darkness of the world
has broken in on us, poisoning the very air we
breathe and befouling the pure water with the
stale, nauseating taste of blood.

—CARL G. JUNG
Collected Works

"Bring whatever you need to feel safe in session so that we can talk," Stanley had said.

Adam appeared in the waiting room with Hawk and his small chanunpa. Stanley was surprised that the boy hadn't brought more with him.

"Are you ready?" He indicated to the boy that he should follow Stanley back to the therapist's office. Both Hawk and Adam rose from the couch, the boy clutching his fringed pipe bag. Stanley was about to give Mr. Spelman permission to stay in the waiting room when it suddenly dawned on him that Meggie O'Connor's husband was part of Adam's safety network. The three of them headed to the office.

"Is it all right with you if I ask Mr. Spelman . . ."

Adam interrupted, "His name is Hawk."

Upon hearing the boy talk out loud, Stanley tried not to let his elation show.

"Mr. Hawk then. Would it be okay, Adam, if I put him in this corner chair where you can see him? I will ask him to remain quiet until the very end."

Adam looked at Hawk who nodded his head. Hawk settled into the comfortable corner chair, in a space that would not intrude on the interaction between the boy and his therapist. Adam nervously traded glances with Hawk.

"Are you ready then?" asked Stanley.

The boy shook his head. He turned toward Hawk with beseeching eyes.

Hawk remained silent.

Stalemate, thought Stanley. *What now?*

"Perhaps you can help us after all," conceded Stanley.

Hawk spoke. "Adam Stands-By-Dog needs to purify this room with sage smoke, then fill his chanunpa. When he holds that loaded pipe before him, he is not only safe from the Evil Spirits, he must be truthful in all things."

Stanley turned back to the boy. "Go ahead. Do what you need to do." He sat back and watched as the boy pulled out a small bowl, gray leaves, and a lighter.

Stanley took a deep breath. *God, I hope this works.*

Adam slipped off his shoes. He rolled the sage leaves into a compact ball, placed it in the bowl, and lit it. He wafted the smoke over himself and his pipe bag. He got up and walked around Stanley, fanning the smoke onto the therapist, then over by Hawk. When he returned to his pipe bag, the boy knelt down on the carpet, facing west, and proceeded to assemble his chanunpa, washing it in the smoke of the sage. Carefully, in ritualized fashion, he placed pinches of tobacco in the bowl, praying quietly to himself. When he had finished, Adam compressed a few sage leaves and plugged the top of his loaded pipe. Sitting down in his chair, he faced the therapist, holding the bowl of the pipe in his left hand, close to his heart.

"He is ready now to answer your questions," announced Hawk.

"This is what I understand so far," began Stanley. "You were kidnaped on the Thursday before Easter by a woman you knew. She gave you something to drink. It made you fall asleep. When you woke up, you were in a traveling van. You couldn't see anything due to a blindfold and you couldn't move because your hands and legs were tied. When you finally arrived at the destination, you were placed in a locked room with the young hitchhiker. And his name was Jesus. Am I right so far?"

Stanley held his breath. Much to his surprise, the boy answered, in a voice that was both little and scared.

"In the room, they untied my arms and blindfold. The man scratched 'Jesus' on the wall but said his name was 'Hey-soose,'" the boy recounted.

"That's the Spanish pronunciation," Stanley explained, thinking, *We're having an actual conversation here.*

"Who was the woman?" Stanley asked.

"Emily. She works in town. I forget her last name. I liked her a lot." Adam clenched the pipe firmly.

Stanley was still finding it hard to believe that a simple thing like a pipe could unlock the boy's tongue.

"Do you still like her?"

"I . . . I don't know," Adam answered.

"Tell us in your own words what happened that Thursday. Do you think you can do that?"

Adam bit his underlip. The anxiety shivered off him like flies fluttering above dead carrion.

"Start with the arrival in the room," Stanley suggested.

"At first I was alone in the room. My mouth was all dry. I asked for water but Emily said not yet. I was scared. 'When can I go home?' I asked, an' she didn't answer. That made me really afraid. She told me that I had to pay attention to what she said or I'd never get out alive. They would kill me if I didn't join them. I didn't understand what she was saying. I didn't know who she was talking about."

Adam's little right finger began gouging his left palm. He was swallowing a lot and his grip on the pipe tightened.

"Go on," Stanley urged. "I know this is difficult, but we have to do it. What else did Emily tell you?"

Like a pack of dogs loosed from a kennel, his words came tumbling out in a frenzy, rushing toward freedom while backpedaling from fear. "I was so tired. I only heard some of it. Stuff like God had given up on the world and the only true power was Satan. That evil was good an' that being good was weak. It didn't make sense to me, an' I was really scared. I wanted to cry, but she told me not to. She said if I was really brave, I'd get stronger. I didn't want her to see me crying. But I was so scared. She slapped me on the face when she thought I was gonna cry. I asked for water an' she said no. She said they'd give me something later. I was hungry an' she said no. Not yet. I wanted my Mom and Dad, an' she said if I didn't shut up I might never see them again, that I had to listen to her very very carefully, otherwise she couldn't protect me."

Adam was breathing hard, verging on tears. "I had to go to the bathroom, an' she said not yet. I had to go so bad. I started to unzip my pants, an' then she said, okay, if that's the way you're gonna listen, then a couple of men came in and pulled off all my clothes, and it was cold. An' I kind of wet myself."

Adam bowed his head in shame.

Hawk's face reddened with anger.

"That must have been awful for you," Stanley empathized. "What then happened?"

"Emily threw a blanket over me. She said that I had been disobedient. Now I'd pay the piper. I didn't know what she meant. Then the two men took me to another room an' ordered me to sit down on a chair, an' they put straps on me to hold me there. Then little metal things. An' then, an' then . . ."

Adam came to a total halt in speech, his body rigid but jerking. "I'm gonna be sick," he exclaimed.

Stanley yanked over his wastepaper basket. The boy handed the pipe to Hawk and, clasping the basket with both hands, proceeded to gag dry heaves and low moans of terror.

"Take some deep breaths," Stanley urged. He felt a sickness rising inside his own stomach. Unobtrusively, he placed a hand over his own mouth.

Hawk began to chant the Stone Song quietly in the background. After a few moments, the boy raised his head from the basket.

"I'm sorry," his voice quivered.

"Do you need to stop?" Stanley asked. *Why do I want him to stop?* Stanley silently questioned himself.

Adam glanced over at Hawk and the chanunpa. Hawk handed him

back his pipe. "I am Adam Stands-By-Dog," the boy announced, indicating that he was ready to proceed.

Stanley sighed. "Okay, we'll continue, but when you need to stop, we'll do that." He didn't want to push the boy over the edge.

Adam began again. "Emily told me that they were gonna have to teach me things, so I'd know better. They put some kind of battery thing near the chair. I was cold an' scared. I wanted my Mom. But I remembered what Emily said 'bout not crying. They asked me a bunch of questions. An' when I didn't get it right, they turned on that battery thing an' it zapped me an' it hurt real bad."

An involuntary shiver trembled up Stanley's spine. "What kind of questions?" he asked.

The boy focused on the bowl of his chanunpa. "Like—did I want to be a good boy? An' when I said yes, they zapped me. So, I knew to say no next time. Did I believe in God? I thought they wanted me to say no, so I said no, an' they zapped me again. They called me stupid and said that of course there was God but that He didn't care anymore. If He really cared, He'd be there to help me. That Satan was the only one that really cared and that Satan could help me."

Adam's words came out choppy, with sharp intakes of breath, almost as if he were crying but without the tears.

"Did I want to be a good boy? An' I said no, and they said that was right, that being bad was being powerful, and that the sooner I learned that, the stronger I'd become. They said would I like to be a part of them, an' I knew they wanted me to say yes, and I said yes, an' they zapped me. . . ." Adam broke down into tears but still his words marched relentlessly on and on.

"They said I was lying and didn't really mean it. Again, they asked me if I wanted to join them, so I said no, and they hurt me with that battery thing again. I was naked an' I couldn't stop from crying then. They called me a cry baby, who didn't have the guts to stand a little bit of pain. An' then they took me back to the first room an' left. She came back with a damp washcloth and gave me a blanket to put over myself. She said I better listen to them if I wanted to make it out alive."

"Do you mean Emily?" Stanley asked, gritting his teeth against a rising tide of rage.

"I thought she was my only friend there," Adam confessed. "Even though she was the one who had brought me there."

"What about the hitchhiker?"

"I don't know when, but it was night, an' the door opened an' they pushed him into the room. They said to me, 'Maybe you can help him.' I didn't know what they meant, but he'd been beaten up. His face was all scratched an' he said his nose was broken. His lip was cut an' he had bruises on his cheeks. But he still had his clothes on. He told me his name and asked me mine. He said that he had hooked a ride with some men in a truck and boy, he was sure sorry he had done that. He asked, 'What kind of crazy people are these?'"

Adam's voice briefly dropped into a monotone. "Later, they gave me some green tea an' took me back to the other room. I was so tired an' things weren't real clear. I heard kids' voices in the distance. I could smell a fire. I think we were in a barn or something. They had the wooden chair with the straps and the battery and the wires and stuff. Then they put wires on me again. I knew what they were going to do an' I was so scared. But I didn't say nothing, 'cuz I got it figured out that I gotta keep quiet, you know?"

The boy's breathing came hard and ragged, hurting. "They told me what I already knew, the name of the guy in the locked room, but they said it different. They asked if I was his friend? An' I guessed what they wanted and I said no, I didn't know him. An' they didn't zap me. They asked me if I would help him if he were hurt an' I said no, that I didn't know him an' he was no friend of mine. They asked me if I knew his name an' they waited for me to say something. An' I was afraid. I said I didn't know him an' I had forgotten his name already. An' that was the right answer, 'cuz they didn't hurt me. But then they asked me if I had ever wanted to . . . ." Adam broke off and looked at the therapist, unsure whether to say the words.

"Go on," urged Stanley.

"To beat up my sister an' do bad things to her an' I said no, and they turned on that battery and the pain was so bad I fell asleep. They woke me up by throwing cold water on me an' calling me a liar, that of course I wanted to do bad things to her. An' they asked me that question again, an' I said yes. Then they gave me some more green tea to drink. It tasted pretty bad but I was so thirsty. I can't do it anymore," Adam said, suddenly panting.

"You've said a lot, Adam." *Almost too much*, Stanley thought. "We'll quit today. I'll see you again in two days." The therapist stood up as if to move toward the door but Hawk and the boy continued to sit there quietly.

Stanley looked inquiringly at Hawk.

Hawk motioned for the man to return to the chair. "Adam Stands-By-Dog has spoken truthfully and with great courage. We must now smoke the pipe with him. You will learn, over time, how we do this pipe ceremony."

Stanley nodded and returned to his chair. The session had exhausted him. Truthfully, he wanted the boy and the man out of his office. He craved a break from the therapy, but he had to be respectful of the boy's wishes.

Adam lit the pipe and offered it to All The Directions, then he passed it to Hawk who smoked it and then handed it to Stanley.

"Hold the bowl in your left hand, your heart hand," instructed Hawk.

Stanley tried not to inhale. The smoke made him dizzy. *This is crazy*, he thought. *This is modern day America. What kind of world is it, where a boy is tortured to believe in the devil and a pipe, full of tobacco, restores him?*

The boy's words had been harsh and shocking, disgusting in their description of human depravity. The story made Stanley's teeth grind together and he felt full of hot fury. *How could adult human beings do that to a child?*

Stanley checked the boy's face, the calmness that had returned to his eyes. The pipe ceremony really seemed to be helping Adam. *And not just the boy*, Stanley acknowledged to himself. The cleansing of the sage smoke, the smell of the pipe tobacco burning, the reverence of the ceremony, and the weight of the pipe in his hand was bringing him face to face with the Sacred too.

Stanley thought back to the days of his bar mitzvah at age thirteen. *A long long time ago*, he thought. *I, too, once believed.*

* * * *

"I need to talk with you. My husband is the boy's guardian. I am also a clinical psychologist, so I am trying to understand the boy's behavior at home. I need to ask you some questions." Meggie carefully chose her words over the telephone lest the investigators sense that she knew more than she was saying.

"Like what?" asked one of them.

"Do you have any information on who kidnaped him?"

"Yes," came the clipped reply.

"It would be helpful if you could share that with me."

There was a long pause. "Understand, we don't want to jeopardize our investigation or warn off potential suspects."

"Yes." Meggie waited.

"So, you must keep this quiet."

"Okay," Meggie agreed.

"We happen to think that an Emily Bassett was the one to transport the boy south into Illinois."

"Clyde Bassett's wife?" Meggie knew of the reputation of Clyde Bassett as the town drunk and incestuous father.

"Yes. She's skipped town with the children. Except for the oldest daughter. Not only does Mr. Bassett claim that he has no idea where his wife has gone but he says 'Good riddance.' Seems like the marriage was on the rocks. The daughter's been real helpful to us."

Meggie wondered if that was the same girl Sam Waters had hired at the Suttons Bay Veterinary Clinic.

"Any idea why she would have taken the boy?" Meggie probed.

"Some sort of cult thing. But you know, people are always claiming stuff about Satanic cults and a lot of the time it's just adults playing games. Deadly games." The investigator sounded weary. "We've got an all-points bulletin out on her and the kids. We'll pick them up sooner or later."

Emily Bassett. Satanic cult or pseudo-cult. The pieces are beginning to fall into place, thought Meggie.

"Anything about June Tubbs and her murder?"

"Dead end there," sighed the officer on the phone. "But I'd bet my bottom dollar that she fits into this somewhere. Now you keep this information quiet, you hear?"

"My lips are sealed," replied Meggie. "You've been very helpful."

"Anything you want to share with me?" he asked.

"Not yet," Meggie cheerfully answered, "but when we have something we'll be sure to let you know right away." *It wasn't so hard to lie after all*, thought Meggie.

As soon as Hawk returned from the therapy session, Meggie dragged him into a bedroom and shut the door so that Adam couldn't eavesdrop.

"Wait until you hear what the investigator told me," Meggie whispered.

But Hawk already knew what Meggie had just learned. He told her of the session, his face sterner than Meggie had ever before seen.

He swore, "If it weren't for the Pipe, Meggie, I think I would kill those people."

"Then it's lucky that they've not been found. I don't want my new husband locked up for the rest of his life," Meggie chided.

"You don't understand, Meggie. I'm not talking about killing them the white man's way."

"Well, then what do you mean?"

His face grew rigid with anger. "I could take the Black Pipe and call the Evil Spirits. I could kill them with that Pipe. But I won't," he reassured her.

Meggie looked at him as if he were somebody she did not know, a man with murder in his heart.

"You didn't hear the boy's words," he continued. "They carved themselves into me deeper than a knife could go. I will never forget them. He has more courage than you or I, Meggie. For one reason only, I won't use that power."

"What?" She had to ask.

"My respect for the Chanunpa Wakan. If I ask for the power to hurt those people, I'd be turning my back on why the White Buffalo Calf Woman brought us the Chanunpa in the first place. I'd be putting you in danger when those forces demanded payment."

"Why?"

"The old ones say that when you call upon Evil Spirits, They will come back and take away those you love the most. I have seen it happen with my own eyes, Meggie, when people make that choice. I have seen family members sicken and die when one of their own decides to summon those evil energies. We are always given the choice on how to use the Pipe, but it never comes free of charge."

Meggie reached out and placed both hands on his shoulders. "You're doing the right thing, Hawk. Violence only breeds violence and there is enough of that in the world already."

"But in my heart, Meggie," he swore, "I still want to kill those sons of bitches."

FORTY-SIX

No Choice

In order to be successful, treatment must address not only the whole complex of the post-traumatic stress disorder that results from the child's abuse, but the mind control as well. . . .

For example, the child will be drugged, terrorized, physically and sexually tortured, and made to witness or participate in the perpetration of similar abuse of someone else, all of which combine to create an an altered state of consciousness in which he or she dissociates and becomes willing to do, think, or believe anything that will cause the pain to stop.

—CATHERINE GOULD, PH.D
Diagnosis and Treatment of Ritually Abused Children

"What's going on, Meggie? You look worried and distracted much of the time. Is it your father's death?" Despite grief and the confusion of being a new widow, Meggie's mother still retained her sharp, observant eye.

"No, that's not it." Meggie couldn't disclose confidential information to her mother.

"If you're concerned about me, then rest easy. I can take care of myself even if I am a bit slower these days. If I get to a point where I can't manage the house by myself, I'll call you. You can then help me find a retirement community. I'll not be a burden to you kids."

"You'd never be a burden, Mom."

"It's time for me to go back home and get used to being alone. The focus of your fretting is Adam, isn't it?"

Meggie nodded.

Her mother patted her arm. "Last few nights, when you were bringing food to the table, the boy was watching your every move."

"He was?"

She smiled. "I know that you are trying to help Adam recover from the kidnaping incident. But you never told me why he couldn't live at home." She held up her hand. "No, that's okay. I don't need to know everything."

"He was violent, Mom." She thought that was the simplest explanation.

"Still," her mother continued, "I think when it is time for him to return home he'll find it very difficult to leave you."

Meggie looked into her mother's face for clarification.

"Meggie, it's obvious that you have won over that boy's heart."

If only that were enough to heal him, thought Meggie.

*   *   *   *

They said if I talk,
Satan will listen.
Wherever I go,
The Evil Eye will follow me.

Above me, below me
Around me, inside me
Satan lives.

They said that if I told,
I'd be killed.

Today is a good day to die.

*   *   *   *

"Good morning, Adam." Stanley forced himself to sound cheerful. "Good morning, Mr. Hawk."

The two of them accompanied him back to the office area, the boy clutching the pipe bag in his right hand.

"Are you ready to begin again?" Stanley wasn't quite sure to whom his question was addressed—the boy or himself.

Adam nodded. He knelt down on the carpet and proceeded to fill his small chanunpa in the ways of respect, first smudging himself with the sage smoke, then Hawk, then the therapist. When he had finished, he settled back into the big arm chair, holding his pipe out before him.

Hawk, too, found his place in the corner where he served as silent witness to the boy's story.

Stanley quickly summarized the previous session. "After having been drugged and bound by Emily, you arrived at some place where two men stripped you naked, shocked you, and forced you to answer questions that could not truthfully be answered." Picking his words carefully, Stanley was slowly trying to drive a wedge between the words of the Satanists and the meanings to be derived from their actions.

"Then you encountered a young man by the name of Jesus. He had hitchhiked a ride with the wrong people. They beat him, drugged him, and threw him into the locked room with you. When the two thugs asked you if you knew the young man's name, you were smart to try and figure out what they wanted you to say. Inside, you knew that what these men were doing was wrong."

Uncertainty riddled across Adam's face. He gave a tentative nod to Stanley's interpretation of events.

"Is there more to the events of that Thursday evening?"

"Yes." Adam heaved a sigh, saturated with resignation.

"Go on." Stanley urged.

"They made us go outside in the dark. There was a big fire an' lots of people. Grown-ups an' another kids. I couldn't see them too well. Everything was kind of fuzzy an' I felt real dizzy. Everybody was drinking stuff, making lots of noise."

Stanley interrupted. "Were there other houses around?"

Adam shook his head. "No. It was a farm or something. I know, 'cuz there were cows and sheep and a ram. A guy in a black robe called everybody together. He said words I didn't know. Then he pointed out the guy next to me and said that they were real lucky 'cuz they had Jesus with them this year. But the guy whispered to me that he didn't feel so lucky, you know?"

Stanley nodded for Adam to continue.

"Then he said something about Satan being an Equal Opportunity Employer and that they had an Indian boy, me, an' he told them my name was Adam and that I would have first choice."

"First choice?" Stanley didn't understand.

Adam looked down at his feet. "They were going to kill one of us, they said. Something about a gift to Satan. An' I could pick whether it would be me or . . ." Adam stopped, unable to say the words.

"The hitchhiker?" Stanley inserted.

Adam nodded. "But that if I chose him, then I would have to join them. I didn't know what that meant. So, they asked me in front of everybody, what's your choice? An' I didn't want to say anything but they told me I had to. I closed my mouth and prayed for my grand-mother to come and rescue me."

He paused a moment. "But she didn't come."

"Then what happened?" Stanley knew it must have seemed like an eternity to the boy.

"Jesus finally shouted at them to stop doing this to me, that it wasn't right. They tried to gag him but he continued to yell at them. An' that made them really mad. The guy in the black robe said that if I was going to keep quiet, then I was choosing to die, and I said no, don't take me, an' they said okay, they'd take Jesus. But they said I'd have to prove my allegiance or something like that. They, they . . ."

Adam began to writhe in the chair. He blurted out, "Grabbed me and dragged me to a wooden table. They slapped my hand down on the table. They took a knife and cut off the top part of my finger with a knife." He lifted the pipe and his left hand, displaying the maimed finger.

Hawk's hands bunched into fists. Stanley's hand went to his mouth as if to prevent himself from getting sick.

Adam rushed through the telling, trying to find an end to that long night. "It hurt so bad. Jesus screamed at them when he saw what they had done to me. They laughed an' told him that now I was part of them, traveling the Left Hand path. They put a bandage on it an' put the fingertip in a cloth. Then they took the blood of some animal an' passed around a silver cup. I had to drink from it, an' it tasted awful. Then they passed around some kind of shredded meat. They said it was from my finger and other fingers. I got sick. Jesus refused to drink it but they forced his jaw open and poured the drink down his throat, saying this is my blood, this is my flesh, something like that. Then, after a long time, after singing and other words, I was so tired and thirsty, they locked the two of us up in the room again."

"And then what happened?" Stanley was relentless in pushing the boy to conclusion.

"Jesus said he was going to pray all night long, that he would look after me, and that I should go to sleep. An' that's what I did."

"Did anything else happen that night?"

Adam shook his head.

Stanley spoke quietly. "At least for that night, you had a friend, Adam. A man who knew right from wrong."

Adam hung his head in shame.

Stanley guessed at his feelings. "It was a set-up, Adam. They were planning to kill him no matter what you said."

Adam looked up. "But they told me I had the first choice."

Stanley shook his head. "No, Adam. They wanted you to *think* there was a choice. They were playing head games with you. The hitchhiker was marked for death the first time he told them his name."

"Still, I . . ." Adam protested.

"Chose life over death. That's what you did, Adam." Stanley's words were crisp and affirmative. It was not enough to assuage the boy; Stanley could see that, but he didn't know what else to say. Hawk caught his eye. Stanley nodded. Maybe the man could help the boy with his guilt.

But Hawk did not make a statement. Instead, he asked the boy a question. "Who came into the sweat lodge, Adam Stands-By-Dog?

The boy stared at his pipe and answered, "Jesus, the guy in the room with me."

"And what did he tell you?"

"That he had arrived and that it wasn't my fault." Adam expelled a large breath of air. Then, for a few minutes, all was quiet in the therapy room as the two men let Adam work it out in his head.

"Mitakuye oyas'in," the boy finally said. "Okay, I'm ready to do the pipe ceremony."

FORTY-SEVEN

THE TRIAL

*For the highest spiritual working one must accordingly choose
that victim which contains the greatest and purest force. A male
child of pure innocence and high intelligence is the most
suitable victim. . . .*

—ALEISTER CROWLEY
Magick In theory and practice

NO sooner had Meggie's client left her office than the telephone rang.
It was Hawk, calling from the Gertrude Gold Clinic.

"What's up?" he asked her. "The receptionist said that it was important for me to contact you."

"Shunka's dead, Hawk."

"That's going to be tough on Adam."

"It's worse than that. His throat was cut. The killer left the body."

"At Lucy's?"

"Yes, early this morning."

"Did Lucy call the tribal police?"

"They said they'd interview the neighbors and let the federal officers
know about the incident. Do you think it's all connected with Adam's
disappearance, Hawk? What are we really dealing with here?" Fiery
anger and shrill anxiety colored her voice.

After listening to the content of the past hour, Hawk wouldn't put
anything past the kidnappers. "Is Fritzie okay?"

"Not according to him. He's locked up in the kitchen and furious about it too. He'll try to shred the door, one claw at a time." Meggie paused on the phone. "Do you think it wise to tell Adam about Shunka? Couldn't it interfere with what's happening in the therapy?"

"It might stop him cold. That's a chance we'll have to take. I'm not going to start lying to him or keeping things from him. He deserves the truth even if it's harsh. I'll tell him as we drive home."

"I want to see him," Adam announced.

Hawk drove Adam to his mother's house. Lucy pointed to where they had covered up Shunka's body. Hawk pulled aside the tarp. The boy sank to his knees and cradled the dog's head in his lap. He stroked the soft hair around Shunka's ears. Large tears fell, anointing the open, unseeing eyes of his old pal.

"Why?" Adam looked up into his cousin's face. The question resonated with anger, fear, and genuine puzzlement.

Hawk shrugged. "I suppose somebody wanted to scare you, keep you quiet."

You have to pay the piper, she told me.
I didn't keep my promise.

The boy bit his lip.

"To prevent you from telling what happened," Hawk added.

Pay the piper.
Pay the piper.
Pay the piper.

Slowly, Hawk coaxed Shunka's body from Adam's hands. Into the wheelbarrow he maneuvered the dog's corpse while noticing the far-away look in Adam's eyes. He handed Adam two shovels. They dug a grave and gently lowered the body into the pit. Adam bent over and sprinkled tobacco into Shunka's open mouth. Hawk spoke a prayer, offering tobacco to Unci Maka. When the boy signaled with his head, they picked up the shovels and returned Shunka back to the Grandmother.

Grim lines of tension shuttered Adam's mouth. He was angry at them. He was angry at himself.

I didn't keep my promise.
Shunka was my friend. Why did they have to kill him?
Why couldn't it have been me to pay the piper?

And he was scared.

They know where I live.
Satan knows everything. He knows I've talked.
He will send them to come get me.

Interrupting the boy's thoughts, Hawk placed a hand upon his shoulder. "You're protected by my medicine, Adam. Nobody can hurt you directly, so they killed your dog. It's up to you if you're going to let them win by scaring you back into silence. Or stand up like a warrior and make them pay for Shunka's death. It's up to you, Adam. We can go back to Chrysalis right now and lock all the windows and doors and hide inside. Or we can try to track down the person who did this cowardly thing. It's up to you, Nephew."

Hawk waited, leaning against a shovel. He wouldn't move until Adam made a decision.

The boy stood there, his feet splayed in opposite directions, his face a wrench of emotions.

You will have to pay the piper, a voice resonated within him. Adam didn't have the slightest doubt as to who was the Piper. The only way to assuage the Prince of Darkness would be in blood.

It was a compromise. He would show Hawk that he was brave and a warrior, that he would not keep quiet.

But later, when the house had gone to sleep, he would take his hunting knife and . . .

Pay the piper.

* * * *

Something about Adam's eyes disturbed Meggie as she tucked the boy in bed. She sat down on the edge of the mattress. Adam didn't move to make more room for her. He kept his arms hidden under the blankets. His body was unnaturally stiff and his eyes were wary, observing her without the usual warmth. She wondered if he was regressing from the shock of Shunka's death.

"Did I ever tell you the story of Pandora?" she began.

Adam shook his head.

"It's an ancient Greek myth. Long time ago, the first race of people had been fashioned out of clay. After they received the stolen gift of fire, they made sacrifices to the gods but over time, they began to keep the best part of the meat for themselves. They offered only leftovers to the gods. Well, you can imagine how that made Zeus, the ruler of the Universe, very angry."

Adam's eyes flickered with interest. This was a story of divine fury.

Meggie continued. "So Zeus decided to punish the people. He had Hephaestus fashion a beautiful woman—Pandora. The gods and goddesses helped in her creation. Apollo gifted her a voice so sweet that even the birds hushed when she sang. Hermes endowed her with eloquent speech and the Graces infused her with captivating charm. Athena dressed her in elegant clothes and Aphrodite adorned her in jewels and taught her the art of healing. Her eyes were like deep blue sapphires, her mouth the color of rubies. When she smiled, the whole world around her smiled."

She glanced at Adam but, to her surprise, he did not smile back. There was grim business behind his watchful eyes.

Meggie returned to the subject of anger. "Zeus was furious at the human beings and he had a plan to get back at them. Not only had Zeus made Pandora beautiful beyond compare but he filled her with insatiable curiosity. He then sent her down to earth with a sealed jar and instructions that she was never to open that jar. Men, far and wide, were struck by her beauty. Pandora married and had a daughter, Pyrrha. But she was always restless and unhappy. More than anything, she wanted to know what was in that jar."

Meggie's eyes twinkled in mischief but Adam kept his head glued to the pillow. Meggie instinctively knew something bad was brewing in Adam's mind.

"Unable to stand it any longer," Meggie said, "Pandora opened the jar to take a quick peek. Whoosh! Out flew all manner of misery. Greed, vanity, gossip, deceit, jealousy—evils of all kind that human beings hadn't known until then. Pandora was horrified at what she had uncorked. She slapped a lid onto the jar just in time. Because at the bottom of that jar had lingered Hope, and if Pandora had let Hope fly away, the other miseries would have surely killed it."

Out of the corner of her eye, Meggie could see that she had caught Adam's full attention. He lifted himself up on his elbows, away from the pillow.

"As it was," Meggie said, "these miseries swarmed around the human beings, stinging and biting them. You see, Adam, Zeus badly miscalculated. He thought that all that pain and suffering would bring the people to their knees, make them pious and obedient, return them to the ways of goodness. But it didn't do that at all. Instead, the unleashed misery and evil made the human beings lie, steal, kill, and be very hurtful toward each other."

Adam was listening to every word.

Meggie continued, "Fed up, Zeus then sent a nine-day flood to destroy the evil human beings but Pandora's daughter, Pyrrha, and her husband, Deucalion, had built an ark. And that ark rode out the terrible flood that killed everybody else. When the waters receded, the ark came to rest on Mt. Parnassus."

"Like the story of Noah," interjected Adam.

"That's right. When they emerged from their ark, Pyrrha and Deucalion did the respectful thing. In ceremony, they gave thanks and honored Zeus for letting them live. He was pleased by their piety and touched by their loneliness. So Zeus said to them, 'Gather up the bones of your mother and throw them over your shoulder."

Meggie stood up. "What he meant was Gaia, Grandmother Earth, and Her bones are, of course, the stones. So Pyrrha picked up rocks and tossed them over her shoulder. When they touched the ground, each one of the stones became a woman." Meggie moved her arm as if to pitch something backwards.

"Likewise, when Deucalion threw stones over his shoulder, a score of men arose. And the couple was no longer lonely."

Meggie looked down at Adam whose eyes had been tracking her gestures. "This was a new race of people, born not out of clay but out of stone. Thus, when visited by all the miseries that had survived the flood, they were a sturdier group of human beings. They could better stand the sting of evil."

Adam stammered, "But . . . what happened to Hope?"

"It's a good question. We must always protect Hope from being overwhelmed. We need Hope to live. Sometimes things can hurt so bad that we lose touch with Hope. But if you look deep enough, you'll discover it, sealed inside of you. Don't ever let it slip away, Adam."

The boy looked at her strangely, as if lost in thought. He then sat up and rolled back the sleeves of his pajamas. Running down his arms were bloody tracks.

"Oh Adam, what have you done?" Meggie exclaimed.

"I . . . was going to kill myself," he confessed.

"How? Carving up your arms? With what?" The questions anxiously tumbled out of Meggie.

He turned and looked at his pillow. Meggie reached over and lifted it up. Adam's hunting knife lay there, sharp and deadly. She could see that the jumbled sheets were already lightly stained from the cuts on his arms.

"Oh Adam," Meggie said. "How you must be hurting." She brought him a damp washcloth, antiseptic salve, and a host of Band-Aids.

"I'm glad you showed me the knife. I will keep it safe with me." She cleaned the cuts. "Will you promise me that you will never do this again?"

He nodded.

But I break my promises,
And the piper will demand payment.

* * * *

"Are you scared?" Stanley later asked Meggie. "I'd be."

"We're taking precautions," she replied. "My home is beginning to look like an armed camp, with guns loaded, gates locked, and all senses on high alert. I refuse to cower in the corner."

Stanley smiled at Meggie's bravado. "Does Adam feel safe?"

"Adam isn't going to find a sense of security anywhere right now," Gertrude interrupted. "The killing of his dog was a deliberate attempt to shut him up. Now, I have to find out whether either one of you has told anyone outside of this room that Adam is talking?"

Both Meggie and Stanley shook their head.

"What about your husband, Dr. O'Connor?"

"He knows that disclosure would put the boy into harm's way. I'm sure he's kept what he has heard to himself."

"So," said Gertrude stroking her chin, "this must be an attempt then to maintain his silence. They don't yet know that he's talking to us. For his safety, tell him to play mute in public. I will keep his files under lock and key. Stanley, I want you to write up an account so far of what the boy has said and make several copies. Send it to several of your colleagues with instructions not to open and read the material unless you die unexpectedly."

Stanley's eyes grew large and wide. "Why? Do you think I'm in danger too?"

Gertrude gave a short laugh. "We're all in danger right now. This is a murderous group of people. Safety lies in the whole story being told and then given to the police. But we're not ready to do that yet."

"But who are they?" Meggie asked the crucial question.

Gertrude shrugged her thin shoulders. "We may never find that out, Dr. O'Connor. From reports of other therapists, there appears to be a Satanic underground that stretches across this country, made up of people with normal day jobs—lawyers, police officers, farmers, house-wives, construction workers, ministers—you name it. They recruit teenagers with drugs, sex, and big thrills and, before long, these young people find themselves so mired in the muck that they don't know how to get out. Sometimes you'll find families that have generational ties to the Satanic cults. They're a slippery lot. They know how to cover their tracks well."

Meggie was surprised at the depth of Gertrude's information. "You seem to know what you're talking about."

Gertrude nodded. "You can't work long in the Dissociative Disorders without coming across evidence of these Satanic cults. It appears that they took some of the findings of the CIA-funded research on brain-washing and perfected the techniques on young children. But when these children grow into adults, they walk into clinics across the country exhibiting all kinds of dissociative problems."

"But why doesn't the public or most therapists know more about their activities?" Meggie pushed.

"Why does the FBI deny that there are Satanic cults? Why are there so many facetious law suits against therapists who uncover information on Satanic cults? Why does the police department report the death of that little Tubbs girl as a normal homicide when she had her heart ripped out of her body? You tell me, Dr. O'Connor. What do you think is going on?"

But Meggie had no answer.

"Evil will always have its defenders," Gertrude snorted. "And the complicity of good people who cannot abide the thought that Evil truly exists except in a perverse imagination."

*   *   *   *

"Are we ready?" Stanley was acutely aware of using *we* instead of *you*. After the last supervision session, he had his own reasons for wanting to move through this process as speedily as possible.

Adam nodded. Again, he had brought his cousin, Hawk, to the session. Stanley was growing in respect for the quiet man in the corner whose steadying presence centered them all.

Adam kicked off his shoes, knelt on the carpet, and filled his chanunpa. When done, he rose and sat down in his chair. "I'm ready now." He stared straight ahead, his pipe held out before him. Despite it being warm, the boy was wearing a long-sleeved shirt.

Stanley began once again with a brief summary. "Last session, you detailed for us what happened on that Thursday evening. You were forced to make choices that were not real choices but they succeeded in convincing you that you were guilty of betrayal of your hitchhiking friend, Jesus. They gave you drugs again. They cut off the tip of your finger. They performed a perverted kind of Mass, using human flesh and animal blood."

"Perverted?" Adam didn't know the word.

"It means something that isn't normal, something out of the bounds of human decency." Stanley's voice took on a monotone quality, deadening his own feelings in preparation for the rest of the session.

He could feel a numbness creep across his emotions and mistook it as evidence of greater objectivity.

Adam nodded but Stanley wasn't sure he really understood the definition of perversity.

"After the Mass, you were finally allowed to go to sleep. Your friend, however, stayed up praying and watching over you." At the risk of inciting more guilt in the boy, Stanley wanted him to know that there were still good people in the world, adults who would look out for him the best that they could.

Stanley waited for the boy to begin. Nothing happened. *Is he frightened? Did the killing of his pet succeed in silencing him?* "I heard about your dog, Adam. I'm sorry that happened. Dr. O'Connor told me about the scratches on your arms and your wish to die. She said you promised you wouldn't do that again. I have to warn you that more suicidal behavior might force us to return you to the hospital."

Adam flinched at that threat. He then turned around to look at Hawk. Angrily, the boy announced, "We're going to find the person who did it."

Stanley suspected that Adam was diverting from the topic of the suicidal gesture. He let it pass, knowing that the boy had heard him. "Let's go back to that Friday morning when you awoke."

Silence.

"Go on," he urged the boy. But inside, Stanley could feel the drag of his own fatigue, his own reluctance to hear more about the perversions of human beings.

Adam coughed, then resumed the narrative: "They tied the hitchhiker to a tree and held a trial. They told him he was the king of the Jews. He said no, he was a Mexican and they were all crazy. He told them that God would strike them dead. But He didn't."

"Didn't what?"

"Strike them dead. They said, see that proves God is weak and Satan is strong. If God really cared, then He would strike them dead. But He didn't." Adam seemed to have found the argument somewhat convincing.

"Then what happened?" Stanley didn't have an adequate defense for why horrible things happen to good people.

"They put a bunch of vines on his head."

"Vines?"

"Yeah, the kind with thorns. They pressed it down on his head an' he began to bleed. It ran into his eyes an' they wouldn't let him wipe it off. They pulled off his clothes."

Adam looked away. "He swore at them in another language. They said look at him standing there naked as a jay bird. They made fun of him. They put Halloween clothes on him an' a gorilla mask. There was a lot of laughing. I tried not to look at him. One time he was crying and begging for his life. I wanted to go up and tell him not to do that."

"Why? Because it would make it worse for him?"

Adam nodded, then hung his head.

"The main guy, he kept asking him, are you the king of the Jews? At first, he'd yell back, no, I'm not Jewish. I'm a Mexican. But they wouldn't listen to him. He said I don't want to die, stop doing this to me, but they kept on asking him that question. They punched him in the gut and slapped his face. Finally, he got real quiet and told them that it didn't do any good to answer them, they were going to do whatever the hell they wanted with him. He looked at me an' said remember my name. But they told him I'd forget it."

After the rush of these words, Adam stopped cold.

Stanley waited. The air hung heavy with Adam's struggle to talk.

"I forgot his name," the boy stammered.

"And then you remembered," Stanley asserted. "Then you remembered," he repeated.

Adam looked up at Stanley with appreciation. "You helped me to remember."

"*He* helped you to remember." Stanley was referring to the vision in the sweat lodge. *Vision or hallucination, I don't care*, thought Stanley. *I will use whatever the boy presents for the healing process.*

"Was there a small group of people there?" Stanley asked.

Adam shook his head. "No. There were lots of people and more coming all the time."

"Adults only?"

Again, Adam shook his head.

"So, there were children there as well?" It was more of a statement than a question.

"And teenagers," Adam added.

"Didn't anyone protest or try to stop what was happening at this mock trial?" Stanley pushed.

"Mock?" Adam was confused.

"Adam, this was not a real trial." The therapist leaned forward to explain.

"But they were adults," Adam said. It was obviously real to him.

Stanley sat back for a moment. "When you watch television and you see one person shoot another, is that real?"

Adam shook his head. "But this wasn't television."

Adam's right, Stanley concluded. *The blood that ran down the man's face was real. The jeering and the lust for the drama was real.*

"Okay," Stanley conceded the point. "You said that there were children and teenagers there, as well as adults. Did you know any of them?"

Adam nodded. "Emily was there. I knew her. Sometimes she helped me, told me what to do and say, so they wouldn't hurt me. She snuck me some food."

She also kidnaped you, Stanley was tempted to say but held his tongue. *In that situation, Adam needed to believe that someone would look out for him.*

And then Stanley slowly inquired, "Did you recognize anyone else?"

At first, Adam shook his head.

Stanley pushed a little harder. "Among the children, Adam. Was there anyone among the children whom you recognized?"

The answer came snapping out, like a whip protesting in the brittle air, too fast, much too fast: "I don't remember. I don't remember. I don't remember."

* * * *

The investigation into Shunka's death yielded nothing. A neighbor of the Arbres had noticed a green truck cruising up the road early that morning. Neither Hawk nor Adam ever found conclusive proof about who had killed Shunka, but they did discover tracks in the woods— those of a heavy-set man.

FORTY-EIGHT

RECONSTRUCTING HOME

Love is not love until love's vulnerable.

—THEODORE ROETHKE
The Dream

Bleary-eyed, Daisy sat glumly on the bar stool by the kitchen counter, bare feet splayed on the lower rung, her hair wild and uncombed, her sleeveless shirt half in and half out of her denim shorts. She was bent so low over the counter, that her nose was almost dipping into her cup of coffee.

"You look like something the cat dragged in," Jillian commented.

"I *hate* my name," the teenager exclaimed.

"Why? Would you rather be a Rose, a Tulip, or a Daffodil?"

"No-o-o," Daisy whined. "I mean my last name. I hate being known as the Bassett kid."

"Oh." Jillian couldn't really blame her.

"You know my Dad's disappeared?"

"Oh?" Jillian hadn't known. "Maybe he's just away for a couple of days."

"You mean drinking? No, he's taken his clothes, that old green

Chevy pick-up, and all his stuff. I went up to the house yesterday. He's gone. I told you he doesn't give a damn about me."

Jillian couldn't refute that conclusion either. She went up to the morose teenager and wrapped her arms around Daisy. "Well, I give a goddamn," she asserted.

Normally Daisy would have tightened up against the embrace but this time it felt warm and loving and good. The sourness in her began to sweeten. "Jillian?"

The woman pulled back and looked into the girl's face. "Yes?"

"I'm seventeen now. I've got an idea."

Instinctively, Jillian knew that Daisy was about to ask for a favor. "Ideas at seventeen are always dangerous," she said.

"I want the courts to declare me an independent adult."

Isn't she happy here with us? Jillian didn't know where Daisy's ideas were taking her.

Daisy continued, "I want to tell them what my father has done to me."

Oh, oh, confession time. Jillian guessed at what was coming next.

"I want to tell the courts that my Dad forced me to have sex with him when I turned thirteen and that my mother knew about it."

Jillian put her hands on Daisy's shoulders and looked her straight in the eyes. She had known that the time would come when Daisy had to face her past. "Okay, if that's what you want to do, I'll stand behind you or beside you, whatever you need."

But Daisy hadn't finished. "I want the court to protect me from any further contact with my parents."

"Sounds reasonable to me," Jillian agreed.

"And then, I want to take your last name."

"You want us to adopt you?" Jillian was confused.

"No," replied Daisy. "I just want to have your last name. I want to be known as Daisy Townsend, not Daisy Bassett."

"People will think that I have adopted you as my daughter," Jillian cautioned.

"That's all right with me," said Daisy.

Jillian smiled. She touched the girl's cheek. "Then it's all right with me."

* * * *

"I'm proud of our son," Larry commented. His long black hair flared off his shoulders. "Hawk tells me that he's standing tall, like a warrior. He's counting coup on those who kidnaped him."

"I'm scared for our family," Lucy said. "How is it that people think they can come onto our property and steal my child, then take our dog and kill him? I don't feel safe anymore, Larry."

"This is our home. Nobody's going to drive us out of here," he replied.

"I'm scared for my son. Maybe they'll slit his throat next." Lucy couldn't shake off her fear.

"What would you have us do, Lucy? Run away from them?"

"Maybe we ought to think about going home to Pine Ridge. I've got lots of family there."

Larry shook his head. "Yeah? Well, kids can disappear there as well. We're already on a reservation, one that gives us good jobs, good medical care. It's unlike you to be so afraid."

"I worry about Eva. What's going to happen to her when her brother comes home? Will she be safe from him? You know what I'm talking about, don't you?"

Larry knew she worried that Adam might touch his little sister again. "I guess we'll have to take it day by day."

"That's not good enough, Larry."

Frustration and impatience raised his voice, made it louder. "Well, goddamn it, what do you want, Lucy? A perfect world?"

To his surprise, a sour, wry laugh greeted him. "Yes," she answered. "I want my family back the way it used to be."

* * * *

Seated around Hawk's inipi fire, Larry complained, "I don't know how to make my wife feel safe anymore. I feel so goddamn helpless these days."

Hawk studied the flames curling around the wooden foundation for the stones. He pointed to the blaze. "Fear is like that fire. Starts with a spark, then soon it's blazing all over the place."

"I've got a big favor to ask of you, Bro'." Larry's reluctance was marked by the hesitation in his speech.

Hawk watched the flames reach up over the base, fingers flickering toward the dark night sky.

"Lucy wondered if . . ." Larry stopped, then started again. "Could you and Meggie keep Adam?"

Hawk nodded toward the boy who was over by the wood pile, splitting wood. "Seems to me he's here already."

"Yes, but I mean, after he's finished with the therapy. Lucy figures if he stays with you, she can see Adam every day but not have to worry about Eva. It's a lot to ask of you," Larry acknowledged.

Hawk turned and briefly looked at Larry. "Adam's family."

In the world of Native Americans, that was all that needed to be said.

*   *   *   *

Adam liked to work with the wood while his father and cousin were talking by the fire. Wood had taught him many things: If you go against the grain, the log splinters and the cut grabs the blade. But if you go with the grain, the log willingly yields to the axe's energy. He liked the smell of resin, the curlicues of the grain around knots, the slabs of rough bark, the inner red cores leaching into the white flesh.

They were talking about him. He could tell by the way his father unnaturally hushed his voice, below Adam's range of hearing. It didn't matter. It simply meant his father and his cousin loved him. That's what mattered.

Thwack! Another piece split open to reveals its innards. The axe surged with his energy. With all the fence-building, he had grown strong over the summer. Adam had even learned to enjoy the low-fat cooking of his cousin's wife. But, most of all, he liked the stories she would tell him at night.

Sometimes the stories were personal and came from her childhood at Chrysalis. Sometimes he'd let her into his world. He even told her about how he had experimented with alcohol but she never criticized him or wagged a finger at him. Instead, she told him tales that always curled around to whatever he had just confessed, but not in any way he could put his finger on. Those were the stories that left him thinking.

She not only taught him about the Greek gods and goddesses but also about the Norse gods. Gosh darn, they fought more than his parents ever did!

"You see, there are many ways that people have tried to understand their human experience and the Sacred," Meggie had said. "It's like a diamond, brilliant in reflection, but turn that diamond just a bit and you will see a whole new facet."

But what he saw was that in every culture there were always people who didn't get it. People who misunderstood their purpose in life and the Trickster Spirits out to cause them mischief. People who thought that their way was the only way to understand life.

Best of all, he loved the Lakota stories and traditions. It wasn't just that his grandmother, mother, and Hawk all came from that tradition. There was something special in the sweat lodge and the Pipe ceremonies. They were a way he could reach out, in his own story, and touch into the Sacred. He didn't need any book or Bible, fancy clothes, or fancy words. All he needed was a good heart.

He looked at his broad-shouldered father, so strong and handsome, the fire flicking gold glitter onto his black hair. Adam wanted to look exactly like him when he got older. But deep in his heart he thought he might follow in his cousin's footsteps, in the way of his grandmother, and learn more about Lakota medicine. Some day he wanted to go up on the hill and ask for a vision for his life. He kept these wishes to himself.

Later, when they piled into the sweat lodge, closed the door, and began the first round of the inipi, Adam settled into the warm darkness, the only light coming from the glow of hot, red stones. It was bright enough that he could make out the comforting and shadowy presence of Hawk to the left of the door and his father to the right. He was proud to be with them. He felt safe in the lodge.

During the first round, after Hawk had sung his Spirit-calling song, Adam overheard a sound that astonished him: His father was quietly weeping. In all his life, Adam had never witnessed his father cry. He wondered if it had to do with him.

Hawk broke into a Stone song, a chant that brought courage to those who felt weak, endurance to those who were suffering, and compassion to those who had kept their griefs to themselves. He sang the prayer song over and over until Adam's father finally emptied himself of his sorrow.

In the hot steam, Adam prayed quietly for strength to come to his dad.

Hawk spoke words of gratitude for all the things that went into the making of the ceremony—the way the Stone Nation invited the two-leggeds into their lodge, the Lightnings who gifted the fire, the tree nations who provided the wood, and the water without which the human beings could not live.

His dad uttered a simple prayer, over and over: "Wopila, Wopila for my son."

After the door had been raised and the steam had rushed out the door, the three of them drank the water that had been purified in the inipi.

The door came down again and the time for personal prayers began.

Larry prayed first for Lucy, that she might rediscover her power. "It is not like her to be so afraid, Tunkasila." He asked the Good Spirits to watch over his little girl. He gave thanks for the love and care Hawk and Meggie were showing to his son.

Last, but not least, he made strong prayers for his son. "Adam Stands-By-Dog is my son. I am proud to be his father. He shows courage when others would have run away. Grandfather, it is awful what my son had to endure, but I ask that you make it for a reason. That what he has learned from this experience be something that he can take into manhood, something to make him a better human being. In the old days, some of the most powerful medicine people were those who had gone through a great sickness or ordeal when young. They came back from those experiences stronger, wiser, better able to listen to the Spirit world. I ask you, the Grandfathers, to help Adam Stands-By-Dog take what he needs from this experience. I ask you, Unci Maka, to help him bury those things he no longer needs. Mitakuye oyas'in."

Adam sat quietly, his eyes adjusting to the blackness around him. He welcomed his father's prayers and was deeply moved. On his left, he felt a strange sense of peace settle over him as if there were a protective Presence next to him. He could see nothing; he knew the men were waiting for him to pray. Hawk had already offered water to the stones. But his silence continued as he grew in strength.

I am here, the Voice whispered into his left ear.

It was not the voice of the hitchhiker. It was a woman's voice, an old woman's voice.

Adam smiled. His old world was beginning to reconstruct itself. "Wopila," the boy exclaimed.

For the third round, the Pipe round, Larry brought in new stones searing red with heat. He pulled down the door. Except for the sizzling, faint glow from the stone pit, all was dark again.

Hawk gave thanks for the Chanunpa and the gift of the White Buffalo Calf Woman to the Lakota people. "All our Pipes are the children of that original buffalo pipe," he said.

"We ask for healing for our young cousin," Hawk continued. "He has gone through what no human being should have to experience. In this Pipe round, we ask that You bend over and surround him with your healing energies, make him strong enough to remember what he has to remember, help him to forget what he no longer needs to hold onto. In his veins, he carries the blood of his people, both Lakota and Ojibway. Let him know that to be a warrior is to recognize his fear but not stop from doing what has to be done. Adam Stands-By-Dog, tell the Grandfathers what you need to stand strong. Mitakuye oyas'in."

Hawk put water on the stones and waited.

"Tunkasila Wakan Tanka, Grandfathers of the Four Winds, Unci Maka, Grandmother, Wanbli Gleska, this is Adam Stands-By-Dog. I ask that You hear my prayer. I ask that you send me the help that I need, so that I can live as a human being. Tunkasila, onsimala ye." It was a short prayer but Adam didn't know what else to say.

"Hau!" Hawk grunted approval that Adam was learning the language of his people. He poured water on the blistering stones. They threw hot, hissing steam into the air until it was almost impossible to breathe without scorching one's lungs.

But Adam continue to sit up straight and tall with his eyes peering into the darkness. He paid special attention to the left of him, the space between himself and Hawk, where he had previously sensed a hidden Presence. At first, all he could see was a swirling pattern of energy in that space and then slowly that energy converged and condensed. Adam had to wipe the sweat off his eyelids to make sure that what he was seeing was truly there, not just a wish or fantasy.

In that space between Hawk and himself sat his grandmother, Winona. She had come back to him.

She smiled. *I told you I was here.*

"Can they see you?" Adam was referring to Hawk and his dad.

Hawk can. If he is paying attention.

"Hau!" Hawk answered.

"Will you stay with me? Will you come to see me again?"

Will you pray with your chanunpa? she asked.

Adam nodded.

Then I will come. When you no longer need to see me, you'll find me in your heart. Adam watched as the vision of his grandmother dissolved back into the blackness.

"Wopila," exclaimed Hawk, pouring more water on the stones. "This is a very hard thing that your grandmother does for you. It is not easy to cross back Over. She does it because she loves you and you need her right now."

Adam turned toward his left and vowed, "With your help, I'm going to remember."

FORTY-NINE

To Sleep or Not to Sleep

*The meaning of my existence is that life has
addressed a question to me. Or, conversely, I
myself am a question which is addressed to the
world, and I must communicate my answer, for
otherwise I am dependent upon the world's answer.*

—Tess Gallagher
Borrowed Strength

"Tell me," asked Meggie, stretching out on the bed next to the napping Hawk, "why didn't Winona come earlier? During the kidnaping, Adam said he called out to her several times but she never showed herself to him. More than anything else, I think her absence drove Adam to the final despair of capitulation."

A midnight philosophical discussion was the last thing Hawk desired. The inipi ceremony, the week of listening to Adam's story, had exhausted him. Sleep weighted his eyelids but he struggled to respond. It was an honest question. "I don't really know," he said. "Isn't that what everyone asks? Why doesn't the Creator come down and lift up my burdens? How can bad things happen to good people?" He lifted himself up on his elbows.

"But why does Winona appear now?" Meggie was determined to talk about it.

"She came in the middle of ceremony, when the Chanunpa was filled and on the altar," he said.

"Do you mean that she needs help to cross back over?" Meggie knew nothing about the movement of Spirits.

Hawk sat up and stroked Meggie's hair. He tried to find the words to explain what little he understood. "I think that They won't come unless we make a place for them. When Adam entered into the inipi, anything became possible for him. His eyes, his ears, his mind opened up and there she was."

"And so, if a person doesn't believe in the Spirits . . ."

"Then he won't see or hear Them." Hawk finished her sentence.

"It's as simple as that?" Meggie was astonished.

"Well," he tempered his statement, "it's one thing to believe in the Spirits, but if you're not open to Them, how will you ever welcome Them with your eyes and ears? Fear will shut down your awareness. When you're afraid, it's often impossible to trust that They are there, all around you."

"So you think Winona was with him during the whole trauma and he just didn't know it?"

Instead of answering her question, Hawk pulled a strand of her hair with his teeth. "If I die before you, Meggie, I'll come back and haunt you. That's a promise."

Meggie didn't know if he were being serious or not. "Why would you do that? I thought the dead had to make a long journey south."

"Oh," Hawk stretched, then wrapped a leg over hers. "Do you think I would ever let you be with another man? No way. If I were cold in the ground and you started dating, all you'd need to do is to look at the end of the bed. There I'd be, shaking my head and telling you that I'd better not catch you messing around."

Meggie pushed him over to his side of the bed. "Go to sleep," she said.

But he rolled right back towards her. "Correction. I was going to sleep until my love decided that we had to stay up to talk."

She laughed. It was true that she had jostled him awake. And she could tell from his amorous advances that much more than his mind had been awakened.

✳ ✳ ✳ ✳

Adam had filled his little chanunpa. His face was serious as he looked straight ahead at Stanley's window. Hawk perched in the corner, quiet as usual. Adam didn't wait for Stanley's summary.

"I remember now," the boy said.

Stanley waited.

"There were about five other kids there younger than me. One of them was June."

"June Tubbs?"

Adam nodded.

"They said that if I ever talked about her, they would come find me and I would die. They'd take my sister and hurt her, in the way they did to June." Adam cast wild eyes toward Hawk. "Will you tell Mom and Dad, so they can protect her?"

"I will," Hawk promised.

"What did they do to her?" Stanley spoke very carefully, not wanting the boy to rush into quicksand and get swallowed up in the suck of guilt and grief.

"They'd given her the green drink too. It made her sick. She said she was sore and was bleeding."

"Bleeding? Where?" Stanley pushed for detail.

Adam cast his eyes down toward his waist. "Down there," he answered, embarrassed. "She said they had told her she was the bride of Satan or something like that. And that several men had . . . hurt her there."

Stanley could feel his fingers curling into his palms, making involuntary fists. Consciously, he relaxed his muscles. "This was on Friday, right?"

The boy nodded and continued. "They kept us kids together, gave us peanut butter sandwiches. I didn't see the hitchhiker guy. They let us fall asleep on the floor. We were pretty tired. A couple of the kids were crying. I wanted to sleep a long, long time."

"Were you hoping that when you woke up, you'd find that it had just been a bad dream?" Stanley asked.

Adam nodded. "At sundown, more grownups came. Lots of them dressed up in robes. We were told that somebody was going to be 'sacrificed' an' we were all scared that it might be one of us kids. There was a big bonfire an' then they dragged out the hitchhiker. He was naked and had red marks across his face and back, like he'd been whipped. He was screaming but the guys pinned him down on a large wooded cross. They tied his arms an' took nails an' hammered his hands and feet to the wood." Disgust and fear rippled across Adam's face. His breathing came short and fast.

"Then they raised that cross toward the fire. People were clapping their hands and cheering. Some even picked up burning sticks and hit him. They raised the cross with him on it an' then . . ."

Adam stopped cold.

The image of the crucified man dangled between them in the therapy room. Hawk rested his chin in the palms of his hands, his fingers cupping his cheeks, as if his brain had gotten too heavy to be supported solely by his neck. Stanley gripped his hands together, a forced calmness. And Adam kept staring straight ahead, his pipe held out before him.

"They told us kids that each one of us had to take this knife they had an' . . . they made us, they made me, they made me stab the hitchhiker in the side. They held my hands. They pushed the knife in. I could feel the blade pushing in. It made a squishy sound. An' he screamed."

Adam's words could hardly be heard between each hiccupping breath.

"Take a break and breathe deeply," Stanley suggested, practicing it himself.

Adam did as he was told, inhaling and exhaling as if his very life counted on it. But the pus was demanding release and so Adam resumed the telling of his story:

"He was bleeding a lot. But he was still alive. With ropes, they lifted up the cross and pulled it into the fire. An' then his screams became like a dog howling in pain. An' I could smell it. I could smell him burning. I could see him on fire. And even when I couldn't see him anymore, 'cuz of the fire, I could hear him. I heard him all night long. I can even hear him now." Adam nestled the pipe on his lap and brought his hands up to his ears as if to block out the sound of the man's agony.

Adam closed his eyes, picked up the chanunpa, and forced himself to continue. "Then there was all this kind of dancing and eating. An' people were drinking a lot of stuff. Some guy came and took June and the other kids away. I remember how she called out to me, but I couldn't follow her. They wouldn't let me. Then, sometime later, I went to sleep."

Much to Hawk's and Stanley's surprise, Adam's head dropped against the back of the chair, his hands still clutching the pipe, lowered to his lap, and his breath came deep and peaceful. Stanley signaled to Hawk that the two of them should tiptoe out of the room and let the boy have a brief nap.

Outside of the office, Hawk scratched his head. "Never seen him do that before."

Stanley replied, "Sleep was his main defense at that time. It was the only way out for him. Maybe something even worse was about to be revealed today."

"How could there be anything worse?" Hawk asked.

*   *   *   *

That evening, Hawk took Meggie aside and recounted the psychotherapy session to her. Meggie shook her head, incredulous, saying, "The details make me feel dirty."

Hawk could understand that feeling. The knowledge of what was done to Adam and June was like a creeping stain that seeped everywhere into his own consciousness.

Man and boy had returned home, exhausted from the session. Like two maniacs, they drove themselves to hard work on the fence, pounding in the last fence poles. Now it was simply a matter of stringing up the barbed wire. The physical labor had been cleansing. It had distracted their minds, made them feel like they had accomplished something worthwhile.

Over dinner, Meggie announced, "School will be starting soon. Your Mom and I talked. We thought that you'd probably want to go the school on the reservation."

"Where did the summer go?" Hawk asked, but not a one of them wanted to answer the question.

Later that night, Meggie tucked Adam in bed. "That's a fine fence you two have built. That reminds me. Did I ever tell you the story of the two farmers, best friends, who grew up next to each other?"

Adam nestled down under the covers to hear the story.

Meggie sat on the edge of his bed and began the tale. "As kids, they played together, went to school together, grew up, got married, helped each other with farming, raised their children, and spent most of their free time together. They were the best of friends. It was difficult to know where the land of one began and the other ended. As they got older, their own kids moved away and their wives both died. Still, on a summer's evening, the two old men would sit on each other's porch and reminisce about the good old days.

"One day, a tawny cat pranced up on the porch. One of the old guys said, 'How do you like my new cat?' but the other fellow got really angry. 'That's my cat, not yours.' Well, wouldn't you know it, but they got into the worst fight of their whole relationship. Before long, one of them stormed off to his own home."

Adam smiled. He had experienced fights like that with his own friends.

Meggie continued. "Well, the first man was so furious, he cranked up his tractor and changed the course of the creek so that it clearly divided the two properties. There would no longer be any simple strolling over for a visit.

"When the second farmer saw what his neighbor had done to the creek, he said, 'This is war!' Around that time, a young man arrived at his door and asked for food and overnight lodging, promising to work it off the next day. Well, the farmer welcomed him. 'I'm going to town tomorrow, but I've got a project for you.'

"The next morning, the farmer pointed out the creek bed and a bunch of wood. He told the young man, 'I want you to build me a six-foot-high fence along the creek so that I never have to see that ugly face of my neighbor again.'

"The young man agreed and the farmer took off for market. At dusk when he returned, he found the young man putting away the tools. But there wasn't any fence there! No, what the young man had done was to build a bridge. And who should be coming across that bridge but his old friend? 'I'm so sorry,' the first farmer cried out. 'I should never have let myself get so angry at you.' The two old men hugged each other and wept.

"Finally, the second farmer turned to the young man. He said, 'You did a good piece of work there, young fellah. I could use a man like you around my place.' But you know what the young man said?"

Adam shook his head.

Meggie smiled and brushed a lock of hair off the boy's face. "He said, 'Thanks but I need to head on up the road. I've got more bridges to build.'"

A puzzled expression knitted across Adam's eyebrows.

Meggie leaned over and kissed him on the cheek. "Sometimes we need to build fences. Sometimes we need to construct bridges."

*   *   *   *

Hawk was optimistic that finally he was going to get a good night's sleep. Meggie seemed tired and that boded well for him. His eyes were slipping to half mast. The book that rested between his hands and on his chest kept tilting precariously, then jerking upright. "Are you ready for sleep now?" he asked, hope trilling in his voice.

Meggie climbed into bed and pulled the sheet up to her shoulders. She turned out the light and snuggled, spoon-fashion behind him. He could feel the synchronicity of their breathing. It would be but a moment before he would slip into the deliciousness of unconsciousness.

"Honey," her voice grated in his ear.

He ignored her, pretending to be asleep.

"Sweetie," she whispered again, her breath tickling his right ear.

He gave up a sigh that was really a surrender. "Yes?" But he refused to open his eyes. It was a compromise.

"I have a question to ask you," she said.

"Only one?" he answered. He knew that Meggie could never restrain herself to just one question.

She began, "If we don't believe in Spirits, They won't come. So, why would anyone choose to believe in Evil Spirits? Why not just believe in Good Spirits?"

Hawk groaned. He opened one eye. "I didn't say that They wouldn't come. They're around us all the time, Meggie. It just depends whether we let ourselves see or hear Them." *Now maybe she'll let me sleep.*

No such luck.

"What if I take the position that I don't believe in Evil Spirits? A lot of people do that."

Meggie still didn't get it. Hawk opened up his other eye as well. "It doesn't matter what you believe. Evil is always there, just as are the Good Spirits and Trickster Spirits. Either you pay attention or you don't."

"And you think it dangerous to be ignorant, don't you?" Meggie said.

"Yes and no," he replied.

Sleep was going to be out of the question unless he could give her a more satisfactory answer. "There are those people who know nothing about the Sacred, about Good Spirits or Bad Spirits. That world doesn't exist for them. The Creator is dead to them. And since they don't make entry into the Sacred, they're of little interest to the Evil Spirits. But when you're a person who is involved in matters of the spirit and the Sacred, then the Evil Ones come around. They are attracted by all things wakan. The power pulls Them toward you."

Hawk was wide awake by this time. He turned toward Meggie to see if his explanation met with her approval. Her eyes were firmly closed.

She had fallen sound asleep.

Perhaps ignorance is bliss, he thought, his own eyes wide open.

FIFTY

DEATH AND REBIRTH

It's not that I'm afraid to die. I just don't
want to be there when it happens.

—WOODY ALLEN
Death

Meggie was between sessions when the office telephone rang. She picked it up, surprised to find Katja on the other end of the line.

"Are you busy? I can call you back later." Katja sounded excited.

Meggie consulted her watch. "I've got about five minutes before my next client."

"Guess who's going to school this fall?"

Before Meggie could answer, Katja continued. "Paul's accounting firm feels so sorry for Robert and me that they've hired me part-time. I'm already filing and learning their data entry system. Before long, they're going to teach me how to do simple tax returns. And, best of all, they're going to pay my tuition to go back to school in accounting. Luckily, I've already got my Bachelor's degree; otherwise it would take the rest of my life to become a CPA."

"Wonderful! Does Paul know yet?"

"No, and I'm not going to tell him," snorted Katya. "He's down in Illinois, setting up house with his new sweetie-pie. Who, I might say, is about half his age." Katya did not try to disguise the disgust in her voice.

Katja added, "It really hit me this summer that either I was going to turn into one of those frumpy, bitter divorce gals, spreading out at the hips and wallowing in the boredom of depression, or else I was going to stand up and do something with my life. The firm was none too happy with Paul's extended absences and eventual departure. We had mutual grievances. So, Paul has his new woman and I'm aiming for his old job," she declared.

It sounds like the old Katja, rising out of the ashes like the phoenix, thought Meggie.

"I have a question for you," Katja said.

"What's that?"

"What do you think a forty-three-year-old man talks about with a twenty-two-year-old woman?"

Meggie laughed. "I doubt that he's with her for the intellectual conversation."

"Men are real strange, aren't they? A woman's sexual energy doesn't even peak until she gets to thirty-five, yet their eyes are on the twenty-year-olds. The fire burns brighter, the conversation is better, the friendship is deeper with women their own age, yet they leave all that to chase the young female. It doesn't make sense." Bitterness punctuated each sentence.

But Meggie knew their marital problems ran deeper than that. *The dead child stands between them. They can see her in each other's reflection. She enters the fabric of their memories and, pulling threads of guilt, unravels their future dreams. It was more June than Katja from whom Paul was running.*

Meggie kept her thoughts to herself. She congratulated Katja again before rising from her desk to greet the next client.

* * * *

"Are you awake?" Stanley had decided to begin Adam's session with a bit of humor.

Adam nodded. After smudging himself, Hawk, and his therapist, Adam knelt down on the carpet and loaded his chanunpa. Then he resumed his place on the chair.

"Your falling asleep last time was not accidental," Stanley commented. "Did anything else happen the night of Good Friday?"

Adam stared at the bowl of his pipe and nodded.

"Are you ready to talk about it with us?"

But the boy didn't know if he would ever be ready to talk about the terror he felt. Adam squirmed in his chair as if his clothes were clawing at his skin.

He began, his voice distant, emotionless, "They said they'd won a great victory; they'd killed Jesus. Did I see that? Satan is all powerful, they told me. Did I believe in Him now? I said yes, I believed."

Adam hung his head, embarrassed by his quick acquiescence. "But they had more questions. They asked me if I loved my mother more than Satan. If I said no, they'd call me a liar. If I said yes, they were going to do something terrible to me."

Adam looked up at Stanley, his eyes searching for the right answer. "So, I told them that I loved my mother more than Satan."

Anxiety wrinkled across his forehead. Adam stared at his pipe. "They grabbed me. Said I was Mister Goody Two Shoes and needed to learn a lesson. They dragged me outside, yanked off my clothing. I was scared stiff. I tried to tell them, I love Satan, I believe in Satan, He's all powerful, but they wouldn't listen to me. They slapped my face and told me that I was going to die."

Adam bent over, fixated, concentrating on the carpet. "There was this big hole in the ground and a long black box. I tried to fight them but there were too many of them. The men opened that box and shoved me inside. I was on my back. There was no place to sit up. I . . . I couldn't move. It was all black inside."

Suddenly Adam's eyes glazed over, unseeing, remembering only that which was now in his inner vision. He screamed, "Let me out. Let me out!" His heels kicked at the floor. He was back on the farm and it was the night of Good Friday.

Quickly, Stanley reoriented him. "You're in my office, Adam. You're safe here."

Adam looked around the room, lost and confused. He had not let go of the pipe.

"Take some deep breaths now," Stanley ordered.

Adam's breathing slowed down. The pupils of his eyes refocused. He came back into the room with them peering all around like a buck sensing unseen danger in the woods.

"You found yourself in the box." Stanley picked up the threads of the unraveling story.

Adam exhaled. "I banged on the top of the box. I begged them, please open up, please. I'll be good. I'll be bad. I heard them laughing. Okay, they said. The top opened a little bit and a hand came in, shaking a paper bag upside down over my head and chest."

Adam's shoulders scrunched up as if to protect his neck. The bowl of the pipe was almost touching his chin. His face flinched and goose bumps shivered across his arms.

The boy swallowed hard, distastefully. "Bugs. There were bugs in that bag. They were moving all over me, crawling on me. They shut the box. I couldn't see what kind of bugs they were. They were in my hair, on my face, my chest, my arm pits, walking on me, biting me every-where." His elbows began to rub against his sides.

"I couldn't turn in the box. I cried out, please, please, please, I begged them. But they didn't open the box. Then I heard the sound of a key turning in the lock. An' I knew they were making sure I'd never get out."

The boy's voice went dead. "Then I could feel them lifting the box, 'cuz it was moving back and forth. For a second I thought oh good, they're going to let me out of here. But then the box began to drop and bump against something on both sides. An' I remembered the hole. They were putting the box into the hole."

Adam's breath began to get patchy. "I yelled. I screamed. I wet myself 'cuz I knew what they were doing." His voice rose higher into a controlled hysteria. "I heard the dirt hit the top of the box, falling like rain. An' they were laughing. Then I couldn't hear anything.

"An' I banged an' yelled at them to let me out, 'cuz there were all these bugs on me. An' it was dark an' I knew they were never coming back to get me."

Adam wriggled in his chair as if his flesh were on fire. His legs and knees banged against each other, his shoulders moved up and down, his whole body twitched.

"Some of the bugs had little feet. I think they were spiders. Some were slimy. They bit into me. They sucked on me. I tried to squish them but there were too many. I could feel them on my lips, trying to get into my mouth. They were on my eyes. I couldn't breath. I could feel them trying to get inside my nose."

Adam looked around the room, panic riding high in his voice. "It was dark in there. I was scared. An' I was afraid they were going to leave me there. My mom and dad would never find me. I was never going to get out of there."

Tears were running down his cheeks. His breath seized up and he began to cough, sucking in air. Adam couldn't stop wiggling about in the chair. With his right hand, he reached up and started scratching large gashes on his neck.

"They were crawling in my hair an' I couldn't get them offa me." His left hand, holding the pipe, began to jerk until a rippling motion seized his whole body.

Without warning, Hawk stood up and retrieved Adam's pipe bag. He fished a wad of sage leaves, rolled them into a ball, dropped it into the smudge bowl, and lit the sage. The leaves burst into flame, then smouldered. From his hat in the corner, Hawk pulled out an eagle feather and plumed the smoke all over his little cousin.

Stanley watched in fascination as the boy's patchy breathing calmed and his body relaxed in the chair. Hawk touched the boy with the eagle feather, saying, "With the power of the chanunpa, your grandmother comes back to be with you."

Adam's eyes once again refocused. Hawk returned to his chair but left the sage ball smoking in the center of the room.

Stanley waited a few minutes. "How long were you in that box, Adam?"

Adam shrugged his shoulders. His words issued forth measured and monotone, without emotion. "When they let me out, it was dark again. I was in the box a long, long time. One day at least. After awhile, I kind of gave up, you know."

Stanley shook his head. "No, I don't know. What do you mean when you say you gave up?"

Adam turned and looked briefly at his cousin, then back to Stanley. His voice sagged. "I thought I was dead."

Then Stanley knew. *It wasn't a box. It was a coffin.*

Adam continued. "When they pulled me out, they told me I had died. That now I was coming to life again as one of Satan's servants. But that I would still have to prove to them that I was one of them. They gave me some black bread and milk and then some white pills. They said it would make things clearer to me."

Adam kept looking at his pipe. "Emily asked me if I wanted anything else. She was real kind to me. She'd gotten me some clothes. I told her I wanted to be with June. So she took me over to the other kids and there was June."

Stanley hated to ask, "How was June?"

Adam answered, "She said they told her she was really special to them. They made her lie down on a cold rock. They painted something on her body an' there were candles all around. She told me she didn't want to be special, you know. They gave her some real food, then that yucky stuff to drink. It made her feel dizzy. She was happy to see me."

"Then what happened?" Stanley asked.

Adam shook his head and turned back toward Hawk.

Hawk spoke up. "I think my little cousin has said enough today. He wants both of us to kneel down with him while he does the pipe ceremony."

Stanley understood that it would be counter-therapeutic to push the boy faster than he was willing to go. Following Hawk's lead, he slipped off his shoes and sat down on the floor next to Hawk. Together, the three of them smoked the chanunpa in silence.

* * * *

"It sounds like you've gotten up to Saturday night in the boy's story," Gertrude observed.

"How much of it is true?" Stanley asked.

"What do you mean?" Gertrude fired back.

"Do you think that they really killed the hitchhiker? Do you think they really ate human flesh?" Stanley's face contorted into creases of revulsion.

"Does the boy have all of his ten fingers?" Gertrude asked the rhetorical question.

Stanley shook his head.

"Can people be depraved enough to do this kind of thing? Sure they can. Can people stage such events to make it appear that they are more powerful than they really are? That happens all the time, Stanley. But it is up to the police to determine what really happened, not us. We're involved in the battle for the boy's mind."

For his soul, Meggie silently amended.

"By that Saturday night," Gertrude continued, "Adam was believing everything they told him. It was clear to him that these people would kill him unless he willingly agreed to convert, to join them as Satan's servant. They'd taken him from his home, stripped him naked, given him electric shock, deprived him of food, water, and sleep, drugged him, forced him to participate in the murder of his only adult friend, then lowered him into a coffin filled with insects. Alongside all these actions, they offered explanations which, in the logic of the cult, began to make sense to him."

"But isn't it important that we know the truth of what really happened?" Stanley persisted.

Gertrude snorted and lifted her hands. "Stanley, you should have been a police officer."

"So we'll probably never know?" Meggie said.

"What was the *truth* for the boy? That is our concern. It is always nice to have corroboration, but it rarely happens. We are therapists, not FBI agents. And what do people do nowadays, when they don't like what therapists uncover? They sue the therapist." Gertrude was shaking her head.

"Kill the messenger," chorused Stanley.

"It's like those three little monkeys. . . ." Gertrude began.

"Hear no evil, see no evil, speak no evil," Meggie interjected.

"Precisely," pronounced Gertrude.

* * * *

"You know who called the other day?" Bev peered round into Meggie's office as she was filling out a stack of insurance forms.

"Who?" Meggie looked up at her friend.

"Jillian Townsend. You know, that straight-laced woman at the animal clinic. The one that barks at you if you leave the door open or arrive late for an appointment."

Meggie chuckled. She was well acquainted with Jillian's ways. "I thought the only time you went there was last year, when you were trying to domesticate Sam." Meggie's eyes twinkled with mischief.

"Well, Karl's given me a female kitten. He thinks it may create more maternal aspirations in me. All I know is that the fluffy little thing is costing me an arm and a leg for shots."

"The kitten has a name, doesn't she?" Meggie could see that Bev was trying to keep her distance.

"Well, I'm thinking of calling her 'Kat.'" Bev studied the diamond ring on her finger.

"Kat?"

Bev grinned. "Aren't you the one who told me that names are important. That one should have a name to grow into?"

"So, when are you getting married?" Meggie asked the crucial question.

"Before the end of the year. Karl wants it to be in the church with the bishop presiding. I asked if there were any way we could do the ceremony without mentioning God. Karl thinks I'm just being stubborn. But you know, Meggie, I haven't had the experiences you've had. I'm still uncertain. I don't want to believe something just because others believe. I'm a scientist. You told me last New Year's Day that this would probably be the year I'd uncover my spiritual side. But you know what I really want?"

Meggie didn't have the slightest idea.

"Proof. I want some kind of proof that God exists. Without it, I'd be a fool to sign on to any religious belief."

"What does Karl say?" Meggie wondered how the two of them would negotiate the demands of the church upon their lives.

"He asks me if I believe in love. Of course, I do. He tells me that is proof enough, and that I'll realize it some day. The man is a true optimist." Bev was shaking her head. "But I absolutely adore him."

"That's plain to see."

"Anyway," Bev continued, "Jillian called me. I thought maybe her husband could no longer tolerate her bossiness, but that wasn't it at all.

She asked if I could see the girl that is living with them—Daisy Bassett. You know anything about her?"

What Meggie knew, she couldn't tell. "I hear that she's a tough teenager," Meggie said, shuffling her papers.

"Good. That's the way I like them. Spunky. All Jillian said was that Daisy wanted to see a therapist, that she came from an incestuous family." Bev was still on a fishing expedition.

"I'm glad she's coming to see you. The two of you will work well together. I just hope . . ." Meggie paused.

"Yes?"

"I hope that the girl has good insurance," Meggie finished.

Bev cocked her head. "Why do you say that?"

Meggie shrugged her shoulders, indicating that she didn't want to say much more. "I think she's going to be in therapy with you for a good long time."

FIFTY-ONE

POKEWEED TEA

*If you are forced to live in a nightmare, you survive
by realizing that you can reimagine it, that some day
you can return to reality.*

—LAWRENCE THORNTON
Imagining Argentina

"Are you okay, Mom?" Meggie crooked the phone receiver between
her ear and her neck as she prepared to sample Hawk's bean soup
bubbling on the back burner.

"Meggie, you must stop worrying about me. Of course I'm going to
be all right. I have my moments of crying, but you don't live this long
without having developed routines. And right now, those routines are
providing me with a lot of stability and comfort. I miss your Dad all the
time. So, I'm thinking of getting a puppy. Would you recommend someone like Baby?"

Meggie didn't know whether to be amused or dismayed that her
mother was mentioning her father and a dog in the same breath.
"Mom," she cautioned, "terriers are for young people. They're crazy,
hyperactive creatures. Fritzie's my old buddy and I wouldn't take anything for what we've shared together these past few years, but will I
ever get another fox terrier? Not on your life."

Meggie dipped into the pot again and blew on the spoon. She took a quick sip. "Too spicy."

"Spicy? You think Baby is too spicy?" Meggie's mother was confused.

"Get yourself a sweet dog, an intelligent dog. One that won't bite porcupines. One that will make friends with other dogs instead of attacking three German shepherds all at once. One that won't burrow deep into a rabbit den and get trapped or thrust his nose into a rattlesnake hole." Meggie knew what she was talking about. Her little furry delinquent had already bounced into the kitchen and was now sitting on his haunches before her, his front two legs up, shamelessly begging.

"Did Fritzie do all that?" Her mother's voice shimmered with admiration.

"Get yourself a sheltie, Mom. They aim to please. They'll adore you without running you ragged."

"But Baby is so cute," her mother persisted.

Meggie deposited the tasting spoon on the stove and looked down at her feet. Almost as if on cue, Fritzie cocked his head with a kind of goofy expression that only a wire-haired fox terrier can manage.

"Definitely too spicy for you," Meggie reiterated.

*   *   *   *

Stanley sighed. He was weary. For the first time in his life, he was experiencing insomnia. He also had to fight against his own wish to block out what the boy was telling him. But Gertrude had faith in him. So did Meggie. And most importantly, so did Adam Arbre.

"How are you this morning?" he asked both Adam and Hawk.

The boy and the man nodded in turn. *Native American stoics*, reflected Stanley. *These are people who know how to endure without the hyperbole.*

Adam slipped off his shoes, smudged the office with the sage smoke, and prepared the pipe. Hawk took off his hat and placed it on his lap. Stanley used the time to breathe into a more relaxed, open state. When Adam was finished, the boy resumed his seat upon the chair.

"That Saturday night, you were finally released from the box."
Stanley had wanted to say *coffin* but it was prudent to stick to the boy's
wording. "Then you saw June again. She told you about some ritual
where they had painted her body. They had given her some yucky drink
that made her dizzy."

"The green stuff," Adam interjected. "They made me drink it also."

"What effect did it have on you?"

"Made me want to puke. My heart got to pounding real fast. Everything seemed real loud. Couldn't see straight. They also gave us
alcohol. 'Cuz I recognized the taste. My mind got real fuzzy."

"Can you remember what happened that evening?" Stanley started
nudging the narration.

Adam looked at the pipe. "Sort of."

"Sort of," Stanley repeated.

Adam then turned beseeching eyes upon Stanley, a look that said *Do
I really have to go through this?*

Stanley nodded, aware of a headache beginning its progression
across his brain.

Adam sighed a breath of resignation. He began. "There was a big fire
an' lots of people. They were all drinking an' having a good time. They
kept talking to us kids, telling us about how lucky we were to be with
them. They said that we mustn't ever tell anybody 'bout what we saw,
'cuz nobody would believe us and Satan would know. He knows everything. He's *in you*, they told us."

"In you?" Stanley didn't understand.

Adam bit his lower lip. He breathed deeply and stayed silent a full
four minutes.

He finally broke the silence. "They took all us kids and put things in
us."

"In you? Where in you?" Stanley wasn't sure what the boy meant.

Adam stood up, turned around, and bent over. With his right index
finger he pointed toward his rump then sat down, averting his eyes from
Stanley's gaze.

"How?" *Do I really want to know?* Stanley asked himself.

Adam stared at the carpet. "There was a long tube. They pulled my
pants down an' made me kneel on the ground. They told me to spread
my legs. They had a plastic bag with little squirmy snakes and spiders

in water an' then they pushed my head down." Adam gripped onto his pipe and closed his eyes.

The temperature in the room suddenly dropped.

Adam shuddered. "I felt it coming into me back there, water and things. It just kept coming, all wet and such. The men said now Satan's spies were inside of me forever. He knows what I do or what I say. I felt those things come into me. I can still feel them." Adam began to scooch around in the chair as if he had a bad case of worms.

"They're still crawling around inside of me." The boy grimaced. Then he rushed ahead, flushing out the rest of the story, his speech compressed and pressured. "They took the girls and did the same thing to them down there." He pointed to his front.

"Afterwards the adults took us off, one by one. A bearded man yanked me outside. Back of the barn. He shoved me down against the wall an' said it was time to show him I was Satan's servant. He told me to keep my head down and I did. He put his thing inside of me an' it hurt back there something awful, but I didn't cry. I bled, but I didn't cry. He wouldn't stop banging against me. It hurt so bad." Adam bent over, his body clenching against the remembered pain. He paused, to catch his breath.

"Later, they took me back to Emily. I started crying then an' she pulled me on her lap. I was crying like a baby an' she was saying poor thing, poor thing an' holding me. She was the only nice grownup there an' . . ." Adam started sobbing. The tears dribbled down his cheek.

Stanley stood up and retrieved the box of tissues. "Would you like me to take your pipe while you wipe your eyes?"

Adam nodded and exchanged the pipe for the tissues. When he had finished wiping his tears, Stanley handed back the pipe.

"Do you remember going to the hospital, after you were found?" Stanley asked, sitting back down.

The boy nodded.

"The doctors did an examination of you, inside and out. They found that there had been some tearing around your rectum."

"Rectum?" Adam didn't know the meaning of that word.

"Your asshole," Stanley explained. "But there were no snakes or spiders anywhere in your colon area."

"But it happened!' the boy protested.

"Adam, listen carefully. The body has its own way of rejecting things that don't belong there. They may have put little snakes inside of you, but your body got rid of them. They're not there now." Stanley spoke with as much medical authority as he could muster.

"Maybe they climbed up further," Adam guessed.

"It doesn't matter how far they went. The intestines would reject them as well. You don't have the snakes of Satan inside of you now," Stanley said.

He could see that the boy remained unconvinced.

In the corner, Hawk caught the therapist's eye. "I'll take care of it," Hawk said, fingering his hat. "We'll do a ceremony that'll purify my cousin inside and out."

Adam sat up straight.

Stanley took a deep breath. "Okay." He turned his attentions back to the boy. "After the man sexually assaulted you, what then happened?"

"I fell asleep."

"And then?"

"They woke us up right before dawn."

"Dawn on Easter morning?" Stanley wanted to make sure of the sequence of events.

Adam nodded.

"And?"

"They said that there had to be another sacrifice to the Lord and Master of Darkness."

Stanley could feel his stomach begin to twist.

"Another sacrifice?"

Adam's voice flattened. "They said it had to be one of us kids."

Stanley looked up at the clock on the wall, judging that there wasn't enough time in the session to process the new information.

"Adam," he said, "you've worked really hard today. But we're going to have to stop now. It's important that the three of us honor your pipe."

The boy nodded. It was okay with him to wait. He didn't want to talk about it anyway.

Stanley looked at Hawk.

"When we smoke the chanunpa together," Hawk said, "we put ourselves back into balance with the Creation and with each other."

The plume of smoke spiraled toward the ceiling as Adam lit and offered his pipe to All the Directions.

* * * *

"You're going to purify him inside and out?" Meggie was curious. She was cooking up a couple of chickens for the community sweat lodge ceremony that night.

Hawk hovered over the stove, steeping pokeweed tea. "Long ago, Winona told me this will clear out anything that ails you."

"Why not just give him Ex-lax or something like that?"

"Because this tea comes to him from his grandmother," he answered. He poured the hot liquid into a cup and sweetened it with honey, sampling it with his finger. Then he left the room to find his little cousin.

Hours later, emptied and somewhat weak from the laxative effect of the tea, Adam entered the sweat lodge. It was crowded with men. The community hadn't gathered together for some time and there was great spiritual hunger.

Despite the press of male bodies in the lodge, when the stones centered and the door came down, Adam sat up straight. The heat settled into him. He knew his grandmother was sitting there by his left side. He could feel her presence and it was making him grow stronger. He could hear his father begin the Spirit-calling song while his cousin intoned the opening prayers.

He was coming home.

"Is he going to be okay, Meggie?" Lucy fretted while setting the table. Her face knotted into a frown. Her hair was wet and stringy from the women's inipi ceremony.

Meggie, her cheeks shiny and red from the heat, put down the napkins and gave her a big hug. "Yes. You should be proud of him."

"Can't you tell me what he's been saying in the therapy?" Lucy still didn't know what had happened.

"It's better this way. He'll tell you when he's ready." *When the story is no longer so raw in the telling. When he is able to construct meaning from the events*, she thought.

"I feel guilty, Meggie."

"Guilty?" Meggie had never known Lucy to apologize or display weakness.

"Like I'm not being a good mother to him. Sometimes I think I'm overprotective of Eva, but . . ." The *but* spoke volumes.

"He's welcome to stay at Chrysalis as long as he wants and as long as you need him to be there, Lucy. It's not as if he doesn't get to see you and his dad a lot."

"I know," she said, pulling back from the hug.

"I have a confession to make too," Meggie said.

Lucy looked at her, curious.

Meggie said, "Despite our best efforts, I'm not getting pregnant. Maybe I'm past my fertile years, I don't know. So, despite all my professional success, there's been a kind of emptiness in my life. And then you asked us if we could take Adam and let him live with us. I could never replace you as a mother in his life nor would I want to . . . ."

Lucy waved her hand. "Hush. I'm not threatened by that. You're helping Adam and he loves you back. What goes around comes around."

For just the briefest of moments, Meggie felt Winona invade her thoughts. *Pay attention, the gifts of Unci Maka are all around you.*

Meggie smiled.

All she had to do was to keep her eyes open.

FIFTY-TWO

THE LAST BETRAYAL

The stupid neither forgive nor forget;
the naive forgive and forget; the wise
forgive but do not forget.

—THOMAS SZASZ
The Second Sin

With a flushed face, Stanley was pacing in the room when Meggie arrived for their supervision session with Gertrude. Onto the table he slapped the large file of Adam Arbre, exclaiming, "What am I supposed to do with this?" His voice was a mixture of anxiety and anger.

Gertrude spied Meggie at the door. "Come in, come in. Stanley has some things to say to us."

Meggie took her seat at the conference table. With a nod of her head, Gertrude encouraged Stanley to continue.

"I'm not sleeping well at night." He apologized for his frazzled appearance.

"Your dreams are bothering you?" Gertrude asked, tapping her fingers together.

"Yes," he conceded.

"And you find yourself angrier than usual?" The old woman pressed.

Stanley leaned over the table, his arms splayed to each side of the thick file, his hands clenched into knobby fists. "It makes me sick to think that there are people who can do this to a child. They make incest look tame."

With piercing eyes, Gertrude spoke. "I warned you, Stanley. I warned both of you that this would be difficult material to hear. While the typical perversions get acted out in such a setting, what these people are really after is to distort the child's whole personality, to twist the mind into believing what the cult believes."

"But why?" demanded Stanley. "Why do they involve children? Why not just consenting adults in their sick little games?"

"Stanley, Stanley," Gertrude chided. "Don't you understand that these Satanic cults see themselves as a religion? To them, they are simply setting up powerful conversion experiences. They use sleep and food deprivation, pain, terror, sacrifice, self-betrayal, degradation, and complicity in criminal acts as powerful incentives for a belief in Satan. They even turn the child's own physiology against him. Whose minds are easier to convert: Individuals with a lifetime of experience or children who trust the adult world?"

"But it's so evil," he pronounced.

"Yes. It is evil," Gertrude agreed.

"And . . ." There was more that Stanley had to say.

"Yes?"

"I feel like something has been stolen from me." Stanley thumped the table with his fist.

"Ach," said Gertrude. "Your trust in the essential goodness of the human race is kaput."

"Yes." He glared at the older woman who could zero into his psyche so quickly.

"So now, Stanley, you have to make a new accounting, do you not? A new way of understanding what life is about. You have to fit evil into your scheme of things. You can no longer say that evil is an abstract construct, concocted by dry theologians. You have to accept that evil and dark coexist with good and light. It is not an easy thing to do, and it makes you very mad."

Stanley heaved himself back up into a standing position. "I keep on bumping into my own rage." He gave a wry laugh. "I'm suffering from secondary post-traumatic stress disorder. And I can't even talk about or process this material with anybody but the two of you. It's confidential information and so it stays with me, inside of me, undigested and raw."

Meggie well understood Stanley's feelings. They matched her own.

Gertrude leaned forward from her wheelchair and spoke softly with compassion for Stanley's pain. "And even if you could speak about it with your friends, Stanley, most of them wouldn't believe you."

* * * *

"So we come to Easter morning then." Stanley could hear the fatigue weighing down his voice.

The boy nodded. He sat there on the chair in Stanley's office, his pipe loaded, the acrid scent of sage smoke still lingering in the air.

"It was still dark," Adam began. "They woke us all up. There were five of us kids."

"How old were the others?" Stanley asked.

"Younger than me. Five, six, or seven."

"Do you know if they were kidnaped like you? Or were their parents there?"

Adam shrugged his shoulders. It was obvious that he didn't have that information.

Stanley knew he was asking too many questions. He asked himself whether he was unconsciously delaying the story or whether the details were really necessary. He warned himself to keep quiet and let the boy continue.

"Go on," he said.

"They lined us up. Said that there was going to be one more offering to Satan. An' that one of us would be the one to have that honor. They said that another would do the choosing. An' when they asked who wanted to do the choosing, I raised my hand."

Adam peered around at Hawk in the corner. "I thought if I could choose, then I could save June."

Hawk nodded that he understood.

Adam then looked back at his pipe. "An' I thought I could save myself as well." He dropped his head, ashamed.

Stanley intervened, "You did what most people would do in that situation, Adam."

"But it didn't work out the way I thought it would," Adam continued. "They asked me who should be sacrificed, an' I pointed out the little one. I thought, she's not gonna understand what this is all about anyway. But they shook their heads and said no, she's too young. Satan wanted someone older. So I pointed out the other boy. But they said no, Satan wanted a girl child. That left only two, June and the other girl, so I said the other girl. And then they told me that she was too young or too old or something and that June was the perfect one. I told them no, I didn't pick her. They said yes, you did. They said I had chosen her by the process of elimination or something like that."

Adam's voice filled with indignation. He turned back towards Hawk. "I didn't choose her, did I? They said I did."

Hawk looked to Stanley, not wanting to speak unless the therapist gave his okay.

Stanley redirected the boy back to himself. "They were playing mind games with you, Adam. They wanted you to think that you were responsible for choosing June."

"But I did, didn't I?" The boy rubbed his head with his right hand, the left maintaining the grip upon the pipe bowl.

"No," Stanley answered. "Adam, they had already chosen June. These people were telling you that good is bad, that bad is good. They wanted to confuse you into thinking you chose her."

"But why?" the boy asked.

Stanley could hear the echoes of his own questions to Gertrude. He had to give an answer that a nine-year-old could understand. "Because when a person is truly confused, he'll be much more likely to accept what others are telling him. And these people wanted you to believe in Satan's power."

Stanley waited for that to sink in, then carefully, slowly inserted the crucial insight. "Because what they were telling you was wrong and, on some level, you knew it was wrong."

Bingo! In a slight physical lifting of the boy's shoulders, Stanley watched the suggestion impact Adam. He was righting the upside down world, reasserting the moral order. *On some level, Adam knew it was wrong.* He was putting back into the boy the old knowledge of right and wrong by telling him it had never truly gone away. It had simply gone underground *on some level.*

What seemed like minutes passed and then the boy nodded. He understood, accepted what Stanley had said.

"Are you ready to go on?" the therapist asked.

Adam sighed. "She cried when they took her away. I was really scared. The other kids wouldn't talk to me. Emily said I had made a good decision, an' she was glad it wasn't me. She said something about my being spiritual already an' that made them want me more, or something like that. I wanted to know what was happening to June. But when I next saw her, she was . . . she couldn't move her arms and legs."

"Was she dead?" Stanley asked.

"No." Adam shook his head.

"Was she paralyzed?"

"She was breathing an' didn't have any clothes on. An' the guy with the black robes was singing and speaking words I didn't understand. June was on a table. It was made of stone or something. He had a huge knife that he held over her. An' they were waiting. There were candles and the people kept saying things back to the guy. An' then when the sun started coming up, they began to yell an' he took that knife. . . ."

Adam stopped. He stood up and thrust the pipe into Hawk's hands. "I'm gonna be sick," he gasped.

Stanley grabbed the waste paper basket and plunked it down before the boy. Adam knelt down, leaned into the basket, and was violently ill.

Stanley could feel his own gorge rise because it always made him nauseous to see someone vomit. He opened a window.

Quietly in the background, Hawk began to chant. Stanley didn't know anything about Native American music but it didn't sound to him like the words meant much. Everything was being carried by the softness of the notes, the way they wrapped around the three of them, singing the boy back into balance.

Adam lifted his head out of the basket and accepted tissues from Stanley. Stanley placed the wastepaper basket outside the office door. But the boy didn't get back into the chair or retrieve his chanunpa. Instead, he sat on the floor and drew up his knees, encircling them with his arms and burying his head. He spoke in muffled tones. "He took that knife and he cut out her heart."

Adam tightened his muscles. "He said that Satan was now real happy. They cut up her heart an' passed it around on a plate. An' everybody had to eat a little piece an' I got sick and threw up."

With Adam's mouth buried in his knees, Stanley had trouble hearing the boy. But he knew Adam was describing a Satanic mass. *No transubstantiation* here, thought Stanley. *What a crazy time for my psyche to be cracking internal jokes.*

"Then people started to clean up the place," Adam said.

"Clean up?" Stanley was jarred by the presence of normal activity in the narration.

Adam wearily rested his forehead against his knees. "They were gonna burn June's body but somebody said that someone was coming back to the farm, so they decided to do something else with it. Cut it up, take it somewhere, an' dump it in the woods. Then they all kind of rushed about, packing things up."

"What about you?"

"People kept talking to me. Some were nice. They gave me food and water to eat. They told me they were glad that I was one of them. Others were not so nice."

"What do you mean?" asked Stanley.

"They said if I told anyone what happened, that Satan would know an' it would get back to them. They would come find me. They would hurt somebody I really loved. Again and again, they asked if I was gonna tell, an' I swore to them, on my mother's life an' my sister's life that I'd never tell. They said that wasn't good enough. I was so tired but they wouldn't let me sleep. They took me away from the farm to another place an' they kept on talking to me. Don't talk or else, they said. Again and again. I fell asleep once an' when I woke up, one guy was saying, don't talk, don't talk, don't talk. I swore I wouldn't."

Adam pulled himself up onto his feet. Almost proudly, he stated, "An I kept my promise. I didn't talk for the longest time." He accepted the pipe from Hawk's hands and sat down.

"They said that I should be waiting for them. Some day they were gonna come back into my life an' that I should be ready for them. That there were things they'd want me to do."

"Like what?"

Adam shrugged his shoulders.

"Emily came and got me. She drove the van way back in the woods and told me to get out. But it was dark an' I was scared. She told me to sit by a tree an' when the sun came up to walk toward it. She said that I shouldn't tell anybody, 'cuz the police would arrest me for the death of the hitchhiker guy and put me away for the rest of my life. I was really scared."

"I bet you were," empathized Stanley.

"I asked her to drive me back home but she said I'd never see her again. She kissed me goodby. I walked a long long time, until I got to that big road."

"Was that where the police found you?"

Adam nodded.

Stanley let out a huge sigh of relief.

*　*　*　*

On the way home, Adam sat quietly in the front seat of Hawk's pick-up.

"You did good," Hawk said, glancing over at his young cousin.

At first Adam said nothing. Then, to Hawk's surprise, he spoke. "Are they going to kill me, Hawk?"

"Do you believe in the Chanunpa Wakan?" Hawk asked.

Adam solemnly nodded.

"Do you trust that your grandmother is there guarding your back?"

Again Adam dipped his head up and down.

Hawk kept his eyes on the road, not sure what else to say. He knew what lay ahead were many more inipi ceremonies with the boy, teaching him about Lakota medicine, making him strong in the Pipe Road, embedding him in community. The healing would take time, but Hawk no longer doubted the outcome. The boy was going to be okay.

Adam peered out the window as they drove north on M22 toward Suttons Bay and Chrysalis.

"When will we get home?" the boy asked.

"It won't be long now," Hawk answered.

*　*　*　*

"How long is Adam's healing going to take?" Stanley asked Dr. Gold.

"As long as it takes for the boy to go from being a victim to a survivor to someone who encountered a very evil group of people when he was but nine years old."

"But that could require a lifetime," Stanley protested.

"And how long will it take for you to heal, Stanley?" Gertrude's eyes bored into him.

He didn't reply, because he didn't have an answer.

Gertrude turned toward Meggie. "That's not the same question as to the length of the boy's psychotherapy. What first had to occur was for you, Stanley, and your husband to win the boy's trust. Then Adam had to tell you the sordid story of that awful week. All along, the three of you have been helping him reframe his assumptions about people and the Sacred world while countering the garbage the Satanists fed him."

Both Stanley and Meggie nodded in agreement.

Gertrude continued. "It's not just a matter of restoring the boy's mental and emotional balance. You also have to desensitize his body to triggers in his environment that may set him off, flip him back into that Easter week. But, over the months of treatment, he will learn how to stay more grounded in present time." In an unconscious gesture, Gertrude Gold pushed back her sleeve revealing the tattooed numbers on her arm.

She said, "The boy is strong, and he's fortunate to have a spiritual tradition available to him. He's also surrounded by loving people. Adam will come to terms with the trauma. He will forge his own lessons from what happened. When you encounter Evil and the forces of Death, you make a different appraisal of life's meaning. It becomes important to make your life count for something."

"But will he ever be safe from them?" Meggie asked. "Or will he always be in danger?"

Dr. Gold rubbed her ancient eyes. "This is not simply a question about Adam Arbre. It is a question each one of us must address in our own lives. If we don't ask that question, then the answer is that we all remain at peril."

FIFTY-THREE

THE END IS ALWAYS THE BEGINNING

Because, more than anything, it is the road
and its turnings that is the traveler,
that comes back and remains unexplained
and even sits in the doorway and looks over
the hills and sees sunsets and calls you
to see them too. . . .

—ROBERT CREELEY
Poem for Beginners

At the first hint of fall the fudgies fled south. In their wake, the leaves on the Leelanau Peninsula fluttered their last and glorious farewell. Almost overnight, the pallid green hardwood trees blushed fiery red, Halloween orange, and lemon yellow as if the tallest trees had reached up into the sky's curtain at sunset, loosened the bold and delicate filaments, and shaken them down upon their spreading branches.

Days whispered warm but nights harkened to the distant whistle of arctic currents. In the absence of lake-side cottage lights, the evening skies sparkled a pristine infinity. There was a greater quiet on the roads and a slower mood to the town's business. Some stores had boarded up, following the summer trade south. Most had simply switched their wares to winter.

School had begun and mothers breathed more easily. Every morning, Lucy arrived to pick up Adam for the reservation school. Not only did the new school offer him an opportunity to celebrate his heritage but it spared him painful reminders of June Tubbs.

Therapy sessions reverted to twice a week, much to everybody's relief. After Adam's first telling of the entire story, Stanley informed the boy that he would have to talk to the investigators. "Do you want Hawk there with us? Do you want the pipe with you?" the therapist asked.

Stanley was surprised when Adam shook his head. "I want Meggie."

Around a large table, Meggie sat on one side of him, Stanley on the other side. The investigators peppered the boy with questions, backtracking in detail where and when and how. In this second telling, a day-long interrogation which Meggie thought would never end, Adam spoke clearly, his emotions wrung dry and knotted in control. A couple of times, he reached under the table for her hand.

After it was over, Meggie told Adam, "I have never been more proud of you than I was today."

For several nights thereafter, the boy woke up in a sweat, crying out, and Meggie went to him. Once he even wet the bed and the two of them simply followed the old routine. Each time he woke up in the middle of a nightmare, Meggie tucked him back into bed. "It's okay. You're safe here with us," she said, brushing away the hair from his eyes. On the side of his bed, she sat softly talking him back to sleep.

During the days afterwards, Meggie occasionally caught Adam staring off into the distance as if trapped by an old image, a scene playing and replaying itself in his imagination. But he was easily distracted back into the present and those moments of dissociation became less and less frequent.

On a third occasion, Adam had to tell the story and this time it was also very very hard. He had to share it with his parents. Clearly afraid that his account would shatter their loving view of him, he asked that he be allowed to tell them in a family inipi ceremony.

Meggie kept the door and Hawk poured the waters. No sooner had Meggie lowered the sweat lodge door than Adam began to cry and tell the tale of those horrible five days. In the cleansing steam of the old ways, with his parents on both sides of him, the boy trembled and vented his fear and his shame. From the first through the fourth round of the ceremony, the tears would not stop flowing. To his astonishment, his parents wept alongside him. And when, together, they smoked the Chanunpa, Adam knew he had been forgiven.

Later that night, after Lucy and Larry had left and Adam had gone to bed, Hawk and Meggie slumped down on the living room couch. Shadows, cast by the last dying embers in the fireplace, played over their faces and onto the ancestral paintings. All around them they could feel the chill of oncoming winter but the coals and the heat of their own bodies wrapped them in a cocoon of warmth.

Meggie leaned her head against Hawk's shoulder and stared into the glowing fireplace. "It's been a rough year so far, hasn't it?"

He smiled, kissing her on the cheek. "But it's been the year that we got married, Meggie. So it's also been the best year of my life."

"You never got to do your four-day, four-night vision quest," she said. "You never took up the medicine altar. Any regrets?"

Hawk shrugged his shoulders, seemingly unconcerned. "Maybe I never will. I don't know what Wakan Tanka has in mind for me." He looked toward the staircase, obviously thinking of Adam. "I don't know what lies ahead, Meggie. But this year, I learned the true meaning of courage from a young boy. He had no doubts that to tell us the story meant a death sentence for him."

Then, to Meggie' surprise, she could feel a heaving ripple through Hawk's chest. At first she thought he was laughing until she turned and saw the tears streaming down his cheeks. "It's been so awful for him," his voice choked.

In the tears of her lover, it all came flooding back to Meggie—the days and nights of hard work with the boy, watching him struggle, feeling his panic, hearing his words and nightly telling him stories of suffering and redemption, calling him home the best way she knew how.

*   *   *   *

By early November, the rain and northwestern winds began blasting the leaves off the trees. The stalwart evergreens stood their ground but the rest of the land simmered into lukewarm browns and damp purple. Small animals scurried about in last preparation before the snows brought a winter's purification.

Adam was thriving in his new school. With Stanley Schwartz, he worked and reworked the meaning of what had happened to him: Not all grown-ups are good and not all power is bad. Sometimes life takes away people you love and it's okay to grieve their loss. Evil exists but so does strong medicine. There are ways you can protect yourself.

The police informed him that the trail of Emily and Clyde Bassett had simply disappeared into the wooded areas of Oregon. Nor had any of the other cult members been found.

It was not safe for him to dwell in the past, but he now knew that he wanted to walk the traditional path of his grandmother, Winona. She was always near him and he didn't need to keep calling her from the Other Side. Hawk was teaching him about the Chanunpa Wakan and the Red Road.

From Meggie, Adam had learned that there were many roads leading up the Sacred mountain and that he had to walk the road that made the most sense to him. His therapist told Adam that he, too, was starting to learn more about his own journey—as a Jew.

As his tenth birthday approached, Adam grew increasingly excited. There had been a lot of hush-hush whisperings between Hawk and Meggie and his parents. Hawk and his dad had been busy with a secret project. During the weekends, Lucy and Meggie kept taking him off on day trips. He kept his fingers crossed and his mouth shut about his real desire. Over the past year, he had learned that it was safer to say less than more.

On the morning of his tenth birthday, his parents and his sister arrived for breakfast. They woke him up singing *Happy Birthday*. His mother told him to dress warmly. After they had eaten their eggs and bacon and drunk their coffee, his family—his mom, dad, Eva, Hawk, and Meggie—escorted him down to the field. Way back, out of sight of the house and the driveway, he spied a newly constructed, small barn.

Across the fenced, stubbled field, Hawk trotted ahead of the group. He flung open the large barn door and out into the morning's bright November sunlight stepped the most beautiful pinto pony that Adam had ever seen.

Adam blinked. He couldn't believe his eyes. A grin spread from one ear to the other. "Is that horse mine?"

Hawk handed him a halter and rope. "She's all yours, provided you can catch her. She's got a strong fence to keep her safe."

"Does she have a name?" Adam asked. He couldn't believe that they had finally given him what he had always wanted—his own horse.

"No. Nor is she saddle-broke. There are a lot of things you're going to have to teach her but if you do it with love, she'll give you her heart," Hawk answered.

"Then I'm gonna call her Shunka Wakan," the boy announced.

Hawk laughed. "It's a good name to grow into."

Adam approached the pinto.

She stepped back, her ears flickering with interest, her eyes fixated on the halter.

"Whoa," he said, lifting up his free hand.

The motion spooked her. The pony tossed her head, backing up a few steps.

"Go easy on her. Don't make any sudden movements. Come from the side. Talk to her," Hawk advised.

"I'm not going to hurt you," Adam whispered. In a dance between the boy and his new pony, he followed Hawk's instructions. But no matter how hard he tried, the pinto wouldn't let him get within halter distance.

Frustrated, Adam returned to Hawk. "What am I gonna do now?"

Hawk smiled. "Here." He pulled out a couple of long carrots from his denim jacket and handed them to Adam.

"Now, I want to give you a little advice." Out of the corner of his eye, Hawk checked to make sure that Lucy and Meggie were listening. "All of us males like to think that we are in charge when it comes to courting the female."

Adam solemnly nodded.

"But it just isn't true. When we make the frontal approach, they get to side-stepping and proudly rearing their heads at us. You've got to learn sooner or later, Adam, that the best way to catch the female is to let her come after you."

"Ha!" Lucy retorted.

Larry sported a grin a mile wide.

"So, while we return back to the house for another cup of coffee, I think you ought to sit down in this field and hold up those carrots so that Shunka Wakan can see them. Women are always wanting whatever a man has in his possession."

"Okay," said Adam, heading out into the field.

"Watch out," his mother yelled after him. "There seems to be a lot of horse shit around here."

Lucy always liked having the last word.

It had been a wonderful tenth birthday for Adam. He had spent the majority of the day in the field, learning about the limited powers of male persuasion.

As Meggie tucked the tired boy into bed that night, Adam said, "I love being here with you and Hawk."

"And Shunka Wakan," she added.

"I feel at home here."

She pulled the warm covers over his shoulders. "You'll always be at home here. And if the time comes that you're ready to move back with your parents, I hope you'll continue to see Chrysalis as your other home." She kissed him good night.

Meggie descended the stairs to the second floor bedroom. Hawk's back was to her; he was pulling off his socks and shirt by the bedroom hamper. She tiptoed up behind him and grabbed him around his bare midriff.

"Hey," he shouted, startled. "Is Adam asleep already?"

"He says he feels at home here," she whispered, happy.

"So do I," said Hawk. "Home will always be wherever you are, Meggie." He scooped her up with strong arms and pressed her into him.

"Put me down," she protested, laughing. "I've got something important to say. Earlier this year, the Spirits instructed me to tell you and Adam what is *home*."

Hawk let her feet touch the ground but kept a strong hold upon her as if he were never going to let her go.

Meggie would not be deterred. "At first I thought *home* was simply Chrysalis, this place of my mother, my grandmother, and my great-grandmother. Then Winona taught me about the Pipe and prayer and that, too, became a coming home for me. Along you came and captured my heart and I put it all together as one—you, Chrysalis, and the Chanunpa creating a home for me. But now I know that *home* carries even deeper meanings."

He kissed her eyelashes. He nuzzled her nose, but Meggie kept on talking.

"Listen, Hawk," she insisted.

"I am listening," he answered. "You're about to tell me what *home* really means."

She looked into him. Her eyes shone with excitement, joy, curiosity. *Her face*, he thought, *is young and old and beautiful. Her words are like the eagles spiraling through invisible breaths of wind. Around and around they rise, always turning toward the sun, the gold glinting off black wings and the awesome silence unfolding in the after.*

"When and where," Meggie began, "the heart can celebrate each awakening day—that becomes home. When and where the spirit can mine for nourishment in the little moments—that becomes home. When and where the mind can distill meaning from the shadows as well as the light—that also becomes home."

Mitakuye Oyas'in

GLOSSARY OF
LAKOTA WORD

Chanunpa Wakan – sacred pipe
Hanbleciya – crying for a dream, vision quest
Hanhepi wi – dark sun, moon
Ikcewicasta – a simple earth man, Indian
Inipi – sweat lodge, ceremony
Inyan – rock, stone nation
Itokaga, Itokagata – Grandfather of the south, toward the noonday sun
Iya – An evil Being, the second son of the mythological Inyan.
Maka – the great disk whose edge is where there is no beyond
Maka-akan – the spirit imparted to Maka
Mitakuye oyas'in – all my relations
Mni – water
Onsimala ye – mercy
Ptesan Wi – White Buffalo Calf Woman
Skan – the Sky Being, the sky
Sungmanitu – wolves
Tunkasila – Grandfather
Unci Maka – Grandmother Earth
Unk – Water Being, associated with evil
Wakan – sacred, mysterious, a spiritual power
Wakan Tanka – Grandfather, Great Spirit
Wakanpi – All things that are above mankind, Spiritual Forces
Waziya, Waziyata – Grandfather of the north, toward the pines
Wasna – pemmican
Wicasa Wakan – holy man
Wiyohpeyata, Wiyohpeyatakiya – Grandfather of the west,
    toward where the sun falls off
Wiyohiyanpa, Wiyohiyanpata – Grandfather of the east,
    toward where the sun rises
Wanbli – eagle
Wanbli Gleska – spotted eagle who takes the prayers to the grandfathers
Wopila – thank you to the Creator, the Spirits

I *want to* acknowledge the following works whose voices of history and reflection, healing and redemption, poetry and wisdom are cited throughout *Crack at Dusk: Crook of Dawn*:

Allen, Woody. *Death.* New York: S. French, 1975, p. 63.

Beckett, Samuel. 1952. "The Unnameable" from *Samuel Beckett: Molloy, Malone Dies, The Unnamable.* London:Calder Publications, 1994, p. 418.

Borland, Hal. 1964. "February-February 1." from *Sundial of the Seasons.* Cutchogue, NY: Buccaneer Books. (Out of print).

Brooks, Francis. "XXIX." from *Margins.* Chicago: Searle & Gorton, 1896, p. 69.

Browning, Elizabeth Barrett. 1844. "The Lady's Yes." from *Elizabeth Barrett Browning: Selected Poems.* Baltimore: John Hopkins University Press, p. 150.

Browning, Robert. 1842. "The Pied Piper of Hamelin." from *Robert Browning: The Poems.* Ed. John Pettigrew. London: Penguin Books, 1996. p. 389.

Creeley, Robert. "Poem for Beginners." from *The Collected Poems of Robert Creeley, 1945-1975.* Berkeley: University of California Press, 1982, p. 9.

Crowley, Aleister. 1924. *Magick in Theory and Practice.* Paris: Lecram Press, 1929, p. 95.

Dickinson, Emily. 1862. "The Difference between Despair" (#305). from *The Complete Poems of Emily Dickinson.* Ed. Thomas H. Johnson, Boston: Little, Brown and Co., 1960, p. 144.

Frost, Robert. 1914. "The Death of The Hired Man." from *The Poetry of Robert Frost.* Ed. Edward Connery Lathem. New York: Holt, Rinehart, & Winston, 1979, p. 38.

Gallagher, Tess. "Borrowed Strength." from *The Generation of 2000.* Ed. William Heyen. Princeton: Ontario Review Press, 1984, p. 55.

Gould, Catherine Ph.D. "Diagnosis and Treatment of Ritually Abused Children" from *Out of Darkness: Exploring Satanism and Ritual Abuse.* Ed. David K. Sakheim and Susan E. Devine. New York: Lexington Books, 1992, p. 240.

Gray, Thomas. 1747. "Ode on a Distant Prospect of Eton College." from *The Works of Thomas Gray, Vol.I.* Ed. Edmund Gosse. London: MacMillan Co. 1884, p. 18.

Hawthorne, Nathanial. *The Marble Faun, Vol. I.* Boston: Houghton, Mifflin Co., 1860, p. 240.

Herman, Judith Lewis. *Trauma and Recovery.* New York: Basicbooks, 1992, p. 1.

Hillman, James. "Betrayal." from *Loose Ends:Primary Papers in Archetypal Psychology.* Dallas: Spring Publications, 1975, p. 69.

Hopkins, Gerard Manley. 1918. "No Worse, There Is None." from *The Poems of Gerard Manley Hopkin.* Eds. W. H. Gardner and N. H. MacKenzie. Oxford: Oxford University Press, 1970, p. 100.

James, William. "The Importance of Individuals." from *The Philosophy of William James.* New York: The Modern Library, Inc., 1925, pp. 242-243.(Also in *The Will To Believe.*)

Jacket, Red. 1792. "Brother, the Great Spirit Has Made Us All." from *Indian Oratory.* Comp. W. C. Vanderwerth. New York: Ballantine Books, 1971, pp. 40-41.

Jung, Carl G. *Collected Works*, 2nd ed., Vol 10. Princeton: Princeton University Press, 1970, p. 199.

Lowell, James Russell. 1848. "The Vision of Sir Launfal." Pt. 2, St.8. from the *Poems of James Russell Lowell.* London: Oxford University Press, 1917, p. 155.

Maggid of Dubno (1741-1804). One version of this traditional story can be found in *The Maggid of Dubno and his Parables* by Benno Heinemann, Jerusalem: Feldheim Publishers, 1967, pp. 250-251.

Ondaatje, Michael. *The English Patient.* New York: Vantage Books, 1992, p. 21.

Pope, Alexander. 1744. "Essay on Criticism." from *Pope: Complete Poetical Works.* Ed. Herbert Davis, Oxford: Oxford University Press, 1978, p. 79, line 559.

Roethke, Theodore. 1958. "The Dream." from *The Collected Poems of Theodore Roethke.* New York: Anchor Books, 1975, p. 115.

Shakespeare, William. 1602. *Hamlet* (Act I, sc. 5). from *The Complete Plays and Poems of William Shakespeare.* Boston: Houghton Mifflin Co., 1942, p. 1055

————. 1606. *Macbeth* (Act III, sc. 2). from *The Complete Plays and*

Poems of William Shakespeare. Boston: Houghton Mifflin Co., 1942, p. 1197.

Shelley, Percy Bysshe. 1819. "The Cloud." from *Shelley's Poetry and Prose*. Eds. Donald H. Reiman and Sharon B. Powers. New York: W.W. Norton & Co., 1977, p. 226.

Shreve, Anita. *The Weight of Water*. Boston: Back Bay Books (Little Brown and Co.), 1997, p. 71

Sidney, Sir Philip. 1581. *The Old Arcadia*. Bk.3. Ed. Katherine Duncan-Jones. Oxford: Oxford University Press, 1985, p. 167.

Singer, Isaac Bashevis. "Mirror." from *An Isaac Bashevis Singer Reader*, New York: Farrar, Straus and Giroux, 1979, p. 24.

Swift, Jonathan. 1711. "Thoughts on Various Subjects." from *The Choice Works of Dean Swift*. N.Y: Lovell, Adam, Wesson & Co., n.d., p. 401.

Szasz, Thomas. *The Second Sin*. New York: Doubleday & Co., 1973, p. 51.

Thornton, Lawrence. *Imagining Argentina*. New York: Bantam Books, 1987, p. 79.

Von Franz, Marie-Louise. *Shadow and Evil in Fairytales*. Dallas: Spring Publications, 1987, p. 270.

Walker, James R. *Lakota Belief and Ritual*. Eds. Raymond J. DeMaillie and Elaine A. Jahner. Lincoln: University of Nebraska Press, 1980, pp. 198, 214.

Webster's Third New International Dictionary. Springfield, Mass: G.& C. Merriam Co., 1971, p. 1895.

Woodman, Marion. *The Pregnant Virgin*. Toronto: Inner City Books, 1985, p. 83.

Wordsworth, William. 1818. "Inscriptions" (Hermit's Cell). from *The Complete Poetical Works of William Wordsworth*. London: MacMillan & Co., 1889, p. 570.

Yeats, William Butler. 1919. "Lines Written in Dejection." from *The Collected Poems of W. B. Yeats*. London: Macmillan, 1985, p. 164.